I LOOKED again. I could see now that the figure was limp and lifeless. There was something about the way it sagged that told me that.

I stared at it in horror, for it had swung round and I was looking at a grotesque face . . . a face that was not human. It was white . . . white as freshly fallen snow, and it had a grinning gash of a mouth the color of blood.

It was not a man. It was not a human being, though the corduroy breeches and the tweed cloth cap were those of a man who worked on the land.

I moved forward but every instinct rebelled against my going near the thing.

I suddenly felt I could not stay there a moment longer. I banged the door and called out, "Let me out. Help."

I kept my back on the thing that was hanging there. I had an uncanny feeling that it might come to life, come over to me, and then . . .

Fawcett Crest Books
by Victoria Holt:

VICTORIA HOLT

The Mask of the Enchantress

FAWCETT CREST • NEW YORK

THE MASK OF THE ENCHANTRESS

Published by Fawcett Crest Books, a unit of CBS Publications, the Consumer Publishing Division of CBS Inc., by arrangement with Doubleday and Company, Inc.

ISBN: 0-449-24418-0

Featured Alternate Selection of the Literary Guild Selection of the Doubleday Book Club.

Printed in the United States of America

First Fawcett Crest printing: September 1981

10 9 8 7 6 5 4 3 2 1

CONTENTS

Three Wishes in an Enchanted Forest

I am trapped. I am caught in a web, and it is small comfort to me that that web is of my own weaving. When I think of the magnitude of what I have done I am overcome by a numb terror. I have behaved in a wicked manner, I know, perhaps a criminal manner; and every morning when I wake there is a heavy cloud over me, and I ask myself what fresh disasters there are in store for me this day.

How often have I wished that I had never heard of Susannah, Esmond and the rest—particularly Susannah. I wish that I had never had that glimpse of Mateland Castle, so noble, so gracious, with its massive gatehouse, its gray walls and battlements like something out of a medieval romance. Then I should never have been tempted.

In the beginning it had all seemed so easy and I had been desperate.

"Dat ole Debil be at youse elbow tempting you," my old friend Cougaba on Vulcan Island would have said.

It was true. The Devil had tempted me, and I had succumbed to temptation. That is why I am here in Mateland Castle, trapped and desperate, seeking a way out of a situation which every day is becoming more and more dangerous.

It all goes back a long way—in fact it started before I was born. It is the story of my father and mother; it is Susannah's story as well as mine. But when I first began to be aware that there was something unusual about me, I was just six years old.

I spent those early years in Crabtree Cottage on the village green of Cherrington. The church dominated the green and there was a pond in the center where every fine day the old men would take their places on the wooden seat there and talk the morning away. There was a maypole on the green, too, and on May Day the villagers chose a queen and there were wonderful celebrations which I used to watch through the slats in the wooden venetian blinds at the parlor window if I could escape the stern eyes of Aunt Amelia.

Aunt Amelia and Uncle William were very religious, and they said that the maypole should have been removed and such pagan ceremonies done away with; but I was thankful to say that that was not the view of the rest of us.

How I used to long to be out there, bringing in the green from the woods, and taking one of the strands and dancing round the maypole with the May Day frolickers. I thought it must be the height of bliss to be chosen as the May queen. But one had to be sixteen at least to qualify for that honor, and at the time I was not yet six.

I accepted the strangeness of my life and I suppose would have gone on doing so for a while if it had not been for the nods and hints going on around me. Once I heard Aunt Amelia say: "I don't know if we did right, William. Miss Anabel begged me and I gave way."

"There's the money," Uncle William reminded her.

"But it's condoning sin, that's what it is."

Uncle William assured her that no one could say they had sinned.

"We've condoned a sinner, William," she insisted.

William replied that no blame could be attached to them. They had done what they were paid to do and it might be that they could snatch a soul from hellfire.

"The sins of the fathers are visited on the children," Aunt Amelia reminded him.

He just nodded and went out to his woodshed where he was carving a crib for the church at Christmas.

I began to realize that Uncle William was less preoccupied

with being good than Aunt Amelia was. He smiled now and then—true, it was rather a twisted sort of smile as though he was ashamed of it, but it sometimes threatened to emerge; and once when he had found me looking through the blinds at the May Day celebrations he had gone out of the room and said nothing.

Of course I am writing after a lapse of years, but I think I very soon began to realize that there was speculation about me in the village of Cherrington. Uncle William and Aunt Amelia were an incongruous pair to have charge of a young child.

Matty Grey, who lived in one of the cottages on the green and used to sit at her door on summer days, was what was known as a "character" in the village. I liked to talk to Matty whenever I could. She knew it and when I approached she would make strange wheezing noises and her fat body would shake, which was her way of laughing. She would call to me and bid me sit at her feet. She called me a "pore little mite" and bade her grandson Tom be kind to little Suewellyn.

I rather liked my name. It was derived from Susan Ellen. The *w*, I think, was put in because of the two *e*'s coming together. I thought it was a good name. Distinctive. There were Ellens in plenty in our village and there was a Susan called Sue. But Suewellyn was unique.

Tom obeyed his grandmother. He stopped other children teasing me because I was different. I went to the dame school, which was run by a lady who had been a governess at the manor house where she had taught the squire's daughter, but when that young lady no longer required her services she had taken a small house not far from the church and opened a school to which the village children went, including the squire's daughter's son, Anthony. He was going to have a tutor when he was a year or so older and after that he would go away to school. We were a mixed community who gathered in Miss Brent's front parlor and scratched out letters in trays of sand with wooden sticks and chanted our tables. There were twenty of us from the ages of five to eleven and of all classes; some would finish their education at the age of eleven; others would go on to further it. In addition to the squire's heir, there were the doctor's daughters and three children of a local farmer, and then there were those like Tom Grey. Among them I was the only one who was unusual.

The fact was, there was some mystery about me. I had

arrived in the village one day, already born. The coming of most children was a much-discussed event before the newcomer actually put in an appearance. I was different. I lived with a couple who were the most unlikely pair to have the charge of a child. I was always well clothed and sometimes wore garments which were more costly than the status of my guardians warranted.

Then there were the visits. Once a month *She* came.

She was beautiful. She arrived at the cottage in the station fly, and I would be sent into the parlor to see her. I knew it was an important occasion because the parlor was only used at very special times—when the vicar called, for instance. The venetian blinds were always drawn to keep out the sun for fear it might fade the carpet or damage the furniture. There was a holy atmosphere about it. Perhaps it was the picture of Christ on the cross or that of St. Stephen, I think it was, with a lot of arrows sticking in him and blood trickling from his wounds, side by side with a portrait of our Queen when young, looking very stern, disdainful and disapproving. The room depressed me and it was only the lure of such occasions as May Day which tempted me to peer through the slats at the frolicking on the green.

But when *She* was there, the room was transformed. Her clothes were wonderful. She wore blouses that always seemed to be adorned with frills and ribbons; she wore long bell-shaped skirts and little hats trimmed with feathers and bows of ribbon.

She always said: "Hello, Suewellyn!" as though she were a little shy of me. Then she would hold out her hand and I would run to her and take it. She would lift me up in her arms and study me so intently that I wondered if the parting of my hair was straight and whether I had remembered to wash behind my ears.

We would sit side by side on the sofa. I hated the sofa at most times. It was made of horsehair and tickled my legs even through my stockings; but I did not notice this when she was there. She would ask me a lot of questions, and they were all about me. What did I like to eat? Was I cold in the winter? What was I doing at school? Was everybody kind to me? When I learned to read she wanted me to show her how well I could do it. She would put her arms round me and hold me tightly, and when the fly came back to take her to the station, she would hug me and look as if she were going to cry.

It was very flattering, for although she did talk awhile to Aunt Amelia, when I would be sent out of the parlor, it did seem as though her visits were especially for me.

After she had gone it would seem different in the house. Uncle William would look as though he was trying hard to stop his features breaking into a smile; and Aunt Amelia would go about murmuring to herself: "I don't know, I don't know."

The visits were noticed in the village of course. James, who drove the fly, and the stationmaster whispered together about her. I realized later that they drew their own conclusions on the matter, which could hardly have been called obscure, and I have no doubt that I should have learned earlier but for Matty Grey's injunction to her grandson to look after me. Tom had made it clear that I was in his charge, and anyone offending me would have to answer to him. I loved Tom though he never deigned to speak much to me. For me, however, he was my protector, my knight in shining armor, my Lohengrin.

But even Tom could not stop the children putting their heads together and whispering about me, and one day Anthony Felton noticed the mole just below my mouth on the right side of my chin.

"Just look at that mark on Suewellyn's face," he cried. "It's where the Devil kissed her."

They all listened with wide eyes while he told them how the Devil came at midnight and picked out his own. Then he kissed them and where he had touched them there was left a mark.

"Silly," I said. "Lots of people have moles."

"There's a special sort," said Anthony darkly. "I know it when I see it. I saw a witch once and she had one just like that right near her mouth....See?"

They were all looking at me with horror.

"She don't look like a witch," Jane Motley ventured, and I was sure I did not, in my prim serge dress and mid-brown hair severely scraped back from my forehead and drawn over the top of my head to be plaited into two ropes, each tied with a piece of navy-blue ribbon. A nice neat suitable style, as Aunt Amelia had often commented when I wanted to wear it loose.

"Witches change shapes," explained Anthony.

"I always knew there was something different about Sue-wellyn," said Gill, the blacksmith's girl.

"What's he like...the Devil?" asked someone.

"I don't know," I answered. "I've never seen him."

"Don't you believe her," said Anthony Felton. "That's the Devil's mark on her."

"You're a silly boy," I told him, "and no one would listen to you if you weren't the squire's grandson."

"Witch," said Anthony.

Tom was not at school that day. He had had to go and help dig up potatoes for his father.

I was afraid. They were all looking at me so oddly; and I was suddenly aware of isolation, of being different from the herd.

It was a strange feeling—exultation in a way because I was different—and, in another way, fear.

Miss Brent came in then and there was no more whispering, but when lessons were over for the day I ran out of school quickly. I was afraid of those children. It was due to something I had seen in their eyes. They really believed that the Devil had visited me in the night and put his mark on me.

I ran across the green to where Matty Grey was sitting at her door; there was a pint pot beside her and her hands were folded in her lap.

She called out to me: "Where you running to then...like you've got the Devil at your heels?"

Cold fear touched me. I looked over my shoulder.

Matty burst out laughing. "Just a way of talking. There ain't no Devil behind you. Why, you look real skerried out of your wits, that you do."

I sat down at her feet.

"Where's Tom?" I asked.

"Still digging taties. It's a good crop this year." She licked her lips. "A good tatie is hard to beat. All hot and floury in a nice brown jacket. Nothing like it, Suewellyn."

I said: "It's this mole on my face."

She peered at me without moving. "What's that?" she said. "Oh, that's a beauty spot, that is."

"It's where the Devil kissed me, they said."

"Who said?"

"At school."

"They've no right to say that. I'll tell Tom. He'll stop 'em."

"Why is it there then, Matty?"

"Oh, sometimes you's born with it. People is born with all sorts of things. Now my aunt's cousin was born with what looked like a bunch of strawberries on her face...all along of her mother having a fancy for strawberries before she was born."

"What did my mother fancy for me to be born with a spot like that on my face?"

I was thinking: And where is my mother? That was another strange thing about me. I had no mother. I had no father. There were orphans in the village but they knew who their parents had been. The difference was that I did not.

"Well, there's no knowing, is there, ducky?" said Matty comfortably. "We all of us get these things now and again. I knew a girl once born with six fingers. Now that wasn't easy to hide. What's a mole nobody's noticed before? I'll tell you something. I think it's sort of pretty there. There's some people that makes a lot of that sort of thing. They darken 'em to call attention to them. You don't want to worry about that."

Matty was one of the most comforting people I ever knew in my life. She was so content with her lot, which was nothing much but living in that dark little cottage—"one up, one down, a bit at the back where I can do the washing and cooking, and a privy at the bottom of the garden," was the way she described it. It was next door to that of her son, Tom's father. "Near but not too close," she used to say, "which is as it should be." And if the days were dry enough for her to sit outside and see what was going on, she asked no more.

Aunt Amelia might deplore the fact that she sat at her door bringing down the tone of the green, but Matty lived her life as she wanted to and had reached a contentment which few people achieve.

When I went to school the next day Anthony Felton came up to me and whispered in my ear: "You're a bastard."

I stared at him. I had heard that word used in abuse and I was ready to let him know my opinion of him. But Tom came up at that moment and Anthony slunk off at once.

"Tom," I whispered, "he called me a bastard."

"Never mind," said Tom and added mysteriously: "It wasn't the kind of bastard you think." Which was very confusing at the time.

Two or three days before my sixth birthday Aunt Amelia

took me into the parlor to talk to me. It was a very solemn occasion and I waited with trepidation for what she was going to tell me.

It was the first day of September and a shaft of sunlight had managed to get through one of the slats in the blinds which had not been properly closed. I can see it now all so clearly—the horsehair sofa; the horsehair chairs to match, which, mercifully, were rarely sat on, with the antimacassars placed primly on their backs; the whatnot in the corner with its ornaments which were dusted twice a week; the holy pictures on the wall with that of the young Queen looking very disagreeable, her arms folded and the ribbon of the Garter over her very sloping shoulders. There was no gayety in that room at all and that was why the shaft of sunshine looked so out of place. I was sure Aunt Amelia would notice it and shut it out before long.

But she did not. She was obviously very preoccupied and rather concerned.

"Miss Anabel is coming on the third," she said. The third of September was my birthday.

I clasped my hands and waited. Miss Anabel had always come on my birthday.

"She is thinking of a little treat for you."

My heart began to beat fast. I waited breathlessly.

"If you are good," went on Aunt Amelia. It was the usual proviso, so I did not take much notice of that. She continued: "You will wear your Sunday clothes although it will be a Thursday."

The wearing of Sunday clothes on a Thursday seemed full of portent.

Her lips were firmly pressed together. I could see that she did not approve of the meeting.

"She is going to take you out for the day."

I was astounded. I could scarcely contain myself. I wanted to bounce up and down on the horsehair chair.

"We must make sure that everything is all right," said Aunt Amelia. "I would not want Miss Anabel to think that we did not bring you up like a lady."

I burst out that everything would be all right. I would forget nothing I had been taught. I would not speak with my mouth full. I should have my handkerchief ready in case it were needed. I would not hum. I would always remember to wait until I was spoken to before speaking.

"Very well," said Aunt Amelia; and later I heard her say to Uncle William: "What is she thinking of? I don't like it. It's unsettling for the child."

The great day came. My sixth birthday. I was dressed in my black button boots and my dark blue jacket with a mercerized cotton dress beneath it. I had dark blue gloves and a straw hat with elastic under the chin.

The fly came from the station with Miss Anabel in it and when it went back I was in it as well.

Miss Anabel was different that day. The thought occurred to me that she was a little afraid of Aunt Amelia. She kept laughing and she gripped my hands and said two or three times: "This *is* nice, Suewellyn."

We boarded the train under the curious eyes of the stationmaster and were soon puffing away. I did not remember ever having been on a train before and I did not know what excited me most, the sound of the wheels which seemed to be singing a merry song or the fields and woods which were rushing by; but what gave me most pleasure was the presence of Miss Anabel pressed close beside me. Every now and then she would give my hand a squeeze.

There were a lot of questions I wanted to ask Miss Anabel but I remembered my promise to Aunt Amelia to behave in the manner of a well-brought-up child.

"You are quiet, Suewellyn," said Miss Anabel, so I explained about not speaking until I was spoken to.

She laughed; she had a gurgling sort of laughter which made me want to laugh every time I heard it.

"Oh, forget that," she said. "I want you to talk to me whenever you feel like it. I want you to tell me just anything that comes into your mind."

Oddly enough, with the ban lifted, I was tongue-tied. I said: "You ask me and I'll tell you."

She put her arm round me and held me close. "I want you to tell me that you are happy," she said. "You do like Uncle William and Aunt Amelia, don't you?"

"They are very good," I said. "I think Aunt Amelia is more good than Uncle William."

"Is he unkind to you?" she asked quickly.

"Oh no. Kinder in a way. But Aunt Amelia is so very good that it's hard for her to be kind. She never laughs...." I stopped because Miss Anabel laughed a good deal and it seemed as though I were saying she was not kind.

She just hugged me and said: "Oh, Suewellyn...you're such a little girl really."

"I'm not," I said. "I'm bigger than Clara Feen and Jane Motley. And they are older than I am."

She just held me against her so that I couldn't see her face, and I thought she didn't want me to.

The train stopped and she jumped up. "We're getting out here," she said.

She took my hand and we left the train. We almost ran along the platform. Outside was a dogcart with a woman sitting in it.

"Oh, Janet," cried Miss Anabel, "I knew you'd come."

"'Tain't right," said the woman, looking at me. She had a pale face and brown hair drawn down the sides of her face and fastened in a bun at the back. She had on a brown bonnet with ribbon tied under the chin and reminded me of Uncle William suddenly because I could see she was trying to stop herself smiling.

"So this is the child, miss," she said.

"This is Suewellyn," answered Miss Anabel.

Janet clicked her tongue. "I don't know why I..." she began.

"Janet, you're having a wonderful time. Is the hamper there?"

"Just as you said, miss."

"Come on, Suewellyn," said Miss Anabel. "Get up into the trap. We're going for a ride."

Janet sat in front holding the reins. Miss Anabel and I were behind. Miss Anabel held my hand tightly. She was laughing again.

The dogcart started off and we were soon riding through leafy lanes. I wanted this to go on and on forever. It was like stepping into an enchanted world. The trees were just beginning to turn color and there was a faint mist in the air which made the sunshine hazy, and this seemed to give a certain mystery to the landscape.

"Are you warm enough, Suewellyn?" asked Miss Anabel.

I nodded happily. I did not want to speak. I was afraid of breaking the spell, afraid that I would wake up in my bed and find that I had been dreaming it all. I tried to catch each moment and hold it, saying to myself, *Now*. It is always now, of course, but I wanted this moment of now to stay with me forever.

I was almost unbearably excited, almost unbearably happy.

When the trap stopped suddenly, I gave a gasp of disappointment. But there was more to come.

"This is the spot," said Janet. "And, Miss Anabel, I reckon it's a whole lot too close for comfort."

"Oh, get away with you, Janet. It's perfectly safe. What time is it?"

Janet consulted the watch pinned to her black bombazine blouse.

"Half past eleven," she said.

Miss Anabel nodded. "Take the hamper," she said. "Get everything ready. Suewellyn and I are going for a little walk. You'd like that, wouldn't you, Suewellyn?"

I nodded. I should have liked anything I shared with Miss Anabel.

"Now you watch out, miss," said Janet. "If you was to be seen..."

"We're not going to be seen. Of course we're not. We're not going all that near."

"I should hope not."

Miss Anabel took my hand and we walked away.

"She seems rather cross," I said.

"She's cautious."

"What's that?"

"She doesn't like risks."

I didn't know what Miss Anabel was talking about but I was too happy to care.

"Let's go into the woods," she said. "I want to show you something. Come on. Let's run."

So we ran over the grass, dodging between the trees. "See if you can catch me," said Miss Anabel.

I almost did; then she would laugh and slip away from me. I was breathless and even happier than I had been in the train and the dogcart. The trees had thinned and we were on the edge of the woods.

"Suewellyn," she said softly. "Look."

And there it was, just about a quarter of a mile away from us, set on a slight incline with a ditch all round it. I could see it clearly. It was like a castle out of a fairy tale.

"What do you think of it?" she said.

"Is it...real?" I asked.

"Oh yes...it's real."

I have always had a good visual memory and could look at something and remember it in detail after a glance or two and thus was able to carry the image of Mateland Castle in my mind through the years to come. I describe it now as I know it to be. When, at the age of six, I first saw it there was something magical on that day which was to stand out in my mind for some years to come, almost like a dream.

The castle was magnificent and mysterious. It was enclosed by tall curtain walls and at the four angles there were massive drum towers; on each flank was a square tower and there was the traditional machicolated gatehouse. Long narrow slits of windows were set in the ashlar walls. The postern tower parapet defending the portal below was a formidable reminder that once boiling oil had been poured from it on anyone who dared attempt to break down the defenses. Behind the battlements were wall walks from which the defenders of the castle would have sent their arrows raining down. I learned all this and much more later; I came to know every corbel, every machicolation, every twist of the spiral staircases. But from that moment it fascinated me completely. It was almost as though it took possession of me. I liked to think later that it willed me to act as I did.

At this time I could only stand beside Miss Anabel staring, speechless.

I heard her laugh and she whispered: "Do you like it?"

Like it? It seemed a mild word to express my feeling about the castle. It was the most wonderful thing I had ever seen. There was a picture of Windsor Castle in Miss Brent's parlor and that was beautiful. But this was different. This was real. I could see the September sunshine picking out sharp bits of flint in the walls and making them sparkle.

She was waiting for me to answer.

"It's...beautiful. It's real."

"Oh, it's real all right," answered Miss Anabel. "It's been standing there for seven hundred years."

"Seven hundred years!" I echoed.

"A long time, eh? And think, you've only been on this earth for six. I'm glad you like it."

"Does anyone live in it?"

"Oh yes, people live in it."

"Knights..." I whispered. "Perhaps the Queen."

"Not the Queen, and they don't have knights in armor these days...even in seven-hundred-year-old castles."

Suddenly four people appeared—a girl with three boys. They were riding across the stretch of grass before the castle moat. The girl was on a pony and I noticed her particularly, for she seemed to be about my age. The boys were older.

Miss Anabel caught her breath sharply. She laid her hand on my arm and drew me back into the bushes.

"It's all right," she whispered, as though to herself. "They're going in."

"Do they live there?" I asked.

"Not all of them. Susannah and Esmond do. Malcolm and Garth are visitors."

"Susannah," I said. "That's a bit like my name."

"Oh yes, it is."

I watched the riders pass over the bridge which crossed the moat. They went under the gatehouse and into the castle.

Their appearance had affected Miss Anabel deeply. She took my hand suddenly, and I remembered Aunt Amelia's injunctions not to speak unless I was spoken to.

Miss Anabel started to run through the trees. I tried to catch her and we were laughing again.

We came to a clearing in the woods and there Janet had undone the hamper, spread a cloth on the grass and was putting out knives and forks and plates.

"We'll wait awhile," said Miss Anabel.

Janet nodded, her lips tight as though she were holding back something she wanted to say which was not very pleasant.

Miss Anabel noticed, for she said: "It's none of your business, Janet."

"Oh no," said Janet, looking like a hen with ruffled feathers, "I know that well enough. *I* just do as I'm told."

Miss Anabel gave her a little push. Then she said: "Listen."

We all listened. I could hear the unmistakable sound of horses' hoofs."

"It is," said Miss Anabel.

"You be careful, miss," warned Janet. "It might not be."

A man on horseback came into sight. Anabel gave a cry of joy and ran towards him.

He jumped off his horse and tied it to a tree. Miss Anabel, who herself was a tall lady, looked suddenly very small beside him. He put his hands on her shoulders and looked at her for some seconds. Then he said: "Where is she?"

Miss Anabel held out her hand and I ran to her.

"This is Suewellyn," she said.

I curtsied as I had been taught to do to people like the squire and the vicar. He picked me up and held me in his arms, scrutinizing me.

"Why," he said, "she *is* a little thing."

"She's only six, remember," said Miss Anabel. "What did you expect? An Amazon? And she's tall for her age. Aren't you, Suewellyn?"

I said that I was taller than Clara Feen and Jane Motley, who were older than I.

"Well," he said, "that's a mercy. I'm glad you surpassed those two."

"But you don't know them," I said.

And they both laughed.

He put me down and patted my head. My hair was loose today. Miss Anabel did not like it in plaits.

"We're going to eat now," said Miss Anabel. "Janet has it all waiting for us." She whispered to the man: "Most disapproving, I assure you."

"I don't need to be assured on that point," he said.

"She thinks it was another of my mad schemes."

"Well, isn't it?"

"Oh, you know you wanted it as much as I did."

He still had his hand on my head. He ruffled my hair and said: "I believe I did."

At first I was rather sorry that he and Janet were there. I should have liked Miss Anabel to myself. But after a while I began to change my mind. It was only Janet I wished to be without. She sat a little apart from us and her expression reminded me of Aunt Amelia, which in its turn recalled the unpleasant truth that this magical day would come to an end and I should be back in the house on the green with only memories of it. But in the meantime it was Now and Now was glorious.

We sat down to eat and I was between Miss Anabel and the man. Once or twice she called him by his name, which was Joel. I was not told what I was to call him, which was a little awkward. There was something about him which made it impossible not to be aware of him all the time. Janet was in awe of him, I sensed. She did not speak to him as she did to Miss Anabel. When she did address him, she called him Sir.

He had dark brown eyes and hair of a lighter shade of

brown. There was a cleft in his chin and he had very strong white teeth. He had white, strong-looking hands. I noticed them particularly, and there was a signet ring on his little finger. He seemed to be watching me and Miss Anabel; and Miss Anabel was watching us both. Janet, sitting a little distance away, had brought out her knitting, and her needles were clicking away, registering disapproval as clearly as her pursed lips did.

Miss Anabel asked me questions about Crabtree Cottage and Aunt Amelia and Uncle William. Many of them she had asked before and I realized that she was asking them again so that he could hear the answers. He listened attentively and every now and then nodded.

The food was delicious, or perhaps I was so enchanted that I found everything different from everyday life. There was chicken, crusty bread and some sort of pickle which I had never tasted before.

"Why," said Miss Anabel, "Suewellyn has the wishbone." She picked up the bone on my plate and held it up. "Come on, Suewellyn, pull with me. If you get the bigger half you can have a wish."

"Three wishes," said the man.

"It's only one, Joel, you know," replied Miss Anabel.

"Today it's three," he retorted. "It's a special birthday. Had you forgotten that?"

"Of course it's a special day."

"So special wishes. Now for the contest."

"You know what you have to do, Suewellyn," said Miss Anabel. She picked up the bone. "You twist your little finger round that side, and I twist mine round this side, and we pull. The one who gets the bigger bit gets the wish."

"Wish three times," said Joel.

"There's one condition," said Miss Anabel. "You must not tell your wishes. Ready?"

We curled our little fingers about the bone. There was a crack. The bone had broken and I cried out in delight, for the larger part was in my hand.

"It's Suewellyn's," cried Miss Anabel.

"Shut your eyes and make your wishes," said Joel.

So I sat back holding the bone in my hand and asked myself what I wanted most of all. I wanted this day to last forever, but it would be silly to wish for that because nothing, not even chicken bones, could make that come true. I was

(21)

thinking hard. What I had always wanted was a father and mother; and before I had realized it I had wished for that—but not just any father and mother. I wanted a father like Joel and a mother like Miss Anabel. There was my second wish gone. I did not want to have to live in Crabtree Cottage. I wanted to live with my own father and mother.

The three wishes were made.

I opened my eyes. They were both watching me intently.

"Have you made your wishes?" asked Miss Anabel.

I nodded and pressed my lips together. It was very important that they should come true.

We then ate tarts with cherry jam in them, and they were delicious, and as I bit into the sweet tart I thought there could not be greater happiness than this.

Joel asked me if I rode.

I told him I did not.

"She ought to," he said, looking at Miss Anabel.

"I could speak to your Aunt Amelia," said Miss Anabel.

Joel stood up and held out a hand to me. "Come and see how you like it," he said.

I went with him to his horse; he lifted me up and put me on it.

He walked the horse through the trees. I thought it was the most thrilling moment of my life. Then suddenly he leaped up behind me and we started going quickly. We came through the trees in the woods and out to a field. The horse cantered and galloped and I thought for one moment: Perhaps he *is* the Devil and he has come to take me away.

But oddly enough I did not care. I wanted him to take me away. I wanted to stay with him and Miss Anabel for the rest of my life. I did not care if he was the Devil. If Aunt Amelia and Uncle William were saints I preferred the Devil. I had a feeling that Miss Anabel would not be far away from where he was, and if I were with one I would be with the other.

But that exciting ride came to an end and the horse was going slowly again through the trees to the clearing where Janet was packing up the remains of the picnic and putting the hamper into the dogcart.

Joel dismounted and lifted me down.

I was indescribably sad because I knew that my visit to the enchanted forest with its distant castle was over. It was like a beautiful dream from which I was trying hard not to wake up. But I knew I should.

He lifted me in his arms and kissed me. I put my arms about his neck. I said: "It was a lovely ride."

"I have never enjoyed a ride more," he said.

Miss Anabel was looking at us as though she did not know whether to laugh or cry but, being Miss Anabel, she laughed.

He mounted his horse and followed us to the dogcart. Miss Anabel and I got in. He went off in one direction and we went off in another to the station.

We alighted there.

"Don't forget to meet my train, Janet," Miss Anabel said.

It was a sad reminder that the day was almost over, that I would soon be back in Crabtree Cottage and this day's events would move into the past. We sat side by side in the train, holding hands tightly as though we would never let go. How the train rushed on! How I wanted to hold it back! The wheels were laughing at me, saying: "Soon be back! Soon be back!" over and over again.

When we were nearly there Miss Anabel put her arm around me and said: "What did you wish, Suewellyn?"

"Oh, I mustn't tell," I cried. "If I did they would never come true and I couldn't bear that."

"Were they such important wishes then?"

I nodded.

She was silent for a while and then she said: "It's not quite true that you mustn't tell *anyone*. You can tell one person. That's if you want to... and if you whisper, it won't make any difference about the wishes coming true."

I was glad. It is very comforting to be able to share things and there was no one I wanted to share with more than Miss Anabel.

So I said: "I wished for a father and mother first. Then I wanted you and Joel to be them; and after that I wanted us all to be together."

She did not speak for a long time and I wondered whether she was rather sorry I had told her.

We had come to the station. The fly was waiting for us, and in a very short time we were at Crabtree Cottage. It looked more dismal than ever now that I had been in the magic forest and seen the enchanted castle.

Miss Anabel kissed me and said: "I must hurry to catch my train." She still looked as though she were going to cry although she was smiling. I listened to the clop-clop of horses' hoofs which were carrying her away.

There were two parcels in my room which Miss Anabel had left for me. One contained a dress of blue silk with ribbons on it. It was the prettiest dress I had ever seen and it was Miss Anabel's birthday gift to me. There was a book about horses in the other parcel and I knew this was from Joel.

Oh, what a wonderful birthday! But the sad thing about wonderful occasions was that they made the days which followed seem more drab.

Aunt Amelia's comment to Uncle William on the outing was: "Unsettling!"

Perhaps she was right.

For the next few weeks I lived in a dream. I kept peeping at the blue dress, which was hung in my cupboard. I had not worn it. It was most unsuitable, said Aunt Amelia; and I had come to the conclusion that she was right. It was too beautiful to be worn. It was just to be looked at. At school Miss Brent said: "What's come over you, Suewellyn? You're very inattentive these days."

Anthony Felton said that I went to covens at night and took off all my clothes and danced round and round and kissed Farmer Mills's goat.

"Don't be silly," I told him; and I think the others agreed that he was romancing. Aunt Amelia would never have allowed me to go out at night and take off my clothes, which was indecent, and to kiss a goat would be unhealthy.

I read as much as I could of the book about horses. It was a little advanced for me; but I was always hoping that one day Miss Anabel would come again and I would be taken to the enchanted forest. I should want to know something about horses by the time I met Joel again. Then I thought how foolish I was not to have wished for something which would have been easy to grant—like perhaps another day in the forest, instead of a father and mother. Fathers and mothers had to be married. They were not in the least like Miss Anabel and Joel.

I grew interested in horses. Anthony Felton had a pony and I begged him to allow me to ride on it. At first he laughed me to scorn, and then I think it occurred to him that if I tried to ride I should surely fall off and that would be great fun. So I was taken to the paddock adjoining the manor house and I mounted Anthony's pony and rode round the field. It was a miracle that I was not thrown off. I kept thinking of Joel and imagined he was watching me. I wanted so much to shine in his eyes.

Anthony was very disappointed and wouldn't let me ride his pony after that.

It was November when Miss Anabel came again. She was paler and thinner. She told me she had been ill; she had had pleurisy and that was why she had not come before.

"It was only that which kept me away," she told me.

"Are we going to the forest again?" I asked.

She shook her head, rather sadly, I thought.

"Did you enjoy that?" she asked eagerly.

I clasped my hands together and nodded. There were not enough words to convey how much I had enjoyed it.

She was silent, looking a little sad, and I said: "It was a wonderful castle. It didn't look like a real one. I think it is one of those which are not there sometimes. Though there was that girl with the boys and they went into it. And there was the horse. I rode on that horse. . . . We galloped on it. It was exciting."

"You liked it all so much, Suewellyn?"

"Yes, I liked it better than anything I have ever done."

Later I heard her talking to Aunt Amelia.

"No," Aunt Amelia said, "I do not, Miss Anabel. Where would we keep it? We could not be in a position to afford such a thing. There would be more talk than there already is, and there is enough now, I can tell you."

"It would be so good for her."

"It would cause talk. I don't think Mr. Planter would agree to it. There are limits, Miss Anabel. And in a place like this . . . There are your visits for one thing. In these cases there are not usually visits."

"Oh, I know, I know, Amelia. But you'll be paid well. . . ."

"It's not a question of money. It's a question of appearances. In a place like this . . ."

"All right then. Leave it for a bit. Only I'd like her to ride and she would love it."

It was all very mysterious. I knew that Miss Anabel wanted to give me a pony for Christmas and Aunt Amelia would not allow it.

I was so angry. I should have wished for a pony. That would have been sensible. I had just been silly and wished for what was not possible.

Miss Anabel went away, but I knew she would come again

soon, although I heard Aunt Amelia telling her not to come too often. It looked bad.

I asked Anthony Felton to let me have another ride on his pony, but he refused. "Why should I?" he asked.

"Because I nearly had one," I answered.

"What do you mean? How could *you* nearly have one?"

"I nearly had one," I insisted.

I imagined riding out past the Felton paddock on a pony which was far handsomer than Anthony Felton's and I was so angry and frustrated that I hated Anthony and Aunt Amelia. I couldn't tell Aunt Amelia this but I could tell Anthony and I did.

"You're a witch and a bastard," he said, "and it's a terrible thing to be both."

Matty Grey no longer sat outside her cottage. It was too cold.

"That wind cutting right across the green blows itself into my bones," she said. "It's bad for me screws." Her screws were her rheumatism, and in the winter they were so bad that she could not stray from the fire. "The old screws is getting me today," she used to say. "No joke, they ain't. Still, Tom'll make me a nice fire, and what's nicer than a good wood fire? And when there's a kettle singing on the hob...well, you couldn't get nearer the angels in heaven, I say."

I made a habit of going into Matty's cottage when I came home from school. It could not be for long because Aunt Amelia must not know of these visits. She would not have approved. We were "better class" than Matty. It was rather complicated, for although we were not on the level of the doctor and the parson, who themselves were not quite up to the rank of squire, we were some way above Matty.

Matty would get me to cut a slice of bread from the big cottage loaf. "The bottom half, ducks." And I would put it on a long toasting fork which Tom's uncle had made at the forge, and hold it before the fire until it was a golden brown.

"A good strong cup of tea and a nice thick slice of good brown toast; your own fireside and the wind whistling outside and you shut away from it all....I don't reckon there could be better than that."

I didn't agree with Matty. There could be an enchanted forest, a cloth spread on the grass; there could be chicken wishbones and two beautiful people who were different from anyone I knew. There could be an enchanted castle seen through the trees and a horse on which to gallop.

"What you thinking about, young Suewellyn?" asked Matty.

"It depends," I said, "on you. Perhaps some people wouldn't want toast and strong tea. They might like picnics in forests."

"Now that's what I mean to say. It's what you fancy, eh? Well, this is my fancy. Now you tell me yours."

And before I realized it, I was telling her. She listened. "And you saw that forest, did you? And you saw this castle? And you was took there, was you? I know, it was by the lady who comes."

"Matty," I said excitedly, "did you know that if you break a wishbone and get the bigger half you can have three wishes?"

"Oh yes, that's an old trick, that is. When we was little now and then we'd have a bird...a regular treat that was. There'd be the plucking and the stuffing...and when it was done a regular fight between us little 'uns for the wishbone."

"Did you ever wish? Did your wishes come true?"

She was silent for a while and then she said: "Yes. I reckon I had a good life. Yes, I reckon my wishes come true."

"Do you think mine will?"

"Yes, I reckon so. One of these days it'll all come right for you. She's a mighty pretty lady what comes to see you."

"She's beautiful," I said. "And he..."

"Who's he, dearie?"

I thought: I'm talking too much. I mustn't...even to Matty. I had a fear that if I talked I would discover that it had not really happened and that I had only dreamed it.

"Oh, nothing," I said.

"You're burning the toast. Never mind. Scrape that black off in the sink."

I scraped the burned part from the bread and buttered it. I made and poured out the tea. Then I sat for a while watching the pictures in the fire. I saw the wood there glowing red and blue and yellow. And there was the castle.

Then suddenly the ashes fell into the grate and the picture collapsed.

I knew it was time I went. Aunt Amelia would be missing me and asking questions.

Christmas was almost upon us. The children went into the woods to gather holly and ivy to decorate the schoolroom.

Miss Brent set up a postbox in the hall of her house and we would slip in our cards to our friends. The day before Christmas Eve when school broke up Miss Brent would act as postman, open the paper-covered postbox, take out the cards and, sitting at her desk, call out our names, when we would go up and collect those which were addressed to us.

We were all very excited about it. We made our own cards in the classroom and there was much whispering and giggling as we painted on scraps of paper and with great secrecy folded them and wrote on the names of those for whom the offering was intended and slipped them into the box.

On the afternoon there would be a concert. Miss Brent would play the piano and we would all sing together and those among us who had good voices would sing solos; and others would recite.

It was a great day for us all and we looked forward to it for weeks before Christmas.

More exciting to me was Miss Anabel's visit. She came the day before the school party. She had brought parcels for me which had written on them "To be opened on Christmas Day." But I was always more excited by Miss Anabel herself than what she brought.

"In the spring," she said, "we'll have another picnic."

I was delighted. "In the same place," I cried. "Will there be chicken bones?"

"Yes," she promised. "Then you can have more wishes."

"I might not get the bigger piece of bone."

"I should think you would," she said with a smile.

"Miss Anabel, will he... will Joel be there?"

"I think he might be," she said. "You liked him, did you, Suewellyn?" she asked.

I hesitated. Like was not exactly a word one could apply to gods.

She was alarmed. "He didn't... frighten you?"

Again I was silent and she went on: "Do you want to see him again?"

"Oh yes," I cried fervently, and she seemed satisfied.

I was sad when the fly came to take her to the station; but not so sad as usual because, although the spring was a long way ahead, it would come in time and then I had the glorious prospect of the forest before me.

Uncle William had finished the Christmas crib he had

made in his woodshed and it was now in the church with a model of the Christ child lying in it. Three of the boys from school were going to be the three wise men. The vicar's son was one, because I supposed it was natural that the vicar should want him to be; Anthony Felton was another because he was the squire's grandson and his family gave liberally to the church and allowed all the garden parties and sales of work to be held on their lawns or, when it was wet, in the great hall; and Tom was the other because he had a beautiful voice. To hear that angelic voice proceeding from that rather untidy boy was like a miracle. I was glad for Tom. It was an honor. Matty was delighted about it. "His father had a voice. So did my granddaddy," she told me. "It runs in families."

Tom had stuck an enormous sprig of holly over *The Sailor's Return* in Matty's room, which gave it a jaunty air. I had often studied *The Sailor's Return* because it was the sort of picture I should not have expected Matty to have. There was something gloomy about it. It was a print and there was no color for one thing. The sailor stood at the door of the cottage with a bundle on his shoulder. His wife was staring blankly before her as though she were facing some major disaster instead of the return of a loved one. Matty had talked about the picture with tears in her eyes. It was strange that one who could laugh about the trials of real life should shed tears over the imaginary ones of someone in a picture.

I had badgered her to tell me the story. "Well," she said, "it's like this. You see the cot there. There's a little baby in it. Now that baby didn't ought to have been born because the sailor had been away for three years and she's had this little baby while he was away. He don't like that...and she don't like either."

"Why doesn't he? You'd think he'd be glad to come home and find a little baby."

"Well, it means that it's not his and he don't like that."

"Why?"

"Well, he's what you might call jealous. There was a pair of them pictures. My mammy split them up when she died. She said, '*The Return* is for you, Matty, and *The Departure* is for Emma.' Emma's my sister. She married and went up north."

"Taking *The Departure* with her?"

"She did. Didn't think much of it either. But I'd have liked to have the pair. Though *The Departure* was very sad. He

(29)

killed her, you see, and the police was there to take him away to be hanged. That's what *The Departure* meant. Oh, I'd have loved to have *The Departure*."

"Matty," I asked, "what happened to the little baby in the cot?"

"Someone took care of it," she said.

"Poor baby! It had no mother or father after that."

Matty said quickly: "Tom was in here telling me about that there postbox you've got at school. I hope you've done a nice one for Tom. He's a good boy, our Tom is."

"I've done a lovely one," I said, "of a horse."

"Tom'll like that. He's a rare one for horses. We're thinking of putting him to learn with Blacksmith Jolly. Blacksmiths have a lot to do with horses."

Sessions with Matty always came to an end too soon. They were always overshadowed by the knowledge that Aunt Amelia would be expecting me home.

Crabtree Cottage was cheerless after Matty's. The linoleum on the floor was polished to danger point and there was no holly propped up over the pictures of Christ and St. Stephen. It would have certainly looked out of place there and to have stuck a piece over the disagreeable Queen would have been nothing short of lese majesty.

"Dirty stuff," had been Aunt Amelia's comment. "Drops all over the place and the berries get trodden in."

The day of the party came. We did our singing, and the more talented of us—I was not among them—recited and did their solos. The postbox was opened. Tom had sent me a beautiful drawing of a horse and on the paper was written: "A merry Christmas. Yours truly, Tom Grey." Everyone in the school had sent everyone else a card, so it was a big delivery. The one I had from Anthony Felton was meant to wound rather than carry good wishes. It was the drawing of a witch on a broomstick. She had streaming dark hair and a black mole on her chin. "Wishing you a spellbinding Christmas," he had written on it. It was very badly drawn and I was delighted to note that the witch on it was more like Miss Brent than like me. I had had my revenge by sending him the picture of an enormously fat boy (Anthony was notoriously greedy and more than inclined to plumpness) holding a Christmas pudding. "Don't get too fat to ride this Christmas," I had written on it; and he would know that the card carried with it the hope that he would.

A few snowflakes fell on Christmas Eve and everyone was hoping it would settle. Instead it melted as soon as it touched the ground and was soon turning to rain.

I went to the midnight service with Aunt Amelia and Uncle William, which should have been an adventure because we were out so late; but nothing could really be an adventure when I walked between my two stern guardians and sat stiffly with them in the pew.

I was half asleep during the service and glad to be back in bed. Then it was Christmas morning, exciting in spite of the fact that there was no Christmas stocking for me. I knew that other children had them and thought it would be the height of fun to see one's stocking bulging with good things and plunging one's hand in to pull out the delights. "It's childish," said Aunt Amelia, "and bad for the stockings. You're too old now for such things, Suewellyn."

Still I had Anabel's presents. Clothes again—two dresses, one very beautiful. I had only worn the blue one she had given me once, and that was when she came. Now there was another silk one and a woolen one and a lovely sealskin muff. There were three books as well. I was delighted with these gifts and my great regret was that Anabel was not there to give them to me in person.

From Aunt Amelia there was a pinafore and from Uncle William a pair of stockings. I could not really feel very excited about them.

We went to church in the morning; then we came home and had dinner. It was a chicken which brought reminders, but there was no mention of wishbones. Christmas pudding followed. In the afternoon I read my books. It was a very long day. I longed to run across to the Greys' cottage. Matty had gone next door for the day and there were sounds of merriment spilling out on the green. Aunt Amelia heard it and tut-tutted, saying that Christmas was a solemn festival. It was Christ's birthday. People were meant to be solemn and not act like heathens.

"I think it ought to be happy," I pointed out, "because Christ was born."

Aunt Amelia said: "I hope you're not getting strange ideas, Suewellyn."

I heard her comment to Uncle William that there were all sorts at that school and it was a pity people like the Greys were allowed to send their children and mix with better folk.

I almost cried out that the Greys were the best folks I knew, but I was aware that it was no use trying to explain that to Aunt Amelia.

There was Boxing Day to follow... another holiday and even quieter than Christmas Day. It was raining and the southwest wind gusted over the green.

A long day. I could only revel in my presents and wonder when I should wear the silk dress.

In the New Year Anabel came. Aunt Amelia had lighted a fire in the parlor—a rare event—and she had drawn up the venetian blinds, for she could no longer complain of the sun's doing harm to her furniture.

The room still looked dismal in the light of the wintry sun. None of the pictures took any cheer from the light. St. Stephen looked more tortured, the Queen more disagreeable and Christ hadn't changed at all.

Miss Anabel arrived at the usual time, which was just after dinner. She looked lovely in a coat trimmed with fur and a sealskin muff, like the big sister of mine.

I hugged her and thanked her for the gifts.

"One day," she said, "you're going to have a pony. I am going to insist."

We talked as we always did. I showed her my books and we discussed school. I never told her about the teasing I received from Anthony Felton and his cronies because I knew that would worry her.

So the day passed with Anabel and in due course the fly came to take her back to the station. It seemed like just another of Anabel's visits, but this was not quite the case.

It was Matty who told me about the man at the King Willian Inn.

Tom was working there after school, carrying luggage into rooms and making himself generally useful. "It's a second string to his bow," said Matty. "In case it don't work out with the blacksmith."

Tom had told her about the man at the inn and Matty told me.

"A regular shindy-do there was up at the King William," she said. "He was a very high and mighty gentleman. Staying there in the best room. He arrived in a temper, he did. It was all along of there being no fly to take him to the King William when he got off the train. Well, how could there be? The fly was in use, wasn't it?" Matty nudged me. "You had a visitor yesterday, didn't you? Well, Mr. High and Mighty had to wait, and there's one thing that kind of gentleman don't like much . . . and that's being kept waiting."

"It doesn't really take long for the fly to come to Crabtree Cottage and go back to the station."

"Ah, but rich important gentlemen don't like waiting one little minute while others is served. I had it from Jim Fenner." (He was our stationmaster, porter and man of all work at the station.) "There he was standing on the platform ranting and raging while the fly went off carrying your young lady in it. He kept saying, 'Where is it going? How far?' And old Jim he says, all upset like, because he could see this was a real gentleman, Jim says, 'Well, sir, it won't be that long. 'Tas only gone to Crabtree Cottage on the green with the young lady.' 'Crabtree Cottage,' he roars, 'and where might that be?' ''Tis only on the green, sir. There by the church. Not much more than a stone's throw. The young lady could walk it in ten minutes. But she always takes the fly like and books it to bring her back to catch her train.' Well, that seemed to satisfy him and he said he'd wait. He asked Jim a lot of questions. He turned out to be a talkative sort of gentleman when he wasn't angry. He got all civil like and gave Jim five shillings. It's not every day Jim sees the likes of that. He says he hopes that gentleman stays a long time."

I couldn't stay talking to Matty, of course, so I left her and ran back to the cottage. It was getting dark early now and we left school in twilight. Miss Brent had said we should leave at three o'clock in winter because that would give the children who lived farther away time to get home before darkness fell. In the summer we finished at four. We started at eight in the morning instead of nine as in the summer and it was quite dark at eight.

Aunt Amelia was putting some leaves together. She said: "I'm going to take these to the church, Suewellyn. They're for the altar. It's a pity there are no flowers at this time of the year. Vicar was saying it looked bare after the autumn flowers were finished, so I said I would find some leaves and we would use them. He seemed to think it was a good idea. You can come with me."

I put my school bag in my room and dutifully went downstairs. We crossed the green to the church.

There was a hushed silence there. The stained glass windows looked different without the sun or even the gaslight to shine on them. I should have been a little scared to be there alone, afraid that the figure of Christ on the cross might come down and tell me how wicked I was. I thought that the pictures in the stained glass windows might come alive. There was a good deal of torturing in them and there was my old acquaintance St. Stephen up there, who seemed to have such a bad time on earth. Our footsteps rang out eerily on the stone flags.

"We shall have to hurry, Suewellyn," said Aunt Amelia. "It will be quite dark very soon."

We mounted the three stone steps to the altar.

"There!" said Aunt Amelia. "They'll make some sort of show. I think I had better put them in water. Here, Suewellyn, take this jar and fill it at the pump."

I took it and ran out of the church. The graveyard was just outside. The gravestones looked like old men and women kneeling down, their faces hidden in gray hoods.

The pump was a few yards from the church. To reach it I had to make my way past some of the oldest gravestones. I had read the inscriptions on them many times when we came out of church. People had been laid under them a long, long time ago. Some of the dates on them went back to the seventeenth century. I ran past them to the pump and vigorously began pumping the water and filling the pot.

As I did so I heard a sudden footstep. I looked over my shoulder. It had grown darker since Aunt Amelia and I entered the church. I felt a shiver run down my spine. I had the feeling that someone...something was watching me.

I turned back to the pump. One had to work hard to get the water and it wasn't easy working the pump with one hand and holding the jar with the other.

My hands were shaking. Don't be silly, I said to myself. Why shouldn't someone else come to the churchyard? Perhaps it was the vicar's wife returning home to the vicarage or one of the devoted church workers who also had the idea of adorning the altar.

I had filled the jar too full. I tipped a little water out. Then I heard the sound again. I gasped with horror. A figure was standing there among the gravestones. I was sure it was a ghost who had risen from the tomb.

I gave a startled cry and ran as fast as I could to the church porch. The water in the jar slopped over and splashed down the front of my coat. But I had reached the sanctuary of the church.

There I paused for a moment to look over my shoulder. I could see no one.

Aunt Amelia was waiting impatiently at the altar.

"Come along, come along," she said.

I handed the jar to her. My hands were wet and cold and I was shivering.

"There's not enough here," she scolded. "Why, you careless girl, you've spilled it."

I stood firmly. "It's dark out there," I said stubbornly. Nothing would have induced me to go back to the pump.

"I suppose it will have to do," she said grudgingly. "Suewellyn, I don't know why you can't do things properly."

She arranged the leaves and we left the church. I kept very close to her as we crossed the graveyard and came out to the green.

"Not what I should have liked for the altar," said Aunt Amelia. "But they'll have to do."

I could not sleep that night. I kept dozing and thinking I was at the pump in the graveyard. I imagined the ghost starting up from the ground and coming out to frighten people. It had certainly frightened me. I had always thought of ghosts as misty white transparent beings. When I came to think of it, as far as the gloom and my fear would allow me, this one had been fully dressed. It was a man, a very tall man in a shiny black hat. I hadn't had time to notice very much else about him except the steadiness of his gaze. And that had been directed straight at me.

At last I slept and so deeply that I awoke late next morning.

Aunt Amelia surveyed me with a grim expression when I went down to breakfast. She had not given me a call. She never did. I was supposed to wake at the right time myself and get to school at the appointed hour. It was something to do with Discipline, for which Aunt Amelia had as great a reverence as she had for Respectability.

I was, consequently, late for school and Miss Brent, who believed the teaching of the necessity of Punctuality was as important as the three Rs, said that if I could not come on time I should stay behind for half an hour and write out the Creed before I left school.

It would mean, of course, that I shouldn't have time to call on Matty.

The day passed and at three o'clock I was seated at my desk writing out "I believe in God the Father..." and when I came to "conceived" saying the little rhyme to myself, "I before E except after C," and I had finished it in twenty minutes. I then took it to Miss Brent's sitting room upstairs, knocked on the door and handed it to her. She glanced through it, nodded and said: "You'd better be quick. You'll be home before dark. And, Suewellyn, do try to be on time. It's bad manners not to be."

I said: "Yes, Miss Brent," very meekly and ran off.

If I took the short cut across the churchyard, which would save a few minutes, I might just have time to look in on Matty and tell her about the ghost I had seen in the churchyard on the previous day. If I were late home I could tell Aunt Amelia I had been kept in to write "I believe." She would nod grimly and show her approval of Miss Brent's action.

To go across the churchyard after the previous day's experience seemed a little strange. But it was typical of me—and perhaps this goes a little way to explain what happened later—that the fact of my fear gave the churchyard special fascination for me. It was not quite dark. It had been a brighter day than yesterday and the sun was a great red ball on the horizon. I was afraid; I was tingling with a mixture of apprehension and excitement, but somehow I felt myself drawn almost involuntarily to the churchyard.

As soon as I entered it I called myself stupid for coming. Fear took a firm grip of me and I had a great desire to turn and run. But I wouldn't. I would skirt the ancient part and make my way among the whiter stones whose inscriptions had not yet been obliterated by time and weather.

I was being followed. I knew it. I could hear the footsteps behind me. I started to run. Whoever was behind me was hurrying too.

How foolish of me to have come here. I was playing some game of bravado with myself. I had had my warning yesterday. How scared I had been then and Aunt Amelia had not been far away. I would only have had to get to her. And yet I had come back...alone.

I could see the gray walls of the church. Whoever was following me was faster than I. It...he...was right at my heels.

I looked at the church door. I remembered hearing something about churches being a sanctuary because they were holy places. Evil spirits could not exist there.

I hesitated at the door of the church...whether to go in or run?

A hand reached out and touched me.

I gave a little gasp.

"What's the matter, little girl?" said a musical and very friendly voice. "There's nothing to be afraid of, you know."

I swung round and faced him.

He was a very tall man and I noticed the black hat which he had worn yesterday. He was smiling. His eyes were dark brown and his face was not a bit as I imagined a ghost's would be. It was a living man who confronted me. He took off his hat and bowed.

"I only wanted to talk to you," he went on.

"You were in the graveyard yesterday," I accused.

"Yes," he said. "I like graveyards. I like reading the inscriptions on the tombs, do you?"

I did, but I said nothing. I was trembling with fear.

"That pump was a bit stiff, wasn't it?" he went on. "I was coming to help you with it. You needed one to hold the jar while the other pumped. Don't you agree?"

"Yes," I said.

"Show me the church, will you? I'm interested in old churches."

"I have to get home," I told him. "I'm late."

"Yes, later than the others. Why?"

"I was kept in...to write the Creed."

"'I believe in God the Father.' Do you believe, little girl?"

"Of course I believe. Everybody believes."

"Do they? Then you know God will watch over you and protect you from all dangers and perils of the night...even strangers in graveyards. Come along...just for a moment. Show me the church. I believe they are rather proud of their stained glass windows here."

"The vicar is," I replied. "They have been written about. He has a lot of cuttings. You can see them if you like. He would show them to you."

He was still holding my arm and drawing me towards the church door. He glanced cursorily at the notices in the porch about the various meetings.

I felt better inside the church. That air of sanctity restored

(37)

my courage. I felt nothing terrible could happen here with the golden cross, and the stained glass windows portraying the life of Jesus in lovely reds, blues and gold.

"It's a beautiful church," he said.

"Yes, but I must go. The vicar will show you round."

"In a moment. And I had better see it in daylight."

"It will soon be dark," I said, "and I..."

"Yes, you must be home by dark. What is your name?"

"Suewellyn," I told him.

"That's a pretty and unusual name. What else?"

"Suewellyn Campion."

He nodded as though my name pleased him.

"And you live at Crabtree Cottage?"

"How did you know?"

"I saw you go in there."

"So you watched me before."

"I just happened to be near."

"I must go or my Aunt Amelia will be angry."

"You live with your Aunt Amelia, do you?"

"Yes."

"Where are your father and mother?"

"I must go. The vicar will show you about the church."

"Yes, in a moment. Who was the lady who visited you two days ago?"

"I know who you are," I said. "You're the one who was angry about the fly."

"Yes, that's right. They told me she had only gone to Crabtree Cottage. She's a most attractive lady. What is her name?"

"Miss Anabel."

"Oh, I see, and does she call to see you often?"

"Yes, she does."

Suddenly he took hold of my chin and looked into my face. I believed then that he was the Devil and that he was looking for the mole on my chin.

I said: "I know what you're looking for. Let me go. I must go home now. If you want to see the church ask the vicar."

"Suewellyn," he said. "What's wrong? What am I looking for? Tell me?"

"It's nothing to do with the Devil. It's something you're born with. It's like having a strawberry on your face when your mother fancied strawberries."

"What?" he asked.

"It's nothing, I tell you. Lots of people have them. It's only a mole."

"It's very nice," he said. "Very nice indeed. Now, Suewellyn, you've been very kind to me and I am going to see you home."

I almost ran out of the church. He was beside me. We walked swiftly through the graveyard to the edge of the green.

"Now, there's Crabtree Cottage," he said. "You run along. I'll watch from here until you are safely in. Good night, Suewellyn, and thanks for being so kind to me."

I ran.

As I was going to my room, Aunt Amelia came out of hers.

"You're late," she said.

"I was kept in."

She nodded with a smile of satisfaction.

"I had to write out the Creed," I told her.

"That'll teach you to lie abed," she commented.

I went to my room. I could not tell her about the stranger. It was all so odd. Why had he followed me? Why had he wanted me to show him the church? For when he was in it he seemed hardly interested in it. It was rather mystifying. At least I had not given way to my fear. I had braved the graveyard and discovered that the ghost was only a man after all.

I wondered if I should ever see him again.

I did not.

When I looked in on Matty the next day she told me that the gentleman had left the King William. Tom had carried his bag down for him to the fly; and he had gone off on the train traveling first class.

"He was a real proper gentleman," said Matty, "traveling first class and having all the best at the King William. John Jeffers don't have many like him there, and he gave Tom a shilling for carrying his bags up and another for bringing them down. A regular gentleman."

I pondered whether to tell Matty about my encounter in the graveyard with that regular real proper gentleman.

I hesitated. I wasn't quite sure about it myself. Perhaps I'll tell her one day, but not yet...no, not yet.

At the end of the week I had ceased to feel that vague apprehension which had come to me since I first saw the man in the graveyard. After all he had seemed kind in the church.

He had one of the handsomest faces I had ever seen. He reminded me a little of Joel. His voice had been similar and he had smiled in the same way. He had been a visitor to the church and had thought that I, who lived in the village, could tell him something about it. That was all.

I knew he had not gone to the vicar the next day because it was the next morning he left.

It had been a cold day. Miss Brent had lighted a fire in the schoolroom—even so, our fingers were cramped with cold and that was not good for our handwriting. We were all glad when three o'clock came and we could run home. I looked in on Matty, who was seated before a roaring fire. The kettle, which was covered with black soot, was on the hob and it would not be long before she was making her tea.

She welcomed me as she always did with her wheezy laugh which shook her plump body.

"This is a day and a half," she said. "Wind coming straight in from the east. Even a dog wouldn't go out on a day like this...unless he had to."

I nestled at her feet and wished I could stay there all the evening. It would not be nearly so cozy in Crabtree Cottage. I knew there was a layer of dust on the mantelshelf and crumbs under Matty's chair; but there was a coziness in these things which I missed at home. I thought of my icily cold bedroom, going up there to undress and walking carefully over the dangerously polished linoleum, and leaping into bed to shiver. Beside Matty's fireplace was a stone hot water bottle which she took to bed with her.

Tom came in and said: "Hello, Granma." He nodded towards me. He was always shy of me.

"Ain't you wanted at King William?" asked Matty.

"Got hour off to myself before we get busy. Not that there'll be much...night like this."

"Oh, you don't get them fine gentlemen every day."

"Wish we did," said Tom.

I found myself telling them about the encounter in the graveyard. I had not meant to, but somehow it made me seem important to tell. Tom had carried his bags and had his shilling. I wanted them to know that I, too, had made his acquaintance.

"His sort is always interested in churches and suchlike," said Tom.

Matty nodded. "There was a man come down here

once...after the tombs he was. There he would sit...down by Sir John Ecclestone's graven image, and rub it off on a bit of paper. Oh yes, you get that sort."

"When I was kept in late I went home through the grave-yard. He was there...waiting."

"Waiting?" echoed Tom. "What for?"

"I don't know. He wanted me to go into the church with him and I told him the vicar would tell him all he wanted to know."

"Oh, Vicar would like that. Once he gets started on the arches and the windows you can't stop him."

"It was funny," I said. "It was really as though he wanted to see me...not the church."

Matty looked sharply at Tom.

"Tom," she said sternly, "I told you to keep your eye on Suewellyn."

"I do, Granma. She was kept in that day, wasn't you, Sue-wellyn, and I had to go to work at the inn."

I nodded.

"You don't want to go looking into no churches with strange men, ducks," said Matty. "Not churches nor nothing."

"I didn't really want to, Matty. He somehow made me."

"And how long was you in the church?" asked Matty intently.

"About five minutes."

"And he just talked to you, did he? He didn't...er..."

I was puzzled. Matty was trying to tell me something and I wasn't sure what.

"Never mind," she went on. "You just remember, and His High and Mighty Nibs is gone away, I believe. So there won't be no more visiting churches for him."

There was silence in the cottage. Then the center of the fire collapsed and sent out a shower of sparks onto the hearth.

Tom took the poker and knelt down, poking the fire. His face was very red.

Matty was unusually silent.

I could stay no longer but I made up my mind that when I was alone with Matty I was going to ask her why she was so disturbed about this man.

But that opportunity never came.

It had been a mild and misty day. It was almost dark just after three o'clock when I came home from school. As I came to the green I saw the station fly outside Crabtree Cottage and I wondered what it could mean. Miss Anabel always let us know when she was coming.

So I did not call in on Matty as I had intended but ran as fast as I could into the cottage.

Aunt Amelia and Uncle William came out of the parlor as I entered. They looked bewildered.

"You're home," said Aunt Amelia unnecessarily; she gulped and there was a brief silence. Then she said: "Something has happened."

"Miss Anabel..." I began.

"She's upstairs in your room. You'd better go up. She'll tell you."

I ran up the stairs. There was chaos in my room. My clothes were on the bed and Miss Anabel had begun putting them into a bag.

"Suewellyn!" she cried as I entered. "I'm so glad you're early."

She ran to me and hugged me. Then she said: "You're coming away with me. I can't explain now.... You'll understand later. Oh, Suewellyn, you do want to come!"

"With you, Miss Anabel, of course!"

"I was afraid...after all, you've been here so long...I thought...never mind....I've got your clothes. Is there anything else?"

"There are my books."

"All right then...get them...."

"Is it for a holiday?"

"No," she said, "it's for always. You're going to live with me now and...and...But I'll tell you about it later. At the moment I want us to catch the train."

"Where are we going?"

"I'm not sure. But a long way. Suewellyn, just help me."

I found the few books I possessed and those with my clothes went into the traveling bag which Miss Anabel had brought with her.

I was quite bewildered. Secretly I had always hoped for something like this. Now it had come I felt too stunned to accept it.

She shut the bag and took my hand.

We paused for a second or so to look round the room. The sparsely furnished room which had been mine for as long as I could remember. Highly polished linoleum, texts on the walls—all improving and all slightly menacing. The one which I had been most conscious of was: "Oh, what a tangled web we weave, when first we practise to deceive!"

I was to remember that in the years to come.

There was the small iron bedstead covered by the patchwork quilt made by Aunt Amelia—each patch surrounded by delicate feather stitching, a sign of commendable industry. "You should start collecting for a patchwork quilt," Aunt Amelia had said. Not now, Aunt Amelia! I am going away from patchwork quilts, cold bedrooms and colder charity forever. I am going away with Miss Anabel.

"Saying good-by to it?" asked Miss Anabel.

I nodded.

"A little sorry?" she asked anxiously.

"No," I said vehemently.

She laughed the laugh I remembered so well, although it was a little different now, more high-pitched, slightly hysterical.

"Come on," she said, "the fly's waiting."

Aunt Amelia and Uncle William were still in the hall.

"I must say, Miss Anabel..." began Aunt Amelia.

"I know...I know...," replied Anabel. "But it has to be. You will be paid...."

Uncle William was looking on helplessly.

"What I am wondering is this," went on Aunt Amelia, "what are people going to *say?*"

"They've been saying things for years," retorted Miss Anabel lightly. "Let them go on."

"It's all very well for them as is not here," said Aunt Amelia.

"Never mind. Never mind. Come on, Suewellyn, or we'll miss our train."

I looked up at Aunt Amelia. "Good-by, Suewellyn," she said, and her lips twitched. She bent down and touched the side of my face with hers, which was as near as she could get to a caress. "Be a good girl...no matter where you find yourself. Remember to read your Bible and trust in the Lord."

"Yes, Aunt Amelia," I said. "I will."

Then it was Uncle William's turn. He gave me a real kiss. "Be a good girl," he said, and pressed my hand.

Then Miss Anabel was hurrying me out to the fly.

* * *

(43)

Of course I am looking back over the years and it is not always easy to remember what happened when one is not quite seven years old. I think the picture gets colored a little; there is much that is forgotten; but I am sure that a wild excitement possessed me and I felt no regret at leaving Crabtree Cottage except for Matty, when I came to think of it, and Tom of course. I should have liked to sit once more by Matty's fire and tell her how I found Miss Anabel in the cottage packing my things with the fly waiting to take us to the station.

I do remember the train going on and on through the darkness and now and then the lights of a town appearing and how the wheels changed their tune. Going away. Going away. Going away with Anabel.

Miss Anabel held my hand tightly and said: "Are you happy, Suewellyn?"

"Oh yes," I told her.

"And you don't really mind leaving Aunt Amelia and Uncle William?"

"No," I answered. "I loved Matty, and Tom a bit, and Uncle William I liked."

"Of course they looked after you very well. I was very grateful to them."

I was silent. It was so difficult for me to understand.

"Are we going to the woods?" I asked. "Are we going to see the castle?"

"No. We're going a long way."

"To London?" I asked. Miss Brent had often talked about London and it was marked with a big black spot on the map so that I could find it straight away.

"No, no," she said. "Far, far away. On a ship. We're going to sail away from England."

On a ship! I was so excited that I started to bounce up and down on the seat involuntarily. She laughed and hugged me and I thought then that Aunt Amelia would have told me to sit still.

We got out of the train and waited on a platform for another train. Miss Anabel brought bars of chocolate from her bag.

"This will stay the pangs," she said and laughed; although I did not know what she meant I laughed with her and dug my teeth into the delicious chocolate. Aunt Amelia had not allowed chocolate in Crabtree Cottage. Anthony Felton had sometimes brought it to school and took great pleasure in eating it before the rest of us and letting us know how good it was.

It was night when we left the train. Anabel had traveling bags of her own and with mine there seemed to be a good deal of luggage. There was a fly which took us to a hotel where we had a big and luxurious bedroom with a double bed.

"We must be up early in the morning," said Miss Anabel. "Can you get up early in the morning?"

I nodded blissfully. Some food was brought up to our room—hot soup and cold ham, which was delicious; and that night Miss Anabel and I slept in the big bed together.

"Isn't this fun, Suewellyn?" she said. "I always wanted it to be like this."

I didn't want to go to sleep. I was so happy but so tired that I soon did. I awoke to find myself alone in the bed. I remembered where I was and gave a cry of alarm because I thought Miss Anabel had left me.

Then I saw her. She was standing by the window.

"What's the matter, Suewellyn?" she asked.

"I thought you'd gone. I thought you'd left me."

"No," she said, "I'm never going to leave you again. Come here."

I went to the window. I saw a strange sight before me. There were a lot of buildings and what looked like a big ship lying in the middle of them.

"It's the docks," she told me. "Do you see that ship? It will sail this afternoon and we are going to be on it."

The adventure was getting more and more exciting every minute. Not that anything could be more wonderful than being with Miss Anabel.

We had breakfast in our room and then the porter took our bags down and we went in a fly to the docks. All our luggage was taken and we went up a gangway. Clutching my hand tightly in hers, Miss Anabel took me up a flight of stairs to a long passage. We came to a door on which she knocked.

"Who's there?" said a voice.

"We're here," cried Miss Anabel.

The door opened and Joel was standing there.

He just caught Miss Anabel in his arms and held her tightly. Then he picked me up and held me. My heart was beating very fast. I could only think of the wishing bone in the forest.

"I was afraid you wouldn't be able to..." he began.

"Of course I would be able to," said Miss Anabel. "And I wasn't coming without Suewellyn."

"No, of course not," he said.

"We're safe now," she said, a little anxiously, I thought.

"Not for another three hours...when we sail...."

She nodded. "We'll stay here till then."

He looked down at me. "What do you think of this, Suewellyn? A bit of a surprise eh?"

I nodded. I looked round the room, which I learned was called a cabin. There were two beds in it one above the other. Miss Anabel opened a door and I saw another very small room leading from it.

"This is where you'll sleep, Suewellyn."

"Are we going to sleep on the ship then?"

"Oh yes, we're going to sleep here for a long time."

I was just too bewildered to speak. Then Miss Anabel took my hand and we sat together on the lower bed. I was between the two of them.

"There's something I want to tell you," said Miss Anabel. "I'm your mother."

Waves of happiness swept over me. I had a mother and that mother was Miss Anabel. It was the most wonderful thing that could happen. It was better even than going on a ship.

"There's something else," said Miss Anabel; and she waited.

Then Joel said: "And I am your father."

There was a deep silence in the cabin. Then Miss Anabel said: "What are you thinking, Suewellyn?"

"I was thinking that chicken bones *are* magic. All my three wishes...they've come true."

Children take so much for granted. It was not long before I felt I had always been on a ship. I was soon accustomed to the rolling and lurching, the pitching and tossing, which had no effect on me though it made some other people ill.

As soon as the ship had been a day at sea and England was far behind us I noticed the change in my parents. They had lost a certain nervousness. They were happier. I vaguely sensed that they were running away from something. But I forgot about that after a while.

We were on the ship for what seemed like forever. Summer

had come quite suddenly and quickly when it shouldn't have been summer at all—moreover it was a very hot summer. We sailed on calm blue seas and I would be on deck with Joel or Miss Anabel...or perhaps both...watching porpoises, whales, dolphins and flying fish—such things which I had never seen outside picture books.

I had a new name. I was no longer Suewellyn Campion. I was Suewellyn Mateland. I could call myself Suewellyn Campion Mateland, suggested Anabel. Then I wouldn't lose the name I had had for seven years altogether.

Anabel was Mrs. Mateland. She said she thought I shouldn't call her Miss Anabel any more. We discussed what I should call her. Mother sounded formal. Mamma too severe. How we laughed about it. She said at last: "Just call me Anabel. Drop the Miss." That seemed best and I called Joel Father Jo.

I was so happy to have a father and mother. Anabel I loved slavishly. I worshipped her. Joel? Well, I was very much in awe of him. He was so tall and important-looking. I think everyone was a little afraid of him...even Anabel.

That he was the finest, strongest man in the world I had no doubt. He was like a god. But Anabel was no goddess. She was the most lovely human being I had ever known and nothing could compare with my love for her.

I discovered that Joel was a doctor, for when one of the passengers fell sick he cured her.

"He has saved a lot of people's lives," Anabel told me. "So one..."

I waited for her to go on but she did not, and I was too busy thinking how wonderfully it had all turned out for me to ask. I had gained not ordinary parents but these two. It was indeed a miracle after having none.

The journey continued. It was always hot and I had to think hard to remember the east wind blowing across the green and how in winter I had to break the thin layer of ice to get the water to wash from the ewer in my bedroom.

That was all far away and becoming more and more hazy in my mind as my new life imposed itself on the old.

In time we came to Sydney, a town of beauty and excitement. As we passed through the Heads, I watched with my parents on either side of me and my father told me how many years ago prisoners had been brought here to get them out of England. This coast was rather like the one we had in

England...or Wales rather, and it had therefore been named New South Wales.

"The finest harbor in the world," said my father. "That's what they called it then and it still is."

It was too much for a child of my age to absorb. A new family; a new country; a new life. But because I was so young, I just lived from day to day and each morning when I awoke it was with a sense of excitement and happiness.

I learned a little about Sydney. We were there for three months. We found a house near the harbor, which we rented for a short period, and there we lived very quietly. A vague uneasiness had crept into the household which had not been there when we were on the ship. Anabel was more frequently affected by it than my father. It was almost as though she were afraid of too much happiness.

I felt a twinge of fear too.

I said to her once: "Anabel, if you are too happy can something take it all away from you?"

She was very perceptive. She understood at once that some of her anxiety had come through to me.

"Nothing is going to take us away from each other," she said at last.

My father went away for what seemed like a long time. Each day we would watch for the return of the ship which would bring him. Anabel grew sad, I knew, though she tried not to let me see it. We went on living as we had when the three of us were together; but I could see she was different. She was always looking across the sea.

Then one day he came back.

He was very pleased. He held her tightly in his arms and then he picked me up, still holding her with one arm.

He said: "We're going away. I've found the place. You'll like it. We can settle there...miles out in the ocean. You'll feel safe there, Anabel."

"Safe," she repeated. "Yes...that's what I want...to feel safe. Where is it?"

"Where is a map?"

We pored over the map. Australia was like a circle of dough which had been kneaded slightly out of shape. New Zealand was two dogs fighting each other. And there right out in the blue ocean were several little black dots.

My father was pointing to one of these.

"Ideal," he was saying. "Isolated...except for a group of

the same islands. This is the largest. Little goes on there. The people are inclined to be friendly...easygoing...just what you would expect. There has been some cultivation of the coconut, but little now. There are palms all over the place. I called it Palmtree Island but it is already named Vulcan. They are in need of a doctor there. There is none on the island...no school...nothing....It is the place where one can lose oneself...a place to develop...a place to offer something to. Oh, Anabel, I like it. You will too."

"And Suewellyn?"

"I've thought of Suewellyn. You can teach her for a few years and then she can go to school in Sydney. We're not all that far. A ship calls once now and then to collect the copra. It's the place, Anabel. I knew it as soon as I saw it."

"What shall we need?" she asked.

"Lots and lots of things. We have a month or so. The ship calls every two months. I want us to be on the next one that goes. In the meantime we are going to be busy."

We were busy. We bought all kinds of things—furniture, clothes, stores of all sorts.

"My father must be a very rich man," I said. "Aunt Amelia said she always looked twice before she spent a farthing." Take care of the pence and the pounds will take care of themselves was one of her favorite sayings. Waste not, want not was another. Every crust of bread had to be made into a bread and butter pudding, and I was often in trouble for feeding the birds in winter.

My father talked a great deal about the island. Palms grew in abundance, but there were other trees as well as breadfruit, bananas, oranges and lemons.

There was a house there which had been built for the man who had made a thriving industry out of the cultivation of coconuts. My father had taken over the house at a bargain price.

All our baggage was put on board the ship and we set sail. I don't remember what time of year it was. One forgot because there were no seasons as I had known them. It was always summer.

What I shall never forget is my first glimpse of Vulcan Island. I immediately noticed the enormous peak which seemed to rise up out of the sea and was visible long before we reached the island.

"It has a strange name, that island," said my father. "It

is called something which when translated means the Grumbling Giant."

We were standing on deck, the three of us hand in hand, watching for the first glimpse of our new home. And there it was—a great peak rising out of the sea.

"Why does it grumble?" I asked eagerly.

"It's always grumbled. Sometimes when it gets really angry it sends out a few stones and boulders. They are boiling hot."

"Is it really a giant?" I asked. "I have never seen one."

"Well, you are going to make the acquaintance of the Grumbling Giant, but it's not a real giant," answered my father. "I'm afraid it is only a mountain. It dominates the island. The native name is Grumbling Giant Island but some travelers came by long ago and called it Vulcan. So on the maps it has become that."

We remained there looking and in due course the land seemed to form itself about the great mountain and there were yellow sands and waving palms everywhere.

"It's like a paradise," said Anabel.

"We are going to make it that," answered my father.

We could not go right in to the island and had to anchor quite a mile out. There was a tremendous bustle of activity on the shore. Brown-skinned people paddled out in light slim craft which I afterwards learned were called canoes. They were shouting and gesticulating and mostly laughing.

Our possessions were loaded into some of the ship's lifeboats and they and the canoes brought them ashore.

When the goods had all gone, we were taken.

Then the little boats were drawn up and the big ship set sail, leaving us in our new home on Vulcan Island.

There was so much to do, so much to see. I could not entirely believe it was all happening. It seemed like something out of an adventure story.

Anabel was aware of my bewilderment.

She said: "One day you will understand."

"Tell me now," I begged.

She shook her head. "You would not understand now. I want to leave it until you are older. I am going to start writing it down now so that you can read it when you are older and understand. Oh, Suewellyn, I do want you to understand. I don't want you ever to blame us. We love you. You are our very own child and, because of the way it happened, it only makes us love you more."

She could see that I was very puzzled. She kissed me and, holding me close to her, went on: "I'm going to tell you all about it. Why you're here... why we're all here... how it came about. There was nothing else we could do. You must not blame your father... nor me. We are not like Amelia and William." She gave a little laugh. "They live... safely. That's the word I was looking for. We don't. It's not in our nature to. I have a feeling that you might be as we are." Then she laughed again. "Well, that's the way we're made. And yet... Suewellyn, we're going to settle here... we're going to like it. We're going to remember all the time if we feel home-sick... that we're together and this is the only way we can stay together."

I put my arms round her neck. I was overwhelmed by my love for her.

"We're never, never going to leave each other, are we?" I asked fearfully.

"Never," she said vehemently. "Only death can part us. But who wants to talk about death? Here is life. Don't you feel it, Suewellyn? It's teeming with life here. You only have to lift a stone and there it is...." She grimaced. "Mind you, I could do without the ants and termites and suchlike.... But there's life here... and it's our life... the three of us together. Be patient, my dearest child. Be happy. Let's live for each day as it comes along. Can you do that?"

I nodded vigorously, and we walked together through the palm trees to where the warm tropical water rippled onto the sandy beach.

Anabel's Story

Jessamy had played a big part in my life. She had always been there. She was rich, petted and the only child of doting parents. I never envied her her pretty clothes and her jewelry. I am not, I believe, envious by nature. It is one of my virtues, and as I have few others it is advisable to record it. In any case I always believed I had so much more than she did.

It was true I did not live in a mansion surrounded by servants. I did not have several ponies which I could ride as the fancy took me. I lived in a rambling vicarage with my widowed father—my mother had died giving birth to me— and we had two servants only, Janet and Amelia. Neither of them exactly doted on me, but I think Janet was fond of me in her way, though she would never admit it. They were both quick and eager to tell me of my faults. But I was happier, I think, yes, a great deal happier than Jessamy.

The fact was that Jessamy was decidedly what kind people call "homely" and those uncomfortable people like Janet, who could never tell a lie however much it might save someone's feelings being hurt, called downright plain.

"Never mind," Janet used to say. "Her father will buy a nice husband for her. You, Miss Anabel, will have to find your own."

Janet pursed her lips when she said this as though she was certain that my hopes of finding one were very frail.

Dear Janet, she was the best soul in the world but she was obsessed by her own unshakable veracity from which she would never diverge.

"It's a good thing you're not brought up before the Inquisition, Janet," I said to her once. "You'd still stick out for the silliest little truth in face of the stake."

"Now what are you talking about, Miss Anabel?" she replied. "I never knew anyone who took such flights of fancy. And, mark my words, you'll come a cropper one of these days."

She had seen that prophecy come true; but that was later.

So there I was in my vicarage home with my absentminded father, down-to-earth honest Janet and Amelia, who was every bit as virtuous as Janet and even more aware of it.

Some people might wonder how I could enjoy life thoroughly but I did. There was so much to do. There was interest all around me. I helped my father quite a bit. I even wrote a sermon for him once and he was halfway through it before he realized it was not the kind of sermon his parishioners wanted to hear. It was all about what constituted a good person and I had unwittingly illustrated my meaning by describing some of the failings of the people who were sitting in the pews listening. Fortunately Father changed to one he kept in a drawer about God's gifts to the land, which was really one for the harvest festival, but as he changed over before my revolutionary words had aroused the congregation from its usual slumber, no one noticed.

I was not allowed to write sermons after that. It was a pity. I should have liked to.

I remember Sundays well. The Seton family were always there in the family pew right in the front under the lectern. They were the big family who lived in the manor and it was to them my father owed his living. They were related to us. Lady Seton was my aunt, for she and my mother had been sisters. Amy Jane had married "well" when she took Sir Timothy Seton, for he was a rich man owning a great deal of land and, I believe, had many possessions as well. It was a very satisfactory match apart from one thing. They had no son to carry on the illustrious Seton name and their hopes rested on their only daughter, Jessamy. Jessamy was constantly indulged, but oddly enough that did not spoil her. She was a rather timid child and I always got the better of her when we were alone. Of course when we were not and there were adults present, they always saw fair play, which meant putting Jessamy in the ascendant.

When we were young and before Jessamy had a governess, she came to the vicarage for lessons because then my father had a curate who used to teach us.

Let me start at the beginning though. There were two sisters—Amy Jane and Susan Ellen. They were the daughters of a parson and when they grew up the younger of the two, Susan Ellen, fell in love with the curate who came to assist her father. He was poor and not in a position to marry but Susan Ellen had never been one to consider the practical side of life. Acting against the advice of her father, the entire village community and her forceful sister, she eloped with the curate. They were very poor because he had no living and they opened a little school and taught in it for a while. Meanwhile Amy Jane, the wise virgin, had made the acquaintance of the wealthy Sir Timothy Seton. He was a widower with no children and he desperately wanted them. Amy Jane was a good-looking, very capable young lady. Why should they not marry? He needed a mistress for his house and children for his nurseries. Amy Jane seemed well equipped to provide them both.

Amy Jane believed she was a suitable wife for him and, what was more important, that he would be the right husband for her. Riches, standing, security—they were three very desirable goals in Amy Jane's eyes. And after the disastrous marriage of her sister there must be someone to reinstate the family fortunes.

So Amy Jane married and in her forceful way set about performing the tasks she had undertaken. In a short while Sir Timothy's household was managed with the utmost skill, to his delight and to slightly less of that of the domestics, for those whom Amy Jane considered not worth their salt were dismissed, and the rest, realizing their fate lay in their ability to please Amy Jane, proceeded to do just that.

It was not long before a living was found for the curate and his reckless bride; and they were to live right under the shadow of Seton Manor.

Amy Jane then set about the next project, which was to fill the nurseries at Seton Manor.

In this she was less successful. She had one miscarriage, which she believed to be an oversight on the part of the Almighty as she had prayed, and set the whole village praying, for a son. But she was almost immediately pregnant and this time that pregnancy was brought to a conclusion and, although it might not be entirely satisfactory, it was at least a start.

Sir Timothy was delighted with the puling infant who, Nurse Abbott declared, had needed an extra smart slap on the posterior to start its breathing. "The next will be a boy," stated Amy Jane, in a voice before which Heaven itself would have quailed. Opposition came from the doctor; Amy Jane would risk her life by trying again. Let her rest content with her girl. The child was responding to treatment and was going to survive. "Don't risk it again," said the doctor. "I could not answer for the consequences." And as neither Amy Jane nor Sir Timothy wished to face such a disaster, there were no more children; and Jessamy, after clinging to life somewhat precariously for a few weeks, suddenly began to clamor for food and to kick and cry the same as other children.

A few months after the birth of Jessamy, life and death came to the vicarage hand in hand. Amy Jane was shocked. My mother had always been a great disappointment to her. Not only had she made a disastrous marriage, but just when her capable sister was putting her on her feet in a very pleasant living which Sir Timothy had secured with some effort, for there were others who were in fact more deserving than my father, she had given birth to a child and died doing it. A small baby in a vicarage with a man who was more than usually helpless was inconvenient to say the least, but a woman of Amy Jane's caliber was not to be deterred. She found Janet and installed her. Henceforth I was cared for, and Amy Jane, as my mother's closest relative, would of course keep an eye on me.

This she undoubtedly did and her own precious Jessamy was a part of my childhood and girlhood. It was Jessamy's clothes which came to the vicarage and were made over for me. I was slightly taller, which would have made them short, but she was broader-shouldered and took them up more. Janet said it was child's play to take them in a bit and there was better stuff in them than any that would find their way into this house from the shops.

"You look a sight better in them than Miss Jessamy," she would say and, coming from can't-tell-a-lie Janet, that was gratifying.

So I was accustomed to wearing castoff clothes. I can remember very few that did not come via Jessamy. Spending such a lot of time with her, wearing her old garments, did make me become a part of her life.

There was one time when Aunt Amy Jane thought it was fashionable to send girls to school, and there was talk of our going. I was excited at the idea. Jessamy was terrified. Then Dr. Cecil, he who had suggested that there should be no other Seton child in the nursery but Jessamy, decided that she was not strong enough for a boarding school. "Her chest," was all he said. So no school it was, and as Jessamy's chest was too weak to let her go, mine, strong as it might be—and it had never given me or Dr. Cecil any indication that it was not—could not take me there. Fees would have to be paid by Sir Timothy, and it was not to be thought of that I should be sent and paid for while his daughter remained at home.

When there was entertaining at Seton Manor, Aunt Amy Jane always did her duty and invited me. When she came to the vicarage she rode over in the carriage with a foot warmer in the winter and a parasol in the summer. On winter days she would pick up her beautiful sable muff and alight from the carriage while the Seton coachman held open the door with the utmost display of deference and she would march into the house. In the summer she would hand her parasol to the coachman, who would solemnly open it and hold it out in one hand while he helped her to alight with the other. I used to watch this ritual from one of the upstairs windows with a mixture of hilarity and awe.

My father would receive her in a somewhat embarrassed way. He would be frantically feeling for his spectacles, which he had pushed up on his head. They always slipped too far back and he would think he had put them down somewhere—which he did now and then.

The purpose of her visit was certain to be me, because I was her Duty. She had no reason to bother herself about a man who owed his living to her benevolence—or Sir Timothy's, but all blessings which fell on our household came through her, of course. I would be sent for and studied intently. Janet said that Lady Seton did not really like me because I looked healthier than Miss Jessamy and reminded her of her daughter's weak chest and other ailments. I was not sure whether Janet was right but I did feel that Aunt Amy Jane was not really fond of me. Her concern for my welfare was out of duty instead of affection, and I have never relished being the object of duty. I doubt anyone ever does.

"We are having a musical evening next Friday," she said one day. "Anabel should come. She should stay the night as it will be late before it is over, and that will be much simpler. Jennings has the dress she will wear in the carriage. He will bring it in."

My father, struggling with his self-respect, said: "Oh, that isn't necessary, you know. I dare say we can buy a dress for Anabel."

Aunt Amy Jane laughed. I noticed that her laugh was rarely mirthful. It was usually intended to dismiss or denigrate the folly of the one to whom it was directed.

"That would be quite impossible, my dear James." When she said "my dear" that was very often a term of reproach. I was struck by that. Laughter was supposed to express gayety; endearments were for expressing affection. Aunt Amy Jane turned them about. I supposed it came of being such an efficient, highly respectable, always-right sort of person. "You can hardly be expected to buy suitable clothes on your stipend." A repetition of the laugh as her eyes swept round our humble sitting room and mentally compared it with the fine hall at Seton Manor, which had been in the Seton family for hundreds of years with the gleaming swords on the wall and the tapestries which had been in the family for generations and were reputed to be Gobelins. "No, no, James, leave this to me. I owe it to Susan Ellen." The hushed note in her voice indicated that she was speaking of the dead. "It was what she would have wished. She would never have wanted Anabel to be brought up like a savage."

My father opened his mouth to protest but by this time Aunt Amy Jane had turned to me. "Janet can adjust it. It will be quite simple." Other people's tasks always were in Aunt Amy Jane's eyes. It was only those she undertook herself which demanded so much. She was regarding me somewhat malevolently, I thought. "I hope, Anabel," she went on, "that you will behave with decorum and not upset Jessamy."

"Oh yes, Aunt Amy Jane, I will and I won't."

I felt an irresistible desire to giggle, which I am afraid came to me quite frequently in the presence of a number of people.

My aunt seemed to sense this. She said in a low funereal voice: "Always remember what your mother would wish."

I was on the point of saying that I was not sure what my mother would wish, for I was argumentative by nature, and I could never resist the temptation to get a point cleared up. I had heard from some of the servants at Seton Hall that my mother had not been at all the saint Aunt Amy Jane was turning her into. My aunt seemed to have forgotten that she had been so headstrong in making a marriage with a poor curate. The servants said that Miss Susan Ellen had been "a bit of a caution. Always got a finger in some pie and making a joke of it. Come to think of it, Miss Anabel, you're the spitting image of her." That was damning enough.

Well, I went to the musical evening in Jessamy's watered silk, which was really very beautiful. Jessamy said: "Yes, you look prettier in it than I did, Anabel."

She was a sweet girl, Jessamy was, which makes what I did to her all the more reprehensible. I led her into constant mischief. There was the affair of the gypsies, which will give you a good idea of what I mean.

We were forbidden to walk in the woods alone, but the very fact that the woods were out of bounds made them specially fascinating to me.

Jessamy did not want to go. She was the sort of girl who liked to do exactly what she was told; she saw it all as for her own good. Heaven knew that was the explanation given to us often enough. I was exactly the opposite; and I took a great delight in trying to prove which was the stronger—my powers of persuasion or Jessamy's desire to keep to the paths of righteousness.

I invariably won because I went on worrying her until I did. So at length I persuaded her to venture into the woods where some gypsies were camping. We could have a quick look, I said, and go away before they saw us.

The fact that there were gypsies in the woods made it all the more important that we should not venture into them. However, I was determined and I taunted Jessamy with cowardice so mercilessly that at length she agreed to accompany me.

We came to a caravan. There was a fire smoking nearby with a pot boiling on it. It smelled quite good. Seated on the steps of the caravan was a woman in a torn red shawl and with brass rings in her ears. She was a typical gypsy, with a tangle of black hair and big sparkling dark eyes.

"Good day to you, pretty ladies," she cried out when she saw us.

"Good day," I replied, gripping Jessamy's arm, for I had a feeling she was going to turn and run.

"Don't be shy," said the woman. "My! You are two fine little ladies. I reckon there's a bonny fortune waiting for you."

I was enthralled by the prospect of looking into the future. I always have been. I could never then and cannot now resist a fortuneteller.

"Come on, Jessamy," I said, dragging her forward.

"I think we ought to go back," she whispered.

"Come on," I said, holding her firmly. She did not like to protest. She was afraid it might seem ill-mannered towards the gypsies. Jessamy was always considering what was good and bad manners, and she was terrified of committing the latter.

"Now you two has come from the big house, I reckon," said the woman.

"She has," I told her. "I'm from the vicarage."

"Oh, holy, holy," said the woman. Her eyes were on Jessamy, who was wearing a fine gold chain with a gold locket in the shape of a heart attached to it. "Well, my pretty," she went on, "I'm sure you've got a good fortune waiting for you."

"Have I?" I asked, holding out my hand.

She took it. "You'll be the one who makes her own fortune."

"Doesn't everybody?" I asked.

"Oh, clever, are you? I see. Yes, we do . . . with a little help from fate, eh? You've got a great future, you have. You'll meet a tall dark stranger and you'll sail across the seas. And gold . . . yes, I see gold. Oh, you've got a great future, you have, missy. Now let me look at the other little lady."

Jessamy hesitated, and I held up her hand. I noticed how brown and grubby the gypsy's was compared with Jessamy's.

"Oooh. Now you're going to have the luck, you are. You're going to marry a lord and have silk sheets to sleep in. There'll be gold rings on your fingers . . . finer than this here chain." She had taken the chain in her other hand and was examining it. "Oh yes, you've got a fine and bonny future before you."

A man had strolled up. He was dark like the woman.

"You been telling the ladies' future, Cora?" he asked.

"Bless their little hearts," she said softly, "they wanted to hear their fortunes. This little 'un comes from the big house."

The man nodded. I did not much like the look of him. His

eyes were sharp like a ferret's, whereas the woman was fat and comfortable-looking.

"Hope they crossed your palm with silver, Cora," he said. She shook her head.

The little ferret eyes were gleaming. "Oh, that's terrible unlucky, that is. You must cross the gypsy's palm with silver."

"What will happen if we don't?" I asked with curiosity.

"It would all turn topsy-turvy. All the good would be bad. Oh, that's terrible unlucky...not to cross the gypsy's palm with silver."

"We haven't got any silver," said Jessamy, aghast.

The man had his hands on the chain. He tugged at it and the clasp came undone. He laughed and I noticed what unpleasant teeth he had; they were black, like fangs.

It occurred to me that our elders had been right and it *was* unwise to go walking in the woods.

The man was holding up the chain and looking at it intently.

"It's my best chain," said Jessamy. "It was given to me by my papa."

"Your papa is a very rich man. I reckon he'll give you another."

"That was for my birthday. Please give it back to me. My mother will be angry if I lose it."

The man nudged the woman. "I reckon Cora would be angry if we didn't have it," he said. "You see, she's given you a service. She's read your fortunes. Now that's something that has to be paid for. You have to cross the gypsy's palm with silver...if you don't terrible disaster will befall you. That's so, ain't it, Cora? Cora knows. She's got the powers. She's in touch with them that knows. The Devil's a great friend of hers, too. He says to her, 'If any don't treat you right, Cora, you just let me know.' Well, telling fortunes without crossing the gypsy's palm is all against the rule. But gold will do...gold will do just as well."

Jessamy was standing as though transfixed with horror. She was staring at her chain in the man's hands. I sensed danger. I could see his little eyes looking at our clothes, particularly Jessamy's. She was wearing a gold bracelet too. It was mercifully hidden by her sleeve.

I suddenly knew we had to get away quickly. I seized her hand and dashed away, running as fast as I could, dragging

(60)

her with me. From the corner of my eye I saw the man start after us.

The woman shouted. "Let 'em be. Don't be a fool, Jem. Let 'em go, and put the horses on the van."

Jessamy was panting behind me. I stopped and listened. The man had taken Cora's advice and we were not being followed.

"He's gone," I said.

"So is my chain," said Jessamy mournfully.

"We'll tell them he came up to us and snatched it."

"That's not quite true," said Jessamy. Oh dear, I thought, these sticklers for the truth, how trying they could be!

"He did snatch it," I insisted. "We mustn't tell them how far into the woods we went. We'll just say he came up and snatched it."

Jessamy was very unhappy. However, I was the one who told the story, keeping to the truth as far as I could, not telling them how deeply we had penetrated into the woods and eliminating the woman and her fortunetelling.

There was great consternation—more, I realized, because we had been molested, as Aunt Amy Jane put it, than because of the loss of the chain. They sent men into the woods, but the caravan had gone, though there were the wheel marks and the remains of the fire to show where they had been.

Aunt Amy Jane, who managed most things in the village as she did at Seton Manor, had "Trespassers Will Be Prosecuted" put up on signboards all over the woods, and from then on gypsies were not allowed to camp there. I felt overawed to contemplate that this had been brought about by my waywardness, but I consoled myself with the thought that I had not made a thief of the gypsy; he had been that already, so I did not feel there was anything much to worry about.

It was poor innocent Jessamy who worried. She blushed every time gypsies or fortunetelling were mentioned. We had acted a lie, she said, and the recording angel would make a note of it. It would have to be answered for when we got to heaven.

"That's a long time yet," I comforted her. "And if God is what *I* think He is He won't like that sneaking little recorder very much. It's not nice spying on people and writing down what they do in a little book."

Jessamy was always expecting the heavens to open and God to inflict something terrible upon me. I used to reassure her that He had had plenty of opportunities and He hadn't done anything so far, so it must mean that He thought I was not so very wicked.

Jessamy was unsure. Her life was fraught with fears and indecisions. Poor Jessamy, who had so much and never seemed to take advantage of it.

I was always very interested in Amelia Lang and William Planter. They had been a part of the vicarage household for as long as I could remember, and they had always been the same through the years. Then I discovered that there was, as Janet put it, "something between them." No sooner had I heard this than I was consumed with curiosity to discover what. I used to discuss it with Jessamy and make up all sorts of wild stories about them. William's name delighted me. It was William Planter, which, I said to Jessamy, was a lovely name for a gardener. Now did he become a gardener because his name was Planter or was it just a joke of God's...or whoever had given him the name in the first place? For William came from a long line of Planters and they had all been noted for their skill in gardening.

I would roll about with delight and get Jessamy doing the same, forgetting all the rules about deportment, choosing names for people like William Planter's. The cook, I said, should be Mrs. Bakewell instead of Mrs. Wells. Thomas, the butler, should possess the obvious for his name. No one seemed to know what his real one was. He was always called Thomas. The footman should be Jack Foot. The coachman George Horsemare. As for Jessamy, she should be Jessamy Good.

It all seemed hilariously funny to me.

I remained very interested in this "something" between William and Amelia. On one rare occasion I induced Amelia to talk of it. Yes, there was an understanding between them, but William had never spoken and, until he did, things must remain as they were.

I could not understand what was meant, for I had heard William speak many times. He wasn't dumb, I pointed out. "He hasn't spoken," insisted Amelia, and that was all she would say.

I was instrumental in getting him to "speak." I managed to get them together one afternoon. I had lured Amelia into the garden to get some roses when I knew William was working on the rose beds.

So, having them together, I said: "William, you will not speak. You must do so right away. Poor Amelia can do nothing until you *speak*."

They just looked at each other and Amelia went bright pink, and so did William.

Then he said, "Will you then, Amelia?"

And Amelia replied: "Yes, William."

I watched them with satisfaction although they did not seem to be aware of me. But William had "spoken" and now they were engaged.

The engagement went on for several years but it was known that William and Amelia were bespoken from that day, and when Janet told me that meant no one else could have them, I remarked that I did not think anyone else wanted them.

I told her how I had made William "speak."

"Miss Interference!" she said; but I knew she was laughing.

There were always reasons why Amelia and William could not get married. William lived in a small place in the vicarage grounds. It was little more than a hut, and there was not room for two there. The marriage would have to be put off until they could find a place to live.

Amelia chafed under the delay but she was happy that William had spoken. I often reminded her that it was due to my prodding.

Several years passed and then one autumn day William had a fall. He had mounted a ladder to gather apples from the topmost branches when he missed his footing. He broke his leg and it was never right again after that. He limped about the place and developed rheumatism in the afflicted limb and my father spoke to Sir Timothy about him.

Sir Timothy was a kindly man who took a pride in looking after his work people, and of course ours—through Aunt Amy Jane of course —were under his jurisdiction.

It soon became clear that something must be done for William Planter. Sir Timothy, who seemed to have possessions all over the country, owned a cottage on Cherrington green. It was called Crabtree Cottage because of the crabapple tree in front of it.

William was past his best work. He should have an annuity and marry Amelia, whom he had kept hanging about far too long, and they should take up residence in Crabtree Cottage, which should be theirs for their lifetimes.

So William and Amelia married and departed in certain splendor for Cherrington and Crabtree Cottage.

Amelia sent us a card every Christmas and both she and William seemed to have settled into matrimony as comfortably as they did in Crabtree Cottage.

We had a jobbing gardener who also worked at Seton Manor and one of the widows in the village came in to help about the house in Amelia's place.

We were growing up. Jessamy was a few months older than I, but I always thought of myself as the elder.

We were seventeen and there was talk of "coming out." That would not be until we were eighteen and the object would be to find us suitable husbands. Before this great event there were what I called skirmishing parties and it was one of these which did not seem overly significant at the time but which, looking back, I think may have changed the whole course of our lives.

Aunt Amy Jane was inviting some people for a house party. There was to be what she called "a little dance." No, not a ball, just a pleasant evening, a sort of rehearsal, I gathered, for the great campaign which would begin when Jessamy was eighteen.

I was to have one of Jessamy's castoff dresses, made over. My father protested and said I was to go into the town and buy some material and get the village seamstress to make it up for me. Now I knew that any material we could get and any work industrious Sally Summers could put into it would not compare with a made-over garment from Jessamy's wardrobe, for Jessamy's clothes came from London or Bath and they were not only of the latest fashion, which all Sally Summers' neat stitching could not match, but they were of such delicate and expensive materials as we could not hope to acquire.

So I persuaded my father that I was quite happy in Jessamy's castoffs, and when Janet had done with them, no one would notice that they had been altered for me.

It was a beautiful dress—with rather a tight bodice nipped in at the waist and the skirt cascading out into hundreds of frills. It had become too tight for Jessamy and it was ideal for the transformation.

Jessamy was dark-haired and a little sallow; she took after her father and had inherited his nose, which was rather large. She had a sweet expression, though, and lovely dark doelike eyes. I thought that if she could only be a little more animated she would be quite attractive. The dress was pink and it had not matched her complexion. I was fair-haired with light brown eyes and very long gold-tipped lashes; my brows were very firmly defined and of a darker shade than my hair, which made them stand out. My skin was very fair and I had a slightly retroussé nose and a wide mouth. That I was attractive I knew, because people always looked first at me and then looked again. I was by no means beautiful, but I had those high spirits which were irrepressible, for there was little I could do to restrain them. I was always finding something in life so excruciatingly funny that I had to share the joke with someone. To some people—people like Aunt Amy Jane and Amelia—this in me was a decided fault; they shook their heads over it and did everything they could to repress it, but to some people it was amusing and attractive. I knew by the way they smiled when they looked at me.

Well, there we were at this little dance which was to prove so fatal to my future.

The carriage was sent over for me, which was considerate of my aunt, for it would have been awkward to walk from the vicarage to the great house in all my finery.

I arrived before the other guests and went to Jessamy's room. She was in a blue silk dress, all frills and flounces. My heart sank, for it was the wrong color for Jessamy; frills did not really suit her. She looked best in her gray riding habit with its severely tailored coat and the topper with the gray silk band round it.

As usual she was delighted to see me looking so well in the dress.

"It's lovely," she cried. "Why do my things always look better on you than on me?"

"Dear Jessamy, you imagine it," I lied, for I was never haunted by Janet's truth-at-any-price philosophy. "And you look lovely."

"Oh, I don't. Everything is getting so tight. Why do I put on weight? You're as slim as a wand."

"I move about more than you do, Jessamy. Heaven knows I eat as much. But you're only pleasantly plump. Mary Macklin said men like plump women and she should know."

I giggled, for Mary Macklin was our local light lady whom Aunt Amy Jane was trying to shift from the village.

"Did she tell you?" asked Jessamy.

"Oh no, it's only hearsay."

Just at that moment Uncle Timothy came in. He was carrying two little white cardboard boxes.

"For my girls," he said, looking at us with pride.

Inside the boxes were orchids. I cried out with delight. This was just what I needed to add a touch of elegance to my made-over gown. The orchids had been chosen with care, for they matched our dresses to perfection.

Uncle Timothy was standing there looking like a pleased schoolboy and suddenly I thought how good he was. He had given the Planters Crabtree Cottage and to me a beautiful orchid which matched my dress perfectly.

I put down my flower on Jessamy's table and put my arms about Uncle Timothy's neck. I kissed him vehemently. And just at that moment my aunt came in.

"What is going on here?" she demanded.

I withdrew my arms and said: "Uncle Timothy has given us such beautiful orchids."

Uncle Timothy looked slightly red and apologetic and my aunt continued: "You seem to be acting in a very boisterous manner. Now I will pin the flower on your dress, Jessamy. There is a right place and a wrong place."

Uncle Timothy said: "Well, I'll be going. There is a lot to see to."

"There is indeed," replied my aunt coolly.

I went to the mirror and pinned on my orchid. I was delighted with it and I noticed Aunt Amy Jane casting one or two malevolent glances in my direction.

Captain Lauder was one of the guests. He was in his early twenties, I imagined, tall, graceful and debonair. He was the son of Sir Geoffrey Lauder and it was clear that he and his family were among the more important members of the company, for Aunt Amy Jane was very gracious to them.

Captain Lauder was presented to Jessamy and they danced together. He was very charming and put Jessamy at her ease immediately, which was not without its difficulties, for I knew she persistently regarded herself as inferior in some way. However, she blossomed with Captain Lauder and it occurred to me that Jessamy was really quite attractive; all she needed was someone to convince her so strongly of this that she believed it herself.

I had plenty of dances and now and then noticed Aunt Amy Jane watching me cautiously. I hoped I had not done anything amiss, for I did so enjoy gatherings like this and should hate to be banished from them. There was so much to enjoy at the time and laugh about afterwards. I danced the supper dance with a pleasant young man who was a soldier and when we went in to supper we ran into Jessamy and Captain Lauder.

"Here's my cousin," said Jessamy.

Captain Lauder turned and looked at me. Admiration shone from his eyes as he took my hand and kissed it.

"You're Miss Anabel Campion," he said. "Miss Seton has been telling me about you."

I grimaced and Jessamy said quickly: "Only nice things."

"Thank you for keeping back the rest," I replied.

Everybody laughed.

The four of us sat down together and it was a very jolly party, but every time I looked up Captain Lauder's eyes were on me.

When we left the supper room he was at my side.

"I should like to have a dance with you," he said.

"Well," I answered, "they are just starting something."

We danced together.

"You're beautiful," he said.

That was not true but I had long since learned that if people had a good opinion of you, however misguided, it was best to let them keep it.

"I wish I had found you earlier," he went on.

"But I am sure you have been enjoying the evening in spite of the lack of my company."

He laughed: "You're the daughter of the vicar, I hear."

"Oh dear, Jessamy has been supplying you with information."

"She is very fond of you."

"And I of her. She is a delightful person."

"Yes, yes, I gathered that. I am still wishing, though, that I had found the intriguing Miss Campion earlier."

"What charming things you say."

"You sound as though you doubt my veracity."

"Should I? I have such a high opinion of myself that it hadn't occurred to me not to accept all the nice things you are implying about me."

"Do you find it hot? Shall we slip outside?"

Now of course I should have said no. But I did not. I was

too warm and I wanted to discover how outrageous Aunt Amy Jane's cherished guest could be.

There was a half-moon among the stars out there.

"You look enchanting in moonlight," he said.

"It's less revealing," I replied.

He had drawn me under the shade of a tree and put his arms about me.

I withdrew myself. "On sober consideration," I said, "I think we should go back to the ballroom."

"Sober consideration is impossible when you are near me."

He had suddenly seized me in a viselike grip from which I could not extricate myself. Then his lips were on mine.

This had happened far more quickly than I had thought it could. I had no wish to be in the gardens, kissed forcibly by a man whom I scarcely knew. But he was stronger than I.

Then I heard a cough, and so did he, for he released me. To my horror Aunt Amy Jane was coming towards us.

"Oh," she said in a startled voice when she saw who it was she had caught kissing under one of her trees. Then she added: "Captain Lauder...and...er...Anabel. My child, you will catch cold. Go in at once."

I was only too pleased to escape. As I did so I heard my aunt continue imperturbably: "I do want to show you my hydrangeas, Captain Lauder. While we are out here..."

I went straight to Jessamy's bedroom. I was ruffled and slightly pink. There was a red mark on my cheek. I touched it gingerly. It would soon go.

I tidied myself and went back to the ballroom. Jessamy was there dancing with one of the neighboring squires.

The next day I was expecting a reprimand from Aunt Amy Jane. She had actually seen the captain kissing me and I was sure that as he had been one of her favorite guests I should be blamed for what had happened. Captain Lauder was of too good a family, too rich a family, to be in the wrong. He was an eligible bachelor and the discovery of the ideal gentleman in that category was her next project and one which she would pursue with single-minded purpose. Therefore, if he had been seen to act in an unseemly manner, he could only have been led into the indiscretion.

I was amazed that not a word was said to me, although I caught her looking at me rather oddly now and then.

For a while I allowed myself to believe she had forgotten. But Aunt Amy Jane would never forget.

Thus, when Jessamy and her parents were to pay a visit to Mateland Castle, I was not invited, although but for that incident I was sure I should have been, for I often went visiting as a companion for Jessamy, and Jessamy always begged that I should go with them. I was sure she did on this occasion, but Aunt Amy Jane was adamant.

So I did not go to Mateland Castle. If I had gone things might have turned out differently. I *know* it would have been different, and I should not be writing this to you, Suewellyn. Your life and mine would have gone on smoother lines. How the great events of our lives hang on flimsy chances. Yours and mine could have been so different...and all because of an unwanted kiss under an oak tree!

Jessamy returned from Mateland Castle in a state which I can only describe as bemused. For a time I could get no sense out of her; then an amazing truth began to emerge.

Jessamy had wakened up; she had become animated, which was what I always thought she needed to make her attractive. In the place of the gangling girl was a personable young woman.

Of course I lost no time in drawing the story from her.

Mateland Castle, it appeared, was an enchanted place. It was a combination of El Dorado, Utopia and the Elysian Fields. It was inhabited by gods and the occasional goddess; and nothing would ever be the same for Jessamy now that she had set foot within those magic portals.

"I shall never forget my first sight of it," she said. "We alighted from the train and the Mateland carriage was waiting to take us to the castle. I shall never forget riding along those lanes...."

"I'll accept the fact that it has engraved itself in your memory forever. You've mentioned that twice. Get on, Jessamy."

"Well, it's just what you think a castle should be. It's medieval."

"Most castles are. Never mind about the castle. What about the people?"

"Oh, the people..." She half closed her eyes and sighed. "There's Egmont Mateland..."

"Egmont! A medieval name to go with the castle."

(69)

"Anabel, if you are going to interrupt and make fun, I shall not tell you."

I was amazed. Signs of revolt in our docile Jessamy! Yes, something had indeed happened.

"There's Egmont," I went on. "Go on from there."

"He is the father."

"Father of whom?"

"David and Joel. David has the dearest little boy named Esmond. He, of course, will be the heir to the castle."

"How interesting," I said coolly, feigning a complete lack of that state.

"Of course, if you don't want to hear..."

"Of course I want to hear. But you're so slow."

"All right, there are two brothers, David and Joel. David is the elder and he is married to Emerald."

"I like the names."

"You're interrupting again, Anabel. If you want to hear..."

"Oh, I do. I do," I said humbly.

"David manages the estate, which is considerable. Joel is a doctor...."

Ah, I thought. It's Joel. I knew my Jessamy too well not to recognize the change in her voice when she said his name. I also noticed the slight emotional twitch of her lips.

"Tell me about the doctor," I said.

"He's such a good man, Anabel. I mean he really does a lot of good...to a lot of people."

I found my interest flagging a little. People who did a lot of good to a lot of people were, I discovered, often indifferent to individuals. They liked people en masse, not individually. Moreover, they were usually so wrapped up in their good works that they became a little boring outside them. My only interest in Joel was the effect he had had on Jessamy.

"How?" I asked.

"With his work, of course. He has a place in the little town. The castle is outside the town...right in the country. He lives in the castle with his family, of course. The Matelands have lived there for centuries."

"Since the days of the Conqueror, I bet."

"You're laughing at them again. No, it was *not* since the days of the Conqueror. The castle was built one hundred years after he came to England."

"I see you have the family history at your fingertips. Very commendable after one short visit."

"I feel as though I have known Mateland all my life."

"The castle or its fascinating inmates?"

"You know what I mean."

"I believe I do, Jessamy. Tell me more of the intriguing Joel Mateland."

"He is the younger son."

"Yes, you told me that, he having an elder brother, David, with a delightful son, Esmond, begotten in co-operation with the glittering Emerald. I have them and Grandpa Egmont settled in my mind. Now tell me about Joel."

"He is tall and handsome."

"Of course."

"All his life he wanted to be a doctor. There was some opposition in the family because the Matelands had never had a doctor in the family before."

"Certainly not. Too aristocratic, I am sure, to be sullied by a profession."

"Oh, do stop teasing, Anabel. You know nothing about these people."

"Fortunately your knowledge is so great that it positively drips out of you. How old is Joel?"

"He is not so very young."

"I thought he was the younger brother."

"He is. David is about two years older. He was married for ten years before Esmond was born. Joel was married before but had no children. Like all big families, they wanted an heir."

"What happened to Joel's wife?"

"She died."

"A widower, eh?"

"He is the most interesting man I ever met."

"I gathered that."

"My mother liked him very much. My father had met them somewhere...I forget where. That was why we visited."

"It was obviously a successful visit."

"Oh yes," said Jessamy fervently.

Very significant, I thought. A widower. Perhaps the best sort of husband for Jessamy. And Mateland Castle! There was a good possibility of Aunt Amy Jane's approving of that.

It seemed that she did, for after about a month there was another visit to Mateland Castle. It was supposed to be for a few days but it was extended and Jessamy and her parents were away for two weeks.

When they returned a radiant Jessamy came to see me.

I guessed what her news was before she told me. She was engaged to be married to Joel Mateland. Aunt Amy Jane had won the campaign almost before it started. No coming-out balls for Jessamy—and I realized with a pang that that meant none for me either. I would have shared Jessamy's but I could not expect to have one specially for myself.

I shrugged my shoulders.

Jessamy, in the sweetness of her nature, had time to think of me.

"When I am at Mateland Castle you shall come and stay," she told me.

I could see plans forming in her limpid eyes. Jessamy was always one who liked to share good fortune. She was going to have the best husband in the world and it would be her pleasure to find the second best for me.

I kissed her. I wished her all the happiness in the world.

"It's what you deserve, sweet Jessamy," I said, seriously for once.

The Matelands had not come to Seton Manor. Joel was busy working, Jessamy told me. She and her family could always go to Mateland.

The wedding, however, would be held at Seton. Aunt Amy Jane threw herself into the bustle of preparation, for this was going to be the occasion to outdo all others. No expense must be spared. The very desirable marriage of the only daughter should be given all the honor and dignity it deserved.

One afternoon soon after the announcement of the betrothal she came to the vicarage in her carriage. It was early May—neither foot warmer and muff nor parasol weather. The Seton footman helped her out of the carriage and she came straight into the house. Janet took her into our rather shabby sitting room where my father received his parishioners when they came to pour out their troubles to him.

I was summoned too.

Aunt Amy Jane was seated in the only comfortable armchair and even in this the springs were sagging. They were apt to make pinging noises of protest when anyone sat down and I wondered how they would bear my aunt's not inconsiderable weight. She gave her usual disdainful look about our room, but she was not really thinking of it. She was in very high spirits and clearly the marriage of her daughter was going to be one of the great events of her life, rivaling only the triumph of her own marriage to Sir Timothy on which her opulent fortunes were founded.

"As you know," she announced, "Jessamy is to be married."

I could not resist murmuring: "We had heard of it."

Aunt Amy Jane chose to ignore my impertinence and went on: "The wedding will be as great an occasion as we can make it."

She smiled smugly. That meant very great with the might of Uncle Timothy's purse strings behind it, and it was well known who had control of them.

"Timothy and I are determined that it shall be a day neither Jessamy nor we shall forget. There is so much to do between now and the wedding day. How they are going to get her dress done in time, I don't know. But talking of the actual ceremony...Jessamy has made a request. She wants you to be her bridesmaid, Anabel."

"Oh, how kind of Jessamy. She always thinks of others."

"Jessamy has been very properly brought up." A stern glance at my father, who quite missed the shaft and was intent on retrieving his spectacles, which had receded even farther than usual. "The fact is you are to be a bridesmaid. Now we shall have to have you suitably clad. I am arranging for Sally Summers to come and make a dress for you."

"Perhaps we could find something..." began my father.

"No, James. The dress is not to be found. It is to be made. It must be absolutely right for the occasion. I thought of buttercup yellow."

I did not like buttercup yellow. It was not one of the colors which became me most and I had a notion that Aunt Amy Jane might have chosen it for that reason.

"Jessamy wanted shell pink or azure blue," she went on.

Dear Jessamy! She knew that of all colors those suited me best.

"I suppose she, as the bride, will be the arbiter on this occasion," I said.

My aunt did not reply to that. Instead she said: "Sally will be coming over with the material in a few days' time. There must be no delay. I have told her that she will stay here and make the dress. It should only take a day or so. We shall have a houseful of guests for the wedding, so there will be no room for you to stay at the Manor. You will be officiating of course, James, and Anabel can join the party at the church and you will come to the Manor for the celebrations. The bride and bridegroom are going to Florence for the honeymoon. You can return to the vicarage after they have left. I will send the carriage back for you."

"Oh, Aunt Amy Jane, what a wonderful manager you are!" I cried. "Everything planned to the last detail. I am sure it will all go off beautifully."

She gave me a look of rare approval; and when she left I thought how different life was going to be with Jessamy married, how I had taken her for granted and how fond I really was of her.

I should go and see her, though, in this wonderful enchanted castle of hers and I should meet the husband who had been able to work such a miracle in her.

Two days later the material arrived for my dress. It was soft azure-blue silk chiffon.

Dear Jessamy! I thought.

It was a lovely morning. June was the month to marry. Tomorrow would be Jessamy's wedding day.

There would be bustle and excitement at the Manor with all the guests arriving.

"We have a houseful," Aunt Amy Jane declared proudly. "The Matelands will be there in force and naturally all the bridegroom's family are staying in the house."

I had offered to help decorate the church and early this morning roses had come over from the Seton gardens and were now standing in buckets of water in the church porch. Sally Summers was an artistic arranger of flowers as well as a dressmaker and had been assigned to deal with them by my indomitable aunt. Poor Sally, her eyes looked as though they were going to disappear into her head; she had been so overworked, hurried and harried over the last two weeks.

"I'll get a start on it," I told her. "You can come in later and adjust them all. But it will be a help to have them in their various containers."

Sally was grateful and consequently on that June morning, the day before Jessamy's wedding, I made my way to the church immediately after breakfast and set to work on the decorations.

It was a lovely morning, and I felt exhilarated. Tomorrow was the great day. Who would have believed it possible that Jessamy would be married so soon? Shy little Jessamy had found the man of her choice, whose home was a castle—albeit shared by David, Emerald, little Esmond and Grandfather Egmont. And the bridegroom was a doctor. Such a comforting profession. One never need suffer from mysterious ailments, for he would always know what was wrong and to whom should he give his care more assiduously than to his dear wife? Oh yes, Jessamy was a queen of romance. I would never have believed it possible. In fact, I had always thought that, in spite of my overwhelming handicap, I should be the first to marry.

Well, Fate—or Aunt Amy Jane, which I had begun to believe was the same thing—had decided otherwise. And here I was confronted by bucketfuls of beautifully scented flowers which filled the church porch with their exquisite perfume and I was to start on this task—for which I was not really fully qualified; but I should be some help to poor tired over-worked Sally.

I carried the buckets into the church and found the containers in the vestry. Then I set about the task. I sorted the colors and carried in more water from the pump and began on the flowers.

I had been working for an hour, cautiously picking up the prickly stems and arranging the flowers to the best of my ability.

They were so beautiful—only the very best blooms would suit Aunt Amy Jane, and I could imagine how the gardeners had been harassed ever since she knew there was to be a wedding. I decided that the glorious pink roses which had an even more exquisite scent than the others should go on the altar. There was a special pot which was used for this. It was metal and rather heavy. I made the mistake of filling it with water and arranging the flowers and then carrying it up the three carpeted steps to the altar. I should, of course, have taken it to the altar and filled it there. It was a supreme effort on my part and I was not going to dismantle it. I was sure I could never achieve that artistry again. So I picked it up and started up the altar steps.

I am not sure now what happened. Whether I heard the church door creak and open, and turned and so fell, or whether I stumbled and fell and then the door opened. I turned to look towards the door and saw a man standing there as I felt the pot slipping out of my hands. The roses were falling out, stabbing my hands, and I made a frantic effort to save the pot, which failed. I went sprawling up the three steps. It all happened in less than a second. I was lying there, the overall I had put over my dress was soaked with water, the flowers were scattered round me, and the pot had gone rolling down the stairs—bump, bump, bump—scattering Seton prize blooms as it went.

A man was looking down at me.

"What happened? I'm afraid I startled you," I heard him say.

I have often heard of those dramatic moments when one meets people who make a devastating effect from the first. I had never believed it. One had to get to know people before one could judge whether one was going to like them. That was what I had always believed. Deep feeling has to grow. But something happened to me on those altar steps. It meant that I was fast approaching the end of my carefree girlhood when, try as I might to be serious, anything seemed to turn into a joke. Something was about to happen which was no joke at all.

I noticed that he was tall, that he had dark hair with rather heavily marked brows. It was a somewhat inscrutable face but it was one which I wanted to go on looking at.

It could only have been some seconds that I lay there looking up at him, but it seemed to go on for a long time. Then he was kneeling down beside me, helping me up.

"I've spilled the water over the carpet," I said.

"Yes, you have. Let's make sure you're all right, though. Come on. Stand up."

I did so.

"All right?" he asked.

"My foot hurts a bit."

He knelt and touched my ankle. He had a firm yet delicate touch.

"Press down," he said. "Now...put your weight on it. All right?"

"All right," I said.

"No bones broken. What about your wrist? You fell on that, I think."

I looked down at my hands. There was blood on them.

"Only a prick or two from the thorns," I said, taking my hand and working it about.

He smiled at me and for the first time I remembered how untidy I must be looking in the overall, which was too big for me, and my hair escaping from its pins.

"Thank you," I said.

"Shall we pick this up?" he asked.

He stooped and lifted the pot.

"No damage," he commented.

"I hope not. It's one of the church's best."

"It's rather fine. Where do you want it?"

"On the altar. But I shall have to fill it with water now and put the roses back."

"I shouldn't try carrying it up three steps full again if I were you."

"It was silly of me but I had done it before I thought."

He put the pot on the altar and I stooped to pick up the pail of water. He took it from me and carried it up to the altar. I stuck in the flowers in a manner which would have completely shocked Sally Summers.

"There's going to be a wedding here tomorrow," I said. "I'm decorating the church. I'm not very good at it, as you can see, but it will all be adjusted properly before the day. I suppose you came in to look at the church?"

"Yes, it's a fine old place."

"Norman. Part of it anyway. My father would be pleased to show you round. He's got all the history at his fingertips."

He was studying me intently. "So you're the vicar's daughter."

"Yes."

"Well, I'm glad to meet you. I am only sorry that my arrival caused you such inconvenience."

"You can put it down to my carelessness."

"Do you feel all right now?"

"Quite all right, thanks."

"A little shaken?"

"No. I've fallen many times in my youth."

He smiled. "Have you much more to do to the flowers?"

"Lots, but I'll have to go. The dressmaker is due at any moment and I daren't keep her waiting. She's so much to do and she is the local flower arranger too, so she does not only have to assure herself that I shall be right for The Day, but she has to make my dismal handiwork presentable."

"Well," he said, "I must not detain you."

"I should have loved to show you the church," I said regretfully, for I had not at this stage learned to disguise my feelings and I was tremendously stimulated for some reason which I did not understand then; although he was attractive in looks, I had seen other good-looking men, and our conversation had not been particularly sparkling. In fact I felt more tongue-tied than I ever had before. I only knew that I was excited and so glad that he had come into the church.

"Perhaps some other time," he said.

"Do you often come this way?"

"This is the first time," he told me. "But I shall come again. And when I do I shall find you and keep you to your promise."

We came out of the church together. He bowed and put on his hat, which he had taken off when he came into the church. He was in riding kit and he went to his horse, which was tethered by the lych gate.

I went into the vicarage. Sally Summers was already there fidgetingly looking at the clock.

"It's all right, Sally," I said. "I've been to the church. I've got the water for you and put some of the flowers into the containers. Not the right way, of course, but it will be easier for you."

"Oh, thank you, Miss Anabel. Now just let me make sure that this dress is right. I was at the Manor yesterday to see to Miss Jessamy. A regular picture she looks."

I was stripped of my overall and old clothes and put into the blue silk chiffon.

"Why, bless us, Miss Anabel, there's blood on your hands," cried Sally.

"I pricked them on the rose stems. I stumbled up the steps and dropped the pot and flowers and all."

Sally tut-tutted and said: "I don't want any blood on this dress, miss."

"I've stopped bleeding now," I answered dreamily.

And there I was resplendent in my bridesmaid's dress and wishing the strange man could see me now.

I looked into the future and saw him arriving at the church.

"Is the vicar's daughter here? She promised to show me the church."

And we would walk round together and he would come again and again.

I could imagine what it would be like at the Manor that morning. Everyone would be running to and fro and Aunt Amy Jane would be like a captain on the bridge of his ship seeing that orders were carried out.

And Jessamy? She would awaken early, if she had slept at all. They would bring a tray in to her. The wedding dress—pride of Sally Summers' heart—would be hanging in the wardrobe. The ritual of dressing would begin and little Jessamy would be transformed into a beautiful bride.

I should have been there. It was mean of Aunt Amy Jane to keep me shut away. I was Jessamy's natural confidante. I had shared her childhood secrets. It was natural that she should want to talk to me. And there was so much I wanted to know. I was sure that Jessamy was entirely ignorant of the duties of marriage. I was not very knowledgeable on these subjects myself, but I did keep my ears and eyes open and I had gleaned a good deal of information.

The morning wore on. My father was nervous. He was to have the important task of conducting the service and performing the ceremony.

"It's only a wedding like any other," I consoled him. I remembered those words afterwards.

I was gratified to see myself in the mirror. The bridesmaid's dress was most attractive. I had rarely had a dress which had been made just for me. I felt quite important.

At last it was time to go to the church. I was to be waiting there for the bride to arrive. And there she was with Uncle Timothy looking—yes, the only word is radiant—in her white satin gown and the long veil, with orange blossoms in her hair.

She caught my eye and smiled as I stepped out of the back pew to follow her and Uncle Timothy to the altar.

The guests were arriving—the bride's one side, the bridegroom's the other. Our little church was going to be full with very important people.

Then the bridegroom came. And I don't need to tell you, Suewellyn, who he was, for you have guessed. He was the man I had met in the church the day before. He was Joel Mateland, who was to be Jessamy's husband.

I could not understand my emotions then, but I was to analyze them later. All I was aware of was a heavy cloud of depression descending on me. Whenever I smell roses I shall remember that moment in the church when he came forward to stand beside Jessamy. I shall hear their voices taking their vows.

And from then on I knew that nothing would ever be the same again.

I remember vaguely seeing him go down the aisle with

Jessamy on his arm. I can remember the wedding reception at the Manor. All the people, all the splendor; and Jessamy standing there looking lovely and happy; and everywhere the overpowering scent of roses.

He came to me and said: "No ill effects?"

"Oh, the fall," I stammered. "Thank you, no. I'd forgotten."

He stood looking at me—not smiling, just looking.

"Your dress is very becoming," he said.

"Thank you. Rather different from my overall."

"That was becoming too," he said.

It was a strange conversation between a bridegroom and a bridesmaid.

I heard myself say: "I had no idea you were the bridegroom."

"I had an unfair advantage. I knew who you were."

"Why didn't you introduce yourself?"

He didn't answer, for Jessamy had come over.

"Oh, you're meeting each other," she said. "This is my cousin Anabel, Joel." She spoke his name rather shyly, I thought.

"Yes, I know," he replied.

"I do hope you are going to like each other."

"We already do. But perhaps I should not speak for Anabel."

"You may," I said. "It's true."

Aunt Amy Jane was bearing down on us. "Now, you two..." She was arch, the mother-in-law, a new role for her. Instead of being mildly amused by her as I usually was, I disliked her heartily.

It was unfair, I thought. No, it wasn't. She should have let me go to the castle. I should have met him before. What was I thinking? What had happened to me? I knew, of course. Such things did happen sometimes. There was something about him which drew me to him and made me want to laugh and cry at the same time. It was something which happens now and then if rarely. And to me it had happened too late.

The days dragged after the wedding. I felt depressed. I missed Jessamy more than I had thought possible. I went to my father's library and read a book about Florence. I imagined myself there...with him. I tried to picture Jessamy there. She had never been greatly interested in works of art. I imagined them walking along the Arno where Dante had met Beatrice. I imagined their shopping for chunky stone-encrusted bracelets on the Ponte Vecchio.

"What's the matter with you all of a sudden?" said Janet. "You look like a month of wet Sundays."

"It's the heat," I said, for it had turned warm.

"First time I've known it affect you," she replied. "I believe you're jealous."

Oh dear, trust Janet to put her finger on the truth and not hesitate to give voice to it.

"Don't talk nonsense," I snapped.

August passed. The church fete took up a great deal of time. It was held in the gardens of Seton Manor.

"Last year," said Aunt Amy Jane complacently, "Jessamy was here to help."

I tried to throw myself into the life of the village, but my heart wasn't in it. Not that it had ever been, but in the past everything had seemed comical. Now it was just infinitely boring.

At the beginning of September Jessamy came home for a week. I knew she was coming and I could scarcely wait to see her. I wondered what I should feel when I saw Joel again.

I was not invited to Seton Manor. "Jessamy will want to be with her parents for a while," said Aunt Amy Jane. "No intruders...not even family."

She was coyly delighted with the marriage.

But it was like Jessamy to seek the first opportunity to come over and see me. She rode over looking very pretty in a dark blue riding habit and a jaunty hat with a tiny blue feather in it.

There was no doubt that she was happy. We hugged each other.

"Oh, Jessamy, it's been so miserable without you."

She was surprised. "Really, Anabel?"

"Here have I been stuck, doling out cups of tea from the urn at the garden party...one penny a cup, but all in a good cause, and there have you been in romantic Italy with your fairy prince. Let me look at you, my sleeping beauty, who was awakened by a kiss."

"You talk such nonsense, Anabel...you always did. I was wide awake, I do assure you. I was glad. Otherwise I should not have seen Joel."

"And he is all your fancy painted him?"

"Oh, he is...he is."

"Why didn't you bring him over to see us?"

"He's not here. He has his work, you see, Anabel."

"Of course. And he doesn't mind your coming?"

"Oh no. He suggested it. He said: 'They'll all want to see you, your father and mother and your cousin....' He mentioned you, Anabel. I think you made quite an impression on him. It was falling down the altar steps. Trust you."

"Yes, trust me. I must have looked rather peculiar in one of Sally's aprons, rather wet, my hair falling down and myself surrounded by roses."

"He told me about it. He laughed over it. He said he thought you very..."

"Very what?"

"Amusing and...attractive."

"I see you have married a man of discernment."

"He must have been, to have chosen me." Oh yes, Jessamy had changed. She had poise and confidence. He must have given her that. Oh, lucky Jessamy!

"There is so much I want to hear," I said. "I want to hear about Florence and honeymoons and life in the enchanted castle."

"You *are* interested, Anabel."

"Of course I'm interested."

"I'm going to suggest something."

"What?"

"When I go back, you come with me."

"Oh, Jessamy!" I cried. It was as though lights were flashing round me. Joy...indescribable joy and then warnings. No, no. You must not. Why not? You know why.

"Don't you want to come, Anabel?" Her voice was blank. "I thought you were so interested."

"I am but..."

"I thought you would love to come. You were just saying what a bore it was here...."

"Well, it is just that...Do you think I should?"

"What on earth do you mean?"

"Newly married and all that. The third party intruding. Two's company..."

She burst out laughing. "It's not like that at all. We are not alone in a house of our own. We're at the castle and there are the rest of them there. It's not that I see Joel very much."

"Oh, you don't see much of him?"

"He has his place in the town. That's where he works. Sometimes he stays in town. It can be a little lonely."

"Lonely? What about David and Emerald, not to mention little Esmond and Grandpapa?"

"The castle is vast. You have never lived in a castle, Anabel."

"No, I haven't. Nor had you until you made this brilliant marriage."

"Don't talk about it like that."

"How?"

"As though you were making fun."

"You know my flippant ways, Jessamy. They don't mean much. The last thing I would do is make fun of your marriage. You deserve to be happy. You're such a *good* person."

"Oh, nonsense," said Jessamy.

I kissed her.

"You've become sentimental," she said.

"Jessamy," I answered, "I'm coming back with you."

There were of course a great many things to settle.

"Yes, you must go," said my father. "It will do you good. You haven't been quite yourself lately."

"Can you manage without me?"

"Of course. There are plenty of willing helpers in the village."

It was true. As a widower my father always had a stream of middle-aged and elderly ladies eager to ingratiate themselves into his good graces. He never saw through their motives and thought it was the church they were interested in. He was a very innocent man. I did not take after him one bit.

I should need new clothes, said Jessamy, and came over with a pile of dresses. "I was sorting them," she said. "I was going to turn them out."

Janet was pleased and said she was itching to get her fingers on them. She was all in favor of my visit to Mateland. I think she was fond of me in her undemonstrative way and thought my only chance of getting the right sort of husband was through Jessamy. She had been hoping for coming-out balls for me, shared with Jessamy, of course, and assuring herself that I would be the one who would get the suitors.

Aunt Amy Jane was unsure.

"Wait awhile," she said. "Let Anabel visit you later."

But Jessamy was adamant for once and so on a golden September day she and I were seated side by side in a first-class carriage and chuffing along to Mateland.

There was a halt which had been made especially for Mateland and a board stating Mateland Castle was on the platform. We alighted and a carriage accompanied by a man in livery was waiting for us. He bowed and took our hand luggage. He said to Jessamy: "The rest will be collected by the wagon, madam."

And soon we were trotting along the road to the castle.

I shall never forget my first glimpse of it. You have seen it, Suewellyn. I showed it to you and you were as impressed with it as I was. So I will not go into lengthy details describing it to you. You do not need me to tell you of the grandeur of those thick stone walls, of the impressive gatehouse and the machicolated towers and narrow slits of windows.

It enchanted me. There was a golden haze in the air, and I felt as though I were on the threshold of some exciting drama in which I was to play a major part.

"I can see you're impressed by the castle," said Jessamy. "Everyone is. When I first saw it I thought it had come out of one of the fairy stories we used to read, do you remember?"

"I do. There was usually a princess who was a captive in them and had to be rescued."

"And the princesses were all beautiful with long yellow hair. Your color, Anabel."

"I don't think I fit the role somehow. You're the princess, Jessamy. Awakened from years of slumber at Seton by Prince Joel's kiss."

"Oh, I am glad you came, Anabel."

We went under the gatehouse and into a courtyard. Grooms hurried out and we alighted from the carriage.

"Thank you, Evans," said Jessamy, very dignified. I thought that life in a castle suited her.

You have seen the outside of the castle, Suewellyn, but not the interior. Believe me, the inside is equally enthralling. The past seems to rush at you and envelop you when you enter the hall. I am not surprised that the Matelands all seem to revere the place. It has been there for centuries. It was built by one of their ancestors years ago, although in the twelfth century it was little more than a fortress. It has been added to through the ages. I think they loved every stone. It has been cherished by them, enhanced by them. It is their home and their pride. Even I began to feel something of its magnetism although my connection with it was through Jessamy, who had married into it.

The hall was lofty with finely carved stone walls on which weapons hung. There were several suits of armor which had belonged to various members of the family. They looked like sentinels, standing guard. Its timbered roof was very fine and there was a minstrels' gallery at the end; at the other were the screens and near the gallery a beautiful staircase. Jessamy was looking sideways at me to see the effect the place was having, but even I was struck dumb with wonder.

"I'll take you to your room," she said. "It's near mine. Come along."

We walked through the hall and up the staircase. At the head of the staircase was a long gallery. "It's the picture gallery. Here hang the members of the family, illustrious and otherwise."

"Don't tell me there are 'otherwise' Matelands."

"Scores of them," she said with a laugh.

I wanted to linger but she hurried me on. "You'll have plenty of time to look," she said. "Come on. I want to show you your room."

"Do they know you're coming back? Do they know I'm coming?"

"They know I am. I didn't mention you were. You know you didn't decide at once."

"They might not want me here."

"I do," she said, and gave me a hug.

"It's a strange sort of household, isn't it?"

"I think it seems so because it's so big. Everyone goes his own way. Nobody interferes with anyone. It works very well. I thought you wouldn't want to be isolated in the castle. That's why your room is near mine."

"You're right. I shouldn't want to be. I should be imagining all those long-dead Matelands, good and otherwise, were descending on me."

"You were always imagining something. Later on I'll show you everything...the library, the long gallery, the armory, the dining room, the drawing room, the music room...all of it."

"I'm not surprised your mother liked this place and thought it a worthy setting for her precious daughter."

"Oh, my mother was enchanted by it from the moment she set eyes on it."

"It makes Seton Manor look like a farm laborer's cottage."

"Oh, come, hardly that."

"No, of course not. Unfair to dear old Seton. Seton is lovely. I'm not sure I wouldn't rather have it than a castle. There's something about this place. It seems almost alive."

"No more fancies.... This is your room."

I looked round it. It was circular in shape. There were three tall narrow windows at which hung draperies in scarlet velvet. There was a four-poster bed with gold hangings and a gold-colored bedspread. There was an alcove in which were a basin and ewer. Persian rugs covered the stone-flagged floor; there were a table and small bureau, a few chairs and several cupboards. I thought it very well appointed.

"We're in the west front drum tower," said Jessamy, and I looked out of the window. I could see lawns, grassy slopes and woods in the distance.

"I ... we are just along the corridor."

I said suddenly: "May I see your room?" and immediately wished I hadn't. I did not want to see their room. I wanted to forget about them altogether.

"Of course. Come along and see it." I followed her down three steps to a corridor. She flung open a door. It was a large and lofty room and there was a big bed in it with fine silk hangings. There were a dressing table, chairs and two big court cupboards; and an alcove similar to mine.

I kept seeing them there together and I wanted to shut out the picture. It made me unhappy.

I turned away and started back to my own room.

"Where are the rest of them?" I asked.

"Oh, David and Emerald are on the east side. We meet at meals."

"And the grandfather?"

"He has his own apartments. He doesn't leave them very often. Anabel, there's something I have to warn you about."

"Yes."

"It's Emerald. She's an invalid. She has been for some years. She has a companion."

"Oh, I didn't imagine her an invalid."

"She had a riding accident about two years ago. She is in a chair most of the time. Elizabeth is devoted to her."

"Elizabeth?"

"Elizabeth Larkham. She is more like a friend really. She's a widow. She has a son...Garth. He's away at school. He comes here for his holidays to be with his mother. You see...she's like one of the family. You'll meet them all at dinner."

"And...your husband?"

"He will be there, I think."

There was a knock on the door. "Oh, they are bringing your things up. Would you like to wash? They'll bring hot water. Then perhaps you'd like to rest a little. We shall be eating in the small dining room. I'll take you there when you're ready. You'll lose your way in the castle at first. I did."

My baggage came and with it a maid bringing hot water.

I took out a dress—a blue one with a tight-fitting bodice and a rather full skirt; one of the made-over ones of which my wardrobe consisted. It was a fairly large wardrobe and the only one which had been made for me was the blue silk chiffon bridesmaid's dress.

When I had washed I lay on my bed for a while and thought about the strangeness of everything and how quickly it had all come about. This time last year we had been unaware of the name Mateland. Now here we were joined up with the family.

And all the time I lay there I was wondering what it would be like to see Jessamy's husband again. I had only seen him twice—once when I was doing the flowers in the church and the other occasion was that of the wedding; and yet I could remember every detail of his face, how he had looked at me, wonderingly, intently, as though I had the same effect on him as he had on me.

My longing to see him was almost unbearable and yet at the same time I was aware of warning voices within me.

You shouldn't have come, they said.

But of course I must accept Jessamy's invitation to her new home. Even Aunt Amy Jane did not disapprove of my doing so.

There was a tap on the door.

"Are you ready?" said Jessamy. "How nice you look."

"Recognize it?" I asked.

"Yes, but it never looked so well on me."

"It would now. You look very pretty. Marriage suits you, Jessamy."

"Yes," she said. "I think it does."

She slipped her arm through mine.

"Tomorrow I'm going to take you round and show you the castle."

"You are like the monarch of all you survey."

"Oh no. Not me. Grandfather Egmont is very much the lord of the castle...and after him, David. Then Esmond. They are the monarchs. We are on the fringe. Remember, Joel is only a younger son."

"I believe you love your old castle."

"One does, you know, Anabel. Perhaps you can't feel it...not being a Mateland, but it's there. They have fought for it in the past...given their lives for it."

"I am sure they have. Well, you have become one of them, dear cousin. What a long way it is."

"I told you it was a very big castle."

"I look forward to exploring it."

"It's grisly in parts. Dungeons and so on."

"My dear Jessamy, I should have been hideously disappointed if there had been no dungeons."

We had come to a door framed in a pointed stone arch, and I heard voices behind it. Jessamy lifted the latch and walked in. I followed.

It was not a large room. There was a fire in the grate, which gave a welcoming look to the room. I was aware that several people were there and as we entered a man rose and came towards us.

He was not really like Joel, who had haunted my thoughts ever since I had seen him, and yet there was a resemblance, so I knew at once that this was David, the elder brother and heir to the castle. He had dark hair and brilliant dark eyes. He took my hands and held them firmly. "Welcome to Mateland," he said. "I knew at once who you were. Miss Anabel Campion. Jessamy has talked of you."

"And you must be..."

"David Mateland. I have the honor to be brother-in-law to your cousin."

He had slipped his arm through mine. His hands were warm, almost caressing.

"Here she is, my dear," he said. "Jessamy's cousin Anabel. I suppose we may call you Anabel? You're part of the family now."

So this was Emerald of the brilliant name. Anyone less like a precious gem I could not imagine. She was pale and her hair was a dusty brown. Her light blue eyes were sunken, and I wondered if she suffered much pain. Her legs were covered in a blue fleecy rug and her thin blue-veined hands lay limply on it.

She smiled at me and her smile was kind.

"We are glad to have you at the castle," she said. "It will be nice for Jessamy. Elizabeth, my dear, come and meet Anabel."

A tall youngish woman had come into the room. I imagined her to be in her late twenties. She was slender, with sleek dark hair parted down the center and brought to a nob at the nape of her neck. She had large rather sleepy blue eyes and full red lips which somehow did not match the rest of her face. Her nose was rather thin, which gave her a shrewish look. It was an interesting face.

She held out her hand and gripped mine tightly.

"We have heard so much of you from Jessamy," she said. "She has been determined that you should come here for a long time."

"We have always been good friends as well as cousins," I said.

Her eyes were assessing me and I imagined there was a glitter of speculation in the sleepy blue eyes.

"Where is Joel?" asked David. "Is he coming?"

"He knew I was coming home today," said Jessamy. "I am sure he will be here."

"I should hope so," said David. "He has not been a husband long enough to stay away. Let us have a drink while we are waiting. I wonder if Miss Anabel would like to sample our Mateland cup. It's a special brew, I assure you, Miss Anabel."

"Thank you," I said. "I'll try it."

"Don't drink too much of it, Anabel," warned Jessamy. "It's very potent."

"You shouldn't have warned her," said David. "I was hoping to see the gates of restraint opened and the real Anabel emerge."

"I can assure you I'm myself now," I said. "There is no other one to be let out."

He came to stand beside me. I could feel his eyes on me. He made me rather uncomfortable. "Is that so?" he said. "I felt from the first that you were a very unusual lady."

Elizabeth Larkham brought me a pewter goblet in which was the Mateland cup.

"I'm sure you'll like it," she said. "David brews it himself. He won't let anyone else."

"Only I have the magic formula," he said, looking into my eyes.

"I shall be interested to try it," I said, and put it to my lips.

"I hang on your words," he said.

"It's good . . . very good."

"Then drink up and have another."

"I have been warned," I reminded him.

He grimaced and Jessamy came to my side. "I never drink much of it," she said.

"I won't either."

She smiled at me, a little anxiously. Dear Jessamy, I thought. She deserves everything of the best. A castle, a husband who loves her and whom she loves. And surely everyone must love Jessamy.

As we were going in to dinner Joel arrived.

He took my hand and I felt a tremor of excitement run through me. We seemed to stand facing each other for longer than was customary in such circumstances, but perhaps that was my imagination.

"I'm so glad you came," he said.

"Thank you. I'm glad to be here."

Then we went in to dinner. I was seated beside him and I had rarely felt so excited in the whole of my life.

"I hope there were no complications," he said.

For a moment I was bemused and he went on: "The fall. Your ankle . . . your wrist . . ."

"Oh no. None whatsoever." And then I thought: That's not true. There were complications, but not the kind I could mention because I don't think anything is ever going to be quite the same again.

He said to the rest of the company: "The first time I met Miss Campion she was lying on the altar steps."

"There is some significance in that surely," said David.

"I was surrounded by roses."

"A kind of sacrificial lamb?"

"Hardly. I was wearing a big overall. You see, I was about to decorate the altar."

"Ah, bent on good works."

"For Jessamy's wedding," I went on.

"The flowers were lovely," cried Jessamy. "I'll never forget the scent of those roses."

"I am sure they were most artistically arranged," said David.

"They were, but not by me. My talent in that direction is nil."

"But you are very good at falling down altar steps since you came through the ordeal without damage to ankle or wrist."

I could not understand David Mateland. That he was obviously interested in me was a fact which made me feel rather uncomfortable. He seemed eager to be friendly and yet at the same time there was something mocking in his attitude.

"I hope you will be comfortable in the castle," said Emerald.

"I am going to make sure of that," said Jessamy.

"It's a little drafty," Emerald remarked. "Not so bad at this time of the year."

"They say that in the winter when the wind blows from the east you could sail a battleship through our corridors," added David.

"It's not quite as bad as that," Joel told me, leaning towards me and laying a hand lightly on my arm. "Moreover, it's not winter yet."

"I remember when I first came here," said Emerald, "I thought it was quite bleak. I came from Cornwall, Anabel, which is a more benign climate."

"But damp," put in Elizabeth Larkham. "I prefer it here."

"Oh, Elizabeth loves the place and everything connected with it."

"I just think I am lucky to be here," said Elizabeth to me. "Emerald is so good to me. And it is such a relief to have my son here during school holidays."

"Dear Elizabeth," murmured Emerald.

The conversation went on in that vein during the meal. I was conscious of a certain tension in the atmosphere. The setting was so strange to me. To be dining in a room with tapestries on the walls and a suit of armor in the corner, to be in a medieval castle with strangers...all except Jessamy—it was certainly a new venue for me. But it was more than that. I had the feeling that these people were leading complicated lives which were not as they seemed to be.

There was Emerald in her chair, assiduously cared for by

Elizabeth Larkham, who was almost catlike in her movements, with those strange eyes which seemed so sleepy and
yet to take in all that was going on. Then there was David.
I felt I understood him a little better than the others. It was
clear that he was a man who liked the company of women.
His glances were too bold for my comfort; and there was a
hint of cruelty in his mouth and this, I think, showed itself
in his conversation. There was a touch of asperity in his
words, and I could believe that he derived a certain pleasure
in saying wounding things. Perhaps it was wrong to make
hasty judgments; but I had always done that. How many
times had I been obliged to adjust my assessment of someone!
He had an invalid wife and that must be a trial to a man of
his—or so I imagined—sensual nature. But foremost in my
thoughts was Joel. Joel was an enigma. He betrayed little.
He seemed apart from the others. He was a doctor and it
seemed strange to find a doctor pursuing his profession in a
place like this. He had his rooms in the town, which I gathered
was about two miles from the castle. According to Jessamy,
he was dedicated to his work, and sometimes he stayed in his
place in the town. I could not quite understand why he had
married Jessamy.

Again I was jumping to conclusions. Who can know what
it is that attracts people to each other? That Jessamy adored
him was plain and most men enjoy being adored. When he
was present I found my attention was focused on him. I was
conscious of every time he spoke to me, every time he looked
my way; and I do not think I imagined that he did that rather
often.

He excited me. I wanted to be near him. I wanted to attract
his attention, to talk to him, to find out everything about
him. I wanted to know what it had been like to have been
born into a castle, to have lived one's life in a place like this,
to be brought up with brother David. I was obsessed by him.

We went into a small parlor to drink coffee. There was a
great deal of talk. Tomorrow I was to be introduced to Grandfather Egmont and I should meet young Esmond. He was four
years old and, I learned, had been born a year before Emerald's accident.

At ten o'clock Jessamy said she would take me to my room.
She said she was tired after the journey and she was sure I
must be. Tomorrow she would show me the castle.

I said good night and Jessamy took me to my room, lighting me up the stairs with a candle in a brass candlestick.

I felt it was rather eerie walking up that staircase following Jessamy. Along the gallery we went. The pictures looked different in candlelight and one could imagine they were living people who looked down on us.

"We couldn't very well have gaslight in the castle," said Jessamy. "It would be rather incongruous, wouldn't it?"

I agreed.

"On some occasions we have flares in the main hall. I can tell you they look very fine."

"I am sure they do. Jessamy, you love your castle, don't you?"

"Yes. Wouldn't you?"

"I believe I would," I replied.

We reached the room in the tower and she lighted two candles on the dressing table.

I did not want her to go yet. I knew I should not sleep well that night.

"Jessamy," I said, "do you like living here with all these people?"

She opened her eyes wide. "But of course I like it. Joel is here."

"But it's like sharing a home, isn't it? There's David and Emerald....It's two households. You know what I mean."

"Families like this have always lived together. In the old days there were more of them. When Esmond grows up and marries he'll live here with his family."

"And your children too, I suppose."

"Of course. It's tradition."

"And you get on all right with David and Emerald?"

She hesitated a moment. "Yes...yes...of course. Why shouldn't I?"

"Methinks you do protest too much. And why shouldn't you, you say? I should think there is every reason why you shouldn't. People don't necessarily have to get on because they are forced to be together. In fact it is more likely that they don't than that they do."

"Oh, Anabel, that's just like you. I can't say that I'm exactly fond of Emerald. She is rather vague and wrapped up in herself. It's being as she is. It's so dreadful. She was always riding before. It can't be very pleasant for her, can it? And

David...well, I don't altogether understand him. He's too clever for me. He says sharp things...sometimes...."

"Sharp things?"

"Wounding things. He and Joel don't get on well. Brothers don't always, do they? Sometimes I think David is jealous of Joel."

"Jealous! Why? Has he designs on you?"

"Of course not. But there is something....And then ...Elizabeth."

"She seems a very self-contained young woman."

"She's wonderful with Emerald. I think David is very grateful to her for what she does for Emerald. And she of course is so glad to be here. You see, she's a widow with a son. He's about eight...four years or so older than Esmond. He's away at school and she's so grateful that he can come here for his holidays. It solves a big problem for her. Anabel, you *do* like Joel, don't you?"

"Yes," I said quietly, "I do like him. I like him very much."

She put an arm round me.

"I am glad, Anabel," she said. "So very glad."

The next morning Jessamy took me on a tour of the castle. She told me that Joel had already left for the town.

I was enchanted by everything I saw.

She said we should start at the bottom, which we did, descending a stone spiral staircase with a rope banister to which one had to hold firmly as the stairs were not very wide and narrowed almost to nothing on one side.

The dungeons were horrifying with their little cells, small and airless, many of them without even the tiny barred window.

Jessamy said: "I hate it down here. No one ever comes here...except when we show people, that's all. Every castle in the old days had its dungeons. There was one Mateland, in the time of Stephen, I believe, when the country was in a turmoil, who used to waylay travelers and hold them here to ransom. His son was even worse. He tortured them."

I shivered. "Let's go and see the rest," I suggested.

"I agree with you. It's horrible. I suggested having the dungeons walled up, but they won't hear of it. Egmont goes purple in the face at the mere mention of it or any alteration to the castle."

"I can understand it in a way. But as for this place...I should think what happened here is best forgotten."

We mounted the stairs with the aid of a rope banister and were in a stone hall.

"This," explained Jessamy, "is just below the main hall. You ascend that stone staircase and you are in a little passage, and there facing you would be the door to the main hall. This is a sort of crypt. When people die the coffin is kept here for a while."

"It reeks of death," I said.

She nodded. "Look how it is groined with blocks of hard chalk. And just feel these massive pillars."

"Impressive," I said. "This is the very ancient part of the castle, I am sure."

"Yes, it's part of the first structure."

"How grim it must have been to have lived in those days."

I could not get the dungeons out of my mind. I was sure I should think of them even when I went upstairs to my luxurious room.

We went back to the hall where Jessamy pointed out the fine carved stonework and truly magnificent timbers in the vaulted roof. She showed me the exquisite linenfold which had been put in when Queen Elizabeth visited the castle and the intricate carvings at the foot of the minstrels' gallery which depicted scenes from the Bible. Then we went to the long gallery where I studied pictures of ancient and modern Matelands. It was interesting to see Grandfather Egmont there and to have some indication of the man I was to meet. He was remarkably like David. He had the same thick brows and penetrating eyes. There was a picture of Joel and one of David.

"The little boy has not yet been painted," I said.

"No. They are not painted until they are twenty-one."

"How exciting to be able to look back to your ancestors all those years. Oh, Jessamy, perhaps your descendants will inherit all this one day."

"It's hardly likely," she said. "First of all I'd have to have the child...and then of course there's Esmond. His children will inherit. David's the elder."

"Suppose Esmond died...or didn't marry...and therefore had no legitimate heirs."

"Oh, don't talk of Esmond's dying! He's the loveliest little boy."

She seemed eager to get out of the picture gallery.

We explored the rest of the house. There was the drawing room, the dining room in which we had eaten last night, the library, the armory, the gun room—I had never seen such a selection of guns—the Elizabeth room, the Adelaide room—both queens had honored the castle with their presence—and there were all the bedrooms. In fact I wondered how anyone ever learned to find his way about the castle.

Finally we came to the nursery and there I made the acquaintance of Esmond. He was, as Jessamy had said, a beautiful little boy. He was sitting in a window seat with Elizabeth Larkham and she was reading, pointing to the words with her finger as she did so.

He stood up as we entered. He came towards us and Jessamy said: "This is Esmond. Esmond, this is Miss Campion."

He took my hand and kissed it. It was a charming gesture, and I thought how pretty he was with his dark hair and his fine dark eyes...undoubtedly a Mateland.

"You're Jessamy's cousin," he stated.

I told him I was and that I was looking at the castle.

"I know," he told me.

Elizabeth laid a hand on his shoulder. "Esmond has been asking about you," she said.

"It's nice of you to be interested," I said to the boy.

"Can you read?" he asked. "This story is about three bears."

"I believe I know it," I said. "'Who's been sitting in my chair?' 'Who's been eating my stew?'"

"It wasn't stew. It was porridge," he corrected me solemnly.

"I dare say it changes with the years," I replied. "Stew or porridge, what does it matter?"

"It does matter," he insisted. "Stew's not like porridge."

"Esmond is a stickler for detail," said Elizabeth.

"Am I a stickler?" asked Esmond. "What is a stickler?"

Elizabeth said: "I'll tell you another time. I was just going to take him out," she told us. "It's time for his midmorning walk."

"Not yet," said Esmond.

She held him firmly by the hand.

"You'll have more time to talk to Miss Campion," she said.

"Well, we'll continue with our tour," Jessamy replied.

"It's a fantastic place, isn't it?" Elizabeth looked straight at me, and again I felt that she was summing me up.

I agreed that it was.

"We'll go out to the battlements," Jessamy announced. "I want to show you the stone walk."

"I shall see you later then," I said to Esmond, who nodded and said rather sadly: "It wasn't stew."

Jessamy and I climbed the stone stairs—another of those tricky spiral ones—and were on the battlements.

"Esmond is a very serious little boy," she said. "He should be more with boys of his own age. It's only when Garth and Malcolm are here that he sees other boys. And they are both older than he is."

"I've heard of Garth," I said. "Who is Malcolm?"

"He's a cousin of some sort. His grandfather was Egmont's younger brother. You can work it out. I gather there was some feud between Egmont and his brother. They quarreled or something. Egmont has relented and Malcolm pays periodic visits. I think Egmont likes to regard him as an unlikely but possible heir to the castle. You see, if Esmond were to die and Joel and I had no children, I imagine Malcolm would be the next in line. Malcolm's about Garth's age ... sometimes we have them both here together. It's good for Esmond. Elizabeth is of course devoted to him. I think she's a bit jealous if he takes notice of anyone else."

"She needn't be jealous of me. I'm just one of those ships that pass in the night."

"Don't say that, Anabel. I want you to come here often. You don't know how your coming cheers me up."

"Cheers you up! Surely you don't need cheering up?"

"What I mean is that you add that much more."

But she had alerted my senses. Things were not quite what they seemed at the castle. Jessamy was not completely happy. I was sure this had something to do with Joel.

I had been three days at the castle. I had made the acquaintance of Egmont, a rather ferocious-looking old man with the Mateland bushy brows, gray in his case. He was affable to me. "He has taken a fancy to you," said Jessamy.

She told me he had a reputation for being fond of women and in his youth he had had mistresses all over the countryside. There were numerous Matelands all over the district.

"I don't think he ever attempted to deny paternity," she said. "He was proud of his virility. He always looked after them, too."

"What of his wife? How did she react to these bastards all over the countryside?"

"She endured and she accepted. There was nothing else she could do. Of course, in those days that sort of thing was taken as a matter of course, more than it is today. The Queen sets such a good example."

"She sets the fashion for virtue," I commented, "but that sometimes means drawing a veil over immorality rather than suppressing it."

She frowned slightly, and I wondered what she was thinking. I was becoming very sensitive to her moods. For the first time in her life Jessamy was hiding something from me. I was certain that everything was not what it seemed on the surface. But try as I might I could not get her to tell me her innermost thoughts, and the longer I was at the castle the surer I was becoming that there were secrets there.

I saw Joel frequently, but never alone. Sometimes I thought that we both contrived that this should be so. But there did come a day when we were thrown together.

I had done a little riding at the castle. Jessamy rode a good deal. She always had at Seton and Aunt Amy Jane had grudgingly allowed me to share her lessons. I had loved riding and some of the happiest days of my childhood had been spent galloping and cantering over the fields and walking the lanes in Jessamy's made-over riding clothes. There had been nothing quite as exciting in those days as galloping along, a horse beneath me and the wind buffeting me.

So it was pleasant to ride at Mateland, where there was, of course, a large stable and several horses to spare. The right mount was found for me and Jessamy and I rode every day.

Once when Jessamy and I were riding we met David. He had been going round the Mateland estate, which he spent his days looking after, and when he saw us he rode with us.

He chatted amicably, wanted to know what I thought of the Mateland stables and the particular mount which had been found for me, how much riding I had done and so on.

There came a moment when Jessamy slowed down to talk to a woman at the door of one of the cottages. I managed to catch a strange smile about David's lips. He quickened pace a little, and I kept up with him. He turned up a lane, and then I realized that he was trying to get ahead of Jessamy.

I said: "Does she know we're going this way?"

"She'll find out," he answered.

"But..."

"Oh, come on, Anabel. I never get a chance to talk to you."

There was something in the tone of his voice which warned me to take care.

"We shall lose her," I protested.

"That could be the object of the enterprise."

"Not mine," I reminded him.

"Anabel, you are a very attractive young lady. You know it. And you are not as prim as you would have me believe. You have bewitched us all."

"All?"

"My father, myself and my newly wedded brother."

"I am flattered to have made such an impression on your family."

"Anabel, you would make an impression wherever you went. You have something more than beauty. Did you know that?"

"No, but I am interested to hear a catalogue of my virtues."

"There is vitality in you...a response...."

"A response to what?"

"To that which you arouse in men."

"I am learning a great deal, but I think I must say here endeth the first lesson and the first lesson shall be the last."

"You amuse me."

"Another talent? Really, you will make me very conceited."

"I tell you nothing you do not know. Since you have come to the castle you have been constantly in my thoughts. Have you thought of me?"

"Naturally I think of people when I am in their company. Now I think we should join Jessamy."

"Let me show you round the estate. There is a great deal you would be interested in, Anabel...."

I turned and called out to Jessamy, who was looking for us. I rode back to her.

"I didn't see that you had gone up the lane," she said.

I felt very shaken. I thought that clearly I could not stay on at the castle. It seemed to me that there was something a little sinister about this man. I wanted to get away from him.

I thought a great deal about what David had said. The men in the family were all impressed by me. That was what he had stated. I knew that *he* was. What was he looking for? A brief flirtation, a passing affair? He was married to an invalid and for a man such as he was that must be trying. I had no doubt that he attempted to seduce every woman with whom he came into contact, so perhaps I should not attach too much importance to this approach of his. I only had to show him that I was not the type to indulge in brief love affairs with married men...and even if I were he did not attract me.

I liked to sit beside Grandfather Egmont and talk to him. He was complimentary too and made it very clear that he considered me an attractive woman. I hadn't thought much about that before and it was as though I had changed when I set foot in Mateland Castle. A spell had been laid upon me. "Every man who sees you shall desire you." That was the sort of thing. Grandfather Egmont had a wicked twinkle in his eye and was implying that if he were thirty years younger he would be ready to woo me. This amused me and I responded in a lighthearted flirtatious kind of way which delighted him. I did notice that his attitude towards Jessamy, Emerald and Elizabeth was quite different. So it really did seem as though there was something in me which aroused this spark in the Matelands.

That Joel was conscious of my presence I knew, but he seemed to avoid me. But I did meet him one day as I was riding out of the stables. Jessamy had had some duty to perform and she had asked me if I would mind riding alone that day.

I said of course not and when I had ridden through the great gate and down the incline towards the woods Joel joined me.

"Hello," he said as if by surprise. "Riding alone today?"

"Yes. Jessamy is busy."

"Are you going anywhere special?"

"No. Just riding aimlessly."

"Do you mind if I ride along with you for a while?"

"I'd like that," I said.

So we rode through the woods and I was as excited as I had been since our encounter in the church and again at the wedding. It was that particular brand of excitement which only he could inspire in me.

He asked how I was enjoying my visit and then he talked about the vicarage and the church which had so impressed him, and I found myself rattling on. I felt joyous; I wanted to catch and hold the minutes to prevent their passing.

"I suppose all vicars' daughters and wives lead the same sort of existence," I said. "There is always the great concern. Of course it can be the roof, the steeple or the belfry...This is the century of crumbling churches in England, which is very logical, I suppose, since most of them were built at least five hundred years ago. You must have problems with the castle."

"Constant," he assured me. "Our great enemy, deathwatch beetle, is continually summoning us to action. We win a battle or two and then we hear him knocking in another place. That's my brother's concern really."

"And yours is your profession. Are there many doctors in the family?"

"No. I'm the first. It was something of a battle but I was insistent."

"Yes," I said, "you would be."

"Oh, you have summed me up, have you?"

"Yes, as the kind of man who, when he makes up his mind he wants something, gets it."

"I don't think it is quite like that, but there was nothing in the way of my taking up the medical profession. It was just that it had never been done before, and if you know of a sillier reason for not doing something than that it has not been done before, please tell me."

"I know of none," I said. "So you studied and finally qualified."

"I did. It wasn't as though I was the heir. Second sons have more freedom than heirs. It is sometimes not a bad thing to be a second son."

"Certainly it wasn't in your case. Tell me about your studies. Do you specialize in anything?"

"No...just general...." He told me about his apprenticeship and how finally he had set up a practice in the town. "It was not before it was needed," he said. "There's a dearth of doctors in this area. I've plenty to do, I can tell you." He turned to me suddenly. "Would you like to see my quarters? I'd like to show you. I'm hoping soon to build a hospital in the town. It's what we need."

"Yes," I said, "I should very much like to."

"Then come with me. We're nearly there."

We were on the outskirts of the town and we rode on in

silence. I wondered how much he talked to Jessamy. He clearly found pleasure in discussing his work.

Mateland was a small town and as we rode through it several people called a greeting to him. I felt pleased because clearly he was popular. He discussed them with me. "That's an enlarged heart going up there. It's hard to treat. He's far too energetic.... Kidneys," he said of a thin little woman who called, "Good morning, Doctor," as we passed.

I laughed. "So they are hearts and kidneys and whatever is wrong with them to you."

"That's what I'm interested in."

"The rest of us are bodies as a whole, I suppose, until of course you find one of our organs worthy of notice."

"That sums it up, I suppose."

We had come to a house of three stories. It stood apart from the rest of the houses in the street. There was a drive in and a semicircular path which went up to the house and had a gate at each end. We rode in, dismounted and he tethered our horses.

As we went into the house a woman came into the hall. I guessed at once that she was the housekeeper.

"Dorothy," he said, "this is Miss Campion, my wife's cousin."

Dorothy gave me an appraising look.

"Good day to you, miss," she said.

"Are there any messages?" asked Joel.

"Jim Talbot's been in. He says if you could look in on his wife this afternoon he'd be glad. She's better, he says, but not right yet."

"I'll go this afternoon, Dorothy." He turned to me. "Would you like some tea or coffee? There's time, I think, Dorothy, before surgery begins."

"I should like some coffee," I said, and Dorothy went out.

That was an enchanted hour to me. He glowed with enthusiasm for his work and it occurred to me that he did not find it easy to talk to many people as he did to me. His life was so different from that of the other members of the family. A modern doctor in that medieval setting!

As we drank the coffee he explained something of this to me.

"If I had been the elder," he said, "I should never have been able to pursue this and it means a great deal to me. I can't explain how exciting it is. One never knows when one is going to discover something of vital importance...some strange symptom, some cure...something to give one a lead as to how to go on. It was an old doctor who inspired me when I was a boy. He came to the castle to see my mother and I used to watch and listen to him. My father laughed when I said I wanted to be a doctor. 'Why not?' I said. 'There's David to run the castle estate.' In fact, they would have liked me to help him. But David and I never saw things in the same way. There would have been friction. I don't know who is the more stubborn—he or I. We each want our own way and, when two people like us start pulling in different directions, something has to give. Why didn't you come to the castle with Jessamy in the first place? You said you were often at Seton Manor?"

"I wasn't asked," I said.

He looked at me very steadily and then he said something which both alarmed and delighted me. It was just: "A pity!"

I heard myself saying quickly: "Well, I finally came."

He was silent for a moment. Then he said: "We're a strange lot at the castle, aren't we?"

"Are you?"

"Don't you find us so?"

"All people are unexpected when you get to know them."

"So you don't think there is anything specially different about us?"

"No. Except that you can trace your ancestry back hundreds of years and you live in a castle."

"I live quite a lot of my time here." He hesitated.

"Does Jessamy like it here?"

"She...she hasn't been here a great deal. I stay here when I want to be early the next morning or I am working late."

"It's not very far from the castle."

"But it sometimes seems simpler to stay."

I thought it was strange that Jessamy had not mentioned this.

"Talking about our being different," he went on, "there are always rumors about us, you know. There's supposed to be some curse on us. It affects the Mateland wives."

"Oh, what is the curse?"

"It's a long story. Briefly, at the time of the Civil War there was discord between the castle and some of the towns-people here. They were for the Parliament. The castle was of course strictly Royalist. The King's army was in the ascendant here at one time and apparently they raided the town; one of the citizens escaped and came to the castle with his young wife, who was pregnant. He asked for succor. It was refused and one of my ancestors threatened to hand them over to the King's men. They went away; the wife died in a ditch and her husband cursed the Matelands. They had murdered his wife, he said, and they should know no luck in theirs."

"Well, I dare say that has been disproved time and time again."

"I don't know that it has. The odd thing about these legends is that now and then they have a habit of coming true, and when they do they grow in strength."

"And when they don't I suppose they are forgotten."

"My mother went into a decline when I was ten years old," he said. "You know Jessamy is my second wife. I shall never forget the night Rosalie died. She was my wife...my first wife. She was eighteen. We had known each other since we were children. She was dainty and pretty and rather frivolous. She loved to dance and was rather vain about her appearance...rather charmingly vain, you understand?"

"Yes," I said. "I understand."

"There was going to be a ball at the castle. She had talked for days about her gown. It was a mass of frills...lilac color, I remember. She was enchanted with it and tried it on the night before the ball. She danced round and round the room in it. She went too close to the candle flame. We tried to save her...but it was too late."

"What a terrible thing. I am so sorry."

"There was nothing that could be done," he said quietly.

I put out a hand and touched his. "But you are happy now," I said.

He took my hand and held it but he did not answer.

"Then," he went on, "there was a riding accident. Emerald, you know. My mother...Rosalie...Emerald..."

"But now you have Jessamy and luck will change."

He kept looking at me and still he said nothing. But something passed between us. There was so much that did not have to be said. I understood. He had found a certain peace with Jessamy but he wanted something more.

How did I know? Because of a certain longing in his eyes, because of my response to him and my awareness that he knew of this.

I put down my coffee cup.

"Your patients will be arriving," I said.

"I am glad you came," he answered.

"It was all so interesting."

He went with me to the horses.

I rode away thoughtfully and as I was about to enter the woods I heard the sound of horse's hoofs behind me. Then a rider was at my side.

"Good morning to you." It was David.

"Good morning," I said. "I am just returning to the castle."

"No objection to my joining you, I hope. I am going back myself."

I inclined my head.

"Do I detect a lack of enthusiasm? I see I am not as fortunate as my brother. What did you think of that place of his?"

I said: "Have you been following me?"

His smile was malicious. "I just happened to see you emerging with old Joel. You were both looking mightily pleased with yourselves."

"I had met him by chance and he offered to show me his place in the town. It does not seem to me that there is anything in such a natural occurrence to warrant your amusement."

"Quite right," he said. "All very proper and natural. Why shouldn't our noble doctor show his cousin-in-law this practice of his? I just thought I ought to drop a little word of warning into your innocent ears. There's nothing to choose between us, you know. We're all the same. Mateland men all have the same roving eye...they always have...they've been noted for it from the days of King Stephen. They don't change their ways any more than leopards change their spots. Beware of the Matelands, dear Anabel, and particularly beware of Joel."

"You really are letting your imagination run away with you. Both you and your brother are happily married men."

"Are we?" he asked.

"And," I said, "I find this conversation rather distasteful."

"In that case," he said, inclining his head in mock respect, "we must not pursue it."

We went back to the castle in silence. I was very disturbed. I knew that I must get away from there and that I should not come back.

* * *

How dull it was at the vicarage. My thoughts were in the castle.

Jessamy wrote to me.

I do miss you, Anabel. You should come for Christmas. It will be a traditional Christmas in the castle. It has to be as it was celebrated hundreds of years ago...all wassailing and so on, and the great bowl in the hall with steaming punch in it. I heard about it from Esmond. He and I are becoming great friends. There is to be a carol service in the hall on Christmas Eve, and then there will be distribution of baskets of Christmas fare to all the needy villagers. They come up to the castle to collect them. The gardeners are beginning on the decorations. We shall have a house party. Do come, Anabel. It will be spoilt for me if you don't. Joel is kept very busy. I have hardly seen him for several weeks. He says there is a lot of sickness in the town. He works very hard. Grandfather Egmont doesn't like it. He says there has never before been such a thing as a Mateland actually taking money from others for what he does. He thinks it's degrading. Mind you, Joel doesn't take money from the poor. He doesn't need it really. All the Matelands are rich...very rich, I think. Joel is really a very good man, Anabel. He is indeed....

I paused there. I thought she was a little too emphatic. Then I went on thinking about him. He was doctoring and helping the poor, which was very commendable. But there was a certain set of his jaw...I could not describe it but it suggested that he was no saint. He was a man who went out for what he wanted and would not rest, I was sure, until he got it. He could be ruthless. He had obsessed me. I wished I had never seen him. "We are all the same," David had said. Did that mean that they were all philanderers?

Stop thinking about them, I warned myself.

There was enough to do at the vicarage even if I had decided that I was not going to Mateland for Christmas. Aunt Amy Jane and Uncle Timothy had been invited to the castle and were going.

"It will be so interesting to have a castle Christmas," said Aunt Amy Jane. "I hope all goes well here, James." She meant, of course, that it would be the first Christmas that she would not be at home to superintend the festival. "I shall be here for the children's party," she went on. "And I am allowing the Mothers' Union to have their annual gathering in our hall. That is all taken care of. I think I can leave the rest with you and go off with a clear conscience."

How I wished that I were going! Silly, I told myself. It was your own fault. You were invited.

It seemed a long Christmas. It rained all through Christmas Eve. Janet cooked the goose with one of the women from the village to help her. It was too much to do alone, she said, now that Amelia had gone off to that Crabtree Cottage.

The doctor, his wife and two daughters dined with us on Christmas Day. It seemed quiet after our usual Christmas at Seton Manor. The day seemed endless and then there was Boxing Day to follow.

I went for a ride. I had permission to ride one of the horses in the Seton stables. The groom who saddled it for me said: "It don't seem the same without Miss Jessamy. A lovely young lady, she was."

"*Is*, Jeffers," I cried. "Don't talk about her as though she is in the past."

I was depressed. I could find no pleasure in the morning although it was a lovely day, quite balmy, with a faint mist in the air. I noticed that there were lots of berries on the holly, which was a sign of a hard winter, so those who were well versed in country lore told us.

I was uneasy about Jessamy. I did not know why I should be. She had everything. Why should I have qualms about her future? I must stop thinking about Mateland Castle and the people in it. My life would be set in a different direction.

I took the horse back to the Seton stables and from there walked to the vicarage. My father was not in.

"He's not come back yet," said Janet. "I expected him an hour ago. I'm waiting to put the food on the table."

"Is he still at the church, do you think?"

"He said he was going over for something...I don't remember what."

"He's forgotten the time," I said. "I'll go and get him."

I went into the church. I could not enter it now without thinking of myself sprawled on the altar steps and Joel Mateland standing there. I had been a different person up to that time.

I called to my father. There was no answer.

He must be in the vestry, I thought, or in the Lady chapel.

Then I saw him. He was lying very near the spot where I had fallen. I ran to him crying: "Father, what's happened?"

I knelt beside him. At first I thought he was dead. Then I saw his eyelids flicker. I ran out to get help.

He had had a stroke, and he was paralyzed down one side and had lost the power of speech.

With Janet's help I nursed him. A vicar came to take over while my father was ill—so they said; but I knew and so did Janet that he would never preach again.

Tom Gillingham was an earnest young man and a bachelor. Janet reckoned he'd been sent for a purpose.

"Whose purpose?" I asked. "God's or the bishop's?"

"I wouldn't mind reckoning a bit of both," retorted Janet.

Janet, true to the habit of plain speaking, had put the matter clearly before me.

"Your father is not going to get any better," she said. "Pray God he doesn't get worse. And what of you? You've got to think of yourself. Oh yes, you can look at me as if you'd like to tell me to mind my own business. It *is* my business. I work here, don't I? What's going to happen to you and me when your father dies?"

"He may live for years."

"You know he won't. You can see him getting worse every day. Two months...three at the most, I reckon. Then you'll have some thinking to do. I doubt the vicar is going to leave you a fortune."

"Your doubts are confirmed, Janet."

"Well then, what's for you? Companion to some old lady? I can't see that for you, Miss Anabel. Governess to some little 'uns...a bit more likely, but still not right. It's either that or staying on here."

"How could I do that?"

"Plain as a pikestaff, that is, that Tom Gillingham being a bachelor."

I couldn't help smiling. "I wonder what he would say if he knew you were arranging the future for him?"

"He wouldn't mind...seeing as *how* I've arranged it. He's sweet on you, Miss Anabel. I wouldn't be surprised if he's got something like that in mind."

"He's a pleasant enough young man," I agreed.

"And you've been brought up in a vicarage...know all the ins and outs and suchlike."

"It seems very satisfactory but for one thing."

"And what's that?"

"I don't want to marry Tom Gillingham."

"Love can grow, they say."

"It can also diminish, and if it is not there in the first place it can't even do that. No, Janet, we shall have to think of something else."

"It's not that I'm so concerned. I've got my sister Marian I could go to for a spell. We never got on but it would be somewhere to go while I looked round."

"Oh, Janet," I cried, "I should hate to say good-by to you."

Her face twitched but she was always in control of her emotions.

We were silent. It was a bleak future we were looking into.

When Aunt Amy Jane and Uncle Timothy came back they were shocked to hear of my father's illness.

"This puts you in a very awkward position, Anabel," said Aunt Amy Jane.

"You'll have to come to Seton Manor," kind Uncle Timothy told me.

Aunt Amy Jane gave him a cold look. She had never liked him to show affection to me.

"Anabel would never want to live on charity," she said firmly. "She's far too proud."

"Charity!" cried Uncle Timothy. "She's our own niece."

"*My* niece. Therefore, Timothy, I am the one to know best for her. I dare say there would be something for her to *do*."

"I shall know what I have to do when the time comes," I said coldly.

There was speculation in Aunt Amy Jane's eyes. I could see she was beginning to work out a plan of action to decide my future.

When she realized that Tom Gillingham was at the vicarage already, and had in fact been appointed to take over when my father died, she saw the solution even as Janet had. Tom Gillingham should marry me—whether he wanted to or not. He should be made to see reason, as everyone must who had a part to play in Aunt Amy Jane's scheme of things.

I knew that Tom would raise no objection. He was interested in me and I only had to respond, I knew, and he would suggest marriage.

I could not do it. It would be like writing The End to my

life story, because everything that followed would be so predictable.

If only Jessamy had not gone. If I had never seen Mateland Castle, if I had never realized there were other goals in the world than contriving to exist in a degree of comfort, I might have been willing to accept what seemed like the inevitable. But I had glimpsed a different life. I had met Joel Mateland and even though he was my cousin's husband I still went on thinking of him.

Calmly to settle down in the Seton church as the wife of the vicar was not the life for me.

It was spring when my father died. The moment of decision had come.

Tom Gillingham had made it clear that I must not hurry away, although of course I, as an unmarried woman, could not with propriety go on living at the rectory. When my father had been alive—helpless invalid though he might be—it had been different.

It was the day of the funeral. Tom officiated at the service and we filed into the churchyard following the coffin and its pallbearers. We stood round the grave and desolation swept over me as I thought of my dear kindly father with his ineffectual ways and absent-minded but always self-effacing nature.

It was the end of a way of life.

I felt a hand in mine and, turning, I saw Jessamy. The sight of her warmed me, filled me with some sort of hope. A little of my misery lifted.

The mourners had all gone. Jessamy was sitting on the stool in my bedroom, her arms folded about her knees, looking at me. She had always sat like that. To see her there brought back so many memories of our childhood, when I had dominated her, bullied her sometimes, and led her into mischief. Dear, dear Jessamy who had never ceased to love me for all my wickedness to her.

"What are you going to do, Anabel?" she asked.

I shrugged my shoulders.

"You are not going to marry Tom Gillingham, are you? My mother says you are."

"For once she is wrong. I like Tom, but..."

"Of course you can't marry him," she said firmly. "Then what?"

"I think the only alternative is to take some post."

"Oh, Anabel. You'd hate that."

"If you have no money you often have to do something which is not congenial. But I'm worried about Janet. You see, though she can go to her sister for a while, she won't want to stay there. She'll have to get another post...and posts are hard to come by."

"Anabel, I want you to come back with me. Come to the castle. I miss you very much. I'm lonely some of the time. To tell the truth, Joel is away so much...and then...and then...I think he is not very..."

"Not very what?"

"Satisfied with our marriage. He seems almost aloof sometimes. Emerald can say wounding things and so can David...particularly David. Sometimes I think he and Joel hate each other. And then there's Elizabeth....I don't know what to make of her. Sometimes I feel so alone there...a little afraid. No, not exactly afraid...but..."

"I thought you were so happy there."

"Oh, I am...particularly now....Anabel, I am going to have a baby."

I leaped up, took her hand, pulled her up from the stool and hugged her.

"Yes, isn't it exciting?" she said.

"Joel must be pleased."

"Oh yes, he is. Anabel, you must come back with me. I say you must...particularly now."

"I don't think I should, Jessamy."

"But you must. You can't desert me."

"Desert you! You have a husband...and a baby coming. You have everything. What can you want with me?"

"I do want you." She was quiet for a moment. Then she said: "Anabel, I'd feel happier, safer, if you were there."

"Safer? What are you afraid of?"

"N-nothing really." She laughed nervously. "I don't know. Perhaps it's because it's a castle. There's so much of the past there. All the long-dead Matelands...Sometimes it seems as though they are there...watching....Then there is the legend about the wives. It's supposed to be unlucky to be a Mateland wife."

"Jessamy," I said, "you are afraid of something."

"You know I was always a bit silly. Anabel, I need you. I've worked it out. Janet could come with you. She could be your personal maid. It would solve everything if you came."

"But...perhaps the others wouldn't want me. Your husband...your father-in-law..."

"You're wrong. You're absolutely wrong. They were all pleased when I suggested it...every one of them. They said such lovely things about you. Grandfather Egmont said you would brighten up the place. David said it would be pleasant to have you there because you are amusing."

"And Emerald?"

"She is never very enthusiastic about anything but she didn't say she wouldn't want you to come."

"And your husband?"

"I think he would be as pleased as the others. He thinks it would be good for me to have you there. There is plenty of room in the castle. And Janet can come too. Do you think she would like that?"

"She would," I said. "But I don't think it would be wise." I added firmly: "No, Jessamy, I won't come."

But I knew I should go. I could go two ways...one was bleak, offering me nothing, and the other was beckoning me away to adventure, excitement and if it was going to be dangerous, well, it had always been my nature to court danger. It lured me, it fascinated me.

Within a month of my father's death Janet and I were on our way to Mateland Castle.

So there I was installed in my turret room. My new home was now Mateland Castle. Janet was delighted.

"A bit different, this, from that vicarage," she commented. "And here I can keep an eye on that Miss Jessamy, a gentle little thing, and I'm not at all sure that she's been done right by."

"What do you mean?" I demanded.

"I reckon she's neglected, that's what. And there's people here that wants watching."

So there was Janet, happy to be installed as the watchdog of the castle.

I was growing away from the shock of my father's death. I had not realized when he was alive how much I loved him. He had always seemed so ineffectual, so vague, so shut in with his books, going about his duties, delivering uninspired sermons every Sunday to people who came not so much to hear them but because it was expected of them to come. Now that he was gone I knew what an unselfish man he had been. I missed his gentleness.

He had left a little money for me—not enough to live on but sufficient for me to buy a few things I should need and enable me to preserve a modicum of independence.

To have left the vicarage and to have plunged into these new and exciting surroundings was the greatest help I could have to recover from my grief. I had never thought of my father as my guardian; he had never interfered very much and had been a background figure; but now that he was gone I felt alone.

I spent my days with Jessamy and I believe I was as much a comfort to her as she was to me.

There was no doubt of my welcome. Grandfather Egmont came down to dinner on my first evening and made me sit beside him. He seemed to be consumed by some secret enjoyment. "You're going to bring a bit of life into the castle," he said, his chin wagging to express amusement. "Always liked to see a pretty woman around."

David cocked an eyebrow and winked at me. "So you're here," he said. "One of us now. No need for me to say how I feel about that. A thousand welcomes to Mateland Castle, beauteous Anabel."

And Joel? He looked at me steadily, his eyes smiling, telling me more clearly than any words could how pleased he was that I was there.

Emerald showed little feeling either way. "I hope you'll like it here," she said, and her voice was dubious.

Elizabeth Larkham said that there was no doubt of Jessamy's delight in my coming, as though she felt Jessamy was the only one who was going to profit from it.

And so here I was. I had found a refuge for myself and Janet. There was no doubt of Janet's gratification. Even she shared that innate snobbery which most servants seem to have, and the grander the household in which they serve, the better pleased they are. And from a vicarage where certain economies had to be practiced to a castle where there seemed an unending flow of worldly goods was a great step upwards.

I knew from the first that I had to go warily. David had, without doubt, determined to pursue me. There was a gleam in his eyes every time he looked at me. I knew I was already his mistress in his imagination. I was determined that I should never be in reality and I could see that he was equally determined that I should be. He was a ruthless man. Yes, indeed I must take care. Not that I feared I should succumb to his wiles. That could never be; but I believed he would do his best to trap me into an embarrassing situation. As for Joel, I was unsure of his feelings towards me. There were times when I found his eyes on me with the same desire which I had seen in David's. When I was close to him he would touch my arm, my hand, my shoulders and I sensed that he wanted to be close to me.

I would have been insensible if I had not realized that I had aroused great feeling in these Mateland brothers.

There were times when I lay in my turret bedroom and said to myself: If you were a good and virtuous woman, you would go away from here. You know no good can come of this. David is a buccaneer, a descendant of those men who captured travelers and brought them to the castle to ransom or torture them. He would do anything to gain his desires. You are in acute danger from him. And...you are becoming more and more involved with Joel. You are excited by him. In fact sometimes you seek his company. The truth is you are falling in love with Joel Mateland, allowing yourself to become more and more involved every day. To become his mistress would be more shocking than to become David's because he is Jessamy's husband.

It was an uneasy atmosphere. I locked my bedroom door every night. I was glad Jessamy was only a few doors away. I used to think of her and Joel together. But he was more often at the house in the town.

Jessamy was troubled. Once she had a nightmare and called out. I went along to her room, where she was tossing about in her bed. She was saying something about the curse on the Mateland wives.

I aroused her, soothed her and stayed the night in her room.

"You were dreaming," I told her. "You mustn't have these nightmares. They'll be bad for the baby."

Janet and I only had to say something would be bad for the baby and Jessamy would be most concerned. Her life centered round the baby. It was as though she looked upon it as some consolation.

There was so much I wanted to ask Jessamy about her marriage, but I found it difficult to talk of it. I feared I might betray my feelings about Joel.

The inevitable had to happen. I want you to underst
Suewellyn, that neither Joel nor I was wicked. We had
tried hard to stop its happening. But there is something un-
conventional about us both, and during those first months
when I was at the castle we really did try hard, but it was
too strong for us.

Jessamy had had to give up riding and I went out alone.
One day I met Joel in the woods. I knew he had been waiting
for me.

"I had to talk to you," he said. "You know that I love you,
Anabel."

"You must not say that," I told him rather feebly.

"I must say what is true."

"You married Jessamy."

"Why didn't you come with her that first time? Everything
would have been so different if you had."

"Would it?" I asked.

"You know it would. There was a tremendous undeniable
attraction between us from the first moment we met, on the
altar steps. That was significant. Oh, Anabel, if it had only
been you!"

I struggled to remember my loyalty to Jessamy.

"But it wasn't," I insisted. "And you married Jessamy.
Why did you, if you didn't love her?"

"I told you about my first marriage. I had to marry again.
I wanted children. I had waited years. That is what is so
ironical. If only I had waited a little longer..."

"It's too late now."

He leaned towards me. "It's never too late."

"But Jessamy is your wife...soon to bear your child."

"You are here," he said, "and I am here...."

"I think I should leave the castle."

"You must not do that. If you did I should follow you, so
you would achieve nothing by going. Anabel, you and I are
of a kind; we were meant for each other. It was there between
us right from the first. You know that as well as I do. Only
rarely in life does one meet the right person at the right
time."

"But we have met at the wrong time," I reminded him.
"Too late...."

"We're not going to let ourselves be hemmed in by conventions. We'll push aside these man-made barriers. You're
here and I'm here. That's enough."

"No. No," I persisted. "Jessamy is my dear cousin. She is good and quite incapable of disloyalty and unkindness. We must not betray her."

"I tell you we are going to be together, Anabel," he said firmly. "For the rest of our lives, I swear it. Do you think I'm going to let you go? You're not the sort to let conventions ruin your life."

"No, perhaps not. But there is Jessamy. If it were anyone else..."

"Let's tether our horses here and talk. I want to hold you...make you understand...."

"No," I said quickly. "No. And I turned my horse and galloped away.

But it was inevitable. One afternoon he came to my room. Jessamy was sitting in the garden. It was a lovely September day and we were enjoying the sunshine of an Indian summer.

He shut the door and stood there watching me. I had taken off my dress and had been about to change and join Jessamy in the garden.

He took me in his arms and kissed me. He went on kissing me and I was as eager for him as he was for me.

But Jessamy was down there, innocent and unsuspecting, and I clung to the loyalty and love I felt for her.

"No, no," I protested. "Not here."

It was an admission. He held me at arm's length and looked at me.

"You know, Anabel, my love," he said, "that we belong together. Nothing on earth is going to keep us apart."

I did know it.

He went on: "Soon then...."

And he was smiling.

I don't want to make excuses. There is no excuse. We became lovers. It was wicked of us, but then neither of us is a saint. We could not help it. Our emotions were too strong for us. It is rarely, I am sure, that two people love as we did...immediately and simultaneously. I am sure to love like that is the happiest state in the world...if one is free to do so. We tried to forget that we were betraying Jessamy, but of course I could not completely. It was the bitterness in my ecstasy. Perhaps there were times when we were together in closest intimacy when I did forget; but it could not be for long and I found it hard to escape from the memory of Jessamy. She was always in my mind—except for those rare moments—

(116)

and I despised myself for deceiving her because when I looked back I realized that I had known something like this would happen if I came to the castle. I should have been noble and unselfish; I should have taken some post with a disagreeable old woman and pandered to her wishes, taken her nasty little dog for walks, or tried to grapple with the education of little horrors in an alien nursery. I shivered at the thought, and yet, wretched as I should have been, I could have held up my head.

Jessamy had a difficult pregnancy. The doctor said she must keep to her bed, which she did. She was uncomplaining, eagerly looking forward to the day when her child would be born. She was very thoughtful towards me. "You must not stay in all day, Anabel," she said. "Take one of the horses and exercise it."

Dear Jessamy and despicable Anabel! I would take one of the horses and ride to the house in the town, and there Joel and I would be together.

He did not suffer so greatly from remorse as I did. He was a Mateland, and Matelands, I imagined, had never denied themselves the gratification of their senses. That there had been many women before me I was fully aware. Oddly enough I regarded this as a challenge. I was going to keep him devoted to me. I was determined on that. Indeed I was a mixture of contrasts at that time. I was exultant, ecstatic and yet filled with a sense of self-loathing and shame. But one thing I did know and that was that I had to behave as I did. It was as though there was some powerful force driving us together. I think he felt it too. He said there had never been anything like it in his life before, and although this is the sort of thing people say lightly in such circumstances, I believed him.

Understand, Suewellyn, that had this not been a mighty and overpowering emotion in me, a certainty that this was the only man I could ever love, I should not have entered into this relationship. I am not a good woman, but I am not a light one.

So while Jessamy was awaiting the birth of her child, I was making ardent love with her husband. We were completely absorbed in each other and it was only when we were alone in that house that we could allow ourselves to act naturally. In the castle we had to cloak our feelings, and we knew we were involved in a highly dangerous situation. It was not only Jessamy we had to deceive, I was constantly aware of David's watching eyes. He was amused by my rejection of him and at the same time his desires were strengthened by it.

If she knew, Emerald paid no attention to this. I dare say she was accustomed to his philanderings. I often caught Elizabeth Larkham watching me closely. She was Emerald's friend and clearly did not approve of David's interest in me.

As for the old man, he would have been highly amused by the situation if he knew of it, I was sure.

It was a strange household. When I was in the castle I was most at peace with young Esmond. We had become good friends. I used to read to him, and we would sit with Jessamy while she worked at some baby garment and I read aloud. It was a comfort to me to have the boy there; I was very uneasy when I was alone with Jessamy.

I believe that the only person who knew what was happening between me and Joel was Dorothy. She was imperturbable and I could not tell what she thought. It occurred to me that women might have come to the house before. I asked Joel about this and he admitted that it had happened once or twice. He assured me vehemently that that had all been very different. There had never been anything like this, and I believed him.

Elizabeth Larkham's son Garth came to the castle for the summer holidays. He was a noisy boy who behaved as though the castle were his. He was several years older than Esmond and took the lead in their games. I wondered whether Esmond welcomed him. He did not say he did not. He was too polite for that. His mother said it was good for him to have someone near his own age to be with and perhaps it was. There was another boy who came for a short visit. He was a cousin of some sort, named Malcolm Mateland. His grandfather was Egmont's brother.

When I look back now everything that happened seems inevitable. Jessamy's baby was born in November and by that time I had discovered that I was going to have a child.

It was a devastating discovery, although I should have been prepared for it. For several days I kept the information to myself.

Jessamy's baby was a girl. She was called Susannah. It is a custom in our family to give the girls two names by which they are called. Amy Jane for instance. My mother was Susan Ellen. When it came to Jessamy and myself, our names were two strung together. Jessica Amy and Ann Bella. So naturally Jessamy thought of Susan Anna for Susannah.

So wrapped up in her baby was she that Jessamy did not notice my preoccupation.

I discussed my predicament with Joel. He was delighted at the prospect of our having a child and waved aside all the difficulties. I was beginning to understand Joel very well. He was a forceful man, as all the Matelands were. When he was presented with a difficult situation, he always began by assuming that a solution could be found.

"Why, sweetheart," he said, "it's happened millions of times before. We'll find a way."

"I shall have to go away," I said. "I'll find some excuse to leave the castle."

"To go away briefly . . . yes. But you're coming back."

"And the child?"

"We'll arrange something."

It took us some time to work out a plan of action. We then arranged that I should tell them at the castle that a distant relative of my father who lived in Scotland was anxious to see me. I had heard my father talk of these people but apparently there had been some quarrel in the family, and now that they had heard my father was dead they wanted to see me.

I told Jessamy that I thought I ought to go.

Jessamy hated quarrels in families and she said why didn't I go for a week or two?

I left it at that. I would go for a week or so ostensibly and then I would find some reason for lengthening my stay.

I was now three months' pregnant. Janet was in the secret. It was impossible to keep it from her. She had been horrified at first, but that snobbery in her arose in my favor. At least the father of my child was the bearer of a great name and his home was a castle. That made the sin more venial in her eyes. She would come with me.

We did not go to Scotland as we had said we would but to a little mountain village near the Pennines and there we lived while we awaited the arrival of the baby. During that time Joel came twice to see me and stayed a few days each time. They were halcyon days. We were together in the mountains and we played a game of make-believe that we were married and that I was not hiding away so that our child could be born in secret.

Well, in due course you came into the world, Suewellyn, and I want you to know now that no child was ever more loved than you were.

What could I do? I could have set up house somewhere. We thought of that. Joel could have visited us. But I didn't want it to be that way. I wanted to make it as easy as possible for us all. Joel wanted me at the castle. So we decided that you should live with Amelia and William Planter. I could visit you often, keep an eye on you, and the Planters could be trusted to do their duty—moreover they would be well paid for doing it.

They took you and brought you up, and as you know I used to come regularly to see you.

It is a common enough situation. People, of course, began to suspect. The people who lived near the Planters must have guessed. I was always telling Joel that we should take you away. I wanted to have you with me. The Planters would never ill-treat you, I knew, but they would never love you. I used to worry a lot about you.

Do you remember the day I brought you to Mateland? I showed you the castle and Joel came. You were so happy that day, weren't you? You had three wishes. I almost broke down when you told me what they were.

It seems miraculous that they have come true. I wish they could have come true in some other way.

I have told you about David, haven't I? David was a wicked man. I know that Joel and I are no saints. I know that we allowed our senses to overcome our duty. I know that we thoughtlessly brought you into the world when it would be impossible to bring you up as parents should bring up their children. We were concerned first with our selfish desires. But we loved, Suewellyn, we loved. That is my excuse. David could never love anything or anyone but himself. He was concerned with his pride, which had to be satisfied at all costs. There was envy in him too. I quickly sensed that he was envious of Joel. It was true he was the elder son and he had a son to follow him. But Joel possessed some inner gratification. His work among the sick gave him a satisfaction which David lacked. Moreover David was a very sensual man. I do not say that Joel was not. He was. There is a ruthlessness in your father just as there was in David. They had the Mateland traits, both of them. The love of power had been bred in both of them and there is a saying that power corrupts.

But Joel was capable of love. I know that David was not. He was concerned only with the satisfaction of his desires. I had denied him and I fancied that because of that his desire for me increased; but he wanted not only me but revenge.

David was a man of another century. He belonged to an age when the lord of the castle was a feudal lord, when all obeyed him and their fate depended on his whim. I believed he was capable of great cruelty; moreover, that he took a delight in inflicting it.

So, Suewellyn, though you were brought up in Crabtree Cottage, I always promised myself that one day I was going to make up for those early times. They were not desertion. Never that. I ached for you, longed for you. Joel and I talked of you constantly.

I prayed that we could all be together. That was my wish...as it was yours.

The years began to speed by. I knew they were fraught with danger. I knew that David was watching me. I guessed he was aware how it was between Joel and me.

I discovered that Elizabeth Larkham was his mistress. She was a strange woman, an unusual woman. I think she was fond of Emerald but as in the case of Joel and myself her emotions must have been too strong for her. They could exert tremendous power, these Mateland men.

In a way I was grateful to Elizabeth because she turned David's attention away from me. To tell the truth, I was aware of a certain menace in the castle. It had been the scene of many tragedies in the past; many dark deeds had been performed within those walls. Sometimes I believed that violence, passion, death and disaster leave some shadow behind them which generations to come can sense.

There were times when the atmosphere was like a cauldron waiting to boil over. There was David, envious, sensual, seeking to satisfy his insatiable senses; there was Emerald in her chair, quiet and gray like a ghost from the past, and I often wondered what her life with David had been like before her accident. There was Elizabeth Larkham, placating Emerald, making herself necessary to Emerald...and Emerald's husband; and there were myself and Joel indulging in our illicit passion, grasping at something which could never be while Jessamy lived. There was also Jessamy, dear innocent Jessamy, who was aware of something wrong with her marriage, conscious of her husband's indifference and her own inadequacy, living for her child. Then the children: Esmond, bright and intelligent, nearly ready to go away to school; Garth, who came for the holidays; and Malcolm, who paid less frequent visits—a masterful boy, already showing signs of the Mateland strain; and of course Susannah—a beautiful child, screaming to get her own way and chuckling adorably when she got it—another true Mateland.

Even so, there came a time when I was lulled into a sense of security. How foolish of me! David was never going to allow anyone to get the better of him.

Perhaps he was growing tired of Elizabeth, but I grew aware that he was turning more and more to his pursuit of me. When I rode out I would find him following me. I had great difficulty in getting to the house in the town without his seeing me.

I used to slip out at odd times and if I failed to elude him I did not go to the house and Joel would be waiting there in vain.

His hatred of David was intense, I discovered. Joel's emotions were always intense. He never did things by halves. He threw himself wholeheartedly into whatever obsessed him. He was obsessed by his work; he was obsessed by our passion. I often thought how happy we could have been—he, you and I, Suewellyn, in that house in the town away from the castle.

This brings me to the last time I visited you at Crabtree Cottage—no, not the last time, for the last time I came was when I took you away. I mean the time before the last.

I did not realize that I was being followed. I should have done. But he was very skillful. David had become aware that I often left the castle for a day, ostensibly to visit relations of my father. This was supposed to be a branch of the family with whom I had stayed at the time of your birth and whom I had met at that time.

Well, on that occasion David followed me to Crabtree Cottage. He stayed at the local inn for a few days and asked a lot of questions. He saw you...and frightened you, I believe. What he discovered was what he had expected to find. You were there...our daughter, mine and Joel's.

He came back full of delight and the very next day he followed me when I went riding and caught up with me in the woods.

"Now, Anabel," he said, "I have to talk to you."

"Well, what have you to say?" I asked.

"It is about the eternal triangle...you, Joel and myself."

"I don't think I want to hear anything you have to say on such a subject," I retorted.

"Ah, but it is not a question of what you want to hear. It's what I want to tell. I know all, sweet Anabel. I know how you and Joel behave. While he is supposed to be ministering to the sick you and he are sporting in his bachelor bedroom. I am surprised at you, Anabel, though not, of course, at my brother."

"I am going back to the castle."

"Not yet. We'll go back later. I know everything, Anabel. I know of the love nest above the surgery. I know about the little girl too. She's charming...just what I would expect of your daughter...and Joel's, of course."

I felt sick with horror. I guessed that he might have suspected my relationship with Joel but that he should have discovered your existence horrified me.

I heard myself stammering: "You...you went and spoke to her...."

"Don't look alarmed. Little girls don't appeal to me. I like big, beautiful ones like you, Anabel."

"Why are you telling me this? Why did you go spying...?"

"You're clever enough to know. I wonder what Jessamy will say when she hears that her dear friend is her husband's mistress. And she has a little girl too! Do you know your child has a look of Susannah about her? There's not much difference in their ages. There's no doubt that they are Matelands."

I felt ill. I thought of Jessamy. I could picture her stricken face when she knew. That I should be the one...her cousin and her dearest friend! The betrayal was a thousand times more shocking because I was the one who had been disloyal to her.

"You must not tell Jessamy," I said.

"I don't want to, of course. And I won't...for a...consideration."

I felt myself go cold with horror. "What...consideration?"

"I should have thought that to one of your discernment that would have been obvious."

I tried to push my horse past him, but he laid a hand on the reins.

"Well," he said, "isn't it just a question of when?"

I lifted my whip. I could have struck him across his smiling face. He caught my arm.

"Why so outraged?" he asked. "You're no shrinking virgin, are you? I mean, it would not be the first time you have indulged in this kind of adventure."

"You are despicable."

"And you are desirable. So much so, sweet Anabel, that I am ready to go to great lengths for you."

"I don't want to see you again."

"Where shall we go? In the castle? That would be amusing, wouldn't it? When will you come?"

"Never," I said.

"Oh, poor dear Jessamy, she will be upset."

"Haven't you any decency?"

"None," he said.

"I hate you."

"In a way that will make it more interesting. Listen, Anabel, I have been waiting for this... for years. I know about you and Joel. Why be so kind to one brother and so cruel to the other?"

"Joel and I love each other," I said vehemently.

"Very touching. It makes me want to weep."

"I doubt you ever wept for anything but rage."

"There are many things you have to learn about me, Anabel. But you will learn. You are going to have a long time to do it. You have to keep your wickedness from Jessamy, don't you? And there is only one way to do it."

"I shall go to her and tell her myself."

"Will you? Poor Jessamy! She is a very sentimental girl and she has not been well since Susannah was born. She suffers from her chest, you know, and her heart is not what it should be. I hope Joel has not got ideas in his head. Oh dear, the plot thickens. I wonder how she will take the news? This story of your wickedness, I mean. You and her husband... husband and best friend. Alas, it is often like that."

I spurred up my horse and galloped away. I did not know where to go, what to do. Finally I went back to the castle. Jessamy was resting, I was told. I felt frantic with anxiety. I could not bear Jessamy to know.

And the alternative...

I was shivering with fear. There was one thought which kept hammering in my mind. Jessamy must not know.

I kept going over that scene in the woods. I could not forget his gleaming eyes and his full sensual lips. I could read his thoughts so clearly and I knew that he believed he had at last got me into his power.

My door opened slowly. I jumped up startled, for it was Jessamy.

"Did I startle you?" she asked.

"N-no," I answered.

"Is anything wrong?"

"No, why?"

"You look...different."

"I have a slight headache," I told her.

"Oh dear, Anabel, it is so rare to see you not well."

"I'm quite all right really."

"You must get Joel to give you a tonic. Why don't you lie down? I really came to talk to you about Susannah."

"What's wrong with Susannah?"

"She can be very willful, you know, Anabel. She wants her own way all the time and seems to get it."

"She's a Mateland," I said.

"I shouldn't bother you about this now. It's nothing really. I just wanted a talk, I suppose. I was a bit worried about her and when I'm worried it's to you I come. Do you remember, it's about seven years since you came to the castle?"

"I was seventeen then," I said, just to say something.

"That makes you twenty-four now. You ought to have a husband, Anabel."

I closed my eyes; this was becoming unbearable. She went on talking as though musing to herself. "We ought to do something about you. Give parties...balls....I'm going to speak to Joel...when I see him. What's the matter? Are you really all right? I'm chattering away when you've got a headache. You must rest, Anabel!"

She made me lie down. She covered me with a quilt. I wanted to shriek at her: You should hate me. That's what I deserve.

She left me lying there, trying to think what I should do.

I could think of no way out. Jessamy would have to know, and I could not bear her to know. I must tell Joel. Yet I was afraid to tell him. I was afraid of what he would do. I knew that he would be filled with rage against his brother and yet I must tell him.

I came out of my room, still wearing my riding habit. As I entered the hall David called to me. I ran to the door but he was there before me.

"There is a time limit, you know," he said. "Shall we say four hours to make up your mind? I think it would be a nice gesture if you came to my room. It is in the front drum tower. It's a very pleasant room. I will have the fire lighted early. I shall be waiting there for you. I dare say my dedicated brother will be at his surgery. He does not seem eager to be with his wife. We understand why, of course. Other fish to fry. Very well, Anabel, my dear, tonight."

I ran past him. I went out to the stables. I mounted my horse and rode. But I did not go to the town. I dared not tell Joel. But I would have to, of course.

I rode recklessly, galloping over the fields, and all the time asking myself what I was going to do.

It was late afternoon. I must see Joel, I must tell him. One of the things we had said to each other was that we would always share everything.

He had finished with his patients and I saw his pleasure at the sight of me. I threw myself into his arms. I was half sobbing with relief.

I told him everything, and as he listened he grew pale. He said at length: "He's expecting you tonight. He will find me instead."

"Joel," I cried, "what are you going to do?"

"I'm going to kill him," he said.

"No, Joel. We must think about this. You must not be rash. It would be murder...your own brother."

"It would be no more than killing a wasp. I hate him."

"Joel...please...try to be calm...."

"You must leave this to me, Anabel."

"I can't bear Jessamy to know. She would never believe in anyone again. She has always trusted me. We have always been so close...the greatest friends. I can't bear her to know that I have done this, Joel."

I could see that he was consumed by his anger and could think of nothing else. I knew that anger could be fierce, obsessive. I remembered when a child in the town had been illtreated by its parents, how his anger towards them had been uncontrolled. He had had them sent to prison and the child cared for elsewhere. It was righteous anger, of course, but he had not considered that the parents were under strain and that they were not of normal intelligence. I had argued with him about it but he had remained adamant. Now he thought of nothing but revenge on David—not for spying on us, not for going to find you, but because of what he had suggested to me. His blackmail, he called it, as it was most certainly. And, he said, there was only one thing to do with blackmailers and that was eliminate them.

I was afraid of the passions I aroused in these two men. I knew their stormy natures—Joel's no less than David's—and I was afraid.

We returned to the castle together. I went to my room pleading a headache and did not go down to dinner. Jessamy came in after dinner to see how I was. She told me that everything seemed so strange. Joel had scarcely spoken and David seemed in an odd mood. "He was making jokes all the time...obscure ones," said Jessamy. "I couldn't understand them and I was glad when the meal was over. Poor Anabel. It is so unusual for you not to be well. David was saying he didn't remember your ever being unwell before...except that time six or seven years ago when you went to stay with your father's people. He went on about your not looking quite as usual for some time before you went away then but when you came back you had obviously quite recovered. It was a horrible meal, Anabel. I was so glad when it was over. But you're tired." She bent over and kissed me. "'Better in the morning,' that's what old Nanny Perkins used to say. Remember?"

"Thank you, Jessamy," I said. "I do love you. Remember that."

She laughed. "You must be feeling poorly to be so sentimental. Good night, Anabel."

I wanted to reach out to her, to try to explain and ask forgiveness.

I lay there for some time.

Joel had said he would come for me and we would go to David's room together. He did not come though, and as I waited, my eyes on the door, I heard the sound of a muffled shot somewhere outside the castle.

I stood alert, listening. There was no sound from below. I was afraid that shot had something to do with David and Joel. I went to the room which Jessamy shared with Joel and stood at the door listening. I was sure Jessamy was there alone.

Then I could not help it. I made my way to David's room in the drum tower. I stood outside listening. There was no sound from within so I opened the door quietly and looked in. The fire was flickering in the grate. The room shone in the light of several candles. A chair was by the fire and a silk robe lay on the velvet-covered bed.

There was no one there.

My fears were increasing every second.

I ran down the stairs and out to the courtyard. I had to know what had happened and I was terrified of discovering. I heard running footsteps. I held my breath listening.

It was Joel who was running towards me and I knew some terrible tragedy had taken place.

I threw myself into his arms. I could scarcely breathe. There was a great lump in my throat which I suppose was a form of terror.

I stammered: "I heard...a shot...."

"He's dead," he said. "I killed him."

"Oh, God help us," I murmured.

"I went to his room," he said. "I told him I knew and that I was going to kill him. He said we would settle it in a civilized way. He suggested pistols. 'We're both good shots,' he said. So we took the pistols from the gun room. He always thought he was the better shot...that was why he suggested them...but he wasn't this time."

"You've killed him, Joel," I whispered. "Can you be sure?"

"Yes. Right through the heart. That's what I aimed for. It was either him or me...and it had to be him...for you...and myself...and for Suewellyn."

"Joel!" I cried. "What are you going to do?"

"I always thought I'd kill him one day...or he'd kill me. We've come near to it once or twice. Now it's over. I'm going away. I'll have to...tonight..."

"Joel...*no!*"

"You're coming with me. We'll have to get out of the country."

"*Now*..."

"Now...tonight. We've got to think carefully. It is not impossible. I can arrange with my bank when we are well away. We can take valuables with us...everything we can lay our hands on and conveniently take. Go to your room. Get what you can together. Don't let anyone know what you are doing. We'll be well away by morning. We'll ride out a few miles and then get the train to Southampton. We'll get a ship and go out to...Australia most likely...and on from there."

"Joel," I breathed. "The...child."

"Yes," he said. "I've thought of the child. You'll have to go and get her. The three of us will go together."

So I went to my room and within an hour after I had heard that pistol shot I was riding through the night with Joel.

We parted at the railway station. He went to Southampton where I was to join him with you. I had to wait for trains and did not get to you until the following day. You know the rest.

That's my story, Suewellyn. You have come to love us, your father and me, and now that you have heard how it happened you will understand.

The Island

In spite of everything that has happened since that day when my mother came to take me away from Crabtree Cottage, I still remember those years on the island as the happiest of my life. It is still an enchanted place to me, a lost paradise.

Looking back, it is not easy to remember always with clarity. Events become blurred by the years. It seems now that the days were full of sunshine—which I suppose they were except during the rainy season. And how I loved that rain! I used to stand in it and let it fall all over me, drenching me to the skin, soft balmy rain; and then the sun would come out, and the steam would rise from the earth, and I would be dry in a few moments. Each day seemed brimming over with happiness, but of course it was not quite like that. There were times when I sensed a certain fear in my parents. Every time a ship came in during those first years my mother would make a great effort to hide her anxiety from me and my father would sit at the topmost window which overlooked the bay and there would be a gun across his knees.

Then all would be well and when the ship sailed away, having brought us all sorts of exciting packages, we would drink a special wine and we would laugh and be merry. I soon realized that my parents were afraid the ship would bring someone they did not want to see.

When we arrived on the island we were received by Luke

Carter, whose house my father had bought. Luke Carter had owned the coconut plantation which had brought a certain prosperity to the island. He told my father that he had been there for twenty years. But he was getting old and wanted to retire. Moreover the industry had faltered during the last years. Markets had dropped off; the people didn't want to work; they wanted to lie in the sun and pay homage to the old Grumbling Giant. He was going to stay, as he said, to show my father the ropes. When the ship left next time it would take him with it.

He was all alone now. He had had a partner who had succumbed to one of the fevers which were prevalent on the island and grew worse during the wet season.

"You're a doctor," he said. "You'll know how to deal with it, I dare say."

My father said that one of the reasons why he had wanted to come to this particular island was because these fevers were endemic here. He believed he could discover ways of treating them.

"You'll be up against old Wandalo," Luke Carter told him. "He runs the place. He decides who is and who is not going to die. He's the witch doctor johnny and great chief. He sits under his banyan tree and contemplates the earth."

During the days which followed Luke Carter took my father round the island.

My mother never let me go out without her. When we did go she held tightly to my hand and I was rather disconcerted to find that the sight of us filled the islanders with mirth, particularly the children, who would have to be slapped on the back to prevent their choking. Sometimes we found them peering in at the windows at us and, if we looked up, they would shoot away as if in fear of their lives.

In the evenings Luke Carter used to talk about the island and the islanders.

"They're intelligent," he told us. "Crafty though, and light-fingered. They're not respecters of property. You want to watch them. They love color and sparkle but they wouldn't know the difference between a diamond and a bit of paste. Treat them well and they'll respond. They'll never forget an insult and they'll never forget a good turn. They're faithful enough if you can get their trust. I've lived with them for twenty years without being clubbed to death or thrown down the crater as a sacrifice to the old Grumbling Giant, so I've done rather well."

"I dare say I'll manage equally well," said my father.

"They'll accept you...in time. Strangers put them on their guard. That's why I thought it best to stay awhile. By the time I leave they will have come to regard you as part of the island life. They're like children. They don't question much. The only thing you have to remember is to be respectful to the Giant."

"Do tell us about this Giant," said my mother. "I know it is the mountain, of course."

"Well, this island is one of a volcanic group, as you know. It must have come into being millions of years ago when the earth's crust was being formed and it was all internal eruptions. Thus the old Giant was thrown up. He's the god of the island. You can understand it. They think he has power over life and death and he has to be placated. They pay homage to him. Shells, flowers and feathers adorn the mountainside, and when he starts to grumble they get seriously worried. He's an old devil, that mountain. Once it really did erupt. It must have been three hundred years ago and it all but destroyed the island. Now he grumbles from time to time and sends out a few pieces of stone and lava...to warn them."

"We should have chosen another island, I think," said my mother. "I don't like the sound of this Grumbling Giant."

"He's safe enough. Remember he hasn't been what you could call really active for three hundred years. The little grumblings are a safety valve really. He's done his erupting. In another hundred years he'll have settled down entirely."

He introduced us to Cougaba, who had served him well and was willing to do the same for us. He hoped he could persuade us to keep her, for she would find it hard to go from the big house and settle in one of the native huts now. She had been with him for almost the whole of the twenty years he had spent on the island. She had a daughter, Cougabel, who should be allowed to stay with her mother in the house.

"They'll make you good servants," said Luke Carter. "And they'll be a kind of go-between with the natives and yourselves."

My mother declared at once that she would be pleased to have them both, for she had been apprehensive about getting the right servants.

So the first weeks on Vulcan Island passed and by the time Luke Carter was ready to go we were settled in.

My father had already made an impression. He was a very tall man—six feet four in his stockinged feet—and the islanders were a small people. That gave him an immediate advantage. Then there was his personality. He was a man born to dominate and this he proceeded to do. Luke Carter had explained to some of the islanders that my father was a great doctor and he had come to help make the people well. He had special medicines and he believed he could bring great good to the island.

The islanders were disappointed. They had Wandalo. What did they want with another medicine man? What they really wanted was someone to continue marketing the products of the coconut and bring back to the island the prosperity which had once been theirs.

It did seem a pity not to exploit the natural resources. Vulcan Island was the biggest of the group and was all that one imagines a South Sea Island should be—hot sun, heavy rains, waving palms and sandy beaches. My father had said that he wanted to call the place Palm Tree Island when he first saw it, but it had already been named Vulcan, which was equally apt really because of the presence of the Giant.

It was a beautiful island—some fifty miles by ten—lush, luxuriant, dominated by the great mountain. It was grand, that mountain, the more so because it was awe-inspiring and, strangely enough, when one stood close to it—and it was not possible to be far away from it on that island—it seemed to possess those rare qualities with which the natives endowed it. The valleys were fertile, but if one glanced up one could see the ravages on the top slopes where the Giant's anger had boiled over and scarred the earth. But in the valleys trees and shrubs grew close together. Casuarina, candlenut and kauri pine flourished in abundance beside breadfruit, sago plant, oranges, pineapple, sweet banana and of course the inevitable coconut palm.

The Giant had to be watched. He could grow angry, Cougaba told me, for she quickly attached herself to me and became a sort of nurse and maid. I grew fond of her and my mother was pleased by this and encouraged it. Cougaba was grateful because not only did she stay in the house but her daughter did also. She was clearly fond of her daughter, who must have been about my age, but it was difficult to tell with the natives. She was a considerably lighter shade than her mother and her smooth light brown skin was very attractive. She had dancing brown eyes and liked to adorn herself with shells and beads, many of them dyed red with dragon's blood. Cougabel was a very important little girl. A certain respect was shown to her. It was because of her birth. She herself told me that she was a child of the mask. What that meant I learned later.

I discovered a great deal from Cougabel. She took me with her to lay shells and cocks' feathers on the mountainside.

"You come too," she said. "Perhaps Giant angry with you. You come to island and Wandalo not pleased. He says medicine man here. Want man to sell rope and baskets and coconut oil.... Don't want medicine man."

I replied: "My father is a doctor. He is not here to work with coconuts."

"You take shells for Giant," she said, nodding sagely as though it would be wise for me to follow her advice.

So I did.

"The Giant can be terrible angry. Grumble... grumble...grumble.... He throw out burning stones. 'I very angry,' he say."

"It's what is called a volcano," I told her. "There are others in the world. It's quite natural."

The English of Cougaba and Cougabel was better than that of most of the people. They had lived in the big house for a long time. All the same it left much to be desired. Cougaba was expressive in her gestures, though, and we could understand her very well.

"He warns," she told us. "He say, 'I angry.' Then we take shells and flowers. When I was little girl, like you, missy, they throwed man in the crater. He was one wicked one. He killed his father. So they throw him in...but Giant not please. He did not want bad man sacrifice. He want good man. So they took holy man and throw him in. But old Giant still angry. You watch old Giant. He finish all island once."

I used to try to explain to her that it was a perfectly natural phenomenon. She would listen gravely, nodding. But I knew she did not understand a word of what I said and wouldn't have believed it if she had.

Slowly I absorbed the lore of the island from my parents, from Cougaba and Cougabel and from the magician Wandalo, who showed no objection when I went and sat beside him under the banyan tree.

He was very small and thin and wore only a loincloth. I was fascinated by the way in which his ribs stood out. To look at him was like looking at a skeleton. He had a little round hut at the edge of a clearing among the trees and there he would sit all day with his magic stick making lines in the sand.

The first time I saw him was just after Luke Carter had left and my mother's fears had abated a little and I was allowed to go out on my own as long as I did not stray too far from the house.

I stood at the edge of the clearing watching Wandalo, for he fascinated me. He saw me and just as I was about to run away beckoned. I went to him slowly, fascinated yet apprehensive.

"Sit down, small one," he said.

I sat.

"You pry and peep," he said.

"It's just that I was fascinated by you."

He did not understand but he nodded.

"You come from far over sea."

"Oh yes." I told him about Crabtree Cottage and how we came on a ship, while he listened attentively, understanding some of it, I believed.

"No medicine man wanted.... Man for plantation. ...Understand, small one?"

I told him that I did and explained as I had to Cougaba that my father was not a businessman but a doctor.

"No medicine man wanted," he repeated firmly. "Plantation man. People poor. Make people rich. No medicine man."

"People have to do what they do best," I pointed out.

Wandalo drew circles in the sand.

"No medicine man." He brought the stick down on the circle he had drawn and disturbed the sand. "No good come.... Medicine man go.... Plantation man come."

It was very disturbing and difficult to understand, but there was something ominous about Wandalo's actions and words.

Cougabel and I played together. It was good to have a companion. She came to the lessons which my mother gave to me and Cougaba was absolutely overcome with joy to see her little daughter sitting beside me holding a pencil and making signs on a slate. She was a very bright little girl and different from the others on the island with her light chocolate-colored skin. Most of the islanders were a very dark brown, many black. Very soon we were going everywhere together; she was sure-footed and knew which fruits could be safely eaten; she was a happy child and I was glad of her company. She showed me how to cut our fingers with shells and mingle our blood. "We good sisters now," she said.

I sensed that my parents were not as happy as they had hoped to be. In the first place there were the visits of the ships and a few days before they were due to arrive I would be aware of their uneasiness. When the ship left we would be gloriously happy. I used to sit with them and listen to their talking. I would be on a stool leaning against my mother's knee and she would run her fingers through my hair as she loved to do.

I knew that my father had come here to study the malaria, ague, marsh and jungle fevers which abounded. He wanted to see if he could wipe those diseases out of the island. He planned in time to build a hospital.

He said once: "I want to *save* life, Anabel. I want to make up...."

She said quickly: "You have saved many lives, Joel. You will save many more. You must not brood. It had to be."

I wanted to do something. I wanted to show my love for them and how grateful I was to have been taken away from Crabtree Cottage.

In a way I did have a hand in molding the future and, looking back now, I wonder what might have happened if I had not discovered, through my friendship with these people, what was really going on.

We must have been on the island about six months when the Giant started grumbling.

One of the women heard the rumble when she went to lay a tribute on the lower slopes. It had been an angry rumble. The Giant was not pleased. The rumor spread. I could see the fear in Cougaba's eyes.

"Old Giant grumbling," she said to me. "Old Giant not pleased."

I went to see Wandalo. He was sitting with his stick making very rapid circles in the sand.

"Go away," he said to me. "No time. Giant grumbles. Giant

angry. Medicine man not wanted here, says Giant. Want plantation man."

I ran away.

Cougaba was preparing the fish she was going to cook.

She shook her head at me: "Little missy...big trouble coming. Giant grumbling. Dance of the Masks coming soon."

I gradually learned what was meant by the Dance of the Masks—a little from Cougaba, a little more from Cougabel, and I heard my parents discussing what they had discovered.

For hundreds of years, ever since there had been people on Vulcan, there had been these Dances of the Masks. The custom was practiced on Vulcan Island and nowhere else in the world; and the dance was performed when the grumbling was growing ominous and the shells and flowers did not seem to placate any more.

The holy man—now Wandalo—would take his magic stick and make signs. The god of the mountain would instruct him when the Feast of the Masks should be held. It was always at the time of a new moon because the Giant wanted the rites performed in darkness. When the night was decided, the preparations would begin and go on while the old moon was waning. Masks could be made of anything suitable but they were chiefly of clay and they must completely hide the face of the wearer. Hair was sometimes dyed red with the juice of the dragon tree. Then the feast would be prepared. There were vats of kava and arrack, which was the fermented juice of the palm. There would be fish, turtle, wild pig and fowls, all of which would be cooked on great fires in the clearing where Wandalo had his dwelling. The night would be lighted only by the stars and the fires by which the food was cooked.

Everyone participating in the dance must be under thirty years of age and they must be so completely masked that none knew who they were.

All through the preceding day the drums would be beating, quietly at first...and going on throughout the night. The drum beaters must not slumber. If they did the Giant would be angry. All through the feasting they would continue to beat and, when that was over, the drums, which had been growing louder and louder, would reach a crescendo. That was the signal for the dance to begin.

I did not see the Dance of the Masks until I was much older and I shall never forget the gyrations and contortions of those brown bodies shining with coconut oil, with which

they anointed themselves. The erotic movements were cal
culated to arouse the participants to a frenzy. This was tribut
to the god of fertility, who was their god, the Giant of th
mountain.

As the dance went on, two by two the couples would dis
appear into the woods. Some sank where they were, unabl
to go farther. And that night each of the young women woul
lie down with a lover, and neither male nor female woul
know with whom he or she had cohabited that night.

It was a simple matter to discover who had conceived, fo
intercourse between all men and women had been forbidde
for a whole moon before. The reason for Cougabel's impor
tance was that she had been conceived on the Night of th
Masks.

The belief was that the Grumbling Giant had entered th
most worthy of the men and had chosen the woman who wa
to bear his child; so any woman who had a child nine month
from the Night of the Masks was considered to have bee
blessed by the Grumbling Giant. The Giant was not alway
lavish with his favors. If not one child was conceived it wa
a sign that he was angry. There was often no child of tha
night. Some of the girls were afraid and fear made then
barren for, Cougaba told me later, the Giant would not wan
to bestow his favor on a coward. If there was no child of th
night, there would have to be a very special sacrifice.

Cougaba remembered one occasion when a man climbe
to the very edge of the crater. He had meant to throw in som
shells but the Giant had reached up and caught him. Tha
man was never seen again.

I shall never forget the first Feast of the Masks followin
our arrival. Everyone was behaving in a very odd way. The
averted their eyes when we were near. Cougaba was worried
She kept shaking her head and saying: "Giant angry. Gian
very angry."

Cougabel was a little more explicit. "Giant angry wit
you," she said; and her bright eyes were frightened. She pu
her arms about me. "No want you die," she said.

I forgot that for a while but one night I awoke remem
bering it and I thought of the stories I had heard about me
being thrown into the crater to pacify the Giant. It wa
through Cougabel that I realized our danger.

"Giant angry," Cougabel explained. "Mask coming. H
will show on Night of Masks."

"You mean he will tell you why he is angry?"

"He is angry because he want no medicine man. Wandalo medicine man. Not white man."

I told my parents.

My father retorted that they were a lot of savages. They should be grateful to him. He had heard that a woman had died of some fever only that day. "If she had come to me instead of going to that old fool of a witch doctor she might be alive today," he said.

"I think you should open up the plantation," my mother put in. "That's what they want."

"Let them do it themselves. I know nothing of coconuts."

The bamboo drums started. They went on all day.

"I don't like them," said my mother. "They sound ominous."

Cougaba went about the house refusing to look at us. Cougabel put her arms round me and burst into tears.

They were warning us, I knew.

We could hear the drums beating; we could see the light from the fires and smell the flesh of the pig. All through the night my parents sat at the window. My father had his gun across his knees. They kept me with them. I dozed and dreamed of frightening masks; then I would wake and listen to the silence, for the drums had stopped beating.

The silence persisted into the next morning.

Later that day a strange thing happened. A woman came to the house in great distress. I had had her pointed out to me as one who had given birth to a child who had been conceived at the last Dance of the Masks. Therefore it was a special child.

The boy was ill. Wandalo had said he would die because the Giant was angry. As a last resort the mother had brought the child to the white medicine man.

My father took the child into the house. A room was prepared for him. He was put to bed and his mother was to stay with him.

Soon the news of what had happened spread and the islanders came to gather about the house.

My father was excited. He said the boy was suffering from marsh fever, and if he had come in time he could save him.

We all knew that our fate hung on that child's life. If he died they would probably kill us—at best drive us from the island.

My father said exultantly to my mother: "He's responding. I might save him. If I do, Anabel, I'll start their plantation. Yes, I will. I know nothing about the business but I'll find out."

We were up all that night. I looked from my window and saw the people sitting there. They had flaming torches. Cougaba said that if the boy died they would set fire to our house.

My father had taken a terrible risk in bringing the boy here. But he was a man to take risks. My mother was such another. So was I, I discovered later.

In the morning the fever had abated. All through the next day the boy's condition improved and by the end of the day it was clear that his life had been saved.

His mother knelt down and kissed my father's feet. He made her get up and take the child away. He gave her some medicine which she gratefully took.

I shall never forget that moment. She came walking out of the house holding the child and there was no need for anyone to ask what the outcome was. It was clear from her face.

People rushed round her. They touched the child wonderingly and they turned to stare in awe at my father.

He raised his hand and spoke to them.

"The boy will get well and strong. I may be able to cure others among you. I want you to come to me when you are sick. I may cure you. I may not. It will depend on how ill you are. I want to help you all. I want to drive the fever away. I am going to start up the plantation again. You will have to work hard for I have much to learn."

There was a deep silence. Then they turned to each other and put their noses together, which I think was a form of congratulation. My father went into the house.

"And to think that was all due to five grains of calomel, the same of a compound of colocynth and of powder of scammony and a few drops of quinine," he said.

No child had been conceived on that Night of the Masks. It was a sign, said the islanders. The Giant had considered them unworthy. He had sent them his friend, the white medicine man, and they had failed to give him honor.

The white man had saved the Giant's child and, because the Giant was pleased at that and because they had performed

(140)

the Dance of the Masks, he had asked their friend to start up the plantation again.

The island would prosper as long as it continued to pay homage to the Giant.

My father now dominated the island. He became known as Daddajo and my mother was Mamabel. I was known as Little Missy, or the Little White One. We were accepted.

True to his word, my father set about getting the industry of the island working again and because of his immense energy it did not take long. The islanders were wild with happiness. Daddajo was undoubtedly the emissary of the Grumbling Giant and was going to make them rich.

My father immediately started a nursery for coconuts. He had found books on the subject which had been left behind by Luke Carter and they provided him with certain necessary information. He selected a piece of land and placed on it four hundred ripe nuts. The islanders buzzed round in excitement, telling him what to do, but he was going according to the book and when they saw this they were overcome with respect, for he was doing exactly what Luke Carter had done. The nuts were covered with sand, seaweed and soft mud from the beach, one inch thick.

My father had appointed two men to water them daily. They were on no account to neglect to do this, he said, glancing at the mountain.

"No, no, Daddajo," they cried. "No...no...we no forget."

"It had better be so." My father was never averse to using the mountain as a threat when he wished to get something done, and it worked admirably now that they were convinced that he was the friend and servant of the Giant.

It was April when the nuts were placed in the square and they must be planted out, said my father, before the September rains came. All watched this operation presided over by my father, chattering together as they did so, nodding their heads and rubbing noses. They were obviously delighted.

The plants were then set in holes two or three feet deep and twenty feet apart and their roots were bedded with soft mud and seaweed. The waterers must continue with their task for two or three years, my father warned, and the new trees must be protected from the glare of a burning sun.

They plaited fronds of palm which they used to shelter the young trees. It would take five or six years before these trees bore fruit, but meanwhile work would progress with those which were already mature and which abounded on the island.

The nursery was a source of delight. It was regarded as an indication that prosperity was coming back to the island. The Grumbling Giant was not displeased with them. Far from sending out his wrath, he had given them Daddajo to take the place of Luke Carter, who had grown old and not caring, so that everyone neglected his or her work and consequently benefits no longer came to the island.

My father applied great enthusiasm to the project. They accepted him now as the doctor, but he needed a further outlet for his tremendous energy and this supplied it. I see now that both he and my mother were restless. Often their thoughts turned to England. They were shut away from the civilized world and only made contact with it when the ship came in every two months. At first they had sought a refuge, somewhere to hide away and be together. They had found it and, having won a certain security, they were remembering what they were missing. It was only human to do so.

So the coconut project offered a great deal to them both. They became absorbed in it. There was a new mood on the island. There were soon goods to be sent back to Sydney. There was an agent who came to see my father and who was to arrange for the selling of the goods which were produced. Cowrie shells were used as currency on the island. My father paid the natives in these. It was amazing how contented the people were now they had something to do. Instead of a couple of women sitting together idly plaiting a basket under a tree as it had been when we came, there were now groups of them seated on platforms open at the sides but protected by a covering of thatch from the sun; these my father had ordered to be constructed; and in them the women would make baskets and fans and ropes and brushes with the external fiber. My father had also turned some of the round huts into a factory for producing coconut oil.

Life had changed since we came. It was now as it had been in the days of Luke Carter when he had been a young and energetic man.

My father set overseers to look after the various activities, and these overseers were the proudest men on the island. It was amusing to see them strut about, and it became the ambition of every man to be an overseer.

In the mornings my father set aside an hour when the sick

could be brought to our house to be attended and there was no doubt that the health of the islanders had improved since our coming. The people were aware of this and my father was regarded with respect and awe. My mother, I think, was loved; and I was looked on with affection.

We were welcome on Vulcan Island.

In two years since our coming my father had established himself as lord of the island, and my mother told me later that as time passed they realized that it was hardly likely anyone would arrive on the ship to take him away to stand trial for murder. The coming of the boat was then something to look forward to because it brought books, clothes, special foods, wines and medicines.

It was indeed an exciting day when one awoke to see the big ship lying at anchor off the island. Early in the morning the canoes would go out and come back laden with the goods my father had ordered. How beautiful those canoes looked— light, slim and tapering! Some were about twenty feet long, others as much as sixty. Their prows and sterns were high and beautifully carved and they were the pride of their possessors. Cougabel told me that the prows and sterns protected the occupants of the canoes from arrows their enemies might shoot at them, for in the old days there had been much fighting among them.

I said the canoes looked like crescent moons dotted on the sea when they were a mile or so from land. They shone in the sunshine, for their prows and sterns were often decorated with mother-of-pearl. It astonished me how quickly the narrow pointed paddles carried them through the water.

So it seemed we had settled into the life of Vulcan Island.

I was growing up. The years passed so quickly that I lost count of them. My mother was teaching me and each day she insisted that she give me lessons. She was constantly ordering books from Sydney and I suppose I was becoming as educated as most girls of my age of a certain class who depended on governesses for education.

Cougabel continued to share my lessons. She was growing up faster than I physically, for the girls of the island were mature at fourteen and many of them had become mothers at that age.

Cougabel loved my clothes and liked to dress up in them. My mother and I wore loose smocks—a fashion of my mother's devising. Ordinary conventional garments would have been impossible in the heat. We had big hats of plaited fiber which my mother softened a great deal by soaking in oil—a method of her invention. She dyed them—mainly red from dragon tree juice, which we called dragon's blood. But she found other herbs and flowers growing on the island from which she managed to extract dyes. Cougabel wanted smocks and colorful hats such as we wore and she and I would go about together similarly clad. Sometimes, though, she would revert to her native dress and wear nothing but a fringed girdle made of shells and feathers which fell halfway down her thighs, leaving the upper part of her body exposed. Round her neck she would wear strings of shells and ornaments carved out of wood. She looked quite different then and somehow changed her personality. When she sat with me in her smock and did her lessons, I would forget that we were not of the same race. We were then simply two children in a country house.

I guessed, though, that Cougabel did not want me to forget she was an islander and a very special one at that.

Once we wandered to the foot of the mountain and she told me that the Grumbling Giant was her father. I did not see how a mountain could be a father and I laughed this to scorn. She grew angry. She could be passionately angry at times. Her mood changed abruptly and at that moment her great dark eyes flashed with fury.

"He is my father," she cried. "He is...he is....I am a child of the Mask."

I was always interested to hear of the Mask and she went on: "My mother danced at the Mask Dance and the Giant came to her through some man...unknown...like he does at the Mask Dance. He shot me into her so that I grew and grew until I was a baby ready to be born."

"That's just a story," I said. I had not at that time learned when it was wise to keep one's opinions to oneself.

She turned round and flashed out at me: "You don't know. You only small one. You white.... You make Giant angry."

"My father is on very good terms with the Giant," I said somewhat mockingly, for I had heard my parents joke about the Giant.

"Giant sent Daddajo. He sent you to learn me...."

"Teach you," I corrected. I enjoyed correcting Cougabel.

"He sent you to learn me," she insisted, her eyes narrowing. "When I am big and there's a Mask Dance I shall go out to dance and I shall come back with the Giant's baby in me."

I gazed at her in astonishment. Yes, I thought, we are growing up. Cougabel will soon be old enough to have a baby.

I grew thoughtful. Time was passing and we were losing count of it.

I was thirteen years old. I had been six years on the island. During that time my father had built up a flourishing industry and, although many people still died of various fevers, the death toll was considerably reduced.

My father was compiling a book about tropical diseases. He was planning to build a hospital. He was going to put everything he had into the project. All his dreams and hopes were for that hospital.

My mother, I realized, had something on her mind. One afternoon after the intense heat of the day had passed, we sat together under the shade of a palm tree watching the flying fishes skimming over the water.

"You're growing up, Suewellyn," she said. "Have you thought that you have not been off this island since we came?"

"Neither have you or my father."

"We have to stay...but we have talked a lot about you. We worry about you, Suewellyn."

"Worry about me?"

"Yes, your education and your future."

"We are all together. It is what we wanted."

"Your father and I may not always be here."

"What do you mean?"

"I'm just drawing attention to a fact of life. It comes to an end, you know. Suewellyn, you ought to go away to school."

"School! But there is no school!"

"There is in Sydney."

"What! Leave the island?"

"It could be arranged. You would come back to us for holidays. Christmas...and the summer. The boat takes only a week from Sydney. One week there...one week back. You have to have some education beyond what I can give you."

"It is something that has never occurred to me."

"You have to be prepared in some way for the future."

"I couldn't leave you."

"It would only be for a time. When the boat next comes

you and I will go to Sydney. We'll look at schools and decide what is to be done."

I was astounded and at first refused to consider the idea, but after a while they both talked to me and that sense of adventure which lay dormant in me was aroused. Mine was a strange upbringing. For six years or so I had lived in Crabtree Cottage where I had been brought up in rigid convention. Then I had been whisked away and brought to a primitive island. I imagined that the outside world would be very strange to me.

During the weeks that followed my feelings were mixed. I did not know whether I regretted this decision or was glad of it. But I did see the point of it.

When I told Cougabel that I was going away to school her reaction was violent. She stared at me with great flashing eyes and they seemed filled with hatred.

"I come. I come," she kept saying.

I tried to explain to her that she could not come. I had to go alone. My parents were sending me because people like us had to be educated and most of us went to school to receive that education.

She was not listening. It was a habit of Cougabel's to shut her mind to anything she did not want to hear.

A week before the ship was due my mother and I had made our preparations for departure. It was August. I should go to school in September and in December come back to the island. It was not a very long separation, my mother kept saying.

Then one morning Cougabel was missing. Her bed had not been slept in. She occupied a small bed in the room adjoining mine, for she wanted to sleep in a bed when she saw ours. In fact she wanted everything that I had and I was sure that if it had been suggested that she go away to school with me she would have been happy.

Cougaba was frantic.

"Where she go? She have taken her ornaments with her. See her smock here. She go in shells and feathers. Where she go?"

It was pitiful to hear her.

My father calmly pointed out that she must be on the island unless she had taken a canoe and gone to one of the others. It seemed sensible to search the island.

"She go to Giant," said Cougaba. "She go to him and ask him not let Little Missy go. Oh, it is wicked . . . wicked to send

Little Missy away. Little Missy belong...Little Missy not go."

Cougaba rocked to and fro chanting: "Little Missy not go."

My father impatiently said that he did not doubt Cougabel would come back now she had given her mother a fright. But the day went on and she did not return. I was hurt and angry with her because she had shortened the time when we could be together.

But when the second day passed we all became anxious and my father sent search parties up the mountain.

Cougaba was trembling with terror and my mother and I tried to reassure her.

"I frightened," she said. "I very frightened, Mamabel."

"We will find her," soothed my mother.

"I told Master Luke," mourned Cougaba. "I said, 'No sleep in Master's big bed for whole month. Dance of the Masks to be at new moon.' And Master Luke he laugh and say, 'Not for me and you. Do as I say, Cougaba.' I tell him of Grumbling Giant and he laugh and laugh. Then I sleep in bed. Then the night of the Mask Dance and I stay in Master Luke bed and then...I am with child. All say, 'Ah, this child of Giant, Cougaba honored lady. Giant came to her. But it was not Giant....It was Master Luke and if they know...they kill me. So Master Luke he say, 'Let them think Giant father of child,' and he laugh and laugh. Cougabel not child of the Mask. And now I frighten. I think Giant very angry with me."

"You mustn't be afraid," said my mother. "The Giant will understand that it was not your fault."

"He take her. I know he take her. He stretch out his hand and draw her down...down to the burning stones where she burn forever. He say, 'Wicked Cougaba. Your child mine, you say. Now she be mine.'"

There was nothing we could do to comfort Cougaba. She kept moaning: "Dat old man Debil was at my elbow, tempting me. I'se wicked. I'se sinned. I told the big lie and the Giant is angry."

My mother warned her to say nothing of this to anyone and that was a relief to poor Cougaba and something she was ready to listen to. I had seen the natives benign since they had accepted my father as an emissary of the great Giant, but I wondered what they would be like if they turned against us. And what Cougaba had done would certainly be considered an unforgivable sin in their eyes.

That night Cougabel was found. My father discovered her on the mountain. She had broken her leg and was unable to walk.

He carried her back to the house and set her leg. The islanders looked on in wonder. Then he made her lie down and would not let her move.

I sat with her and read to her and Cougaba made all sorts of potions for her distilled from plants, for she had great skill in these matters.

Cougabel told me she had gone to the mountain to ask the Giant to stop my going away and then she had fallen and hurt herself. She took this as a sign that the Giant wanted me to go and was punishing her for doubting the wisdom of his wishes.

We accepted that explanation.

Cougaba said no more about the deception she had practiced concerning her daughter's birth. The Giant could not be very angry, my mother told her, because he had merely broken Cougabel's leg, and my father had said that as her bones were young and strong he could mend her leg and none would guess it had ever been broken.

So the days before my departure were spent mostly with Cougabel and when the time came for me to go she was calm and resigned.

My father was very sad at our going but I knew he thought it was the right thing to do.

So we came to Sydney, my mother and I, and my delight in the beautiful harbor and perhaps my even more intense enchantment by the big city—for I was accustomed to scenic beauty—reconciled me to this new phase in my life. I was excited by all the people. I loved the streets, which wound about in a haphazard way because they had grown from the cart tracks of earlier days. I loved the big streets best and in a few days I knew my way about. I shopped with my mother in the great shops such as I had never seen before. I had never realized there was so much merchandise to be bought.

We should have to buy clothes for my school, said my mother, when we were in the room in our hotel. "First though," she added, "we must find the school."

My mother made inquiries and we looked at three before we decided on one. It was not far from the harbor, right in the heart of the town. My mother saw the headmistress and explained that we had lived on a Pacific island and she had taught me until now. I was given tests from which I was glad to say I emerged in some triumph, so my mother had been a good teacher. Then it was arranged that I should become a boarder at the start of the term, which would give my mother time to leave me at school and catch the next ship back to Vulcan Island.

What weeks they were! We shopped madly. I knew the names of the streets and how to find them. We were able to buy my school uniform in Elizabeth Street. The headmistress had told us where to go. We bought clothes and stores and drugs to be sent to the ship en route for Vulcan Island; and when we had done our shopping we took great pleasure in exploring the town, watching the ships which came into the harbor, visiting the spot where Captain Cook had landed; and I felt I was a child again going with Anabel on a jaunt after she had picked me up from Crabtree Cottage.

Then the day came when I was taken to my school and we said good-by to each other. I was desperately unhappy and missed my parents and the island so much.

Then as the weeks passed I settled in. My strangeness was an attraction. The girls would listen for hours to stories of the island. I was an oddity and as I was bright and able to stand up for myself I began to enjoy school.

By Christmas when I returned to the island I had changed. Everything had changed. Cougabel was better and her leg showed no sign that it had been broken. Another triumph for my father!

But she was no longer a suitable companion for me. She was just an islander and I had been out into the big world.

I questioned a great deal now. What were we doing here? My mother had talked to me and made allusions to the past but she had always been able to brush aside awkward questions. She could do so no longer. I was getting curious. I wanted to know why we must live our lives on a remote island when there were towns like Sydney, when there was a whole world to explore.

I remembered the castle I had seen years ago. It had always held a magical quality for me. Now I became obsessed by it and there was so much I wanted to know. School had aroused me from my lazy indifference to the past. I was consumed by a desire to know what it was all about.

That was why my mother had decided to write it all down to tell me.

When I next returned for my holidays she showed me her account of what had happened and I read it avidly. I understood. I was not shocked to learn that I was a bastard and that my father was a murderer. I wondered a great deal about what had happened after my father left. I thought of Esmond and Susannah. They were the ones who interested me. I wondered if I should ever see them and I was filled with a desire to go to that magic castle and find them.

The Dance
of the
Masks

I was at school for two years and was past sixteen when it was decided that I should leave and go back to the island. In the meantime I had made the acquaintance of the Halmers. At school Laura Halmer and I had become close friends. She had been drawn to me at first by the strangeness of my unusual background and had been an avid listener to tales of the island. I had been attracted by her sophistication. She knew Sydney well and the shops were her happy hunting ground. Her family were farmers and owned a large estate to which they always referred as "the property." This property was some fifty miles north of Sydney. Laura, as the youngest of a family of brothers, was somewhat indulged and it was natural that during my second term at school she should suggest that I go home with her for the half-term holiday, which was just one week and thus not long enough for me to go back to the island. This I was glad to do.

At the Halmers' I was in yet another world. I was received with warmth into the family as a friend of Laura's and in a few days I felt as though I had known them for years. The property was an exciting place to be as there were so many activities going on. They were up at dawn and the Halmer men would be out early and come in at eight o'clock for a breakfast of steak or chops. There were many hands about the place, all with their various duties to perform. It was a very big property.

There I first met Philip Halmer. He was the youngest of Laura's three brothers. The two elder ones were big bronzed men and I could not tell one from the other during those first days. They talked of sheep constantly, for sheep were the main business of the property; they laughed a great deal; they ate a great deal; and they accepted me as one of them since I was a friend of Laura.

With Philip it was different. He was about twenty at that time. He was the clever one, his mother told me. He had soft fair hair and blue eyes; he was sensitive and when I discovered that he was training as a doctor I was immediately drawn to him. I explained that my father had gone to the island to study tropical diseases and that he hoped to build a hospital there. I was very enthusiastic about my father's work and Philip and I were often together talking about the island. It made a special bond between us.

During that mid-term week I spent at the Halmers' I learned a great deal about life in the bush. We would ride out, Laura, Philip and I, and make a campfire in the bush where we brewed tea in a billycan and ate dampers and johnnycakes; and few things had ever tasted so good. Philip used to tell me about the trees and foliage, and I was fascinated by the tall eucalypts, whose branches could fall so swiftly and silently from their great height that they could impale a man, and so they had earned the name of widow-makers. I saw trees and earth scorched by the terrible forest fires and I heard of all the plagues which could beset settlers in this sometimes unwelcoming land.

So after that short week at the Halmers' another change had come into my life.

I went back to school and then Christmas was looming.

"They all want you to come back and spend Christmas with us," said Laura.

But I couldn't, of course; they were expecting me on Vulcan.

When I was on the island now I felt shut in, restricted. It was the first time I had ever been less than contented with my family.

My mother knew what was happening. We spent a lot of

time together. "Ah, Suewellyn," she said one day, "you've changed. You've seen something of the world. You know that being cooped up on a little island is not all there is to life. I was right to send you away to school."

"I was happy before."

"But knowledge is always desirable. You couldn't live your life here on a small island. You won't want to stay here when you grow up."

"What about you and my father?"

"I doubt we shall ever leave here."

"I wonder what is happening...there," I mused.

She did not have to ask where I meant. She knew I was thinking of the castle. For I had read what had happened there, and through her words I had seen it all so clearly.

"After all this time..." I went on.

"We should never feel safe if we left here," she said. "Your father is a good man, Suewellyn. Always remember that. He killed his brother in hot blood, and he will never be able to forget it. He feels he has the mark of Cain upon him."

"It was great provocation and David deserved to die."

"It's true, but there are many who would say that no wrong is righted by another. I feel guilty in a sense. It was because of me that it happened. Oh, Suewellyn, how easy it is to become involved in...horror."

I was silent and remembered those words later. How right she was!

She went on: "One day, perhaps you'll go back to England. You could go to the castle. There is nothing against *you*." Then she started to talk about the castle, and the picture was in my mind as clear as it had been when she showed it to me. I could see it then as I saw it on that day long ago, with its battlemented drum towers and great stone walls.

Then she talked about the inside of the castle. She described those rooms: the main hall, the stone undercroft, the picture gallery, the chapel. It was almost as though there was some purpose in this. I was there...experiencing it all, seeing it through her eyes. It was as though I were being prepared and the Devil was making it easy for me to fall into temptation. I was superstitious perhaps. Was it surprising, living as I did on the island in the shadow of the Grumbling Giant?

My parents liked to hear about my stay on the Halmer property. They were delighted. This was exactly what they wanted for me. They loved me dearly. I had always known

that I had the best father and mother in the world; and that
my father loved me partly because I was hers as well as his
Our devotion had been more marked because we had been
parted in the beginning; and they were ready to let me go
because they believed they knew what was best for me. My
mother told me this, for now that I knew their secret there
was complete confidence between us.

"All these years," said my mother, "we had to hide the
truth. Now there are no more secrets. Oh, how glad I am to
be done with them."

She spoke to me very frankly. "I would do it all again
Suewellyn," she said. "Without your father life would have
been barren for me. I often wonder about Jessamy and little
Susannah. She will be about your age now...a little older
but not much...just a few months. I wonder about Esmond
and Emerald, and Elizabeth too...and then those boys, Garth
and Malcolm. It must all have changed when David died. The
old man must be dead by now. That means Esmond will have
the estate. I have thought so much of Jessamy. She is my
only deep regret. She must have been desolate. She lost her
husband and the one who was supposed to be her best friend
at one stroke. Jessamy is the one I think of most. She is the
one who has made peace of mind impossible for me as his
brother David has for your father. We made a compromise
we two. We had each other, but there were always shadows
between us. Happiness was there but memory took it away
Happiness has just been an hour or two now and
then...sometimes a whole day. But remorse is a bitter enemy
to happiness. That is why your father wants to build this
hospital. Kings in the past used to expiate their sins by en
dowing monasteries and convents. Your father is a king of
a man, Suewellyn. He was born to distinction, born to govern
and rule. Like a king of old, he is going to expiate the murder
of his brother by building a hospital here. He has such plans
and I am going to help him. We shall do this, and I think it
will bring him peace. He is going to put everything into it
You know how we have lived here. He has a good friend in
England, a banker...who has been of great service to him
He is selling everything your father has in England and the
money will go into this hospital. We can live on the profits
from the plantation. Your father would like to get someone
out from England or Australia to help him. He wants to make
a sort of colony here. He wants it to be prosperous. But his

heart is in the hospital. He wants to bring doctors and nurses out here. Oh, it is a great undertaking. That is how he is going to expiate his sin."

My mother was a great talker and since her revelation it was as though floodgates had been opened.

She had always been the most important person in my life ever since the days when she came to Crabtree Cottage as Miss Anabel, but now that she seemed so vulnerable I loved her more than ever. I knew that she was regretting my growing up because she believed that I must be given every chance to have some other life than the island could offer me.

I went to the Halmers' again for the short half-term and I was disappointed because Philip was not there. He was working in Sydney, they told me, and it would not be long before he qualified.

I was determined not to be idle and I insisted on going into the great stone-floored kitchen and helping there. It was the busy time of sheep shearing and there were many men to be fed besides the normal hands; and there were the sundowners who came for a meal and a night's lodging in return for their services. I learned how to make crusty loaves, dampers and johnnycakes. I learned various methods of cooking mutton, for there was a great deal of that on the property. I watched with awe the great pies that came in and out of the ovens. And the days slid by.

I talked to the jackeroos and the aborigines who worked round the property and I enjoyed every minute of it. I loved the tall eucalypts, the yellow wattle and the passion fruit which grew in the garden Mrs. Halmer tended with such care.

I liked the family; I liked their rather casual acceptance of me and the way they welcomed me in the best possible way by almost ignoring me, which meant treating me like one of the family.

I was delighted when Philip came home especially to see me. We rode together for miles. It was all the family property, he told me, and went on to explain how he looked forward to being a qualified doctor so that he could begin to do the work he loved doing.

He asked a great many more questions about my father and I told him more about the hospital. His interest was growing every time we talked.

"It's the kind of project which appeals to me," he said. "To have left England to come out here and do that work is wonderful."

I did not tell him why he had come, but I glowed with pride in my father and told Philip how he had won the respect of the natives after struggle and had even started up the old coconut industry. "My father believes that people are only healthy if they are happily occupied."

"I would agree with that," said Philip. "One day I want to come and meet your father."

I told him I was sure he would be welcome.

"And," he went on, "when you leave school, Suewellyn, you will come and stay with us sometime, won't you?"

I replied that I should have to be asked first. He leaned towards me and kissed me lightly on the cheek. "Don't be an idiot," he said. "You don't have to be asked."

I was very happy. I was realizing that Philip Halmer was beginning to mean a great deal to me.

When I went home that Christmas, workmen were going ahead with the building of the hospital. It was a costly business as all the materials had to be brought out to the island and many workmen were involved. My father was in a state of excitement; my mother was less euphoric. When we were alone together she said: "I just have this uneasy feeling. People will come out here. They will come from home perhaps. I know what it means to have a skeleton in the cupboard. Suppose someone opens the cupboard door which we have kept so satisfactorily shut all this time."

"It will all be forgotten by now," I comforted her; but I was not so sure of that.

She went on: "I just have an uneasy feeling. I can't explain it. I'm afraid of that hospital. I feel there is something ominous about it."

"You're talking like Cougaba...only in a different kind of English, but the sentiment's the same. Dear Anabel, do you think people look for portents and omens when they live for a long time among the superstitious?"

I myself was a little uneasy about Cougabel. I had grown away from her and I found I did not want to spend so much time with her as I once had. Paddling in a canoe no longer seemed adventurous to me. I did not want to hear stories of the islanders. My thoughts were far away in the outside world.

She followed me round for a while looking at me with big

reproachful eyes and sometimes I fancied those eyes held a smoldering hatred. I tried to talk to her then, to tell her about Sydney and school and the Halmer property. She listened but I noticed that her attention wavered. Cougabel could visualize no world but that of the island.

I went back to school and for the short holiday stayed again with the Halmers. There was a great celebration because Philip had passed his finals and was now fully qualified.

"Suewellyn," he said, "I'm going to take up your invitation. I'm coming to Vulcan to see your father and the new hospital."

I was delighted, for I knew my parents would be. They had shown great pleasure when I talked of bringing home my friends.

So it was arranged and the next holidays Philip and Laura came back with me.

That was a wonderful holiday. My parents immediately liked the Halmers and of course my father and Philip had a great deal in common. Philip was enthusiastic about the hospital, which was still not completed. Materials and workmen were still coming over and the islanders were still looking on in awe and wonder. It was true that the building of the hospital had changed the face of the island. This gleaming white modern building erected next to our house had transformed the place from a South Sea island to a modern settlement.

My father had dreams in his eyes. At table he would talk long after the meal was finished. I could see that he planned to turn Vulcan into a kind of Singapore. Stamford Raffles had done it there. Why should he not do it here?

We would all listen entranced by his eloquence and none more than Philip.

"What was Singapore before Raffles persuaded the Sultan of Johore to cede the place to the East India Company? At that time there was hardly anyone there. Who would have believed it possible that it could be what it is today? It was ceded only at the beginning of the century. Raffles made Singapore...introduced civilization to Singapore. Well, that is what I am going to do with this group of islands. Vulcan here will be the center. Here we shall start with our hopsital. I am going to make it into a healthy island. We have only one industry but what a productive industry it is!" He went on to extol the attributes of the coconut. "Not a bit of waste anywhere. Everything produced simply and without a great outlay. Already I am planning to have groves on other islands. I intend to extend...rapidly."

But his great concern was the hospital. "We shall need doctors," he said. "Do you think many would want to come out here? At the moment it will be difficult, but as we develop . . . as there are more amenities . . ." So he went on.

There was no doubt that both Laura and Philip Halmer were greatly interested in my family.

I was very happy that my parents should like them so much. But I was aware of a certain restlessness on the island. I suppose that living so closely with the people in the past and coming among them when I was so young had given me a certain rapport with them. I could sense that all was not well. It was in their looks perhaps, the furtive way in which they avoided meeting my eyes. Perhaps it was old Cougaba, who kept nodding and muttering to herself. Perhaps it was some of the looks I saw cast at the great white building glittering in the sun.

I had a clear warning. I was lying in bed with my mosquito net around me when I heard my door open softly. At first I expected it was Mother, who often came in for the nightly chats which she so much enjoyed; she usually watched and waited for me to tell her to come in.

For a second no one appeared. My heart started to pound suddenly. The door opened very slowly.

"Who's there?" I called.

There was no answer. Then I saw her. She had stepped into the room. She was dressed in a girdle made of shells strung together like beads on a string. The shells were green, red and blue; they made a faint jingling sound as she moved. Around her neck were rows of similar shells strung together; they hung down between the valley of her breasts; she was naked from the waist up as was the custom on the island. It was Cougabel.

I struggled up. "What do you want, Cougabel, at this time of night?"

She came to the bed and looked at me accusingly. "You not like Cougabel any more."

"Don't be silly," I said. "Of course I do."

She shook her head. "You have her...school friend, and you have him. Yes, I know. You love them...not me. I poor half white. They all white."

(158)

"What nonsense," I said. "I like them, it's true, but I haven't changed towards you. We were always friends."

"You lie. That not good."

"You should be in bed, Cougabel," I said with a yawn.

She shook her head. "Daddajo must send them away, Giant says. Daddajo not give you this man."

"What are you talking about?" I cried. But I knew. Cougabel—and that meant her mother and all the island—believed that Philip had come here to be married to me.

"Bad, bad," she went on. "Giant say so. He tell me. I child of Giant. I go to the mountain and he say, 'Send white man away. If he don't go, I angry Giant.'"

She was jealous, of course. I understood. I was to blame. I had ignored her now that Laura and Philip were here. I should not have done that. I had hurt her and this was her way of telling me so.

"Listen to me, Cougabel," I said. "These are our guests. That is why I have to entertain them. That is why I cannot be with you so much as I used to be. I'm sorry, but it is just the same between us as it ever was. I am your friend and you are mine. We have exchanged our blood, haven't we? That means we're friends forever."

"It means the one is cursed who breaks it."

"Nobody's going to break it. Do you believe me, Cougabel?"

Tears started to fall down her cheeks. She just looked at me without attempting to wipe them away. I sprang out of bed and put my arms about her.

"Cougabel . . . little Cougabel . . . you mustn't cry. We're going to be together. I'm going to tell you all about the big city over the sea. We're friends . . . forever."

That seemed to comfort her and after a while she went away.

The next day I told Laura and Philip about her visitation in the night and how when we were little we had played together.

"You must make her join us sometimes," said Philip. "Can she ride?"

I said she could and I loved Laura and Philip for being so kind to her. We went round the beaches in one of the canoes. Cougabel and I paddled and there was a great deal of laughter.

"She is really a very beautiful girl," said Philip. "Being

so much lighter in color makes her stand out against the others."

Cougabel sometimes reverted to the smocks she used to wear. They suited her, but she was really magnificent in her shells and feathers. I often noticed her eyes were on Philip; and she always contrived to be near him. If there was anything to be served, she would serve him first. Philip was rather amused by her attentions.

Then the trouble started. Cougabel told me: "Giant grumbling. He very angry. Wandalo ask him what is wrong. Giant does not like hospital."

My father had been informed of this by Wandalo, though not so precisely. The Giant had been heard to grumble some days before. When one of the women went to the mountain to lay shells there for the Giant, she had heard him rumble angrily. Something was wrong. He did not like something on the island. The Giant had been quiet for a long time, in fact all the time the hospital had been in the process of building and work on the plantation had been progressing satisfactorily. Why, then, should he start to grumble now?

My father was irritated at first. "After all this time," he cried, "are they going to try to put obstacles in my way?"

"Surely they realize the benefits of the hospital and the growing plantation," said Philip.

"They do, but they are hidebound by superstitions. They allow that old volcano to dominate them. I've tried to explain that there are hundreds of them all over the world and that there is nothing special about an extinct volcano which now and then does a little grumbling, as they call it, while it is settling down. There has been no major eruption for three hundred years. I wish I could drive this home to them."

Philip had already heard from me about the Dance of the Masks and how Cougaba had declared Cougabel to be a child of the Giant. He was enormously intrigued by stories of the island and he used to sit with Cougabel and make her talk to him. She was delighted and I felt it had completely set that matter to rights.

"Of course," said my father, "it's that old devil Wandalo who is really making the trouble. He has always resented me. It doesn't matter that we have saved many lives with modern treatment of these virulent fevers which are pests in a climate like this one. I have usurped the place of the old witch doctor and he is longing for a chance to pull down the hospital."

"That's something you will never let him do, I know," said Philip.

"I'll see him dead first," replied my father.

But old Wandalo sat under the banyan tree scrawling on the sand with his old stick, and there were more reports of the Giant's grumbling.

At the next new moon, we heard, there was to be a Dance of the Masks.

Philip and Laura were delighted. That this should have happened during their visit seemed a stroke of good luck to them.

I was more conscious now than I had been before of that mood of frenzy which came over the island. I realized that though my father had introduced so much that was good and which for a time they seemed to appreciate, they could in one night revert to the old savagery. He had never been able to eradicate the fear of the Grumbling Giant and he realized as did my mother that we had been believing he might have done this but it was only because the Giant had been quiet.

Cougabel was in a ferment of excitement. This time she would join the dancers. She prepared herself in secret and my mother said we should have to take special care with a nubile girl in the house. This had not been the case before because at the last dance Cougabel had been very young.

As a daughter of the Giant—which she herself and the islanders believed her to be—this ceremony was of special significance to her. It might well be that the Giant would favor his daughter. "Would that be a matter of incest?" I asked my mother.

"I am sure such a matter would be overlooked in exalted circles such as these," she retorted. Then: "Oh, Suewellyn, we must appear to take this seriously. Old Wandalo is giving your father a great deal of anxiety with these hints."

"Do you really think he could convince them that the Giant doesn't like the hospital?"

"It's Wandalo against your father and I don't doubt that your father will win. But he'll have the weight of centuries of superstition against him."

They were anxious days for us and, while Philip and Laura thought it was all so intriguing, I was deeply conscious of my parents' anxieties.

Cougabel was always beside Philip. She would sit at the door of the house and when he came out run after him. I had seen them sitting under palm trees while she talked to him.

He told me: "I'm collecting all sorts of Vulcan lore. Nothing like getting it from its natural source."

The law had gone out that no husband was to share his hut with his wife for a whole month. Philip was greatly amused, but impressed by the seriousness of the islanders and their determination to bow to tradition. Consequently the women lived together in certain huts and the men in others. Cougaba and her daughter still lived with us and, as we had no male islanders living in, that was considered to be all right.

How the tension mounted during those weeks! My father was impatient. He said there was little work done. They could think of nothing but making their masks.

My mother said: "They'll settle down when it is all past. Your father is disappointed though. He had hoped they were growing out of all this. There are some good men helping him, as you know, and he has been hoping to train them for the hospital, though he first wants a doctor to help him, and he thought he might train some of the women as nurses. But all this makes one doubt he ever will. If they are going to neglect everything for the sake of this ritual dance it shows they are as primitive as ever. Your father is always hoping to explode this foolish Giant legend."

"It will take years to do that," I commented.

"He doesn't think so. He believes that when they see the miracles of modern medicine they will realize that all they have to fear from that mountain is a volcanic eruption . . . and the volcano is most likely dead anyway. I think they imagine these grumblings just to stir up a little excitement. By the way, has Philip spoken to you about what your father is suggesting?"

"No," I said a little breathlessly.

"Really! I expect he is waiting until he has thought about it a little longer. But your father was saying that Philip is tempted. He is most interested in the experiment, and your father will need a doctor. Suewellyn, I should be delighted if Philip decided to join us."

I felt myself grow pink with excitement. If he did that I should be so happy.

I did not have to speak. My mother put her arms about

me and held me tightly against her. "It would be wonderful," she said. "A solution. It would mean that you would stay here...you and Philip. You're fond of him. Of course you are. Do you think I can't see it? If he decides to come I am sure it will be something to do with you. Of course he is thrilled by the hospital. He thinks it is such a wonderful idea. He says it's magnificent and he admires your father so much. And isn't it miraculous that he should be as obsessed as your father with the study of tropical diseases?"

"What you are thinking is that Philip and I will marry. He has never suggested it."

"Oh, darling, there is no need for us to be coy. I know he hasn't yet. It's a big step, this....Probably he wants to talk it over with his parents. He would come out here to live....Oh, I know we are only a week or so from the mainland but it's a bit of an undertaking. I should be so happy. This hospital...this industry we have here is the result of your father's work. It's going to be yours one day. Everything your father has has gone into this island. There's nothing left of his properties in England now. We've been living on his fortune for years and now this hospital has taken everything. What I mean is, it is your inheritance...and what your father and I would like more than anything is to see his successor here before...before..."

"You're both going to live for years yet."

"Of course, but it is nice to see things settled. If only we could get rid of that pernicious old Wandalo and his Grumbling Giant and settle down to the real business of living like civilized people, it would be so simple. Now you're embarrassed. You mustn't be. I shouldn't have spoken perhaps but I did want to tell you how happy we should be if...if it all worked out. Philip is delightful and your father likes him and so do I. And, my dear child, you are fond of him too."

She was right. I was. I could look ahead to a future when we were all here. The island would grow and grow. We would have other amenities here. My father was a man of immense organizing ability. I believe that Philip was not unlike him. They would work well together. Philip was with my father during the hour of the day when he received patients and my father was demonstrating the treatments which were necessary to the diseases indigenous to the islands.

There were at least twelve islands clustered round Vulcan. My father believed that one day they would be a prosperous group. The coconut industry would be developed and they might even set up others. Perhaps then the ship would visit the islands more than once every two months; but his great aim was to discover the source and treatment of island fevers and this he was determined to do.

The beating of the drums had started. Cougabel was shut in her room. I knew that she, like all the girls and men who were to take part in the ritual, was working herself into a frenzy of excitement.

Everywhere we went we could hear the drums. They were quiet...like a whisper during the first hours, but it would not be long before the noise began to swell.

I lay in my bed and thought of Cougabel coming in to tell me she was jealous. I had seen a look in her eyes then which alarmed me. For a second or so I should not have been surprised if she had brought out one of those lanceolate daggers the islanders used and plunged it through my heart. Yes, she had really looked murderous, as though she were planning some revenge for my neglect of her.

Poor Cougabel! When we were children we had scarcely noticed that we were different. We had been the best of friends, blood sisters, and we had been happy together. But it had had to change. I should have been more tender towards her, more considerate. I did not guess that she was so deeply affected by me, but I should have known because she had gone to the mountaintop when I was to go away to school.

The beat of the drums kept us awake all night and we were an uneasy household: my father angry that they should revert to this primitive custom, my mother anxious for his sake and myself faintly worried about Cougabel and at the same time excited by my mother's hints about Philip.

I looked into the future that night and it seemed to me that there was a good possibility of Philip's joining us. It would change everything. And was it really true that he was in love with me and wanted to marry me and share our island life?

It was a pleasant prospect and one which must certainly be shelved for a while. I had another year at school to do yet.

How I wished they would stop beating those drums.

All through the next day they continued. Now we could smell the food cooking in that open space where Wandalo had his dwelling. We were waiting for the dark and the sudden cessation of the drums which was every bit as dramatic as the beating of them.

Silence at last.

It was very dark. I pictured it all, though I had never seen it.

We should stay in the house, my father had always said. He did not know how they would react at seeing a stranger among them and in spite of the fact that we had lived so long among them we were strangers on a night like this.

We tried to go about our normal ways but this was not easy.

Laura came into my room.

"It's so exciting, Suewellyn," she said. "I've never had a holiday like this."

"You have given me some good ones on the property."

"Properties are commonplace," she said. "This is so strange ... so different from anything I have ever seen before. Philip is absolutely wild about the place." She looked at me, smiling. "It has so many attractions. Promise me something, Suewellyn."

"I'd better hear what it is before I answer."

"You'll invite me to your wedding and I'll invite you to mine. No matter what happens, we'll go."

"That's easy," I said.

I spoke lightheartedly. I had little idea how very momentous that promise was going to prove.

"I shan't be going back to school."

"It's going to be deadly without you."

"This time next year it will be your turn to leave."

"What luck it was meeting you! There's only one complaint. You should have been born a year later and then we could both have left school together. Listen."

The silence was over. The drums had started to beat again.

"That means the feasting is over. Now the dance is beginning."

"I wish I could see it."

"No. My father saw it once and so did my mother. It was dangerous. If they had been discovered heaven alone knows what would have happened to them. My father is certain—in fact old Wandalo hinted at it—that they would be very angry. They would discover that the Grumbling Giant was displeased and something dreadful would happen. G.G. would command it—through Wandalo of course." I looked round. "Where is Philip?"

"I don't know. He said he was going to the hospital."

"What for? It's not ready for work yet."

"He just loves to be in the place and plan all sorts of things. Yes, that was where he said he was going."

Fear came to me. Philip was very interested in old customs. Could it be that he had gone to look at the dance? It was dangerous. He didn't realize how dangerous. He had not lived with these people. He had only seen them gentle and eager to please. He did not know the other side of their natures. I wondered what they would do to anyone they found spying at their feast.

"He would never have gone there," said Laura, reading my thoughts.

"No, of course," I agreed. "My father did explain that it would be dangerous."

"That wouldn't stop him," said Laura. "But if he thought it would displease your father he would not go."

I was satisfied.

We sat together for some time. We heard the drums reach their crescendo and then there was silence.

This meant that the clearing would be deserted of all but the old people; the young ones would have now disappeared into the woods. The silence created a greater tension than the noise. I went to bed but I could not sleep.

Some instinct made me get out of bed and go to the window. I saw Philip. He was coming from the direction of the hospital; quietly, stealthily he came.

I felt sure he had been watching the dancers. I could understand that he had found it irresistible in spite of my father's warning.

Cougabel awakened me next morning. She was in her native girdle, wearing the shells and amulets about her neck.

She was different. She had been to the feast last night.

Laughing, she came close to me and whispered: "I know I have the Giant's seed within me. I have Giant's child."

"Well, Cougabel," I said, "for that we must wait to see."

She squatted on the floor and looked at me in my bed. She was smiling and her faraway expression indicated that she was thinking of the night just past.

Cougabel had moved into womanhood. She had had the

great experience of the Mask, and she believed, as I suppose all the women did until they knew they were not pregnant, that she carried the Giant's seed within her.

Cougabel was certainly confident. She kept looking at me as though she had scored some triumph.

Later in the day I saw Philip alone and I said to him: "I saw you come in last night."

He looked embarrassed. "Your father warned me," he said.

"But you went," I said.

"I should hate your father to know."

"I shall not tell him."

"It was something I just could not miss. I want to understand these people. And how could one understand them better than on a night like the one just gone?"

I agreed. After all, my father had watched a Night of the Masks. And so had my mother. They had hidden themselves successfully. My father had said: "They are really too absorbed in what they are doing to look for spies."

Philip went on: "I'm coming back, you know."

"Oh, Philip, I'm glad," I answered fervently.

"Oh yes, I've made up my mind. I'm going to work with your father. I have a year to do in the Sydney hospitals first though. By that time, Suewellyn, you'll have done with school."

I nodded happily.

It was tantamount to an agreement.

When I returned to Sydney I missed Laura. I paid a visit to the property. There was a new manager there and he and Laura had become very friendly. I guessed they were in love and when I taxed Laura with it she didn't deny it.

"You'll be dancing at my wedding before I dance at yours," she said. "Don't forget your promise."

I told her I hadn't.

Philip wasn't there. He was doing his year in the hospitals and couldn't get away.

When I went back on holiday to the island it was nearly time for Cougabel's baby to be born. This was a very special birth because it was due nine months after the Night of the Masks and, as until that time, she told me proudly, she had been a virgin, there could be no doubt whose the child was.

"She Mask child and she have Mask child," said Cougaba proudly.

It was typical that Cougaba should go on assuming that we all accepted the fact that Cougabel had been conceived on a night of the dance although she herself had told us that the girl was Luke Carter's daughter. That was a characteristic of the islanders which we found exasperating. They would state something as a fact in face of absolute proof that it was untrue and stubbornly go on believing it.

I had brought a present for the baby, for I was anxious to make up to Cougabel for my neglect in the past. She received me almost regally, accepted the gold chain and pendant which I had bought in Sydney as though, said my irrepressible mother, she was receiving frankincense and myrrh as well as the gold. There was no doubt that Cougabel had become a very important person. She still lived in our house but my mother said we should not keep her, for when the child was born a husband would be found for her and we could be sure that he would be very acceptable. A girl of the Mask, and therefore sure of the Giant's special protection and one who had been born of the Mask herself, as they all believed she had, would be a very worthy wife. And as in addition Cougabel was one of the island's beauties she could expect many offers.

I told Cougabel how glad I was for her.

"I glad too," she said, and made it clear that she was no longer as eager for my company as she had once been.

One night I was disturbed by strange noises and the sound of hurrying footsteps near my room. I put on a robe and went out to investigate. My mother appeared. She took me by the arm and drew me back into the bedroom, shutting the door.

"Cougabel is giving birth," she said.

"So soon?"

"Too soon. The child is a month early."

My mother was looking mysterious and at the same time concerned.

"You see what this means, Suewellyn. It will be said that the child was not conceived on the night."

"Couldn't it be premature?"

"It could be, but you know what these people are. They will say the old Giant would not have let it be born too soon. Oh dear, this could mean trouble. Cougaba is terribly upset. I don't know what we shall do."

"It's all such a lot of nonsense. How is Cougabel?"

"She's all right. Childbearing comes easily to these people who live close to nature."

There was a knock at the door. My mother opened it to disclose Cougaba standing there. She looked at us with great bewildered eyes.

"What's wrong, Cougaba?" asked my mother hastily.

"Come," said Cougaba.

"Is the child all right?" asked my mother.

"Child big, strong, boy child."

"Then Cougabel..."

Cougaba shook her head.

We went to that room where Cougabel was lying back, triumphant but slightly exhausted. My mother was right. The island women made little trouble of childbearing.

There was the child beside her. His hair was dark brown and straight—quite unlike the thick curly hair of the babies of Vulcan; but it was his skin which was astonishing. It was almost white and that with his straight hair proclaimed the fact that he had white blood in him.

I looked at Cougabel. She was lying there and a strange smile was playing about her lips as her eyes met mine and held them.

There was consternation in the household. First my mother said that none should know that the baby was born. She went at once to tell my father.

"A child that is half white!" he cried. "My God, this is disastrous. And born before the appointed time."

"Of course it could be premature," my mother reminded him.

"They'll never accept that. This could be disastrous for Cougabel...and us. They will say she was already pregnant before she went to the Mask and you know that's a sin worthy of death in their eyes."

"And the fact that the child is half white..."

"Cougabel has white blood in her, remember."

"Yes, but..."

"You can't believe that Philip...oh no, that's absurd," went on my father. "But who else? Of course Cougabel's father was white and that could account genetically for her giving birth to a child which is even whiter than she is. *We* know that, but what shall we do about the islanders? One thing is certain. No one outside this house must know that the child is born. Cougaba will have to keep it secret. It is only for a month. Explain to Cougaba. It is necessary, I am sure...for us all."

And we did that. It was not easy, for the birth of Cougabel's child was awaited with eagerness. Groups of people congregated outside our house. They laid shells round it and many of them went high into the mountain to do homage to the Giant whose child they believed was about to be born.

Cougaba told them that Cougabel needed to rest. The Giant had come to her in a dream and told her that the birth would be difficult. To give birth to his child was not like giving ordinary birth.

Fortunately they accepted this.

My father, always eager to turn disaster into advantage, ordered Cougaba to tell the people that the Giant had come to her in yet another dream and this time he told her that the child would bring a sign for them. He would let them know what he felt about the changes which were coming to the island. In spite of her show of truculence I knew that Cougabel was worried. She understood her people better than we did, and I have no doubt that the premature birth would be as damning in their eyes as the child's color. So both she and Cougaba were ready to follow my father's orders.

The only thing we had to do was keep the birth a secret for a month. In view of the gullibility of the islanders this was not so difficult as it might have been. Cougaba had only to say the Giant had ordered this or that and it was accepted.

But how relieved we were when we could show the baby to the waiting crowd. All our efforts had been worthwhile.

Even Wandalo had to admit that the color of the child indicated that the Giant was pleased by what was happening on the island. He liked the prosperity.

"And most obligingly," said my mother gleefully, "he has stopped that wretched grumbling of his. It couldn't have been more opportune."

So we emerged from this delicate situation. But in spite of my father's assertion that it was not so very rare for a colored person who had had a white father to produce a light-colored child, I kept thinking of Philip and pictures of him and Cougabel laughing together returned again and again to my mind.

I think my feelings toward Philip changed at that time. Or perhaps I was changing. I was growing up.

Susannah
on
Vulcan Island

Soon after that I went back to school for my last term; and when I came back Philip was installed on the island.

To be with him again reassured me that my suspicions were unfounded. Cougabel had planted those thoughts in my mind and she had done so deliberately. I remember Luke Carter's saying that the islanders were vindictive and never omitted to take revenge. I had made Cougabel jealous and, knowing my feelings for Philip, she was repaying me through him.

Silly girl! I thought. And sillier was I to have allowed myself to believe what I did for a moment.

The baby flourished. The islanders brought him gifts and Cougabel was delighted with him. She took him up to the mountain to give thanks to the Giant. It occurred to me that, whatever else Cougabel was, she was very brave, for she had deceived her people and yet she dared go to the mountain to give thanks to the Giant.

"But perhaps she was thanking him because she was extricated from this difficult predicament," my mother suggested. "But in fact she should be thanking us."

I was very happy during the months that followed. Philip

had become like a member of the family. I was finished with school, and my parents were happier than they had ever been before—except for those rare moments which my mother had once mentioned. I realized now that they were at peace. As time passed danger receded and their big anxiety had been on my account. Now I knew they were thinking that I should marry Philip and settle here for the rest of my life. I should not be confined as they had been. I should be able to take trips to Australia and New Zealand and perhaps go home for a long stay. The islands were prospering. Soon they would be growing into a civilized community. It was my father's dream. He wanted more doctors and nurses; they would marry, he said, and have children....

Oh yes, those were dreams he and my mother shared; but it was the fact that they believed my future was settled which delighted them most.

There was another matter. I had noticed one of the plantation overseers, a very tall, handsome young man, was constantly near the house waiting for a glimpse of Cougabel. He liked to take the baby from her and rock him in his arms.

I said to my mother: "I believe Fooca is the father of Cougabel's baby."

"The thought had occurred to me," replied my mother. She laughed. She was laughing a great deal these days.

"You can see how it happened," she went on. "They were lovers. Cougabel probably knew she was with child on the night of the dance. The scheming little creature! Really, one has to admire her. She is bright, that girl. Luke Carter was a shrewd fellow and I think he has passed on some of his attributes to his daughter. It is miraculous the way she has turned this situation to advantage."

So we laughed at Cougabel's deception and, when Fooca came to Cougaba and offered to marry her daughter, we were all delighted.

So was Cougabel.

We were allowed to attend the marriage ceremony as she had lived in our house. She was kept all night in one of the huts with four selected unmarried girls—all virgins—who anointed her with coconut oil and braided her hair. Fooca was in another hut with four young men who tended him. Then in the late afternoon the ceremony was performed in the middle of the clearing. The girls brought Cougabel out of the hut and the young men brought Fooca. Cougaba stood there holding the baby, who was solemnly taken from her by two women and given to Cougabel. The bride and bridegroom held hands while Wandalo chanted something unintelligible to us and Cougabel and Fooca jumped over a palm log together. It was a log which was kept in Wandalo's hut and was said to have been thrown out of the Giant's crater years ago when he had all but destroyed the island. The log had endured as marriage should. It was symbolic.

After that there was feasting in the clearing and dancing, though not of the frenzied kind that took place on the night of the Dance of the Masks.

After we had watched the ceremony of jumping over the log, Philip and I wandered down to the shore. The singing at the wedding had begun and we could hear it in the distance. We sat down on the sandy beach and looked out over the sea. It was a beautiful scene. The palm leaves waved slightly in the balmy breeze which came across the water; the sun, which soon would set, had stained the clouds blood red. Behind us loomed the mighty Giant.

Philip said: "I never dreamed there was such a spot on earth."

"Are you going to be content here?" I asked.

"More than content," he said and, turning on his side, leaned on his elbow and looked at me. "I am so glad," he went on, "that you and Laura were friends. Otherwise you would never have come to the property and we should not be here together like this. Think of that...."

I said: "I'm thinking of it."

"Oh, Suewellyn," he murmured, "what a tragedy that would have been!"

I laughed. I was so happy.

I heard myself saying: "What do you think of Cougabel?"

The suspicion was still lingering, although I almost believed it was nonsense. I wanted to talk of it, though. I wanted to be assured.

"Oh, she's a minx," he said. "Do you know, I wouldn't be surprised if she leads that . . . what's his name? Fooca? . . . a dance."

"She is considered to be very attractive. These people are often beautiful but she stands out because she is different, you see. That touch of white..."

"Ah yes, your father was telling me that her father was a man who used to be here."

"Yes. We were shocked when the baby was born. He is even lighter than Cougabel."

"It happens like that sometimes. The next baby may be quite black. Then perhaps she'll have another of a lighter color."

"Well, she has jumped over the log now."

"Good luck to her," said Philip. "Good luck to everyone on the island."

"It's your future now."

He took my hand and held it. "Yes," he said. "My future...our future."

The sun was low on the horizon. We watched. It always seemed to disappear so quickly. It was like a great red ball dropping into the sea. It had gone. Darkness came quickly. There was no twilight, which I vaguely remembered only from my childhood in England.

Philip sprang up. He held out his hand to help me and I took it.

He put an arm round me as we walked to the house.

I could hear the singing of the wedding party, and I felt that all was well with the world.

A week passed. The ship was due at any time now. My father was looking forward to it. It was bringing the supplies he needed.

It would bring mail too. Not that we received much but Laura was a good correspondent and there was usually a letter to me from her.

I wondered how she was getting on with her love affair and whether she really would be married before I was. I was sure that Philip loved me and would ask me to marry him. I wondered why he hesitated. I had passed my seventeenth birthday but perhaps he still considered me too young. Perhaps I seemed younger than I actually was because I had lived so much of my life shut away from the world. However, although he made allusions to the future, he had not yet asked me to marry him.

That was the state of affairs when the ship arrived.

I woke up one morning and there she lay, white and gleaming, out in the bay. She was about a mile out, for the water round the island was too shallow for her to come closer.

There was the usual excitement but no more than usual and, looking back, I marveled once more that Fate gives one no warning when some great event is going to burst upon one and change one's whole life.

The ship's small boats were being lowered and the canoes were already paddling out to the ship. How they reveled in those days when the ship came in! The noise and babble were tremendous and we could hardly hear ourselves speak.

My parents and I were standing on the shore ready to receive the boats as they came in, when to our amazement we saw someone being helped out of one of the boats which came from the ship. It was a woman. She was climbing down the swinging ladder and being caught by two of the sailors. She settled herself down to be rowed ashore.

"Who on earth can this be?" said Anabel.

Our eyes were fixed on the boat as it came nearer. Now we could see her more clearly. She was young and she wore a big shady hat decorated with white daisies. It was a most elegant hat.

She had turned towards us. She had seen us. She lifted a hand in a rather regal manner, as though she knew who we were.

The boat was scraping the sand. One of the sailors had sprung out. He gave her his hand and she rose. She was about my height, which was fairly tall, and she was dressed in white clinging silk. I thought she was very attractive, and like someone I knew.

And suddenly it hit me. It was like looking into a mirror—a not quite true mirror—and seeing oneself reflected in a flattering way. The person she was like was myself.

The sailor had lifted her out of the boat. He carried her so that she might not get her feet wet.

She stood there looking at us, a smile on her face.

She said: "I'm Susannah."

I think we all felt that we were dreaming—all except Susannah. She was completely mistress of the situation.

My parents appeared to be stunned. Anabel kept looking at her as though she could not believe she was real.

She was aware of it. I came to believe that there was little Susannah was not aware of. And she found the situation very amusing.

"I had to come and see my father," she said. "As soon as I knew where to come I set out. And Anabel...I remember you. And who..."

"Our daughter," said Anabel. "Suewellyn."

"Your daughter and..." She was looking at her father.

"Yes," he said. "Our daughter Suewellyn."

Susannah nodded slowly, smiling. Then she looked straight at me. "We're sisters...half sisters. Isn't it exciting? Fancy discovering you have a sister at my time of life!"

"I knew of your existence," I said.

"Oh, unfair advantage!" Her eyes remained on me. "We are alike, aren't we?" She pulled off her hat. Her hair was cut in a fringe over her forehead.

"We are sisters indeed," she went on. "And we could look more alike...if we dressed similarly. Oh, this is thrilling. How glad I am I have found you at last!"

The sailors put her baggage on the sand beside Susannah.

"You've come to stay," said Anabel.

"For a visit. If you'll have me. I have come a long way."

"Let's go to the house," said Anabel. "There'll be lots to talk about."

Susannah went to my father and slipped her arm through his.

"Are you pleased I have come?" she asked.

"Of course."

"I am so glad. I remember you, you know...and Anabel."

"Your mother..." he began.

"She died...about three years ago. It was pneumonia. Yes, there is a lot to tell you."

Several boys and girls had come to stare at the newcomer. My father shouted at them: "Come on. Give us a hand with these bags."

They giggled and came running, delighted to be included in the adventure.

And so we went into the house, our emotions in a turmoil.

Philip was already there. He came out when he heard us. When he saw Susannah he stopped and stared.

Anabel said: "This is my husband's daughter. She has come out from England to see us."

"This is most interesting," he said, advancing.

Susannah held out her hand. "How do you do?" she said.

"This is Dr. Halmer," my father announced. "Dr. Halmer, Susannah Mateland."

"And have you come to stay?" asked Philip.

"I am hoping to for a while. It is a long way to come for

a day. I believe the ship sails tomorrow. I hope they will like me well enough not to send me back on it."

"You're rather like..."

She turned and flashed her smile at me. "It's natural," she said. "We share a father."

We all went inside. Cougaba came out and behind her was Cougabel. She had obviously been visiting her mother and was carrying the baby whose appearance in the world had been too soon for our comfort.

"Cougaba," said Anabel, "our daughter has arrived from England. Can you see that a room is made ready for her?"

"Yes, yes, yes," said Cougaba. "Cougabel, you come give me hand."

Cougabel stood there smiling, holding the baby in her arms and looking from me to Philip until her eyes rested on Susannah.

"It's a pleasant house," said Susannah.

"It's improved a good deal since we came," replied my father.

"It must have been about eleven years ago. I remember I was seven when...you went away."

"It is eleven years ago," said Anabel quietly. "You must be thirsty. Let me get you something to drink while Cougaba gets your room ready."

"Cougaba! Is that the baleful female who regarded me as though I were some devil escaped from the gates of hell?"

"Cougaba is the elder," I said.

"Oh, I meant the young one with the baby. They're servants, I suppose. I've wanted so long to find you. It was so sudden...your disappearance."

My mother brought some lemonade to which she had added some of the herbs she had discovered; they gave a special and very delicious tang to the beverage, making it a pleasantly refreshing drink.

"We shall dine in an hour's time," said Anabel. "Are you hungry? Should I speed it up?"

Susannah said no. The drink was refreshing and an hour or so would suit her beautifully.

She looked rather roguishly at my father. "I expect you are wondering how I found you. Old Simons, who arranged all your affairs, died last year. His son Alain took over. I made Alain give away your secret. I haven't told anyone but I was determined to come and see you."

"How did Jessamy die?" asked Anabel.

"It was during the cold winter three years back. We were snowed up at the castle for several weeks. You know how the wind whistles down those corridors. It's the draftiest spot I've ever been in. Well, it was too much for my mother. Her chest always troubled her. Elizabeth Larkham—you remember Elizabeth Larkham?—she died a few months after of the same complaint. A lot of people suffered through that winter."

"And how was your mother when..." began Anabel.

Susannah gave that rather secretive smile which I had already noticed. "When you went away?" she asked. "Oh, devastated! She was terribly ill. Another of her colds, which turned to bronchitis. She was too ill to think of anything but getting her breath. I heard her say that it saved her from dying of melancholy."

Anabel closed her eyes. Susannah was opening an old wound and turning the knife in it.

"However," she went on, "that's all in the past. Things are different at the castle now."

Cougabel came down to say that the room was ready. She had only had to make the bed, she said; and she looked at Susannah and continued: "Rooms always clean this house. Mamabel like it so."

"How very commendable," said Susannah.

Cougabel lifted her shoulders and giggled.

"Let me take you to your room," I said. I thought my parents would want to be alone for a while to discuss this shock. Philip would realize this. He was most perceptive and would make an excuse to leave them, I guessed.

Susannah rose with alacrity. I believed she was looking forward to being alone with me.

When we reached her room she took a cursory look round it and turned to me. I obviously interested her far more.

"Isn't this...fun?" she said. "I didn't know I was going to find a sister."

She shook out her hair and looked at her reflection. She laughed and came to me. Taking my arm, she drew me to the mirror and we stood there side by side.

"It's a fair likeness," she said.

"Well, perhaps."

"What do you mean...perhaps! Why, I tell you, sister, that if you cut your hair in a fringe...if you wore a fashionable garment like this one . . . if you were a little less serious

. . . Do you see what I mean? Why, you even have a mole in the same place. Fancy that!"

I stared at it. I had forgotten how long ago that mole had seemed so significant when Anthony Felton tormented me because of it.

"I call it my beauty spot," went on Susannah.

"It's darker than mine," I said.

"Dear innocent Suewellyn! I'll confess to you and to you only. I touch it up a little with a special pencil I have for the purpose. I have perfect teeth . . . you too, sister . . . and the mole being where it is just calls attention to them. That's why they used to wear patches in the past. I wish we did now. How amusing that you should have one just in the same place. I tell you what we'll do. I'll touch yours up to accentuate it and we'll dress up as each other. Oh, it is exciting, finding you, Suewellyn!"

"Yes," I said, "it is."

"You must show me the island. I like the doctor. Are you going to marry him? He's rather handsome, isn't he? Not as distinguished as our dear papa, but then it is hard for anyone to compare with a Mateland. Don't you agree?"

"I think Philip is handsome," I said. "And we are not engaged to be married."

"Not . . . yet," she said. I had a feeling that Susannah could see right through me. She fascinated me and at the same time made me feel very uncomfortable. My thoughts were in such a whirl and I was so entranced by her appearance that I could scarcely take in what she was saying. She was like me and yet so different. She was what I might have been if I had lived in a different world . . . a world of castles and gracious living. That was the difference. Susannah exuded confidence; she believed herself to be fascinating and beautiful and, because she believed it, she was. Her features were so like mine that she could not have been so much more attractive than I without that belief. I was suddenly struck by the fact that I might have been exactly like her.

She was watching me in the mirror and again I had that uncomfortable feeling that she could read my thoughts.

She went on as though I had spoken. "Yes, we are alike . . . taken feature by feature. Your nose is only a trifle longer than mine. But noses are important. Remember Cleopatra's? If it had been a fraction longer—or was it shorter—it would have changed the history of the world, someone said, didn't they? Well, I don't think that difference in *our* noses changes so much. I look slightly more pert than you do...saucier, more irreverent. But perhaps that's my up-bringing. Our mouths are different too. Yours is much sweet-er—a rosebud of a mouth. Mine's wider...it shows I'm very fond of the good things of life. Our eyes...the same shape, the color very slightly different. You are a little fairer than I. Looking at us like this, the resemblance is not so striking, but if we dressed up...if we impersonated each other...oh, that would be another story. Let's do it one day, Sue-wellyn. We'll see if we can deceive them. I doubt we could Anabel. I am sure she knows every inch of your face. You are her little ewe lamb, aren't you? Do you know I was always aware of some secret Anabel was hiding. It's hard to look back all those years. Can you look back, Suewellyn?"

"Yes, I can."

"And you were hidden away, weren't you? And I suppose on the night my father killed Uncle David they swooped down and carried you away with them to this desert island. What exciting lives we Matelands live, don't we?"

"This one's could hardly be described as such."

"Poor Suewellyn, we must alter that. We must make your life amusing."

"I dare say you are the sort of person exciting things hap-pen to."

"Only because I make them. I must show you how to make them happen to you, little sister."

"Not so little," I retorted.

"Younger. How much by? Do you know?"

We compared birthdays. "Ah, I am the senior," she said. "So I may call you little sister justifiably. So you were tucked away, were you? And Anabel used to visit you. It must have been a fearful quarrel they had that night. I shall never forget waking in the morning and feeling that something had hap-pened. There was a terrible hush over the castle and the nurses refused to answer my questions. I kept asking where my father was. What had happened to my Uncle David? And my mother was just lying there on her bed as though she were dead like my uncle. It was a long time before I learned what had happened. They never tell children things, do they? They don't understand that what you can imagine might be far worse than what actually happened."

"There could hardly be a greater tragedy."

"You knew, did you? I suppose they told you. I suppose you know why."

"They will tell you if they think you should know," I said and she burst out laughing.

"You are a very self-righteous little sister. I dare say you always do what is right and honorable, don't you?"

"I shouldn't think so."

"Nor should I...if you are a Mateland. But imagine what it felt like having a murderer for a father. Though, of course, I didn't know this until later. I had to find out myself...listening at doors. Servants are always chattering. 'Where is my father? Why isn't he here any more?' I was always asking, and they would button up their lips, and I knew by their eyes that they longed to tell me. And there was no one in the doctor's house and all the poor patients were sent away empty. And my mother, of course...she was always ill. She would tell me nothing. If I mentioned my father to her she would just get tearful. But I got it out of Garth. He knew everything and he couldn't keep it to himself. He told me I was the daughter of a murderer. I've never forgotten that. I think he found some satisfaction in telling me. He said his mother hated me because my father had killed Uncle David."

She turned to me and laid her hand on my arm.

"I'm talking a great deal," she said. "I always do. But we'll have lots of time for talk, shan't we? There's so much I want to tell you...so much I want to know about you. Dinner is in an hour, Anabel said."

"Shall I help you unpack?"

"Oh, I shall just drag something out of the bag and change now. Do you think the malevolent black woman could bring me some hot water?"

"I'll have it sent up."

"Tell her not to put a spell on it. She looks as though she brews them."

"She's quite benevolent really. It's only if you offend them that you have to take care. I'll have the hot water sent up and shall I come to you when dinner is ready?"

"That would be lovely, little sister."

I went out of her room and it was some time later when I remembered that mail had come with the boat and that there was a letter from Laura waiting for me.

Even as I slit the envelope my thoughts were full of Susannah.

My dear Suewellyn [I read],

It has happened at last. The wedding is to be in September. This will fit in just right for the boat. You can arrive a week before and help with the preparations. It is so exciting. My mother wants a grand wedding. The boys pretend they don't and it's a lot of nonsense. But I think they are thrilled really.

I'm having a white gown made. The bridesmaids' dresses are going to be pale blue. You are to be a bridesmaid. I shall have the dresses made up to a point and all they will need is a quick fitting when you come. I am writing to Philip too. You can travel together. Oh, Suewellyn, I'm so happy. I beat you to the post, didn't I? ...

I put the letter away. On the boat's next call I should be ready to leave with it. Philip could come with me. It might be that Laura's wedding would make him think that I was almost as grown up as his sister and that it was time I married too.

I was smiling to myself. It was all falling so naturally into place—or had been.

I had a feeling that things might change now that Susannah had come.

They did. Her very presence changed the place. There was a great deal of excitement on the island because of her. The girls and women chattered together about her and giggled as we passed by. The men followed her with their eyes.

Susannah enjoyed their interest. She was clearly delighted to be on the island.

She was charming, affable and affectionate; and yet her presence had an effect on us which was the reverse of comforting. ... I knew that she reminded Anabel of Jessamy and that disturbed her peace of mind. She was as conscious now of the wrong she had done Jessamy as she had been in the beginning.

"My poor Mama," Susannah said, "she was always so sad. Janet ... do you remember Janet? Janet said she had no will to live. Janet was impatient. 'What's done's done,' she used to say. 'No use crying over spilled milk.' As if losing your husband and your best friend could be compared with knocking over the milk jug!" Susannah's laugh rang out as she recalled Janet and gave what I believe was a fair imitation of her. But, amusing as it might be, it brought back bitter memories to Anabel.

And my father? "A new doctor came to Mateland. People went on talking about you for years....It was a nine days' wonder, wasn't it? Poor Grandfather Egmont. He used to go about saying, 'I've lost both my sons at a stroke.' He made a great fuss of Esmond after a while and he invited Malcolm to stay more often. We wondered whether Malcolm would be the next in line of succession. We weren't sure because Grandfather Egmont had always borne a grudge against Malcolm's grandfather. He was always rather fond of me and some people thought I'd be the next if Esmond didn't have children. He was always rather fond of girls...liked them a lot better than he liked boys...." She laughed. "It's a family trait in the males which has persisted through the centuries. He seemed to realize that girls might have other attributes than good looks and charm. He used to go round the estate with me and show me things and talk to me about it. He used to say there was nothing like having two strings to your bow. Garth used to call Esmond, Malcolm and me the Three Strings."

Somehow in her seemingly lighthearted conversation she found the spot where best to thrust the barb, and when it came there would be an expression of such innocence on her face that no one could believe that she was aware of what she was doing.

She showed a great interest in the hospital but somehow managed to belittle it. It was wonderful to have such a place on a desert island, she said. It could have been part of a real hospital, couldn't it? They would have to train those black people to be nurses, she supposed. How very intriguing!

She made it all seem like a bit of play acting; and I noticed that there was a change in Philip now. He no longer had that exalted expression on his face when he talked about the work they were going to do.

I wondered whether even my father had begun to think of this project as a wild dream.

Anabel and I sat together in our favorite spot under the palm trees in the shadow of the Grumbling Giant, and as we looked over the pearly blue-green translucent sea and listened to the gentle breaking of the waves on the shore, Anabel said: "I wish Susannah hadn't come."

I was silent. I could not really agree because Susannah excited me. Things had changed since she came and, although I knew they had not done so in the most comfortable manner, I was completely fascinated by my half sister.

"I suppose really," said Anabel, "I'm being unfair. It's natural that she should bring back memories of things we would rather forget. One should not *blame* her. It's just that she makes us blame ourselves."

I said: "It's so strange to me...exciting in a way. Sometimes I feel I am looking at myself."

"The resemblance is not all that marked. Your features are alike. I remember her as a little girl. She was...mischievous. One doesn't take much notice of that in children. Oh, as I say, I'm being unfair."

"She is very pleasant to us all," I said. "I think she does want us to like her."

"Some people are like that. They supposedly mean no harm...and in fact do nothing one can point a finger to, but they act as a disturbance to others while seeming innocent of this. We have all changed subtly since she came."

I thought a good deal about that. It was true in a way. My mother had lost her exuberant good spirits; she was thinking a great deal about Jessamy, I knew. My father was living in the past too. It had been a terrible burden to carry, the death of his own brother. He would never need to be reminded of what he had done but he had begun to work out his salvation and he had dedicated himself to saving lives. And now his guilt sat heavily upon him. Moreover somehow the hospital had been belittled. It seemed like a childish game instead of a great endeavor.

Philip had changed too. I did not want to think about Philip. I had believed that he was beginning to love me. When I first went to the property as his sister's friend I had been just a schoolgirl to him. We had enjoyed being together, had talked together and liked the same things. I had been entranced by everything I saw and he had enjoyed introducing me to the great outback. But he had had to get used to the idea that I was growing up. I thought he had when he came to the island. I had, perhaps conceitedly, thought that I was one of the reasons for his coming. My parents had thought so too. We had all been so happy and cozy. The nightmare of that fearful experience that my parents had undergone had receded, although it could never disappear altogether. Now of course it was right over them, brought by Susannah. She could hardly be blamed for that, except that she made it seem as though it had happened yesterday. But Philip? How had she changed him? The fact was that she had bemused him.

Cougabel said to me one day when she met me on the stairs, "Take care of her, she spell maker and she make big spell for Phildo."

Phildo was Philip. He had been amused when he first heard it. It meant Philip the doctor.

Cougabel laid her hand on my arm and gave me an expressive glance from those limpid eyes of hers. "Cougabel watch for you," she said.

Ah, I thought, we are blood sisters again.

I was pleased, of course, to be on better terms with her, but disturbed by what she was hinting—the more so because I knew it was true.

It was natural that Philip should be attracted by Susannah. He had been attracted by me and Susannah was like me but in a more glittering package. The clothes she wore, the manner in which she spoke and walked...they were alluring. I could imitate her very easily but I scorned to do this. All the same it was rather saddening to stand by and see Philip's interest in me wane while it waxed for Susannah's more sophisticated charms.

My mother was cool to him; so was my father. They must have discussed the change together and it was beginning to occur to them that Susannah—without doing anything but be perfectly charming to us all—was spoiling our plans for the future.

She loved to be with me, and I was fascinated but a little repelled by her.

I felt I had been transported to that magic day when I had seen the castle and there had had my three wishes. There was no doubt that she was obsessed by the castle too. She described it to me in detail...the inside, that is. The outside was imprinted on my memory forever.

"It's wonderful," she said, "to belong to such a family. I used to like to sit in the great main hall and look up at that high vaulted roof and the lovely carvings of the minstrels' gallery and imagine my ancestors dancing. The Queen came once...Queen Elizabeth, you know. It's all in the records.

The Tudor Matelands were ruined by her coming and had to sell some of the oaks in the park to meet the bills for entertaining her. Another ancestor planted more when he was rewarded after the Restoration for being loyal to Charles. You can see them all in the gallery. Oh yes, it *is* exciting to belong to such a family...even though we have robbers, traitors and murderers among us. Oh, sorry. But you mustn't really be so sensitive about Uncle David. He was not a very good man. I'll bet you anything my father had a very good reason for fighting that duel. Besides, a duel is not a real murder. They both agree to fight and one wins, that's all. Oh, I do wish you wouldn't all look so glum when I mention Uncle David."

"It's been on our father's conscience for years. How would you feel if you had killed your brother?"

"Having none, it's difficult to say. But if I killed my half sister I should be very cross with myself, for to tell you the truth I like her more and more every day."

She could say charming things like that and then one believed she never meant to wound.

"Uncle David was a typical Mateland," she went on. "In the old days he would have waylaid travelers and brought them to the castle and made sport with them. There was one who did that long ago in the dark, dark ages. Uncle David would have gone for the women...fate worse than death and all that. Oh yes, he was very fond of the women. He had his mistresses right under Aunt Emerald's nose. Mind you, she was an invalid, poor soul. And a very trying old lady she is too. As for Elizabeth...but she's dead now."

"What about Esmond?" I asked.

Her expression changed. "I'll tell you a secret, shall I, Suewellyn? I'm going to marry Esmond."

"Oh, that's wonderful."

"How do you know?"

"Well, if you love him...and you've been brought up together..."

"Quite good reasons, but there is another. Shall I tell you what it is? You ought to guess. Can you? No, of course you can't. You're too good. You've been brought up by sweet Anabel...who was not too sweet to get a child by the husband of her best friend...."

"Please don't talk about my mother like that."

"I'm sorry, sweet sister. But it *was* my mother who was

her best friend and I was there when she found out. But you're right. It's not fair to speak of it now. It's not really fair to judge anybody, is it? Only priggish people do that, for how can they know what drives people to act as they do, and how do we know what *we* should do in similar circumstances?"

"I agree," I said.

"Then you won't judge me too harshly when I tell you I'm going to marry Esmond because he owns the castle."

"And you wouldn't marry him if he didn't?"

"No. It is purely because he owns the castle and I'd marry anyone who owned the castle. I should get it if Esmond died but as Esmond comes first I'd have to marry Esmond or kill him—and marriage is much easier. There, now you're shocked. You think, She is selling herself for a pile of stones and talking about murder as though it is a natural way of life."

I was silent. I was thinking: If she is going to marry Esmond, she will go away and it will be as it was before. Philip and I will be together again.

But it wouldn't be the same, of course.

"Ever since I was a child I was fascinated by the castle," she went on, for once not seeing that my attention had strayed from her affairs to my own. "I used to force myself to go down to the dungeons. I had the children over from the nearby manor house to play with me and I used to make them enter the undercroft—and the crypt leads from there. You go down a few steps and it is dark and cold...so cold, Suewellyn. It's hard to imagine that cold here. And there are the vaults...long-dead Matelands all lying in state in those magnificent tombs. One day I shall be there. I shan't change my name when I marry. I shall never be anything but a Mateland. It's very convenient Esmond's being my cousin."

"Does he know of your obsession with the castle?"

"To a certain extent. But, like all men, he is vain. He thinks he must be included in the obsession and that is something I have to let him believe."

"You sound very cynical, Susannah."

"I have to be realistic. Everybody does if they are going to get what they want."

"When are you going to marry Esmond?"

"When I go back probably."

"When is that?"

"When I have seen the world. I was in a finishing school in Paris for a year and when that was over I wanted to complete my education by seeing the world. I was going to do something like the Grand Tour. Then I discovered where my father was, so naturally I changed plans and came out here."

"It was a breach of confidence for this man to tell you."

"I had to be very charming to him. I can if I want to."

"You seem to be... quite effortlessly."

"It seems so. That's the art of it... to let it appear effortless. But a lot of work goes into it, you know."

"Sometimes I think you're laughing at me... laughing at us all."

"It's good to laugh, Suewellyn."

"But not at other people's expense."

"I wouldn't hurt you... any of you. Why, I love you all. You're my long-lost family."

Her eyes were mocking. I wished that I understood Susannah.

But there was no doubt that her delight in Mateland Castle was genuine. I was growing as enthralled as she was. It seemed as though I wandered through those vaulted rooms with her. I could feel the cold of the vaults, the terror of the dungeons, the eeriness of the undercroft and the splendor of the main hall. I felt that I had actually walked up the great staircase and stood beneath the portraits of those long-dead Matelands, that I had dined in their company in the dining room with its tapestried walls and needlepoint chair seats which had been worked by some long-dead ancestor. I lingered in the Braganza room which the Queen of that name had occupied when she stayed at the castle. I sat on the bay window in the library with books from the shelves piled beside me—and in the main hall and the little breakfast room which the family used for taking meals when they were alone. Then I walked through the armory at night when it was so ghostly with the suits of armor standing there like sentinels. I felt that I had sat in the solarium catching the last of the sun before darkness fell. It was uncanny. I felt that I knew the castle, that I had lived there. I longed to hear of it and continually I plied Susannah with questions.

She was amused. "You see the power of this castle," she said. "You, who have never stepped inside it, long to be there. You would like to possess it, wouldn't you? Oh yes, you would. Imagine yourself mistress of Mateland. Imagine yourself going to the kitchens every morning to discuss the day's menu with the cooks, bustling round the stillroom, counting your preserves, arranging balls and all the amusements which are part of entertaining in a castle. It's because you belong. You're one of us. Our blood is in your veins and if you acquired it on the wrong side of the blanket, as they say, it's still there, isn't it? It's the home of your ancestors. Your roots are sprouting from those ancient stone walls."

There was a good deal in what she said. I would never forget as long as I lived standing at the edge of the woods with Anabel and seeing it for the first time, and how I had watched the riders passing under the gatehouse—Susannah, Esmond, Malcolm and Garth.

Susannah and I spent a great deal of time together. I told her I was going to Laura's wedding and would be leaving with the ship when next it called. "Shall you be leaving too?" I asked.

"I'll think about it," she said. "You'll be away two months. Oh yes, I must come with you. I'll have to make plans for going home. Why don't you come with me? I'd love to show you the castle."

"Come with you! How would you explain me to Esmond... Emerald and the others?"

"I should say: 'This is my beloved sister. We have become good friends. She is going to stay at the castle.'"

"They would know who I was."

"Why not? You're a Mateland... one of us, aren't you?"

"I couldn't come. They would ask questions. They would find out where my father is..."

She shrugged her shoulders. "Think about it," she said, "while you're dancing at this wedding."

"I am leaving in two weeks' time."

"And Philip will go with you. The bride is his sister, isn't she? I'll have to come, I think."

"I am sure the Halmers would welcome you. It's a big property and there are lots of rooms."

She was thoughtful.

A few days later she said: "Why do you always wear those smocks, Suewellyn? I'd like to see you in something really smart. Come on, try on one of my dresses. Let's see if we can fool them. We'll dress you up as me."

."It would take more than a dress."

She eyed me intently. "I'm going to try," she said.

She brought out the white dress which she had arrived in. It had been freshly laundered.

"Come on, slip it on. Let me see you."

I did so. The dress did transform me. It was an almost perfect fit. I was slightly taller—so slightly that it was only noticeable when we stood side by side; and I was a trifle slimmer.

"What a transformation! Because you live on a desert island, you don't need to look like a native," she said. "There, what do you think of that?"

We stood side by side looking in the mirror. "We're still very much ourselves," I said.

"Here. Let me do your hair for you."

I sat down and she turned away swiftly and came back to me. She had started to cut my hair before I had noticed what she was doing. I cried out in protest but it was too late. I already had the beginnings of a fringe.

She laughed at my dismay.

"I assure you it will be an improvement. You will love it. In any case you are too late to stop me now. Please keep still or you will spoil my handiwork."

I sat there. The image which looked back at me from the mirror had changed from that which usually confronted me.

Susannah stood back. "There! Isn't that exciting?"

She put her face close to mine.

"We might be twins. And now let me make the picture complete."

She turned my face towards her and applied a black pencil to the mole on my chin.

"There. The picture is complete. Do you think you can deceive them?"

"Deceive my mother! Never!"

"Perhaps not, but you could those who don't know you very well."

She was amused. Her eyes gleamed. "I look forward to going down to dinner. You must wear that dress, Suewellyn, and when we are in Sydney we'll buy some clothes for you." I looked down at the white dress and she went on: "Oh, do keep it on. It's most becoming. I always liked that dress. But more on you than on myself."

I kept glancing at myself in the glass. No, I was not really much like Susannah; but it was a different self that looked back at me.

When I came out of Susannah's room I came face to face

with Cougabel. She took one look at me, gave a little scream and fled.

I cried out: "Come back, Cougabel. What's the matter with you?"

She paused and looked over her shoulder, staring at me as though I were a ghost.

"Oh no...no..." she cried, "bad...bad...." And she turned and ran away.

They were astounded when I appeared at dinner.

"Suewellyn!" cried my mother, really dismayed. "What have you done to your hair?"

"I did it," said Susannah, almost defiantly.

My mother just looked at me.

"Don't you like it?" asked Susannah. "And doesn't she look lovely in my white dress? I was heartily sick of those smocks and my sister's going round like a native."

"It looks charming," was Philip's comment. "Why, you look very like Susannah."

That hurt a little. I looked charming because I looked more like Susannah. He was honest at any rate.

My father's comment was: "Whatever have you done to yourself?"

"Susannah did it," my mother told him.

"Oh, Stepmother..." Susannah now and then referred to Anabel as Stepmother; she did it in a somewhat ironical way. Anabel hated it and Susannah knew it. "You make it sound as though I've cut off her head."

"You've cut off some of her beautiful hair," said Anabel.

"It shows it off better that way; and she looks so pretty. You must admit it."

"It looks...neater," said my father.

"There!" cried Susannah. "That is what you call damning with faint praise. Who wants to look neater? That is for maiden aunts. We want to look more fashionable, à la mode, beautiful, don't we, Suewellyn?"

"Oh," I said, "for heaven's sake stop discussing my hair."

"I like it," put in Philip softly.

And then we settled down to a meal.

That night I had two visitors when I was in bed. The first was my mother. She sat on the edge of the bed and said: "What made you let her do it?"

"I didn't realize she was going to until she started. Then she had to go on. In a way, she's right. It is more becoming. My hair was also getting untidy."

"It makes you look like her. It accentuates that faint resemblance."

"Never mind. It's done. It's only hair and I can let it grow in the old way in time."

"You'll be going to Laura's wedding soon. I suppose she will go with you."

"The Halmers are very hospitable. I am sure Philip has asked her."

My mother's face hardened. She said: "Oh, I wish she hadn't come here. She's changed everything...."

"If they changed," I said quietly, "it wasn't really only because of her. If they had been more . . . steady . . . they wouldn't have changed."

I was thinking of Philip and she knew it.

"She's like some sort of siren," said my mother angrily. "She was always a strange child. I remember she always used to be up to some sly sort of mischief. We thought she would grow out of it."

"You mustn't get ideas about her, Anabel."

"She's not a bit/like Jessamy, or her father. I wonder where she gets that mischievous malice from."

"It's the Mateland strain, I dare say. Some of the ancestors were not too nice. There is nothing wrong with Susannah really. Sometimes she can be very charming."

"I always feel she's making trouble. I suppose I don't like her because she is your father's daughter and I don't like the thought of anyone's giving him a daughter except me."

Anabel was always frank with herself and I loved her for it.

"Dear, dear Anabel," I said, "don't worry because I've got a fringe. Nothing can change the way we are together, can it? Whatever happens, you'll always be there for me...and I for you."

She came close to me and put her arms about me.

"You are right, Suewellyn," she said. "There are times when I think I am becoming a silly old woman."

She kissed me and went out.

My next visitor came about half an hour later just as I was dropping off to sleep. This was more dramatic.

The door was slowly opened and a black figure glided in. I could scarcely make her out, for there was no light in the room except that which came from a crescent moon and a sky full of stars.

I started up in bed.

"Cougaba!"

"Yes, Little Missy. Cougaba."

"Is something wrong? Is Cougabel all right?"

"Cougabel very frightened."

"What's happened?"

She pointed a finger at me. "What you do. What you am. There is spell on you."

I put up a hand and touched my new fringe.

"Not good...not good," murmured Cougaba. "Bad spell is put on you."

"Oh, Cougaba, have you wakened me to tell me you don't like the way my hair is cut?"

She came closer to the bed; her eyes were round with horror.

"I tell you," she said, "bad...bad....Cougabel know. You blood sister. She feel it. She feel it here. . . ." Cougaba touched her forehead and the spot where her heart might be expected to be.

"She say: 'Bad things have come to Little Missy. Spell woman take her...make her bad. Make her like spell woman.'"

"Oh, dear Cougaba, you must tell Cougabel not to worry. I'm perfectly all right. It's only that some of my hair has been cut off."

"Bad witch," she said, "Cougaba know. Cougabel know. Cougabel said Giant not like her. He grumbled when this bad thing done."

"The Giant! What has it to do with him?"

"He like island grow big...rich. He like Daddajo and Mamabel and Little Missy. He not like spell woman...and now she take you and make you like her."

"Nobody is going to take me and make me different. I'm myself and I always will be."

Cougaba shook her head sorrowfully.

"You go away. You go on big ship." She came closer to me. "Take Phildo with you. Take him away from her. She put spell on him. You . . . Phildo . . . happy. We like. Have little babies....Grow up on island. More babies...lots of little babies...and make fine rich island. But Giant angry. He does not like. Take her away. . . . Come back . . . come back with Phildo and have babies."

"Oh, Cougaba, it's good of you to care so much."

I held out my arms and she came to me and held me for a moment. Then she drew back, frowning at my hair.

"Not good," she said, shaking her head. "She take you. . . . she make you like her. . . . Cougabel very sad. She feels it in her blood. She says Giant angry. He her father. . . . He father of her child. She very close to Giant."

It was no use reminding Cougaba that this was not so. It mattered not that she had admitted in a moment of stress that Luke Carter was Cougabel's father and we knew that Cougabel's child had not been conceived on the Night of the Masks. Cougaba, like all her race, accepted as truth what she wanted to.

However, I soothed her and, as she thought that Susannah was going away soon, she allowed herself to be comforted.

It was a week before the ship was due to arrive and I was ready to leave.

We were at dinner when Susannah said: "I've decided not to go to Sydney. I'm not really ready to leave the island yet, and let's face it, when I leave I'll have to go home, and when should I get a chance to come and see you all again?"

There was silence. Philip looked completely dismayed.

I said: "Laura would have liked you to be at her wedding. I was looking forward to her seeing us together."

"Fringes and all," cried Susannah flippantly. "No. I've made up my mind. You won't turn me out, will you?" She was looking pleadingly at our father and then she turned and her gaze lingered on Anabel.

"Of course you must stay as long as you want to," said my father.

"I thought the novelty had worn a little thin by now," added Anabel.

"There you are mistaken. The place is so fascinating. Think of all you are doing. When that hospital project really gets under way it will be magnificent. I should love to see it. But I dare say it will take years and years to turn it into a working concern. Perhaps I'll come back someday and see you all. But just yet, I don't feel ready to go. Do you mind, Suewellyn?"

"I was looking forward to introducing you to Laura. She

would have enjoyed meeting you. But I understand, of course."

"You'll be coming back in two months. I shall have to go then, but we'll have a lovely day together before I leave."

"You seem to like the primitive life," said Anabel coldly.

"There are certain things which keep me here." Her eyes swept round the table and rested on Philip.

But he is going with me, I thought, and I wondered how Susannah would like the island without Philip to enslave and me to laugh at.

I was very soon to get an answer to that.

I had come out of the house and was walking down to the shore to sit in my favorite spot under a palm tree where I would read one of the books which had come on the last ship. Philip was beside me.

"I want to talk to you, Suewellyn."

"Yes. What about?"

"Shall we sit down? Under this tree?" He was obviously seeking for the right words. At length he said: "I've been thinking a lot about this...."

"About what?"

"Laura's wedding."

"You do need a lot of prompting, Philip. What about Laura's wedding?"

"Well, there's a certain amount of fever on the island...."

"There always is."

"It...it's rather too much for your father to cope with."

"He coped adequately before you came."

"I think he needs me here."

"Oh," I said slowly, "you're telling me that you don't want to come to Laura's wedding."

"Not don't want to, Suewellyn."

"Well, just that you prefer to stay here."

"It's not a matter of preferring. It's just that I feel I ought...."

I nodded. I looked out over the sea so calmly beautiful, opalescent today, and the water so clear that one could see the sand beneath it.

I wanted to fling myself down on the sand and weep. I did not know until that moment how much I wanted to stay here with my family around me, my deeply loved mother, my revered father...and Philip. I had planned so far ahead. I had seen the hospital working full strength, doing all that I knew it was capable of. I had seen the island a prosperous community and Philip and me bringing up our children here.

I heard myself say: "You feel that . . . that . . ."

"I do," he said earnestly. "I could not happily leave your father here alone . . . now. . . ."

I wanted to shout at him: "You mean you don't want to leave Susannah."

So it was all over. All this time I had been telling myself that she would go away and in time we should forget that she ever came.

Then I thought: Poor Philip. She will never marry you. She is going to marry Esmond . . . for the castle.

The Grumbling Giant

So I went alone to Sydney. One of Laura's brothers came to meet the boat and take me out to the property. The luggage would come the next day by wagon.

I had to explain to Alan, the brother, that Philip had decided there was too much to do on the island for him to come away.

Alan grimaced. "Laura will take a grim view of that, I can tell you," he said.

There was a warm welcome for me at the property. Laura was radiant. She was disappointed not to see Philip but after the initial annoyance she quickly recovered her spirits, for she was too happy to be separated from her absolute bliss for long.

I liked her husband-to-be. They were going up to Queensland where he had inherited a property and they planned to leave immediately after the wedding.

I was fitted for my bridesmaid's dress and she commented that my new hair style was very smart. "It changes you, Suewellyn," she told me. "You've lost that innocent look you had. You look like a woman of the world."

"Perhaps I'm becoming one."

She came to my room as she used to when we were schoolgirls and lay on the floor kicking up her heels and resting her chin in her cupped hands while she studied me sitting in the armchair.

"Doesn't this take you back?" she said. "And now...just think, I'm getting married. I stole a march on you."

"You are a year older."

"Yes, that could account for it. The family is disappointed, Suewellyn."

"You mean about Philip's not coming."

"Yes, and I think they were rather hoping...you know how families are. They have one wedding in the family and they immediately want another. Father says they are catching. In fact, I believe Alan will be the next. But they are thinking of Philip. They are very fond of you, Suewellyn."

"They have always been so nice to me. It meant a lot when I came here on those short holidays. As I couldn't get to the island in time it would have meant staying at school."

"They loved your coming. They thought you were so good for me. I do think it was mean of Philip. Is there so much to do?"

I hesitated.

"Out with it," she said. "What's wrong? You can't fool me. What has gone wrong between you two?"

"There's nothing...."

"There *is* something. Don't you like each other any more?"

"I don't think Philip ever liked me enough to want to marry me."

"He did. He was falling in love with you. We all knew it. My mother used to say it was only a matter of time. They're so disappointed. They wanted an announcement at my wedding."

"No. It wasn't like that at all." She was looking at me steadily and I burst out: "My half sister came to see us on the island. He was, as you might say, swept off his feet by her."

"Oh, is he going to marry *her?*"

"Oh no. She is going to marry someone else."

"What a mess! And what a fool Philip is!"

"These things happen. You can't arrange other people's lives."

"Do you mind?..."

"Oh, I don't think it was ever serious between Philip and me. I suppose I wasn't quite grown up. My parents thought it would be ideal because then I should stay on the island and

(198)

Philip would be working there with my father. It was all too neat really."

"What a pity! It's spoiled things in a way."

"It can't spoil things for you. Everything is perfect. You're going to be blissfully happy, Laura."

"Yes, I am. You'll come and stay with us in Queensland, won't you?"

"I might consider it...if I were asked."

"You're asked here and now."

"All right then, I'll consider."

Then we talked about the wedding preparations and the honeymoon and I let her think that Philip had not really been very important to me.

So Laura was married and I was a bridesmaid and the day after the wedding she and her husband left for their honeymoon. I remained at the property until the ship was due to sail for the island. They tried to persuade me to stay right until the last day but I wanted to do some shopping in Sydney, so I said. The truth was that I wanted to get away. There was too much there to remind me of those happy holidays with Philip and Laura. It occurred to me that I would never visit the property again. I did not want to look very far into the future. I wondered what it would be like on the island when Susannah was gone. Philip might remain unless he made some excuse to follow her to England, which he might well do. I did not want to think of it.

It was quite an adventure staying at the hotel alone, although the proprietors knew me, for once or twice I had stayed there with the Halmers when they came to see me off on the ship. There were quite a number of people staying in the hotel. They were mostly graziers from the outback, who sat about in the big lounge talking wool prices and doing business with each other. I stayed in my rooms and had my meals there. I should only be in Sydney for two days. It seemed a long time, though, and I realized it was the first time in my life that I had really been alone.

I longed to be back on the island, yet I wondered what I should find there. It would not be the paradise it had been on other return journeys in the past. Philip would have learned that Susannah did not regard him with any seriousness. Poor Philip!

How different it would have been if Susannah had never come to Vulcan Island!

It was the morning before the day the ship would leave and I decided to do some last-minute shopping. I came out of one of the shops in Elizabeth Street where I had been to buy some clothes for Anabel and as I emerged into the sunshine a voice said: "Good morning, Miss Mateland."

I turned and saw a young man whom I had never seen before. He took off his hat and bowed. "You don't remember me," he said. "I'm Michael Roston of Roston, Evans. My father, who used to look after your affairs, died three weeks ago and I've taken over from him."

I realized then that he thought I was Susannah. I hesitated.

I heard myself say: "I'm sorry."

"It was sudden," he went on. "A stroke. By the way, something has come in for you. I was going to put it on the ship and send it out to Vulcan Island. I presumed you were there still."

"I was waiting for the ship," I said.

"So you are going back again. Would you like to call in for the mail? You know where we are in Hunter Street. It's a bit of a climb up to the fourth floor. But the firm has been at 33 Hunter for so long. My father would never think of moving."

My heart was beating fast. The name registered very clearly in my mind, so the idea must have been there before I was aware of it. Mr. Michael Roston of Roston, Evans, number 33 Hunter Street on the fourth floor. It would be amusing to collect Susannah's mail and take it out to her.

"Look," I would say. "There must be a strong resemblance. I was accosted by a young man who thought I was you, and I decided to let him believe it and I've brought back your mail."

I said: "I'll collect the mail."

"Very well," he said.

"Perhaps I'll call sometime this afternoon."

"Yes, do. If I'm not there someone else will give it to you. I'll tell them you're coming."

"I'll do that and . . . I'm very sorry about your father."

"We miss him. He had his fingers in everything. It's not always easy picking up the threads. But we shall keep our old connections of course and particularly with your people in England. We have worked with Carruthers, Gentle for over fifty years."

I thanked him and went back to the hotel. I did not notice now the graziers all intent on making negotiations about their wool.

I went straight to my room. I was considerably stimulated by the encounter.

I pulled off my hat. Yes, I did look like her. I *felt* like her. Important. Receiving letters from England through an Australian agent.

My little masquerade had enlivened my spirits.

That afternoon I collected the letters. I saw the young man again. This time I was more prepared for my role. I reminded myself that he had seen Susannah only once and then in passing. His father would have known at once that I was an impostor.

He chatted a little while. "And how are you liking Vulcan Island, Miss Mateland?"

"I find it interesting."

"I suppose you will be returning to England before the year is out."

"Perhaps."

"You must miss a great deal. My father was telling me about that wonderful castle which is your home."

"It's a beautiful place."

He asked a few questions about the island.

"I hear it has changed and, since the hospital has been built and the industry there is flourishing, it's becoming quite a civilized community."

"That is so," I said.

"The Englishman who went there some years ago is to be congratulated, I hear. It's not the most promising spot. I believe it was all but destroyed by volcanic eruption once."

"That was three hundred years ago."

"Extinct now, I suppose."

I said that I must go as I had so much to prepare for the next day. I was afraid he was going to ask questions which it might be difficult for me to answer.

I took the mail to my room and stowed it away in a little hand case which I should carry with me.

I wondered what Susannah would say when I told her I had been mistaken for her in the streets of Sydney.

* * *

It was very hot on the day we sailed. I stood on the deck looking out on the magnificent harbor. I remained there as we went through the Heads and for long after the land had receded and we came out into the open sea.

Then I went to my cabin.

I longed to see my parents but in a way I dreaded getting back to the island. Susannah would be ready to leave. Poor Philip, would he want to go with her?

Oh, Susannah, I thought, why did you ever come to the island to disrupt our lives!

We had been at sea for several days, and the next afternoon we should sight the land. I was awakened in the night by a rocking of the ship. It was unusual on those seas.

When I went down to breakfast I was aware that something was wrong. People were talking together with that mixture of excitement and apprehension which indicated that something extraordinary was afoot.

I asked what was wrong.

"We can't find out. The ship started to rock. We've stopped because the more we go on the worse it becomes."

During the morning we noticed the strange smell in the air; it was acrid, sulphuric, and there was a cloud of smoke hanging in the sky.

Rumors spread through the ship.

I paused to talk to a woman who was leaning on the rail looking out to sea.

"They say it's volcanic action somewhere," she said. "One of the islands...."

A terrible fear gripped me.

"Which one?" I cried. "Which one?"

She shook her head. "I don't know. They are all volcanic in this area."

I felt sick. I had visions of Cougabel's great limpid eyes heavy with prophecies. "Grumbling Giant not pleased...."

A fatalistic certainty came to me. I knew that the Giant had ceased to grumble and give vent to his anger.

The captain was undecided what to do.

He had goods to deliver to the island and he was not absolutely sure which one was affected, and as the rocking of the ship had stopped he decided to venture farther.

I was on the deck. I was looking at the ruins of my home. I could see the mountain peak, flames shooting from it and smoke circling round it.

I went to the captain. "This is my home," I said. "I must go and see for myself."

"I can't let you go," he told me. "It's dangerous."

"It's my home," I repeated stubbornly.

"I am sending two boats ashore to see if there are any people in need of help."

"I'm going with them," I said.

"I'm afraid I can't allow it."

I kept saying: "It's my home, you know." He did know because he had captained the ship several times when I had gone back and forth from school.

"I can't let you go," he said.

"I shall swim then. You can't stop that. I've got to see for myself. My mother may be there . . . my father. . . ."

He could see I was frantic with grief and apprehension.

"It's at your own risk," he said.

I stood there on that once beautiful island. I looked about me but could recognize little. The Giant remained, big and menacing, his sides burned black by the fiery streaks which he had spewed out over the fertile land. On what was left of the huts were strewn cinders and ashes. There were traces of hot pumice and glowing lava. It was dark, almost like night, but I saw that all that was left of the beautiful hospital was a heap of stones.

"Where are you?" I whispered. "Anabel . . . . Joel . . . where are you? Philip, Susannah, Cougaba, Cougabel . . . where?"

There were rivers of pasty mud over everything. The steam from the volcano had evidently condensed into rain and mixed with the light volcanic dust to form this paste. It had clearly flowed down from the slopes and smothered the little houses of the islanders.

Around the island were dust and stones which must have been blown out from the crater for miles around.

I could not believe it. It was a nightmare. I knew that nobody could survive such a cataclysmic experience.

It was lost . . . everything. My whole life had been wiped away.

Why had I laughed at the Grumbling Giant? Why had we all? Why hadn't we listened to the warnings of the natives who knew far better than we did?

He had destroyed us in the end—destroyed my father and

his hopes and dreams, my beloved mother, Cougaba, Cougabel, Susannah, Philip....

I had been saved by some miracle in the form of Laura's wedding. But saved for what?

I was alone...desolate.

I wished that I had been there with them.

The captain looked at me with kindly eyes.

"There is nothing you can do. There's nothing any of us can do. You must return to Sydney with the ship."

My mind was a blank. I could not think of the future. I could think of nothing but that they were gone...they were all dead.

I did not want to go back to Sydney. I wanted to stay there in that spot where we had all been so happy. I wanted to tunnel through the rubble. I wanted to look and look. "Just in case..." I said to the captain.

He shook his head. "None could have survived. Where could they have gone to? Can you imagine what it would have been like?"

I shook my head and cried: "Tell me. Tell me."

He put his arm about me and tried to soothe me. "You mustn't distress yourself," he said.

"Not distress myself! My home ... all that I loved ... all that meant anything to me...gone...and I must not distress myself!"

He was silent and I went on: "Tell me what happened to them. Tell me what it would have been like for them."

"It would have happened quickly," he said. "They might not have had any warning. Just a sudden commotion...inside the crater...."

"Grumbling," I cried hysterically. "It was the Grumbling Giant. We laughed at it ... laughed. Oh, it was evil ... and we laughed. ..."

"My dear Miss Mateland, it is no use going over it," he said. "I doubt they would have suffered. It would all have been too quick."

"All over ..." I said. "Years of hopes and dreams ... and all over."

"Let me take you back to the ship," he said. "We'll go back to Sydney and then you can make plans."

"Plans?" I murmured blankly. "Plans?"

I hadn't thought of the future until then. But of course I had to go on living.

I did not want to think of the future. I did not want to think of living without them. I only wanted to know how it happened. I wanted to think of them in their last moments. My mother, best loved of all, Miss Anabel who had brought such happiness to a little girl in a loveless cottage all those years ago, Miss Anabel with the gayest laughter I had ever heard...and she was gone. I had known what it meant to be dearly loved and I had loved in return. And now . . . and now . . .

I could not imagine a world without her.

"Tell me...tell me how it happened," I cried again.

"Well, it was a volcanic eruption. We thought it was extinct. It hadn't erupted for three hundred years. It only sent out dribbles now and then."

"It grumbled," I said. "It grumbled and grumbled. It was the Grumbling Giant. That's what they called it."

"I know the natives were superstitious about it. They're always superstitious about anything they don't understand. There would have been total darkness. The sea would have been disturbed. You see it has receded from the shores. There are lots of marine animals lying about. There would be flashes of lightning and the lava would start spurting out of the crater and covering the island."

"Hot glowing lava..."

"And the volcanic dust would make the paste. The air would be full of steam. But you are distressing yourself, Miss Mateland. Come, I'm taking you back to the ship. We ought to get away quickly. I just had to make sure there was nothing I could do. Nobody survived. You can see that. Come along now."

"I want to stay," I cried irrationally. "It's my home."

"No more," he said sadly. "Come along. We have to get back. It could be dangerous here. What if it erupted again?"

He took me firmly by the arm and put me into the small boat.

We went back to the ship.

I knew I should never forget the sight of the island . . . smoldering, destroyed. The hospital . . . the plantation . . . all the dreams . . . everything that meant anything to me . . . all gone.

* * *

I must have been in a sort of daze. The captain took me to the hotel. He was a very kind man and I shall always remember his sympathy with gratitude.

Everyone was kind to me, as people seem to be when there is a major disaster. The manager of the hotel gave me my old room and left me alone there. I wanted to be alone.

I stayed there for two days—not eating, just lying on my bed. The only relief was when I slept, which I did now and then very fitfully from sheer exhaustion. Then there would follow the awakening, which was terrible because then the reality would come flooding back.

At the end of two days I awoke from my stupor. Mrs. Halmer came in from the property, for news of what had happened had reached her. She said I must go back with her. I needed to recover from this terrible shock.

I thought about it; I was not sure whether I wanted to go or not. Hers would be a house of mourning too, for her son Philip was one of the victims.

She said we would share our grief, that we would comfort each other.

When she saw that I was still too bemused to make a decision she said she would come back in a week and in the meantime if I wanted to come there would be a welcome for me at any time.

"You'll be able to think about what you are going to do," she said. "We'll work it out together. It'll be quiet on the property. No one will worry you."

When she had gone it was as though she had drawn back the curtain which had shut me in with my misery.

What was I going to do? If I were to go on living I had to have a life to lead. My family and my home were lost to me. Where would I go? What should I do?

I tried to push these questions aside.

I don't care, I kept saying to myself. I don't care what becomes of me.

That was silly. I was here. I was alive. I had to go on living.

How?

With a rush of apprehension I remembered that I was here in the hotel. I had a little money which I had brought with me for my trip but that would not last long.

I was penniless...almost. My father had put everything

into the hospital and the plantation. They were to be my inheritance.

I could remember my mother's saying: "Your father has put all he has into the hospital and the plantation. It will be yours one day, Suewellyn."

The memory of her voice and those beautiful blue eyes all concern for me was too much to bear. I buried my face in my pillow.

"I don't care. I don't care what becomes of me," I muttered.

Then I seemed to hear her voice again: "That's silly, darling. You've got to go on living. You've got to find some way. It's not like you to give up. We're not that sort of people. Your father . . . me . . . you. When life is cruel we just stand firm against it. We fight back, Suewellyn."

She was right. I would have to go on. I would have to fight my way out of this morass of grief and misery. I had to go on living.

I had to have money, so I should have to work. What could I do? What did people in my position do? I had had a good education. My mother had been an excellent governess. I could do something.

I didn't want to. I wanted to take the ship back to Vulcan Island and go up the mountain to the crater and tell the Grumbling Giant to kill me as he had killed them.

I could almost feel my mother's hands stroking my hair. "Suewellyn, you're a Mateland. Matelands never give up."

Yes, I was a Mateland. I thought of my ancestors in the picture gallery. I had always wanted to go to the castle. Even now I could feel that. I was astonished. I had a faint interest in life. I must have, for there was a desire in me to see the castle.

Then I remembered the mail I had collected for Susannah. It was in my bag. What should I do with it now? Take it back to Roston, Evans? Explain that I had pretended to be Susannah? I was in no mood to do that.

I took out the letters and turned them over in my hands. It was such a relief not to be thinking of that devastated island for a few moments.

I don't know when the impulse came to me. It was like clutching at a life line. I had to stop thinking of my parents and Philip. I had to do something which absorbed me to such an extent that I stopped torturing myself.

I opened the letter, telling myself that Susannah was dead now and I should know something of her affairs.

It was an official-looking letter and it was from a solicitor in Mateland, the Carruthers, Gentle whom Mr. Roston had mentioned.

Dear Miss Mateland [*I read*],

We have to inform you of the sudden death of Mr. Esmond Mateland which occurred on Thursday last. According to your grandfather's will, Mateland Castle with its estates now passes to you as the heir named by your grandfather in the event of your cousin's death without issue. Will you please get in touch with us as soon as possible? We shall be in communication with Messrs. Roston, Evans and Company to whom we are sending this letter. On receipt of it perhaps you will call at their offices in 33 Hunter Street, Sydney.

Yours truly,

for Carruthers, Gentle Ltd.

There was a signature which I could not quite decipher.

I sat back. So Susannah was now the owner of the castle. She had intended to be and had planned to marry her cousin Esmond Mateland for that reason. Now Esmond was dead and Susannah had the castle... or would have had she been alive. To whom did the castle belong now?

I think it was at that moment that the idea came into my head. It was so wild, so preposterous that I did not at first receive it. But it was there like a seed, germinating, ready to spring forth and strangle my scruples.

I must have been in a strange mood, for it would not have occurred to me a few weeks earlier to open letters not addressed to me.

I picked up the other letter. It was in a rather thin sloping hand. Before I could stop myself I had slit the envelope.

Dear Susannah [*I read*],

You will have heard the terrible news. As you can guess, I am desolate. He was so well such a short time ago. The doctors are baffled. You can imagine how it is with me. I am prostrate with grief. You must come home at once. I know that you are on the other side of the world and that it will take time. But please leave at once. It seems so long since we have seen you, for, remember, you were away at school that year in

*France at that finishing place, and then home so briefly before
you went away again . . . to Australia. I shall hardly know what
you look like soon. It has been so long.*

*I know how you will be feeling. Your sufferings will be as
mine. After all you were the girl he was going to marry and
I his mother. Who could be closer than that? He had been
threatening to come out to Australia to bring you back. Of
course he did spend all that time in Paris when you were there.
Things are chaotic here. Carruthers, Gentle say you must
come, for only when you are back can everything be settled.
You are the mistress of Mateland now. Oh dear, what tragedies
beset our family. Esmond to die like that . . . so young. And his
father . . . I have had my share of trouble. My eyes, of course,
do not improve. It is a gradual process, but I am warned that
in five years I shall be blind.*

*You must make arrangements to come home at once, Su-
sannah.*

My love to you.

Your Aunt Emerald

I read the letters through again and for a long time sat
staring into space.

When I looked up I saw that I had been sitting there for
half an hour. During that time my thoughts had taken me
back. I was standing on the edge of the woods looking at the
castle. I was there inside, seeing it clearly from what I had
heard from Susannah and my mother.

It was amazing.

I had not thought of my tragic circumstances all that time.

The Great Deception

It is a common human characteristic that when one has decided on a course of action which is wrong, dishonest and even criminal the mind of the offender immediately begins to discover reasons why such action is justifiable.

I was a Mateland. My father's offspring should surely be in the line of inheritance. I was my father's second daughter. Esmond was dead; Susannah was dead. Had my parents been married I should have been the next.

It was no use reminding myself that my parents were *not* married. I was, as I had frankly been told by the children at school, a bastard; and bastards had no rights.

But, said my persuasive mind, my father had loved my mother more dearly than he had loved anyone else. She was his wife in his eyes. I was a Mateland. I had changed my name when I came to them; surely I was entitled to be recognized as such.

The idea was growing.

But for Susannah, Philip would be with me now. He would have accompanied me to his sister's wedding, and we should have married, for he had been in love with me to a certain extent, as I had been with him.

But Susannah had come and stolen my lover. Why should I not take her inheritance? There! It was out.

"It's fantastic," I said aloud. "It's impossible. It's a wild dream."

And the alternative?

I stared the bleak future blankly in the face. I could go to Roston, Evans; I could confess my little deception. It was nothing very serious at the moment. Then I could go to the Halmers and stay with Mrs. Halmer until I worked out what I was going to do. Perhaps I could borrow the money to go to England and there try some post as a governess or a companion, which seemed to be the only course open to women of some education who suddenly found themselves forced to earn a living. I should be utterly miserable.

On the other hand there was this wild preposterous plan which had presented itself to me. All sorts of notions, ideas, possibilities were thrusting themselves into my mind.

It's wrong, I kept telling myself. It's fraud. It's criminal. It's unthinkable.

In some ways to contemplate it acted as a palliative. It took my mind off misery. Of course I won't do it, I told myself, but it would be interesting to see how it could be done...*if* it could be done.

An hour slipped by. I was still thinking of it.

I could go to Roston, Evans. The young man did not know me. He was, in fact, of the opinion that I was Susannah. His accosting me in the street had been the beginning of it all. It would never have occurred to me if that had not happened. It was Fate tempting me. It was like a bait. I had taken the first step down the slippery slope when I allowed him to believe I was Susannah. Why had I done that? It was like some prearranged pattern beginning to show itself.

The first part would be easy. I could go to Mr. Roston and get the money for my passage home. I could tell him that I had set out for the island and been unable to land because of the volcanic eruption. That was all true.

I could go to England...and to Mateland Castle. Then the dangerous part would begin.

One part of Emerald's letter kept coming into my mind: "I shall hardly know what you look like. It has been so long."

Surely it was meant to be!

I thought a great deal about the castle. I believed I knew something about Emerald from what Anabel as well as Susannah had told me. She had said it was long since we met; she referred to her poor vision. That letter of hers was like a beckoning finger, like Fate saying: Come on. It is all made easy for you.

Esmond was the only one who would have been so acutely aware of everything about Susannah that he would immediately recognize an imposture. And Esmond was dead.

Well, it had been diverting to dream and to fabricate such a wild adventure in my mind; and God knew I was in need of some divertissement to draw me out of this hideous depression which enveloped me.

I had done nothing so far except allow Roston to believe that I was Susannah, collect her mail and open it. There was nothing very wicked about that.

I must leave it there and start thinking sensibly.

Misery enveloped me. I kept seeing Anabel coming to visit me at Crabtree Cottage, carrying me off with her on that never-to-be-forgotten night—and most vividly of all, holding my hand as we stood together looking at the castle.

I had no desire to go on living unless . . . unless . . .

I spent a restless night. I kept dozing and dreaming that I had come to the castle.

"It is mine now," I said in my dream.

Then I would awake and toss from side to side, my dream still with me.

In the morning the first thing I thought was: Mr. Roston will be looking for Susannah. He will think she was not on the island. He will know by now that she is the owner of the castle and that that was the purport of the letters he gave me. He would be expecting her to call. I had already created a situation. I had forgotten that. Yes, I was deeper in this than I had at first thought.

Instead of filling me with horror, this thought exhilarated me.

Matelands lived dangerously and I was one of them.

Then I knew that I was going to attempt this outrageous adventure. I was going to enter the biggest masquerade I had ever envisaged. I knew it was wrong. I knew that I would be in acute danger. But I was going to do it. I *had* to do it. It was the only way out of the slough of despond.

The fact was that I didn't care what became of me. The Grumbling Giant had, at one stroke, robbed me of everything I cared for.

I was going to do this desperate thing because, for a host of reasons, it would give me an interest in life.

Besides, I wanted the castle. From the moment I saw it I had felt bound to it, and the urge to take it was growing stronger with every hour because it was only that which could make me want to go on living.

As I walked down Hunter Street I was turning over in my mind what I would say to Mr. Roston, and even as I entered the building and started up the stairs, my mind was not entirely made up. I should not have been surprised if I had blurted out the truth about my deception. But when he received me in his office I did no such thing. He began by saying:

"Miss Mateland, I am glad you've come. I have been expecting you. This is a terrible matter. Of course there was always the possibility of the volcano's erupting, but no one thought it likely, or my father would have advised you against going in the first place. It must have been a shock to you. And now ... this even greater shock. The death of your cousin in England."

"I ... I can't believe it. It's quite terrible."

"Of course. Of course. I gather it was a sudden illness. Most unexpected. A dreadful blow for you." He was gently soothing but, I sensed, eager to get on with the real business.

"I suppose you will be returning to England."

"It's what I must do. I haven't enough money for my passage...."

"My dear Miss Mateland, that presents no problem. We have instructions from Carruthers, Gentle. I can advance you as much as you need. We can book your passage. I hear that your aunt is eagerly awaiting your return."

My resolution was weakening. "The old Debil" was indeed at my elbow.

I suddenly knew, there in Mr. Roston's office, that I was going on with it.

Within three weeks I was sailing to England on the S.S. *Victoria*. My thoughts went back to that journey I had made with my parents over eleven years before. How different that had been and yet both voyages were dominated by a sense of adventure and excitement. In both instances I was going into a new life.

There was something uncanny about this. I was changing

my character. At times I had the strange feeling that I was becoming Susannah. There was a new ruthlessness about me. Was it possible that when someone died that person's soul could find refuge in someone else's body? There was a theory about that, I believed. Sometimes I felt that Susannah had entered mine.

Mr. Roston had given me a trunk of clothes and documents which she had left in the care of his firm. Before leaving Sydney I had gone through it. I had tried on the dresses and chic hats. They all fitted me. I began to walk like Susannah. I began to talk as she had. The girl I had been would never have dared do what I was doing. It was significant that I had ceased to make excuses for myself.

I was a Mateland; I was Susannah's sister; I belonged to the castle. Why should I not take over the role of Susannah? What harm could it do? Susannah was dead. It meant changing my Christian name from Suewellyn to Susannah. They even sounded something alike.

S.M. was imprinted on the trunks. My own initials.

The long sea voyage gave me the time I needed to adjust and to observe the change in myself. People noticed me. I had lost all my diffidence. I had become not only an attractive young woman but one who knew she was.

The fact that there was now no going back added to my confidence. I had to carry on and I was going to. No one should ever know the difference. From now on I was Susannah Mateland, heiress to a castle and a fortune.

This wild adventure had done something for me. It was so preposterous, so fraught with danger, and there was so much to learn that I had no time to brood on my misery. I could even smile to think of Susannah, who had always enjoyed getting the better of me, now gone, leaving me to enjoy what was hers.

There was a certain amount of social life on the ship. The captain took a great deal of notice of me. He knew that I had been going out to visit relations on Vulcan Island and was full of commiseration. But he congratulated me on my fortuitous escape.

"If it had happened a week or so later I should have been there," I said. "I was going out for a last visit before leaving for England."

"A very happy escape, Miss Mateland."

I looked sadly out to the sea. There were moments when

I thought it was far from happy and I still wished that I had been there with them.

He patted my hand. "You must not grieve, Miss Mateland, but it is a tragedy that the island has been ruined."

He sensed that the subject was painful and did not refer to it again. But he was particularly kind to me and I told him that I was going home to claim my inheritance.

"Mateland Castle has come to me on the death of my cousin," I said.

"Ah, you have much to go back to. Is this castle known to you, Miss Mateland?"

"Oh yes . . . yes. . . . It is my home."

He nodded. "You'll feel better when you get home."

I went on to talk about the castle. I glowed with pride in it. I was almost aware of Susannah within me urging me on, applauding me. And I thought: This is the sort of thing Susannah would do. I *am* becoming Susannah.

That was the easy part.

It was April when we docked in Southampton. I took the train to Mateland. It was like retracing that long-ago journey when I sat holding Anabel's hand tightly, my whole being thrilled by the granting of my three wishes.

I remembered the comfort I had derived from Anabel and the lovely new feeling of security. I was far from feeling that now.

In fact with every passing moment I was growing more and more apprehensive.

Mateland Station. How heartbreakingly familiar! I alighted from the train and a man in a peaked cap came towards me.

"Why, Miss Susannah!" he cried. "Welcome home. They're expecting you. 'Tis good to see you. Terrible tragedy, were it not . . . Mr. Esmond going like that?"

"Yes," I said. "Terrible . . . terrible. . . ."

"'Tweren't long afore he died I saw him. He came back home. He'd been away. I can see him now getting out of this train, smiling . . . in that quiet way of his. 'Back again, Joe,' he says. 'You won't catch me staying long away from Mateland.' Not like you, Miss Susannah."

"No, Joe, not like me."

"Well, you've changed a bit."

My heart leaped in sudden fear. "Oh . . . not for the worse, I hope."

"No . . . no. Not that, Miss Susannah. Mrs. Tomkin will be

glad you're back. She said to me only the other day: 'It's time Miss Susannah was back, Joe. That'll make a change up at the castle.'"

"Remember me to Mrs. Tomkin, Joe."

"That I will, miss. Can't wait to get home to tell her. Is the castle sending for you?"

"I wasn't sure of the time...."

"I'll get the fly to take you down. How's that?"

I said it was a good idea.

As I was seated in the fly jogging along those lanes I told myself that this was going to be my first test. I had to keep my ears and eyes open all the time. I must not miss the smallest detail. I had to learn all the time. Even that brief encounter had given me the name of the stationmaster and the fact that he had a wife, and that Esmond had a quiet way with him.

It was scarifying, horrifying and at the same time tremendously exhilarating.

Then, suddenly, there it was ahead of me in all its glory. I was filled with emotion as I gazed at those lofty curtain walls and the strong drum towers at the four angles, at the battlemented gatehouse, the gray flinty walls, formidable, impregnable, and the narrow slits of windows.

I felt a great wave of possessive love for the place. Mateland. Mine.

The fly took us through the portcullis into a courtyard. There we stopped and two grooms ran out to help me alight. I was not sure whether I should know them or not. The elder of the two said: "Miss Susannah..."

"Yes," I answered. "I'm here."

"This is good news, Miss Susannah."

"Thank you," I said.

"It seems so long since you went away, miss, and so much has happened since then. This is Thomas, miss, the new stableboy. He's been with us a month or more."

"Good day, Thomas."

Thomas touched his forelock and murmured something.

"Well, Miss Susannah. I'll have your baggage taken up to your room. And you'll want to go at once to Mrs. Mateland. She's been all impatience for you to come."

"Yes," I said. "Yes."

I walked into the castle. I recognized the hall from Anabel's and Susannah's descriptions as the main hall. I looked up at the magnificent timbered roof, at the stone walls on which some tapestry hung side by side with spears and lances. I knew that high in the wall there was what was called a "peep." It was an aperture scarcely visible from below to those who did not know exactly where it was. Behind it would be a little alcove where the ladies of the house used to look down on the revelries in the hall when they were considered too young to join in or the company was too ribald for them. I knew that it was now used to see what visitors had come and if one did not want to receive them one hurried out of reach.

I had a horrible feeling that I was being watched now, and quite suddenly as I stood there in the hall I was terrified. I had walked into this too glibly. I had not thought of where it could lead me. I was a fraud. I was a cheat. I was taking possession of this magnificent place when I had no legal right to.

It was useless now to tell myself that I had a moral right, which I had been doing since I started on this mad adventure.

I had come here to take the castle. It was as though I had been put under a spell. Now I felt that hundreds of eyes watched me, lured me on, mocked me, urged me to come and see what I could do to take the castle.

I was trapped at this first moment. Here I stood in the center of the main hall and I did not know which way to go. Susannah would have gone straight to her room or Emerald's. Susannah would have known.

There was a staircase at the end of the hall. I knew that it led up to the picture gallery. I had heard both Anabel and Susannah mention it many times. I started up it and was relieved to see a woman standing on the landing.

She was middle-aged, rather self-righteous-looking, with brown hair pulled tightly back from her forehead and rather penetrating light brown eyes.

"Miss Susannah," she said. "Well, my word, and it's about time too."

"Hello," I said cautiously.

"Let's have a look at you. H'm. You've changed. Foreign parts have done you good. Got a bit scraggy though. I suppose it's all this upset."

"Yes, I suppose so."

Who is she? I wondered. Some sort of servant, but a privileged one. A horrible thought struck me. She might be one of those nannies who had been with the child from birth. If so, she would soon find me out.

"It was shocking . . . Mr. Esmond . . . so sudden, too. You going to Mrs. Mateland or your room first?"

"I think I'd better see her first."

"I'll go up with you and warn her you're here, shall I?"

I nodded with relief. "How are her eyes?" I asked.

"They've got much worse. It's cataract over them both. She can see a little . . . but of course it's going to get worse."

"I am sorry."

She looked at me sharply. "Well, you know she was never one to make light of her misfortunes . . . and with Mr. Esmond going . . ."

"Of course," I said.

She had started up the stairs and I gratefully walked beside her.

"I'll warn her you're here before you go bursting in," she said.

We went along the gallery. I felt I knew it well. There were all my ancestors. I would study them in detail at my leisure.

Up the staircase we went. At the top of it the woman paused. She turned and looked at me and my heart felt as though it would burst out of my body.

She said: "Did you see your father?"

I nodded.

"And Miss . . . Anabel? . . ." There was a slight tremor in her voice as she said that and then I knew, for from the first she had seemed vaguely familiar. She was the one who had brought the food when we went on the picnic and who had driven the dogcart for us, the one who, Anabel had told me, always said what she meant, who couldn't tell a lie and rarely said anything good about anything. I struggled a few moments to bring out her name from the recesses of my memory. Then I thought, Janet! It must be Janet, but I was not going to fall into the trap of using her name until I was sure.

"Yes," I said, "I saw them both."

"Were they . . ."

I said fervently: "They were happy together. My father was doing wonderful work on the island."

"We've only just got the news about the explosion or whatever it was."

"It was a volcanic eruption."

"Whatever it was, it killed them both. Miss Anabel...she was a wayward one . . . but she had a sweet nature. . . ."

"You're right," I said.

Again that sharp look in my direction. Then she shrugged her shoulders. "Ought never to have done it."

She turned and we went on our way. She paused by a door, tapped on it and a voice called, "Come in." Janet turned to me and put her fingers to her lips.

I heard the voice say: "Is that you, Janet?"

"It is, Mrs. Mateland."

I was right. It was Janet. I felt I had made some progress.

"Miss Susannah's home, Mrs. Mateland."

I went into the room.

So this was Emerald, the wife of David whom my father had killed in a duel. She was sitting in a chair away from the light. She was evidently a tall woman and very slender; her expression was resigned, her face pale and her hair turning gray.

"Susannah..." She said.

I heard myself say: "Oh, Aunt Emerald, it is good to see you."

"I thought you were never coming." Her voice sounded peevish.

"There were things to settle," I said, and kissed her papery cheek.

"This terrible thing," she began. "Esmond..."

"I know," I murmured.

"It was sudden. That fearful illness. He was well the week before and then he suddenly sickened and was dead in a week."

"What was it?"

"Some sort of fever...gastric fever. If only Elizabeth were alive now. She would have been such a comfort. Malcolm is so practical. He arranged everything. Oh, my dear Susannah, we must mourn together. I know you were going to marry him, but he was my son...my only son. All I had. There's no one now."

"We must comfort each other," I said.

She gave a strange little snort.

"That's a bit incongruous, isn't it?"

I patted her hand because I was not sure what to reply.

"Well," she went on, "we shall have to try and get along now. I take it you don't want to turn me out of my home."

"Aunt Emerald! How can you suggest such a thing!"

"Well, I suppose I haven't the same rights now that Esmond has gone. As his mother, it was natural...oh, never mind now. What is to be will be. It's all so upsetting."

"I didn't intend to disturb anyone," I assured her. "I want it to be the same."

"Your travels have done you good, Susannah."

"Oh, you mean I've changed."

"I don't know. I suppose it's seeing you again after all this time. You seem different somehow. I suppose all that traveling would change a person."

"In what way, Aunt Emerald?" I asked anxiously.

"Just a feeling. I thought you seemed less...well, I always felt you were hard, Susannah. I don't know...."

"Tell me about your eyes, Aunt Emerald."

"They're getting steadily worse."

"Can nothing be done?"

"No, it's an old complaint. Lots of people have it. I've just got to endure it."

"I am sorry."

"There! That's what I mean. You've got gentler. You sound as though you really care. I didn't think you ever gave my eyes a thought."

I turned away. She was thinking my concern for her sight was purely altruistic. I was sorry for her, but I couldn't help seeing this affliction of hers as something to my advantage.

She went on: "Would you like some tea? Or would you like to go to your room first?"

A sudden thought had come to me. I must discover which was my room. If I waited until my bags were put in it I should be able to identify it by them.

I said: "I wonder if my bags have come yet."

"Pull the bell rope," she said. "I'll get them to bring some tea and they can let us know when your bags arrive."

Janet came back.

"Ask them to send up some tea, Janet," said Emerald.

Janet nodded and went out.

"Janet doesn't change much," I ventured.

"Janet...oh. She's too forward if you ask me. Seems to think she is in some special position. I was surprised she stayed after your father went all those years ago. She came with Anabel from her home, you know. You must have seen Anabel with your father."

"Yes."

"On that ridiculous island. Sometimes I think there's a streak of madness in the Matelands."

"Very likely," I said with a little laugh.

"That awful affair. Two brothers...I'll never get over it. I was glad that Esmond was too young to know what it was all about. And then Joel's going off to that island and living there like some nabob or something. Your father always was so flamboyant. So was David for that matter. I married into a strange family."

"Well, that was a long time ago, Aunt Emerald."

"Many weary years ago. There must be a lot you have to tell me . . . about them . . . and everything."

"Sometime I will," I said.

Tea was brought in.

"Susannah, will you pour?" she asked. "I can't see very well. I'm apt to slop the tea over into the saucer."

I sat down, poured out and took a cup to her. There were some little cakes on a plate and some bread and butter.

"Esmond was very restless after you'd gone," she went on. "Really, Susannah, need you have stayed away so long?"

"It was so far away, you see, and having made that long journey, I felt I had to stay a little while."

"Trust you to find out your father's hiding place! And then you went back to Sydney and while you were away the whole thing blew up. What a climax to all that secret melodrama. Fitting in a way."

"It was...horrible," I said vehemently.

"But you were well out of it, Susannah."

"Sometimes I wish..."

She was waiting. I must be careful. I must not show my feelings too intensely. I had a feeling that Susannah had never felt deeply about anything that did not concern herself.

"I wish," I finished lamely, "that they had accompanied me to Sydney. Tell me of Esmond."

There was a brief silence, then she said: "It was a return of that mysterious illness he had before you went away. Do you remember?"

I nodded.

"He was ill then...desperately ill. As you know, we thought that was the end...but he recovered. We thought he would recover the second time. It was a great blow. Malcolm took over estate matters. He's very friendly with Jeff Carleton."

"Oh, is he?" I said.

"Yes. I believe Jeff thinks the place should have gone to Malcolm after Esmond. In fact I thought it might. But your grandfather always had a prejudice against Malcolm because of *his* grandfather. They hated each other, those two brothers. I never knew such a family for feuds."

I felt a tremor of uneasiness. I should know these people. I was skating on very thin ice and I must inevitably come to a spot where the ice was too thin—and then would be disaster.

"I dare say Jeff Carleton will be wanting to see you soon. He's a bit uneasy about things, but of course that's natural."

"Of course," I replied, desperately searching in my mind for some clue received in the past which would tell me who Jeff Carleton was.

"He's hoping everything will be run in the same way. I don't suppose you'll want to change anything. I always thought dear Esmond was a trifle too easygoing."

I nodded. I was building up a picture of Esmond. Quiet. Easygoing.

"I think he gave Jeff rather a free hand and I dare say Jeff is hoping that will continue."

"I dare say," I said.

"There was always such a fuss about the estate and I suppose when David died Jeff assumed authority. He got a taste for it, Esmond being so young."

"And easygoing," I added.

She nodded.

I drank some of the hot tea. It was reviving, but I could eat nothing. I was too overwrought.

Emerald continued to talk and desperately I floundered, trying to catch at some thread and comment sensibly. It was exhausting and when there was a knock on the door and Janet entered to say that my bags were now in my room I rose with alacrity. I was looking forward to a few hours in which to assimilate what I had learned.

I rose and said I would go to my room.

"See you at dinner," said Emerald.

I went out. Now was the moment to look for my room. I guessed it would be on the next floor. I looked over my shoulder furtively. It was important that no one see me. I hurried up the stairs. As I reached the top a figure emerged from the far end of the corridor. It was Janet.

"Just going to your room, Miss Susannah?" she said.

"Er...yes," I replied.

"Well, your bags are there. I went up with them to make sure everything was all right."

"Oh, thank you." Go away, I wanted to shout. What are you hanging about for? It was almost as though she knew what a quandary I was in and wanted to catch me.

I walked past her and she started towards the stairs. There was a window in the corridor. I went to it and loitered as though looking down on the scene below—at the green lawns and the woodlands in the distance.

I thought she had gone and turned towards the first door. I was about to open it swiftly when I heard her voice. "No . . . no . . . I shouldn't, Miss Susannah. I shouldn't if I were you."

She had come back and was standing behind me, her hand on my arm.

"It would be too painful for you. It's just as he left it. His mother wouldn't let us change it. I think she comes up here sometimes. It's not easy for her to get up. I think she just sits there and broods, grieving because he's gone."

Esmond's room! I thought. What a lucky escape! She thought I was going in to brood.

I wanted to get rid of her. I said with what I felt was the right amount of emotion: "I have to go in, Janet."

She sighed and stepped into the room with me. It was very neat. There was his bed, the line of bookshelves along one wall, the bureau in the corner, the armchairs, the bronze-colored curtains with a chrysanthemum pattern on them.

Janet was behind me. "He died in that bed," she said. "His mother won't have anything changed. But I wouldn't advise you to stay in here, Miss Susannah. I don't know. It's eerie. Not good for you."

I answered: "I want to wait here a while, Janet. I want to be alone."

"All right then. You do what you want to." She went out and shut the door.

I sat down on a chair and it was not of Esmond that I was thinking but of Janet and how I was to find my room without her knowing that I was seeking it.

After a while I cautiously opened the door and looked into the corridor. All was quiet and deserted. Stealthily I made my way along the corridor, opening one door after another and looking for my bags.

There were several bedrooms. Cautiously I opened the door right at the end of the corridor, and I found the room which contained my bags.

Strained and nervous, I went in and sank onto the bed.

And this was just the first few hours.

While I was unpacking there was a knock on the door.

"Come in," I called, my heart starting to pound as it did when I was about to encounter some fresh trial.

It was Janet again.

"Can I be of help?"

"No, thanks. I can manage."

"Is there anything they've forgotten to put in your room?"

"I don't think so."

"Grace, that new maid...she's a bit scared of you."

"Why should she be?"

"Oh, she's heard of you and your tantrums. And now you're the mistress, so to speak."

I laughed uneasily.

"Are you going to put these things in the drawer? All neatly folded. That's not like you, Miss Susannah. I never knew anyone so untidy. Things always scattered over the floor. Now you've turned tidy. Is that what travel's done for you?"

"You might say it is. When you're packing and unpacking you realize you have to keep things in some sort of order."

She nodded. "I want to say something to you." She lowered her voice. "It's about Anabel."

"Yes?" I asked uneasily.

"You saw her on that island place. How was she?"

"She was well and happy and seemed satisfied with life."

Janet shook her head. "It was a terrible blow to me when she went away. She was like one of my own. She ought not to have left me like that."

"She could hardly have taken you with her."

"Why not? I came here with her from the vicarage. I belonged with her...not here."

"Well, you stayed here."

"I was fond of her," mused Janet. "She was a bit of a minx ... up to tricks ... you never knew what it would be next ... but she had a sweet nature."

I could not speak. I feared to betray my emotion.

"And they were happy there...her and that Mr. Joel?" she

went on. "I'll never forget that night. All the rushing to and fro . . . all the noise and chatter . . . and then finding him out there. I remember them carrying him in on a stretcher. It didn't seem like real life somehow. But the thing about real life is that it can sometimes be like what is unreal. Oh, my poor Miss Anabel!"

I thought: There is a purpose in all this. She is suspicious. She is testing me. It means something.

"There was a little girl," she said. "I saw her once. A nice little thing. I wonder what became of her."

"She was there... with them," I told her.

"Well, bless me! I might have known. Miss Anabel wouldn't have gone away and left her."

"No, she didn't."

"And you would have seen her on this island then, Miss Susannah."

"Yes, I saw her. She was Suewellyn."

"That's right. They had a picnic once. I was there."

"Did they?" My heart was racing now. I feared it would betray my agitation.

"Yes. A nice bewildered little thing. I could see she was a Mateland. What became of her?"

I could feel Janet's eyes on me and I said quickly: "She was on the island... when it happened. She went with them."

"Poor mite. She reminded me of you when I saw her. About the same age . . . the same build . . . and that something about her which made you say, 'No doubt what stable she came out of!' It's a terrible tragedy . . . and a mercy you were not there when it happened. Funny what made you go over to Sydney just at the right time."

"You seem to know all about it, Janet."

"Well, the news came to Mrs. Mateland, you see, through those lawyers. Mr. Joel would have been the real heir after Esmond had gone if he hadn't been disinherited. It made it neater all the same to have him out of the way, so to speak. Old Mr. Egmont was in a fine way when he realized he'd lost both his sons at the crack of a gun, as it were. He disinherited Master Joel and in any case there was Mr. Esmond. Who would have thought *he* would have died like that? I'm glad the little girl was with Miss Anabel. I was only with them a little while but it was heart-warming to see them together... though it was wrong, of course. My poor Miss Anabel. She deserved better."

"Yes," I said fervently. "She did."

Janet looked at me sharply and I went on quickly: "Well, it's all over now."

"So many deaths," added Janet. "I don't like it. That volcano...well, that's an act of God. Poor Mr. Esmond, too. I wonder how long his room will be left. His mother don't want anything disturbed. Are you going to stick to that, Miss Susannah? The papers in his desk . . . his books and all that . . . not to be touched . . . left exactly as they were when he died. . . . Well, that's the way his mother wanted it."

"We'll see, Janet," I said.

She looked at me dolefully and went out. When she had gone I sat on my bed staring into space.

Does she suspect something? I asked myself.

I got through the evening quite well. I could manage with Emerald, for in the first place she was partially blind and was unable to notice any difference between Susannah and me. Moreover she was a woman who was completely wrapped up in herself, which was a great help in a situation like this one. Any differences she might discover she gave little thought to beyond assuming they were due to the effects of travel.

It was different with the servants. Some of them had known Susannah since her childhood, but I think they were accepting me as Susannah though they thought I had changed.

The one I really had to fear was Janet. Janet knew too much. She knew of the existence of Suewellyn. She might put two and two together. And then what?

That very first evening the fact of how easily I could slip up was brought home to me. Who would have believed I could be betrayed by such a simple thing as a pudding?

The dessert that night was ginger pudding. I felt disinclined to eat anything and I had some cheese and biscuits after the main dish, declining the pudding. Chaston, the butler, must have reported this, for after I had said good night to Emerald and was going to my room, about to mount the staircase, a flustered red-faced woman came from behind the screens and placed her ample body between me and the stairs.

"Is anything wrong?" I asked.

"Yes, Miss Susannah, there is."

"What?" I asked.

"I'd like to know, miss, if you are of the opinion that I am no longer worthy to cook for this household."

Such a verbose statement, delivered in what I can only call a bellicose manner, was an indication that the ire of this lady had been most forcefully aroused.

I wondered why I should be confronted in this way and then I remembered that I was supposed to be Susannah, the mistress of this vast establishment.

"Why, no," I said. "I thought the food was excellent."

"What was wrong with my ginger pudding that it should be sent back untouched?"

"Nothing, I am sure."

"But something for you to turn your nose up at! Why, it was done special for you, knowing as how you had always had a partiality for the same. I go to the trouble to make it on your first night...knowing as how I always did when you come home from anywhere...and there'd always be hardly any left when it came back to my kitchen. Not so much as a sliver taken."

"Oh, M—" I had forgotten that I did not know her name. "I'm sorry. The fact is...I'm too tired to be hungry tonight."

"No," she went on, ignoring my interruption. "It comes out just as it was took in. I said to myself when I see that pudding coming out: 'Well, Mrs. Bates, it seems your cooking ain't grand enough for them that is world travelers.' I could tell you, miss, there's some not very far from here who'd welcome in their houses someone who could make a ginger pudding like that one."

"It's only because I'm so tired, Mrs. Bates."

"You tired! You was never tired. And if that's what traveling's done for you, you'd do better to stay at home...."

"Will you make a ginger pudding tomorrow night, Mrs. Bates?" I begged.

She sniffed a little but I could see she was beginning to be mollified. "I would if I was ordered."

"Then I should be able to enjoy it. I'm just too worn out...and too lacking in appetite to do it justice tonight."

"You had cheese, Chaston tells me," she said accusingly. "You passed by my ginger pudding for cheese! When I think of you, standing on a chair, with your fingers in the basin taking licks when I wasn't looking..." Her face wrinkled into a smile. "You said to me, 'It's the ginger, Mrs. Bates. The

(**227**)

Devil tempted me.' You was a caution, you was, and ginger pudding was always your favorite. Now it seems..."

"Oh no, no, Mrs. Bates, I still like it. *Please* make one tomorrow."

She was beginning to twinkle. "I couldn't make it out," she said, "when I see that pudding going out just as it had come in. It was enough to break any cook's heart."

She was mollified. She accepted my excuses. But what a fuss over a pudding. How careful I had to be!

I was exhausted when I reached my bedroom. I had learned a great deal and the most important thing I had discovered was how easily I could be betrayed.

I slept well. I suppose I was worn out physically and mentally. I awoke with the feeling which was becoming commonplace to me now—a mingling of terrible apprehension and excitement. Any hour could bring my deception out into the open, I realized. I should be lucky to survive for a few weeks.

I rose and went down to breakfast. I had an idea that this was taken any time between eight and ten and that one just helped oneself from the sideboard. I went into the room where we had dined the previous night. Yes, the table was set for breakfast and food was sizzling on the sideboard in silver dishes.

I helped myself and sat down, grateful to be alone. I was hungry in spite of the internal uneasiness.

While I was eating Janet looked in.

"Oh, early," she said in that familiar way of hers. "Not like you, Miss Susannah, to be up at this hour. What's happened to you? Changed your habits since abroad? Miss Lie-abed has become Miss Early Bird."

So once again I had slipped. I must remember that.

"I don't suppose Jeff Carleton will be here till ten," she went on. "He won't be expecting you to want to look round the estate with him at this hour, I can tell you. He was saying how glad he was that you were coming home. He says it's a great responsibility to have when he can't get permission for what he wants. Though, mind you, Mr. Esmond gave him more or less a free hand. He says he doesn't expect that from you."

I listened. So this morning I was to go round the estate with Jeff Carleton, the farm manager. I had to thank Janet for giving me plenty of information. I felt quite exhilarated to pick up so much. I was learning to keep my eyes and ears open.

I said: "I'll be ready when he comes. Ten o'clock, you say."

"Well, that was the time you and Mr. Esmond used to go with him, wasn't it?"

"Oh yes," I said.

"He's told Jim to get Blackfriar saddled for you. He's so certain you'll want to go round the estate at once."

I said again: "Oh yes."

"I don't suppose Blackfriar will have forgotten you. They say horses never forget. He was always good with you, though."

There was a warning in this. I felt a momentary qualm. What if the horse rejected me? There was an implication in Janet's words that Blackfriar, though good with Susannah, was inclined to be less so with others.

"I'll leave you to your breakfast," said Janet.

I went up to my room and changed into riding kit. I uttered a prayer of thanksgiving to my father for bringing a couple of horses to the island and to the Halmers for making me ride so often on the property. They were all such expert riders and galloping through the bush with them and trying to keep up with their skill had given me confidence and a certain expertise.

Just after ten o'clock Jeff Carleton arrived at the house. I went down to meet him.

"Well, Miss Susannah," he said, seizing my hand, "it is good to see you back. We'd been hoping you'd come before. This has been a terrible tragedy."

"Yes," I said, "terrible."

"It was all so sudden. Only a week before I was riding round the place with him and Mr. Malcolm and then ... he's gone."

I shook my head.

"Forgive my speaking of it. We've got to go on from there, haven't we, Miss Susannah, and I'm just wondering if you have any ideas about the estate."

"Well, I'd just like to look at things...." I wasn't sure whether to call him Jeff, Carleton or Mr. Carleton—so I called him nothing.

"You'll be wanting to take a hand, I reckon," he said with a laugh.

"Oh yes, I suppose so."

We came to the stables. The groom stepped forward and said: "Good day to you, Miss Susannah. I've got Blackfriar ready."

"Thank you." I wished I knew the names of these people. It was a great handicap to be in the dark.

I identified the horse. His name was useful. He was beautiful with his black coat in which were a few white flecks about the neck. His name suited him.

"There's one who will be glad to have you back, Miss Susannah. He was always your horse, Blackfriar was. I'll swear he pined when you went away. Of course he got used to your being away when you were in France."

"That's right," I said.

I was thankful that I had always had a rapport with horses and was able to approach Blackfriar confidently. I patted him cautiously. His ears went back. He was alert.

"Blackfriar," I whispered, "it's Susannah . . . come back for you."

There was a tense moment while I was not sure whether he was going to reject me. I patted him and said: "You haven't forgotten. You know me." My voice was soothing. I brought a lump of sugar from my pocket. Susannah had always done that with our horses. They were creatures she was really gentle with.

"That's done it," said the groom. "He remembers that all right."

I leaped into the saddle and, patting him again, murmured: "Good old Blackfriar."

I wasn't sure whether he knew I was not Susannah, but I did know that he liked me; and I felt a sense of triumph as we rode out of the stables.

"Where would you like to go first?" asked Jeff Carleton.

"I'll leave that to you."

"I thought we'd look in at Cringles'."

"Yes," I replied, "if you think that a good idea."

I deliberately allowed him to go ahead. We came into the road which led past the woods and walked our horses side by side.

"You'll find a few changes, Miss Susannah."

"I expect to."

"It's been quite a long time since you were here."

"Quite a long time. Of course there was that short time when I was home after France."

"Yes, and then away again. There'll be certain things you'll be wanting to change possibly."

"I'll have to see."

"You always had ideas about the estate, I know."

I nodded, wondering what ideas Susannah had had.

"Of course we never thought..."

"Of course not. But these things happen."

"Mr. Malcolm was very interested. He was here about a month ago, I think it was."

"Oh, was he?"

"I think he had ideas...he being a man of course. When Mr. Esmond died...he probably thought you wouldn't want to concern yourself with the running of things. I thought to myself, You don't know Miss Susannah!"

I gave a short laugh.

"Of course," went on Jeff Carleton, "with an estate like this people might think if there's a man in the family he should be the one to concern himself with it."

"And you think Malcolm had that notion."

"Sure of it. He thought he might be the next when Esmond died on account of your being a lady, even though he knew, like the rest of us, that your grandfather would hesitate to name him because of that long-ago quarrel."

"Yes," I said.

"Your grandfather's younger brother could, you might say, have a claim on the estate and that claim might go down through his son and grandson. There's some sense in it. Some families don't let the ladies inherit. It's different with Matelands."

"Yes, different with Matelands."

I had at least established Malcolm's claim. He was the grandson of Grandfather Egmont's younger brother. A definite claim. He was the one I was cheating out of his inheritance.

A tremor of alarm ran through me. But it was such a lovely day. The fields were gay with buttercups and daisies; and the birds were going wild with joy because the sun was up there in the sky and spring was advancing into summer.

I couldn't help feeling exhilarated.

"The farms are showing a good profit," went on Jeff Carleton. "All except Cringles'. I don't know what you feel about them and if you could suggest anything."

"Cringles'," I said, as though I was pondering the matter.

"They went to pieces after the tragedy."

"Oh . . . yes."

What tragedy was this? I must feel my way with caution.

"The old man has never been the same since. It seems to have hit Jacob more than any of them. Of course Saul was his brother. They were twins, I think . . . always closer. Jacob always used to depend on Saul. It was a great blow to him."

"It must have been."

"And the farm has consequently suffered. I suggested taking it away from them. They're not getting the best out of the land. Esmond wouldn't hear of it. He had a kind heart, Mr. Esmond. They all knew they could take their troubles to him. I know you used to get a bit impatient with him at times."

"Yes," I murmured.

"So . . . I think they may be expecting changes. There's Granny Bell in the cottages who wants her roof done. It should be attended to. She'll have the rain in if we get any heavy stuff. She was going to ask Esmond to do it, but he was taken ill on the very day I was going to put it before him. So nothing's been done. Would you like to look at the roof?"

"No," I said. "Go ahead and do it."

"It would be wise really. But to get back to Cringles' . . ." I looked about me. I could see fields of wheat and in the distance sheep grazing. The farmhouse lay in a valley. "They don't really take care of the property. Saul was the one. He was a good worker, Saul—one of our best. It was a great pity. No one ever seemed to get to the bottom of it."

"No," I said.

"Well, it's past history now. A year or more . . . It's time it was forgotten. People do away with themselves at times . . . they have their private reasons, and I always say, live your own life and it's not for any of us to judge others. Would you like to see the Cringles?"

I hesitated. Then I said: "Yes, I think so."

We changed direction and rode down between the fields of rye and wheat to the farmhouse.

We dismounted and Jeff Carleton tethered our horses. We walked across a yard where fowls were pecking at worms and whatever they could find.

Jeff Carleton pushed open a door which was slightly ajar.

"Anyone at home?" he called.

"Oh, it's you," said a gruff voice. "You can come in."

We stepped into a stone-floored kitchen. It was hot and baking was in progress at the range. A woman at the table had her hands in a basin. She was kneading dough. Seated in the chimney nook was an old man.

"Hello, Moses," said Jeff Carleton. "Hello, Mrs. Cringle. Here's Miss Susannah to see you."

The woman dropped a grudging curtsy. The old man grunted.

"How are you?" I asked warmly.

"Much as we always are," said Moses. "This is a household of mourning."

"I know," I replied. "I'm sorry. But how is everything going on the farm?"

"Jacob slaves away," said the old man. "Morning, noon and night he slaves away."

"And the children give a helping hand," added the woman.

"Still things aren't what they could be," suggested Jeff Carleton.

"We miss Saul," muttered the old man sourly.

"I know," I said.

"The children will be growing up soon," soothed Jeff. "I was wondering whether it would be a good idea to let Gravel Three Acres lie fallow next year. It's not giving a good yield and hasn't for the last year or two."

"It's all along of Saul," put in Moses.

"Well," was Jeff's mild rejoinder, "Saul couldn't do much about that field if he were here. It should lie fallow a year or so, I reckon."

"I'll tell Jacob," put in the woman.

"Do, please, Mrs. Cringle, and if he wants to consult me at any time I'm always available. Well, we'll be getting on."

We came out and Jeff untethered the horses.

"Hardly a gracious reception," I said.

"Did you expect it at Cringles'? They're all obsessed by what happened to Saul. It's a terrible thing for a man to take his life. They regard it as a disgrace to the family. He's buried at the crossroads. The rector wouldn't bury him in consecrated ground. That means a lot to people like the Cringles."

"I suppose so."

(233)

I had a desire to put as great a distance as possible between myself and the farmhouse.

We had ridden out into the road and were passing a wooded patch when something whistled past my head, missing me by a few inches before it rattled down onto the road.

"What was that?" I said.

Jeff Carleton leaped from his horse and bent down. He held up a stone. "It must have been children playing," he said.

"A dangerous game," I retorted. "If that had caught me . . . or you . . . it could have done quite a bit of harm."

He called out: "Who threw that stone?"

There was silence.

Jeff looked at me and shrugged his shoulders. He threw the stone onto the road. Then he darted among the trees calling: "Who's there?"

I was sure I heard the sound of someone running through the bracken.

Jeff came back and mounted his horse. "No one about," he said. "Shall we go on?"

I nodded.

So we rode round the estate and I saw more of the farms and their tenants. I came through without any serious mistakes but I had been really shaken by that stone. I felt certain it had been thrown at me and by someone from the mysterious Cringle household.

When I came back to the house Janet was in the hall. I could not get out of my mind the thought that she was watching me. She seemed relieved to see me.

"Well, you've had a good morning, miss, that's clear," she said.

"Yes, thank you, Janet."

"There was something I wanted to say to you. It's about Mr. Esmond's room. It's up to you to say what's to be done, of course, but I thought you might like to consider turning out that room . . . like going through the papers in his desk. It ought to be done sometime and Mrs. Emerald hasn't the heart for it . . . and her eyes aren't that good. I thought if you had a mind to it . . . you might want to do it . . . soon."

"Thanks," I said. "I will sometime."

An excitement had come to me. Who knew? I might learn something from those estate papers in Esmond's desk. Yes, it was an excellent idea. It could prove of inestimable value to me. They might give me all sorts of information which was vital to my role.

I washed quickly and took luncheon with Emerald. She was the easiest of all and I found it quite relaxing to be in her company. Her encroaching blindness was a great help—which seemed a callous thing to think of—but I must admit it had to be a relief; moreover her almost complete self-absorption was a blessing too.

She asked how I had spent my morning and I told her I had ridden round the estate with Jeff Carleton.

"Trust you to go into it right away," she said. "You were always urging Esmond to take more interest. I always said it was the castle you were in love with rather than Esmond."

"Oh, Aunt Emerald," I protested, "how can you say that? But I have always loved the castle."

"You need not tell me....So you rode round the estate with Jeff. How lucky you are to be able to get about. I wish I could...."

So we were off on her favorite topic and I was safe for the rest of the luncheon.

I decided to put Janet's suggestion into practice as early as possible and, when Emerald had retired to her room for her afternoon siesta and the household was quiet, I went along to Esmond's room.

I shut the door and stood looking about me. It was an ordinary room—if a room in Mateland Castle could ever be that. The rounded window cut in the wall and the stone window seat alone distinguished it from the rooms I had known before; but it was the furniture in the room which struck me as conventional. There was a sofa, two armchairs, another chair, a small writing table on which stood an oil lamp and the bureau in the corner. The room told me nothing about Esmond.

I went at once to the table. That was where the papers Janet had spoken of would be.

I opened a drawer and saw several notebooks there. I took one out and opened it. A list of names in it was neatly indexed. I turned the pages and saw that it contained information about people and I realized at once that they were people living on the estate.

I saw how useful this information could be to me. If I went

through this book carefully I should know the names and something about those who lived on the estate.

I wanted to cry out: "Thank you, Janet, for leading me to this."

"Emma Bell," I read in the list at the beginning. I turned to the page given in the index.

In her seventies. Lived in cottage since she married fifty years ago. Children married and left. All alone. Depends on what she earns as sewing woman.

Now I knew that this was the Emma Bell whose roof was in need of repair.

Tom Camber. Eighty. Came to Mateland aged twelve. To have cottage till he died. Then consider Tom Gelder when he marries Jessie Gill, housemaid.

This was wonderful. I could go through this book and know all about these people before I met them. I couldn't have a better aid to bolster my position.

I read on with increasing gratification. I decided I would take the book away with me to study. I was enormously exhilarated at the thought of riding round the estate and perhaps meeting Tom Gelder and telling him he should have the cottage when it fell vacant.

These people were coming alive to me and I desperately wanted to make them happy and glad that I had become the lady of the castle. It would ease my conscience considerably and, as I read about them and thought what I could do, part of that overpowering sense of guilt started to slip away from me.

I was deep in the book when I heard the door open. I started and turned sharply, feeling the color flood into my face.

It was Janet standing there.

"Oh, I thought I heard someone here," she said. "But I wasn't sure. So you're going through the papers like I said." She was watching me intently and I felt sure that she was suspicious of me.

"I took up your suggestion," I said. "It's all very neat in here."

"Oh, some of those papers need going through," replied Janet. "I'm glad you're doing it. We don't want Mrs. Emerald starting on it and upsetting herself."

"There seems to be information relating to the estate here."

"That's what it would be. Perhaps inside the bureau..."

"The bureau is locked."

"There must be a key somewhere. Now where did Mr. Esmond keep it?"

She was looking at me with a strange expression on her face—half amusement, half dismay. I could not understand Janet at all.

She clicked her fingers and went on: "I think it was kept in this vase. That's right. I found it when I was dusting in here. I thought I'd better dust in here myself. You know how some of these girls are about dead men's things. As soon as someone dies they think he turns into a hobgoblin—though Mr. Esmond was the mildest of men and never had a cross word for anyone. Oh yes, here it is. In this vase. I think you'll find this one fits."

"Are you sure that it's all right?"

"All right, Miss Susannah?"

"I mean . . . looking into private papers."

Her gaze never left my face and I saw her mouth curl into a smile. For a fearful moment I thought: She knows. She is mocking me. That smile means it's amusing that I who am committing this great fraud should have any scruples at all.

Her face was again set into its usual matter-of-fact expression.

"Well, someone's got to go through them sometime. You're taking over where he left off, aren't you?"

"I suppose that's the way to look at it."

I took the key from her.

"All right then, miss," she said. "I'll leave you to it."

"Thank you, Janet."

"Better lock the bureau and put the key back when you've done."

"I will."

The door shut on her. She was clearly very helpful to me but she did make me somewhat anxious. She was always popping up and giving me the impression that she knew something.

But perhaps that feeling was due to my uneasy conscience.

I opened the bureau.

There were stacks of paper in neat little cubbyholes. I looked at some of them. They were receipted bills and various accounts of the amount of produce that the farms had yielded. There were also accounts concerning the repairs to the castle.

All things I should know about. Then, as I was putting

back one stack of bills, my hand touched a bundle of small leatherbound books. I took them out. They were tied together with red tape; they were diaries and they had been placed in date order. I looked at the bottom one. It had been started last year and the entries stopped abruptly in November. I knew why. That was when Esmond had died.

These were Esmond's diaries and by reading through them I could get some idea of the life he had lived.

I sat with the books in my hands. I felt as though I were desecrating a tomb. The honorable side of my nature would keep popping up to disconcert me. That it still existed might be surprising but it was there.

The instinct for survival, however, was stronger and I could see what a profitable day this was going to be. I was lucky to have found my way into this room so soon and for that I had to thank Janet. What I could learn here was going to be of the greatest value.

I opened the first of the diaries. The entries were brief. For instance:

Tantalus lost a shoe this morning. Took to Jolly. Waited while he shod her and talked about his daughter who is getting married this year. Late for meeting with S. She was furious. Hasn't spoken to me all day.

I glanced through the pages.

Went to Bray Woods with S. Lovely day. S. in good mood, so I was too. Went out with Jeff. He's anxious for me to learn about the estate. Quite enjoyed it.

I turned to one of the more recent ones. There was a good deal about Susannah in it and the entries had taken on a new character. They were more emotional than a brief statement of fact and, reading between the lines, I saw that this was because of Susannah.

I picked up the one which would have been written just before Susannah left for Australia. I thought this would tell me more about recent events. I must discover as much as possible about Susannah.

* * *

S. upsets me. I don't understand her at all. Sometimes she is enchanting. At others I think she enjoys hurting me. Whatever though makes no difference. She was hateful this morning. Argued all the time. She was rude to poor Saul Cringle. He looked absolutely wretched. When I told her she says things that really cut into people's feelings and destroy their pride and self-respect, she laughed at me. She said I was soft and I would never manage the castle. She said: "I suppose I'll have to marry you or the whole place will go to rack and ruin." When she said that I couldn't stop myself. I said: "Do you mean that, Susannah?" And she said: "Of course I meant it." Then she took my face in her hands and kissed me in a strange way. I felt quite dizzy.

The diary seemed to be all about Susannah now. There was no doubt that she had completely fascinated and bewildered him. They had become engaged. He wanted to marry her at once but she had not finished school yet.

The story emerged. I could picture her with her arrogance which came from a deep assurance of her powers to attract. She had something which was irresistible. She could be cruel and be forgiven for her cruelty. I think it was an excessive physical attraction.

I let the book rest on the bureau as the realization of my folly swept over me. How could I ever have thought that I could be like Susannah?

Then I turned back to the book.

Garth came yesterday. He is going to stay awhile. Went riding together, the three of us. S. has taken a dislike to G. It's a pity because he tries to please. "He's an intruder," she says. She was very rude to him and hinted that he was only the son of the companion, a higher servant. Elizabeth would be furious.

Out riding today. Went past Cringles'. Saul C. was cutting the hedge with a scythe. We stopped to look. S. said she thought some of the fences needed repairing. Saul grew quite red in the face. He looked like a schoolboy who has shirked his homework. And the fact that he is so big—he must stand six feet four high—made me all the more sorry for him. He started making excuses. Susannah said in a voice I never like to hear because it frightens people who depend on the castle for their livelihood, "I should see to those fences if I were you, Saul

Cringle." The scythe slipped and he cut himself rather badly.
Susannah changed then. She jumped off her horse, threw the
reins at me and ran to look what damage had been done. She
made Saul go into the cottage and she bound him up herself.
I was glad to see the change in her. But that's Susannah. When
we rode off she said, "It was nothing. Only a little cut. He's
making out it was worse. He wanted me to feel sorry." "Oh,
I don't think so," I answered. Then she turned on me and said
I was soft again and that I should need her to run the estate.
She would know how to deal with people like Saul Cringle.
Then she burst out laughing. No, I don't understand Susan-
nah.

She seems to want to persecute Saul Cringle. She finds
fault with everything on the farm. She acts very strangely. One
night I saw her coming in late. It was raining and she was
wet through. I went out to meet her and she was very angry
with me. "Look here, Esmond Mateland," she said, "if you're
going to spy on me, I won't marry you. I'd never marry a man
who spied."

All day Susannah has hardly spoken to me. She came to
my room last night. She had on a robe and nothing else. She
took it off and slipped into my bed. She kept laughing. She
said, "If you're going to marry me you'll have to get used to
this." Oh, Susannah....

I really could not read any more. He's dead, I kept telling
myself. I am prying into what is for him alone.

I was not surprised that Susannah had gone to his room
like that. Her sensuality was at the very heart of her attraction. There was promise in the looks she cast in the direction of those she wished to enslave; and I had a notion
that if the whim took her she would not be averse to keeping
that promise.

I wondered how it had been with her and Philip. But of
course she had been going to marry Esmond.

I did not want to read any more. And yet I felt impelled
to. If I were going to play my assumed character to perfection
I must know exactly what she was like. The effect she had
had on Esmond told me a good deal; and I had seen her with
Philip.

How had I ever thought that I could be Susannah!

I put together the estate papers and the diaries. I must
take them to my room and study them closely.

I locked the bureau, replaced the key in the vase and shut the door of Esmond's room quietly behind me.

I sat up in bed that night reading through the estate papers. I was sure I should now be able to ride round the estate and talk to people as though I knew them. I was filled with a new confidence. I tried out some of my newly found knowledge on Emerald and I was sure that I did very well. It was easy with her though; she was not one to concern herself with the people on the estate, except of course to provide them with coal and blankets for Christmas and hot cross buns at Easter (a quaint custom which had been carried out for more than a hundred years at Mateland and had been established by a well-meaning dowager) and a goose at Michaelmas. Not that she concerned herself with acquiring these benefits, but she did order that they should be distributed. I supposed I should do that now.

I chatted knowledgeably with Janet, who nodded her head with an air of approval, making me feel like a child who has learned her lessons well.

The next days passed smoothly and I spent the mornings riding round the estate. I stopped and visited some of them, confident in my newly acquired knowledge. Old Mrs. Bell dusted a chair for me and began to tell me about the roof which leaked.

"It is in hand, Mrs. Bell," I was able to tell her. "The thatcher will be along very soon."

"Oh, Miss Susannah," she cried, "I'll be right glad, I will. It ain't nice to be in bed and not be knowing whether the rain is coming in on you or not."

I replied that I was sure it wasn't and she must always let either me or Mr. Carleton know if there was anything else that needed to be done.

"Bless you, Miss Susannah," she said.

"We're going to look after you now, Mrs. Bell," I assured her.

"Well, that's nice. You've come back different, Miss Susannah, if you don't mind me saying so....Softer like. Mr. Esmond he was a soft kind sort of gentleman, always promising though not always doing...if you know what I mean. Praise God, it will be different now...."

"I shall do my best to make everyone comfortable," I replied. "It's a pity if they are not in such lovely surroundings."

"Oh, it's beautiful, miss. That's what I said to Bell when we come here...it's fifty years ago, miss."

I said I hoped there would be another fifty years for Mrs. Bell in her cottage and that made her laugh. "You always were a caution, but if you don't mind me saying so, you're a nicer kind of caution now you've come back."

I came out feeling lighthearted. At least they liked me better than they had Susannah.

After Mrs. Bell, I visited the Thorns. This was a bedridden woman with her daughter Emily, who must have been in her late forties. The daughter was a thin scrawny mouse of a woman, small, with quick movements, graying hair and little dark startled eyes that moved fearfully as though in search of danger. I knew the situation from Esmond's diaries. She had been a lady's maid in a good position until her father died and her mother had become crippled with rheumatism. Then she had to come home to look after her mother. She made a living by doing fine embroidery and making garments for a shop in Mateland, which suited her because she could bring her work home. Poor Miss Thorn, I felt so sorry for her.

She was very nervous when I arrived and she looked at me as though I were some prophet of doom.

"I'm only visiting the estate, Miss Thorn," I said. "I want to know how everyone is getting on, you see."

She nodded and ran her tongue round her lips. She was a frightened woman. I wondered why. I must try to find out without too much obvious probing. Poor Miss Thorn, she was like a frightened mouse.

As I sat talking to her there was a banging on the ceiling. I looked up startled.

"That's my mother," she said. "She wants something. Will you excuse me a moment, Miss Susannah? I'll go and tell her you're here."

I sat looking round the little room with the open fireplace and the table covered with a worn but clean red tablecloth on which lay what I presumed to be needlework wrapped up in tissue paper. I could hear the drone of a voice upstairs, going on and on.

After five minutes Miss Thorn reappeared.

"I'm sorry, Miss Susannah," she said. "I was explaining to my mother that you were here."

"Might I see her?"

"Well, if you would wish to...."

I was not sure whether I should have said that or not. I guessed at once that it was not the sort of thing Susannah would have said. Miss Thorn's startled look assured me of that. However, she rose and I followed her up the stairs. The cottages were more or less all alike. Two rooms downstairs with a kitchen and a staircase leading out of the back room and circling up to the two rooms above.

In one of these lay Mrs. Thorn, a large woman who bore a likeness to her daughter in looks, but there the resemblance ended. I saw at once that Mrs. Thorn was a woman who would have her own way. That accounted for her daughter's cowed looks. It was easy to see that Mrs. Thorn was the dominant character.

She peered at me and for a moment I thought she was going to accuse me of being an impostor.

"Well, it's good of you to bother, Miss Susannah, I'm sure," she said, "and not expected. It's the first time anyone from the castle has come to visit me." She gave a little sniff which I gathered implied resentment. "Not much good to anyone since I got so crippled with the rheumatism. Since Jack Thorn went I've no right to be here, I suppose."

"Oh, Mrs. Thorn, that's no way to talk. I'm sure Miss Thorn won't let you think that."

"Oh, her ..." Mrs. Thorn threw a malevolent glance in her daughter's direction. "Gave up her career, she did, to come and look after her old mother. That's something we ain't going to forget in a hurry."

"She keeps the cottage beautifully," I said, feeling the little mouse daughter was in need of protection from her fierce if crippled mother.

"Finick, that's what she is . . . a regular finick . . . used to living in mansions, that's what it is . . . waiting on highborn ladies."

I was growing sorrier and sorrier for the mouse every minute.

"It was a terrible thing that overtook me, Miss Susannah. Here I lay ... day in, day out. Can't move a muscle without pain. I don't get out. I don't know what's happening. I didn't hear Mr. Esmond had died till a week after it happened. And when there was all that talk about his first illness and Saul Cringle did what he did ... well, I didn't hear of that either. Things like that make you feel shut off ... if you know what I mean."

I said I did and I sympathized wholeheartedly. I had come to see if all was well with the cottages.

"Everything is in order," said Miss Thorn hastily. "I do everything I can...."

"I can see that," I reassured her. "It all looks very neat and orderly."

Miss Thorn said nervously: "They say there are going to be changes now you've come back, Miss Susannah."

"For the better, I hope," I said.

"Mr. Esmond was a very kind landlord to us."

"Yes, I know."

I rose and took my leave of Mrs. Thorn. Miss Thorn conducted me down the stairs and stood at the door, her eyes pleading. "Everything is taken good care of," she repeated. "I do my best."

I wished I knew what was worrying her. I intended to find out.

I rode away and discovered that I was quite near the Cringles'. The farm and its inmates fascinated me. I wondered about Saul. I could picture him, his eyes sullen as he cut the hedge and Susannah taunted him. She had taken a dislike to him, wanted to tease him, show him, I supposed, that he owed his livelihood to the castle.

I dismounted and tied my horse. A boy ran past. He paused to look at me.

I said: "Hello."

He just turned and ran off.

I walked up the path to the farmhouse thinking: I shouldn't have come. It is not very long ago that I called with Jeff Carleton. I thought of quick excuses. I would ask what Jacob (that was his name) had thought about leaving Gravel Three Acres fallow now that he had had time to consider the matter.

I knocked. The old man was sitting in his chair and Mrs. Jacob was washing down the wooden table and a young woman was tying onions into bundles and setting them in a tray.

"Oh, it's Miss Susannah again," said the woman.

The girl looked at me with a pair of beautiful brown eyes, which nevertheless had a haunted look.

"I just came," I said, "to see if you had made a decision about the field."

"'Taint for us to make decisions," said the woman. "It's for us to listen and do as we're told."

"I don't want it to be like that," I protested. "You know so much better about the farm than I do."

"Jacob says that if it lies fallow we'll be short of a crop, and if it ain't so good as it might be, it's still a crop."

"You're right there," I agreed. "I think Jacob and Mr. Carleton ought to get together and make a decision."

"Give Miss Susannah a drop of your cider, Carrie," said the old man.

"Oh, 'twouldn't be good enough for the likes of her."

"Some of us was good enough once," commented the old man wryly; and I wondered what that meant. "Get it, girl," he shouted to the young girl who was dealing with the onions.

"Go on, Leah," said the woman.

The girl rose obediently and went to the cask in the corner. I did not want the cider but I thought it would be impolite to refuse and heaven knew they were touchy enough already.

"It's her own make," said the man, nodding towards the woman. "And it's good stuff. You'll enjoy it, Miss Susannah. That's if you're not too proud to drink with the likes of us."

"What nonsense!" I cried. "Why should I be?"

"There's folks as don't always have to have a reason," commented the old man. "Look sharp, Leah."

Leah was turning the tap of the cask and filling a jug with golden liquid. A pewter tankard was brought to me. I tasted it. I didn't like it much but I realized that I had to drink it or offend the Cringles even more than they seemed to be already, so I put my lips to the tankard and sipped. It was strong stuff. They were all watching me intently.

"I mind you when you was a little 'un," said the old man. "That's years ago...when your uncle was alive and your father was here. It was afore he ran away after murdering his brother."

I was silent but I felt very uneasy. I could feel the hatred in the man and the woman. It was different with the girl. She seemed preoccupied with her own thoughts. She was a dainty, pretty creature and her eyes reminded me of a fawn's—big, appealing and alert, like Miss Thorn's, looking for danger.

I knew instinctively that she was pregnant. There was just the faintest, almost imperceptible bulk below her waist—but it was something in her expression. I could have sworn I was right.

I said: "Do you live here with your husband?"

I was unprepared for the effect those words had. She

flushed scarlet and looked at me as though I were a witch with supernatural powers to search her mind.

"Our Leah...husband! She's got no husband!"

"No . . . I . . . I'm not married." She made it sound as though it were a major calamity.

Just at that moment I was aware of a shadow at the window. I turned sharply. I saw a flash of dark clothing and then whoever had looked in was gone.

My uneasiness increased. Someone had been at the window watching me. It is always disconcerting to be watched when one is unaware of it.

"There was someone there," I said.

The woman shook her head. "One of them rooks flying past the window, I reckon."

I did not think it had been a rook but I said nothing.

"No," went on the woman, "our Leah is not married. She's sixteen. She'll wait a year or so yet, and when she does she'll not be living here. This farm wouldn't support no more. Why, you reckon we don't do well enough as it is."

"I don't reckon that, Mrs. Cringle."

"Then I reckon it's something what brings you here, Miss Susannah. We'd rather you told us outright."

"I want to get to know everyone on the estate."

"Why, Miss Susannah, you've known most of us all your life. Of course, there was that time when you went away when Mr. Esmond was took bad and come near to dying and our Saul..."

"Hush your tongue, woman," said the old man. "Miss Susannah don't want to hear about that. I reckon that's the last thing she wants to hear about."

"I think we want to turn to the future," I said.

The old man gave a hoarse chuckle. "That's a good way, miss, when the past don't bear looking into."

The cider was indeed strong and they had given me a large tankard. I wondered whether I could in politeness leave it. No, I decided, they were too prickly as it was.

I drained the tankard and rose to my feet. The cider was evidently potent. The farmhouse kitchen was looking a little hazy. I was aware of them all watching me with a sort of sly triumph. Not the girl though; she was indifferent; she had too many problems of her own to care for victory over me. I could understand that if she were in fact illegally pregnant. I imagined what that would mean in a household like that.

I was untying the horse when the boy I had seen on my arrival ran up to me.

"Help me, miss," he said. "My cat's caught up in the barn. I can't reach her. You could. She's crying. Come and help me."

"Show me the way," I said.

His face broke into a smile. "I'll show you, miss. Will you get her down for me?"

"I will if I can."

He turned and started to walk quickly. I followed. We went over a field to a barn, the door of which was swinging open.

"The cat . . . she got in . . . high up . . . and she can't get down. You can get her, miss."

"I'll try," I said.

"In here, miss."

He stood aside for me to enter. I did so and the door was immediately shut. I was in complete darkness and could see nothing after the light outside.

I cried out in astonishment, but the boy was gone and I heard a bolt slide. Then . . . I was alone.

I looked about me and suddenly I felt the goose pimples rise on my flesh. I had heard people talk of their hair standing on end. I had never experienced it before, but I did then. For hanging from one of the beams was the body of a man. He was swaying on a rope, turning slightly as he did so.

I screamed. I cried: "Oh . . . no . . . !" I wanted to turn and run.

Those first seconds were terrible. The boy had shut me in here with a dead man . . . moreover a man who had hanged himself or been hanged by others.

Terror gripped me. It was so dark and eerie in the barn. I could not bear this. The boy had done it deliberately. There was no cat . . . only a body hanging on a rope.

I was trembling. I had been lured here for a purpose. That boy must have known what was here. Why had he done this to me?

Panic seized me. I did not know which way to turn.

The barn was some distance from the farmhouse. If I shouted, would they hear . . . and if they did would the Cringles come and help me?

The last thing they would do was that. I could feel the waves of hatred coming towards me in that farmhouse kitchen...from all except the girl Leah. She had too many problems of her own to consider me.

A terrible inadequacy came over me. What should I do? Suppose he wasn't dead. I must try to get him down. I must try to save him. But my first impulse was to escape, to call someone, to get help. I tried to push open the door but it had been bolted from the outside. I shook it. But the barn was a flimsy structure and it shook as I banged on the door.

I had to see whether the man was alive. I had to get him down.

I felt sick and inadequate. I longed to be out in the sunshine, away from this horrible place.

I looked again towards that grisly sight. I could see now that the figure was limp and lifeless. There was something about the way it sagged that told me that.

I stared at it in horror, for it had swung round and I was looking at a grotesque face...a face that was not human. It was white...white as freshly fallen snow, and it had a grinning gash of a mouth the color of blood.

It was not a man. It was not a human being, though the corduroy breeches and the tweed cloth cap were those of a man who worked on the land.

I moved forward but every instinct rebelled against my going near the thing.

I suddenly felt I could not stay there a moment longer. I banged on the door and called out: "Let me out. Help."

I kept my back on the thing that was hanging there. I had an uncanny feeling that it might come to life, detach the rope about its neck and come over to me and then...I knew not what.

The cider was having an effect on me—making me a little lightheaded. It was no ordinary cider. I believed that they had deliberately given me too much of their strongest brew. They hated me, those Cringles. Who was the boy who had shut me in the barn? A Cringle, I was sure. It must be. I had heard there were two sons and a daughter.

I started to hammer on the door again. I went on shouting for help.

My eyes slewed round. It was there...that horrible grinning thing.

I must try to be calm. I asked myself what this could mean. The Cringles had done this. They wanted to frighten me. They must have told the boy to bring me out here and lock me in. For what purpose? Did they intend to keep me here? To kill me perhaps?

That was too preposterous, but I was frightened enough to think anything possible.

I must get out of here. I could not bear to stay in this barn with that horrible grinning thing looking at me as it swayed on its rope.

I shouted again. I banged on the door until it shook under my blows. What a hope! Who would pass this way? Who would hear me? How long must I stay here shut in with that thing?

I leaned against the door. I must try to think rationally, calmly. I had been locked in here by a mischievous boy. But what was the significance of that hanging figure? Why should the boy bring me here with the story of a trapped cat? Boys *were* mischievous by nature. Some of them enjoyed playing unpleasant practical jokes. Perhaps the boy had thought it would be funny to lock me in here with that thing. It was the boy I had seen when I arrived at the farm. He must be a Cringle. He could have hung up the figure there and then waited for me. Why? There was some meaning behind it, I was sure.

I could not stay here forever. I should be missed. But who would know where to look for me?

If I went to that thing...examined it more closely.... But I could not bring myself to do that. It was so uncanny, so horrible in the gloom. It was like a ventriloquist's dummy. But there was something about this one. . . . It seemed alive.

I hammered on the door again. My hands were grazed. I shouted as loudly as I could for help.

Then I listened tensely, and my heart leaped with hope, for I heard a voice.

"Hello. . . . What's wrong? Who's there?"

I banged with all my might on the door. The barn seemed to shake.

Then there came the sound of horse's hoofs and the voice again. "Wait a minute. I'm coming." The horse had stopped. There was a brief silence. Then the voice was closer. "Wait a minute." Then the bolt was being drawn. I heard it scrape out of the sheath. A shaft of light came into the barn and I almost fell into the arms of the man who was coming in.

"Good Lord!" he cried. "What are you doing here, Susannah?"

Who was it? I did not know. In that moment I had time for nothing but relief.

He held me against him for a moment and he said: "I thought the barn was coming down."

I stammered: "A boy lured me here and...bolted the door. I looked up and saw...that."

He stared at the thing swaying on the rope.

He said slowly: "My God! What a trick to play...what a foolish joke."

"I took one look at it and thought it was a man. The face was round the other way then."

"Will they never forget?..."

I did not know what he was talking about, but I was now realizing that I had been brought out of a terrifying situation into a very dangerous one.

He had gone over to the figure and was examining it.

"It's one of their scarecrows," he said. "Whatever made them string it up like this?"

"He told me his cat was trapped in here."

"One of the Cringle boys, was it?"

I took a chance. I gathered I ought to know the Cringle boys. I nodded.

"This is too much. Some people would have had a heart attack. You're made of stronger stuff, Susannah. Let's get out of here, shall we? Have you your horse nearby?"

"Yes, near the approach to the farm."

"Right. We'll go back. I came this morning. Heard you'd gone out round the estate and thought I'd come and look for you."

We came out into the sunshine. I was still trembling from my experience but I had recovered sufficiently to take stock of him. He was tall and what struck me most about him was an air of authority. I had noticed it and admired it in my father and I realized in that moment that it had been lacking in Philip. The man's hair was dark and there was a penetrating look in his brown eyes which would have warned me if I had not been in such a state of shock. He seemed to notice my scrutiny, for he said: "Let me have a look at you, Susannah. Have you changed much since your circumnavigation of the world?"

I avoided his gaze and tried not to look as uneasy as I felt.

"Some people seem to think I have...a little," I said.

He was looking at me intently and I took off my hat,

shaking out my hair as I did so, for because of my fringe I fancied I resembled Susannah more hatless.

"Yes," he said. "You're mellowed. That's what travel does for you. Especially your sort of travel."

"You mean I've grown older?"

"Haven't we all? It's been nearly a year...more than that. I didn't see you when you came back from school. How long were you here then?"

"It must have been about two months."

"And then this wild notion to go to Australia took you. You were going to find your father. You succeeded, I know."

"Yes, I succeeded."

"Let's find the horses and go back. My word, you do look shaken. That wretched scarecrow! They're a vengeful crowd, those Cringles. I never liked them. Why should they blame you for Saul's death? I know you were always getting at him. It's a pity you got on the wrong side of them. All that religious fanaticism. Old Moses is a self-righteous old devil, for all that he fancies himself an angel. I think he gave those boys a dance when they were young. And where has it led them? Saul to a rope in a barn and Jacob...turning into another such as his father. He's a fool too, if he had a hand in playing that trick. He should be more careful now that you're in control. He should think of losing the farm. They're all scared of the changes you'll make. As for that girl of his, Leah...Is that her name?"

"Yes, that's her name. I saw her this morning...."

"I'll bet she has a hard time of it. She looked frightened out of her wits."

I was growing more and more bewildered. So Saul Cringle had hanged himself in a barn! And because of this I had been shut in with that scarecrow hanging from the rafters. There was some secret in the Cringle household and Susannah was part of it.

I suddenly felt very much afraid.

In the meantime I had to discover who my rescuer was.

We rode back to the castle. He was talking all the time and I was desperately working hard not to betray myself.

When we came to the stables I had my first piece of luck of the morning.

One of the grooms called out: "So you found Miss Susannah then, Mr. Malcolm."

Then I knew that my companion was the man whom I had cheated of his inheritance.

As we came into the castle Janet was in the hall.

She said: "Good day, Miss Susannah, Mr. Malcolm."

We acknowledged her greeting and I noticed that she was studying me intently.

"Luncheon's in an hour," she said.

"Thanks, Janet," replied Malcolm.

I went to my room and it was not long before Janet came knocking on my door.

"Come in," I called. She came and I was aware of that alert look on her face which I had noticed in the hall.

"You've no idea how long Mr. Malcolm will be staying, Miss Susannah?" she said. "Only Mrs. Bates was asking me. He used to be fond of saffron flavor and she's run out of it. It's not all that easy to get hold of."

"I've no idea how long he's staying."

"Like him to turn up unexpected. He's been turning up like that...oh, ever since your grandfather used to encourage him after the trouble."

"Oh yes," I murmured. "You can never be sure with Malcolm."

"You never got on very well with him, did you?"

"No. I didn't."

"Too much alike, you two, that's what I used to say. You wanted to take over charge of everything...both of you. I always used to think poor Mr. Esmond got squashed between the two of you."

"I suppose it was a bit like that."

"Well, with you two always at each other's throats...I used to look forward to Mr. Malcolm's visits. I used to say it was good for you." She looked at me quizzically. "You could be a little demon at times."

"I expect I was rather foolish."

"Well, I never thought I'd hear you say that. I always used to say, 'Miss Susannah always sees one point of view and that's her own.' It was rather the same with Mr. Malcolm. There's no doubt about it though, he's got a great feeling for the castle. And the tenants like him too. Not that they didn't like Mr. Esmond. But he was a bit too soft, and then, of course, he had that way of promising and not carrying out. He gave way always because he wanted to please people. He hated saying no, and so he never did. It was yes, yes, yes, whether he could do it or not."

"That was a mistake."

"I'd agree with you on that, Miss Susannah. But he was well liked. It was a shock to us all when he went like that and the people on the estate mourned him."

I thought it was safe to ask about Esmond's death because I knew Susannah had not been here when it happened.

I said: "I'd like to hear more about Esmond's last illness."

"Well, it was like that time when he was ill. You were here when that happened. He had the same symptoms...that terrible weakness that came over him suddenly. You remember how he was when you came back from your finishing school. Mr. Garth was here then. It was at the time Saul Cringle killed himself. After that Mr. Esmond seemed to get better. It was all a bit dramatic, wasn't it? Then you decided to go off and find your father. I know how you felt. I'll never forget the day they found Saul Cringle hanging in the barn. Nobody could say why he'd done it. It might have had something to do with that old Moses. He led them all a dance. Saul and Jacob and now the grandchildren. I reckon young Leah and Reuben and Amos have a terrible life of it. But they got the idea somehow that you had something to do with Saul's taking his life. You'd been bothering him, they said...finding fault.... You were always at Cringles', remember."

"I wanted to see that the estate was running properly."

She looked at me slyly, I thought. "Well, that was for Esmond to see then, wasn't it? They said Saul had been so strictly brought up that he thought he was destined for hell-fire if he did anything that could be the slightest bit wrong. That could explain it."

"How?" I demanded. "If he thought he was destined for hell-fire you'd think he'd delay his arrival there."

"That's just what you would say, Miss Susannah. You were always irreverent, you were. I used to say to Mrs. Bates, 'Miss Susannah cares for neither God nor man.' Your mother went in fear for you."

"Oh, my mother..." I murmured.

"Poor dear lady! She never got over being left like that...and him going off with her best friend."

"They had their reasons."

"Well, doesn't everybody?" She went to the door, pausing there with her hand on the latch. "Well," she went on, "I'm glad to see you and Mr. Malcolm seem to get on better together. It's early days yet. But you used to be like a cat and dog snarling at each other. I think it's got something to do with the castle. In the old days people used to fight over castles.... All that boiling oil they used to pour down from the battlements...and the battering rams and the arrows out the windows...They did all that to capture the castle. Now they have other ways."

"It's all settled now," I said.

She looked wary. "You were always set on being mistress of the castle. I always thought that was why you decided to marry Esmond. Then of course you got it without marrying him. You're mistress of the castle now, and if Esmond had lived you would have had to share it with him. Not that you wouldn't have had your way. I'm sure you would. But it's different now. You're in complete command."

"Yes," I said; and it struck me as very strange that she should always be seeking me out and that she should talk to me in this way. But I dared not discourage her. I had learned more from Janet than from anyone. And I desperately needed to learn.

She said then: "I'll be getting on and you'll want to tidy up for luncheon."

I couldn't help but be grateful to her. So Malcolm and I were old enemies. He wanted the castle. And he had believed that there was a possibility of his inheriting it on Esmond's death. It must have been a blow to him to realize that I—or rather Susannah—had come before him.

I had to be especially careful now. Malcolm knew Susannah but hadn't seen her for some time. Fortunately they had never been very friendly and had in fact disliked each other; still he had all his faculties about him and nothing would delight him more than to discover this fraud.

This was my test. The rest of them had been comparatively easy compared with him. Emerald might have represented difficulties if she had not been half blind; with Malcolm it would be different. He was shrewd; moreover, nothing would please him more than to discover that I was an impostor, for since Susannah was dead he was in fact the true heir. Only a bogus one stood between him and the castle.

There were only three of us to luncheon and I was filled with trepidation. I wished that I had had longer to prepare for Malcolm.

Emerald at the head of the table peered at him. "I guessed you would soon be with us," she said.

"I didn't know Susannah would be here, and I thought I would just take a look at the estate in case there was something I could do."

"Jeff Carleton was pleased to see you, no doubt."

"I haven't seen him yet. He was out so I went in search of Susannah."

"I could not have been more glad to see you," I told him.

"Well, that is unexpected, I'm sure, Malcolm," put in Emerald.

"It was. And in such circumstances! I think the Cringles should be spoken to. This was going a bit too far."

"I hope there is not going to be trouble," said Emerald, "because it makes me feel quite ill. We've had enough, heaven knows."

"It *was* those Cringle boys, I assume," said Malcolm.

I thought I had been silent long enough so I cut in: "I was at Cringles' and one of the boys said his cat was trapped in the barn and asked me to help him free it. He took me to the barn and there was..."

"It was a scarecrow, dressed like Saul," said Malcolm.

"How...horrible!" cried Emerald.

"He was hanging there..." I said.

"And he had one of Saul's old caps on," added Malcolm. "I must say it was realistic until the thing turned and you saw the face. It was a nasty shock."

"I should think so. That's why you've been so quiet, Susannah."

"The Cringles have got to put all that behind them," Malcolm put in. "They've got to stop blaming you ... us ... for what happened. Saul wasn't in his right mind, if you ask me." He was looking at me steadily. "The reason he did it may be known to some...but let it rest, I say."

"Yes," said Emerald, "they should let it rest. The subject makes my head ache."

She then began to talk of a new recipe she had for headaches. She thought it very effective. "There's rosemary in it. Now you wouldn't think that had restful properties, would you?"

I started to talk animatedly about herbs and all the time I was saying to myself: I must find out what Susannah was doing at the time of Saul Cringle's death. That she was involved in it I was sure.

We got through luncheon and Emerald went to her room to rest. I did not ask what Malcolm was doing, but I went to my room with the intention of looking through some of the castle papers.

I wished I could shut out the memory of that horrible hanging figure.

I had avoided reading Esmond's diaries. I had felt reluctant to do so and had laughed at my scruples, which seemed incongruous in one who was perpetrating an imposture which was growing more and more like a criminal act.

At times I had the desire to pack a bag and disappear, leaving a note behind.... To whom? To Malcolm, telling him that Susannah was dead and I had stepped into her shoes. I had no right here and was going away.

But where to? What should I do? I would quickly be without the means to support myself. Perhaps I could do what I should have done in the beginning: stay with the Halmers until I could find some sort of post.

I could not stay in my room. I felt stifled. So I went out and across the fields to the woods. And there I lay down on the spot where I had stood long ago with Anabel and looked at the castle.

The intensity of my feeling amazed and alarmed me. I was caught in the spell of the castle. I would never willingly give it up. If I did I would yearn to be back forever.

It had bewitched me. I realized that it must have had the same effect on Susannah. She had been ready to marry Esmond to get it; and from what I had heard of Esmond it was becoming increasingly clear to me that she could never have been in love with him. She would have that mild, teasing affection for him which I had associated with her and Philip.

I kept imagining her going into Esmond's room, naked beneath her robe. I sensed his bewilderment and delight. Poor Esmond!

And Susannah? She wanted to be admired, adored. I had been aware of that from the first. I wondered why she had stayed so long on the island. Because of Philip, of course.

Somehow in the shadow of the woods I felt safe. It was as though the spirit of my father and mother hovered over me. I thought back to the first moment of temptation and wondered why I who had hitherto been so law-abiding should have become involved in this trickery. I tried in vain to make excuses for myself. I had lost all whom I had loved. I was without means to support myself. Life had dealt me a cruel blow and then...this had presented itself to me. Carrying it out had drawn me out of that depression from which I had felt I could never escape. It had made me forget for moments my parents and all that I had lost. But there is no excuse, I told myself.

And yet, as I lay there in the shadow of the trees, I knew that if I had the chance to go back I would do it all over again.

I was startled by the crackle of undergrowth. Someone was close. My heart started to beat uncertainly as Malcolm came through the trees.

"Hello," he said. "I saw you come this way." He threw himself down beside me. "You're upset, aren't you?" He went on scrutinizing me earnestly.

"Well," I temporized, "it was rather an upsetting experience."

He looked at me quizzically. "In the old days..." he began and stopped. I waited apprehensively for him to go on.

"Yes?" I couldn't stop myself prompting him although I was feeling so uneasy.

"Oh, come, Susannah, you know what you were like. Pretty heartless. Cynical too. I should just have thought you would have looked on it as a sort of practical joke."

"A joke! That!"

"Well, perhaps even you would have balked at that. But I wouldn't have expected you to have the vapors."

"I had no such thing."

He laughed. "An exaggeration. But Garth used to say, 'Susannah's armor-plated throughout. She'll go through life unscathed by the slings and arrows of outrageous fortune. Not that she'd ever let it be outrageous to her.' Do you remember that?"

"Oh, Garth," I said evasively.

"I agreed with him, you know. But it now looks as though that thing in the barn pierced the armor."

I yawned. "I think I should get back."

"Well, you were never very fond of my company, were you?"

"Must you harp on the past?"

"I feel the inclination to because you seem to be different somehow."

"People often seem different after you haven't seen them for a long while."

"Do I?"

"I'll tell you later when I've had time to make up my mind."

I stood up.

"Don't go yet, Susannah," he said.

I stood waiting while he looked at me with that puzzled expression in his eyes which destroyed my peace of mind.

"I wanted to talk to you," he added.

"What about?"

"The estate, of course. You'll have to be serious now."

"I am serious."

"Since you've been away I have been here a good deal with Jeff...and Esmond. Esmond asked me to help. The estate needs a lot of care and attention...particularly care, if you know what I mean. You're dealing with people.... You have to care about them and their troubles."

"I know that."

"I never thought you realized it."

"It seems you thought a lot of odd things about me."

He had leaped to his feet and was standing very close to me. I found his proximity distinctly disturbing.

"Now you are back, do you want me to go?" he asked.

I don't know what possessed me then. It might have been some spirit of adventure in me. I knew very well that his arrival had put me into imminent danger. But he excited me. Perhaps I was a true adventurer and the thought of danger added a zest to my life. In any case I heard myself saying: "N-no. I don't want you to go...yet."

He gripped my hand and held it firmly for a second or so.

"All right, Susannah," he said. "I'll stay. I want to, you know, even now you've come back."

I turned away. I was trying to fight some foolish emotion which would not be suppressed. It was extraordinary, the effect this man had on me.

We walked back to the castle together and we went on talking about the estate.

He did not appear at dinner that evening. He left word that he was dining with Jeff Carleton. I was disappointed yet faintly relieved. It was restful to be alone with Emerald, for she made few demands on me.

She was a little scathing about Malcolm. "He's getting everything out of Jeff," she said. "He's got into the way of acting as though the castle were his over the last years when my poor dear Esmond was so poorly."

"Poor Esmond," I said tentatively. "He never really got over that first illness."

She nodded. "I'll never forget how ill my poor boy was that first time. But you remember as well as I do."

"Oh yes...."

"So ill he was, I didn't see how he could survive and it was painful to watch him. I was with him as much as my own health would allow. And then that recovery...and the horrible affair of Saul Cringle which shook us all so badly. Then you...going off to your father."

"You bring it all back so vividly," I said.

"It's something I shall never forget. It's my belief that, after that illness of Esmond's, Malcolm had hopes. He really believed he must be the next. Your grandfather was a mischievous man. I believe it amused him to let Malcolm hope. He always loathed his brother and he said once that Malcolm was the image of him. I wondered what he said to Malcolm on the quiet. It wouldn't surprise me if he raised his hopes...so when Esmond was ill he naturally thought..."

"He would," I said.

"He was here a great deal while you were away. He did more on the estate than Esmond did. Esmond was glad to leave it to him. Poor lamb, he must have been feeling weak at the time."

"Poor Esmond," I said again.

"You shouldn't have left him so long, Susannah."

"No, I shouldn't have."

I changed the subject by asking about her backache and as usual that never failed to absorb her interest. When I retired to my room I was feeling quite wide awake.

There was something I really must do. I must abandon my remaining scruples and read what Esmond had written about that period when he was taken so ill and Saul Cringle had died, and Susannah had left the castle to go in search of her father.

I undressed, got into bed and took the diaries with me.

I found the one I needed. It was dated some two years ago.

A restless night, [I read]. I waited for S. She did not come. I wish she would agree to our marriage. She keeps saying, "Not yet." Garth is here. He and S. are at loggerheads. I have tried to remonstrate but she calls him an upstart. Feel bewildered by S. She takes such violent dislikes...to Garth and of course Saul C. for instance.

Malcolm has arrived. He and S. seem to dislike each other in a cold sort of way. She is disdainful towards him and he ignores her, or pretends to. I don't believe anyone can be really indifferent to S.

S. out all afternoon. I wonder where. No use asking. She hates what she calls being spied on. Saw her riding in later. She came out of the stables and met Garth. They talked for a while. I watched from my window. I am always uneasy when they are together. I am always afraid she will say something unforgivable to him and there'll be trouble. They seemed to be on slightly better terms though. Then she came in and he went on. I went down to meet her. She looked hot, I thought. I commented on this and she said sharply: "Well, it's scarcely midwinter!" in that sharp voice of hers which she uses when she's angry. "Watching, were you?" she said. "Yes," I answered, "I saw you meet Garth. I was glad you seem a little less irritated with him than usual." "Oh, did I?" she answered. "Yes," I said, "quite affable." "Affable!" she screamed at me. "I'd never be affable with that man." Then she laughed and kissed me. When S. kisses me I don't think of much else. I wish it was always like that.

S. came last night. I never know when to expect her. She does such extraordinary things. She'd brought a bottle of cider which Carrie Cringle had given her. "Poor Esmond, I believe you feel terrible when I come to your room like this. I won't, you know, if you don't want me to." That is like S. She knew that I wanted her more than anything in the world and sometimes that seems to please her, at others it irritates her. She said, "This will arouse your ardor. It will stifle your scruples. Come on. We'll both drink it." She poured it into two glasses which she had brought with her. She brought mine to me, making me drink it, holding it to my mouth and taking a little sip from the glass herself. It was intoxicating. When I awoke next morning she was gone. There is a poem by Keats which reminds me of S. La belle dame sans merci. S. has me in thrall. There is no doubt about that.

I felt ill next morning. I thought it was the cider. S. came in to see me and was dismayed. "It couldn't have been the cider," she said. "I've suffered no ill effects." I reminded her

*that she had only sipped from my glass. "Wrong!" she said
sharply. "I had a glass myself."*

It was a month before Esmond wrote in the diary again.

*Better today. Less feeble. S. getting ready to go away. She
says she must see her father. I think she is upset about Saul
Cringle, who was found hanging in the barn soon after I was
taken ill. There has been a lot of talk and some hinted that
S. had made his life a misery and threatened to persuade me
to take the farm away from them. It is not true. She had never
done that. But she had often gone to Cringles' farm. People
had seen her riding over there. It was all very unpleasant. I
can understand why she wants to get away and she has always
been intrigued by her father's disappearance.*

The entries after that were sparse.

*A letter from S. today. Through someone at the solicitors
she has discovered her father's whereabouts. It is some remote
island, she writes, where he is a sort of great white chief. She
is longing to see it. Garth was here today. Malcolm yesterday.
It was pleasant to have them around.*

*Feeling a little sick today. It reminded me of the illness I
had a few months ago. The same dizziness and cramp. Was
to have ridden round with Jeff. Malcolm went instead.*

*A little better today, but not so well in the evening. I think
I shall have to call the doctor.*

*I wish all the time that S. were here. I wonder when she
will come home. Malcolm says that he will come to the castle
to live if I would like some help. I can see he thinks I'm a bit
of a weakling. I thanked him for his offer. He's staying for a
while. When S. comes back we'll marry. She won't want Malcolm here. I'll have to be careful what I arrange.*

The next entry was a week later.

*Too ill to write before. Too tired to write much now. Think
all the time of S. Malcolm and Garth are both very good. I
wish I could shake off this listlessness.*

That was the last entry. I saw by the date that he died
soon after he had made it.

I shut the book and lay back thoughtfully. It explained little, and I was no nearer to solving the Cringle mystery; but I had a more complete picture of Esmond and Susannah.

I remembered what Cougabel had said of her. She was a witch. She was a spell woman. Perhaps Cougabel was right.

I could not sleep. I was thinking what a dangerous role I had taken on.

Where will it end? I asked myself.

Letters from the Past

The next morning Jeff Carleton came to the castle. He had his own house about half a mile from the castle walls. It had been the residence of the estate manager for generations and it was very pleasant, for Jeff knew how to make himself comfortable. He was a bachelor with a very efficient couple to look after him. Janet said he lived better than we did at the castle, for he didn't have to put up with so many drafts.

Jeff was a man well satisfied with life. He was deeply involved in the castle but not to the point of idolatry. If he had gone to another such estate, in a very short time he would have been as absorbed by it as he was by Mateland. The fact was that Jeff was a very normal man who liked to arrange life to his taste and live it accordingly. We were lucky to have such a good manager.

He had come over to say that he was arranging for the thatcher to call on Granny Bell the following morning. I said I would ride over to tell her.

"That'll please her," he said. "She'll appreciate your telling her. They like to know someone's interested in them."

It was on occasions like this that I felt almost happy. I

wanted to do the best I could for these people, to make life easier for them. I wanted to be able to say to myself: I may be masquerading as someone else but at least I am doing more good than she would.

It didn't excuse me, I knew, but it was something in my favor.

So I rode out in high spirits and almost felt like bursting into song as I looked at the hedgerows and green fields and felt the soft breeze on my cheeks.

I came to Granny Bell's cottage, tethered my horse and knocked at the door. There was no answer so I walked in, for the door was on the latch.

I stepped into the living room. Everything was quiet. The table was covered with a woolen cloth; the clock ticked solemnly on the shelf over the fireplace with the old cloam oven at its side.

"Mrs. Bell," I called, "are you at home?"

This room led into the bedroom. I knew the layout of these cottages now and that Granny Bell used the back room on the ground floor as her bedroom as she could not easily manage the stairs.

I knocked on the dividing door. I heard a low sound and, pushing open the door, went in. Granny Bell was lying on the bed; she looked white and strained and was clutching at her chest.

"Mrs. Bell," I cried, "what's wrong?"

She turned her eyes on me and I could see that she was in pain.

"I'm getting the doctor at once," I said, and was gone.

I rode as fast as I could to Dr. Cleghorn. I knew where it was, for I had passed his residence many times. Anabel and my father had both talked of that house; it was the one where he used to practice all those years ago. By good fortune I found Dr. Cleghorn in and we rode back to the cottage.

Granny Bell was out of pain now. He made her lie very still and said she was not to move. He was going to get the district nurse to come and see her.

"Is there anything I can do?" I asked.

"Nothing really. Just make sure she doesn't try to get up. She must not move. The nurse will come to her and, if everyone keeps an eye on her, that's the best thing to be done."

When we were outside he said: "Not much chance of a recovery, I'm afraid. She's had a heart condition for a long time. And she's an old woman. I give her a few months at most and she'll not get up from that bed."

"Poor old lady," I replied. "We must make sure she does not lack anything."

The doctor looked at me strangely. "It's good of you, Miss Mateland," he said. "It will help her if people call. She needs attention. We want a hospital badly. The nearest one I know is twenty miles off. There was talk of having one here once...."

Yes, I thought, I know. But that hospital was built on an island miles away and destroyed by the Grumbling Giant.

I went back into the cottage and waited for the district nurse. When she came I left and went back to the castle for luncheon. Malcolm was there and I forgot to be nervous. We talked of Granny Bell.

"Cleghorn told me you'd called him," said Malcolm. "He said she would be dead if you hadn't."

I felt immensely gratified.

"I shall go along to see her this afternoon," I said. "They'll have to leave the roof now until she's a bit better. We can't have them doing it while she's ill."

"I'll pass the news to Jeff and he can hold up the work," said Malcolm.

"Oh, please do," I replied.

That afternoon I set out for the Bell cottage and I had not gone far when Malcolm came riding up to me.

"I'm just going to see Granny Bell," I explained.

"I shall come with you."

"As you wish," I replied, trying not to appear too enthusiastic.

"You've certainly taken what I said to heart," he commented.

"What did you tell me?"

"That people need the personal touch. They need to know you think of them as human beings."

"I was well aware of that before," I retorted.

"You gave no sign of it before you went away."

"We grow up, don't we? Even you were a little careless when you were young."

He looked at me searchingly. "I often wonder what happened while you were away," he said.

"I saw something of the world. Travel broadens the mind, they say."

"And changes the character, it seems."

"You do bear grudges, don't you?"

"Not in the least. I'm ready to forgive the new Susannah all the sins of the old."

I thought then: He suspects. He must.

He was looking at me closely and I knew I flushed under his scrutiny.

I said quickly: "Something will have to be arranged about Granny Bell."

"Never fear," he said, smiling. "We'll put our heads together."

We arrived at the Bell cottage where Granny Bell was too ill to notice us, yet she seemed comforted by our presence.

The district nurse looked in. She said she thought someone ought to be in the cottage all day. "Perhaps the Cringles could spare Leah," she added.

"Oh yes, that's a good idea," I cried with enthusiasm. I noticed Malcolm was watching me intently. "Don't you agree?" I asked to hide my embarrassment.

"Excellent idea," he said.

"If the Cringles make any difficulties tell them Leah will be paid for her services," I went on. "She can come to the castle for her money."

"That's a great relief," said the nurse. "I can look in twice a day, but in her condition she needs someone here at least throughout the day. Thank you, Miss Mateland. I'll go straight to Leah."

"I'll stay here till you return with her," I said.

"We'll stay," corrected Malcolm.

When the nurse had gone I said: "There's no need for you to stay."

"I want to," he replied. "I'm interested."

I burst out: "I wish you wouldn't keep looking at me as though I'm some freak."

"Not a freak," he said. "It's just the miraculous change that I can't get over. I like it, of course. I like it very much, but it just puzzles me."

I shrugged my shoulders with assumed impatience. "I have responsibilities now," I said.

Leah came shyly into the cottage. I liked her. She was different from the rest of her family. I had previously sensed she was in what was called "trouble" and now I was sure of it.

I said: "Come in, Leah. You know what we want you to do."

She looked from me to Malcolm and I could see she was more in awe of him than she was of me, which pleased me.

"Nurse told me," she said.

"So you know we want you to stay here and give Mrs. Bell the medicine Dr. Cleghorn has prescribed. If she takes a turn for the worse you can get help quickly. Have you some needlework you can do?"

She nodded and I laid a hand on her shoulder. I was longing to ask her to confide in me. I gathered that few people would have confided in Susannah but there were times when I forgot who I was supposed to be, which was foolish, for with every day Malcolm was growing more and more suspicious. I was aware of the manner in which he kept looking at me. Very soon he would be asking me questions which I should be unable to answer. He gave the impression sometimes that he knew I was deceiving everyone and he was biding his time, waiting for me to betray myself utterly.

"Well," he said as we came out of the cottage, "you handled that rather well. It was as though you have been managing estates all your life."

"I'm glad you think so."

He took my arm as we went towards the horses. I stiffened and would have withdrawn myself but I thought I could not do so without making the incident seem too important.

"The ground is rough here," he said, explaining the affectionate gesture. "It's easy to slip."

I did not speak and when we reached the horses he gave my arm a little squeeze and as he helped me mount he was smiling warmly but the puzzlement in his eyes was as strong as ever.

Malcolm dined with us that night. So did Jeff Carleton.

The conversation dwelt on castle matters, which bored Emerald. She tried to engage one of us in conversation about her interesting illnesses and Dr. Cleghorn's treatment of them, but when each of us was buttonholed by her it was easy to see we listened with only one ear.

"Dr. Cleghorn says Mrs. Bell can't possibly survive," said

Jeff. "She would be dead already but for your timely arrival at the cottage, Miss Susannah. You brought him just in time. However, he says she has been a creaking door for a long time and she can't last more than a few months with all the care in the world. Her cottage will be vacant. There will be the question of who is to have it."

"Who do you think is the most deserving case, Jeff?" asked Malcolm.

"Well, there are the Baddocks. They want to get away from her father's place. There's not enough room there for them. The cottage would come in handy for them and Tom Baddock is a good worker."

"Have you said anything about it to him?" asked Malcolm.

"No, but I know he wants it. No one can say anything until Granny Bell has gone."

"Certainly not," I said. "It would seem as though we were trying to shuffle the old lady out of the way."

"The cottages are really meant for the workers," Jeff reminded me.

"Well, Mrs. Bell's husband worked for us. It seems hard that they have to lose their homes as well as their husbands."

"It's a matter of business," Jeff pointed out. "The cottage is part of the wages. Mr. Esmond let Mrs. Bell stay and so she stayed."

"It was quite right," I said somewhat hotly.

"Of course." Malcolm supported me.

"That's all right," said Jeff, "but it couldn't do the estate much good to have all the cottages occupied by women who had lost their husbands."

"Well, according to the doctor, poor Mrs. Bell won't be here much longer," said Malcolm, "and the question is are the Baddocks going to have the cottage?"

"Let's leave the matter until the cottage is really vacant," I said firmly. "I don't like this talking about Granny as though she is dead already."

I was flushed, I knew, and a little vehement. I kept thinking of being poor and old and rather a nuisance to everybody.

"And," I went on, "don't say a word to the Baddocks. They'll talk and I don't like it. We'll shelve the matter of the cottage until it is really ready to be handed over to someone."

We talked of other matters. Once or twice I caught Malcolm's eyes on me. He was smiling and I felt a brief moment of happiness.

I called on Granny Bell the next day. Leah was there sewing. She hastily pushed what she was doing under a garment on her lap and pretended to be working on that. She was blushing deeply and I thought how pretty she was.

"How has she been?" I asked.

"She does nothing, miss. Just lies there."

"I'll sit with her for a while," I said. "Put your needlework down and go to the farm. You could bring some milk. Tell them to charge it to the castle. It'll stretch your legs a bit."

Leah rose obediently and put her sewing on the table. She went out swiftly and silently. She reminded me of a fawn.

Granny Bell lay still, with her eyes closed. I looked about the cottage and thought of her coming there with Mr. Bell years ago newly married, starting a new life, rearing two children who had in time married and gone far away. The clock ticked noisily and Granny breathed heavily. I rose and went to the pile of needlework which Leah had laid on the table. I turned it over and saw what I had expected. She had pushed the little garment she had been stitching out of the way as I came in.

Oh, my poor child! I thought. Sixteen years old and about to become a mother. No husband and only a terrible self-righteous family to turn to.

Poor little Leah! How I wished I could help her! I will, I promised myself. I will somehow.

I went to the bed and Granny opened her eyes and looked at me. A flicker of recognition appeared there.

"Miss Su . . . Su . . ." she murmured.

"Yes," I said, "I'm here. Don't try to talk. We're taking care of you."

She stared at me, her eyes expressing the wonderment she could not voice. "Bl . . . Bl . . ." she muttered.

"Don't talk," I begged.

"B-bless you."

I took her hand and kissed it and something like a smile touched her lips.

"No . . . not M-Miss . . ."

Not Miss Susannah. That was what she meant. Susannah had never concerned herself with sick old women. She did not sit by their bedsides. I knew I was acting out of character but I didn't care. I so longed to comfort her. I wanted to tell her that we had arranged for the thatcher to come and mend the roof, that everything was going to be taken care of and the last years of her life should be spent without worry.

I think I conveyed that by my presence there.

She kept hold of my hand and we were sitting thus when Leah returned with the milk.

"You could heat a little," I said, "and see if she would take some."

Leah went into the kitchen and lighted the spirit lamp. Granny had fallen asleep and I went out with Leah.

"That's right, Leah," I said.

She lifted her eyes to my face, those big doelike eyes that were so haunted by fear.

"You're good, Miss Susannah," she said, "whatever they say. You're not like you used to be.... You're not the same...."

She did not know how disturbing her words were.

"Thank you, Leah," I said. "I should like you to tell me if there is anything wrong. If you are in need of help... I want to help all the people on the estate.... Do you understand?"

She nodded.

"Well then, Leah, is anything wrong? You're worried about something?"

She shook her head. "I'm all right, miss."

I left her to give the milk to Granny Bell and rode back to the castle.

I was different. I cared about people. Susannah had never cared for anyone but herself. And they were beginning to notice this difference.

At dinner that night Emerald said she must write to Garth. It was a long time since she had heard from him.

I wondered about Garth. I had seen several references to him. All I knew of him was that he was the son of Elizabeth Larkham, who had been Emerald's companion in the old days. She had been a widow and Garth was her only son.

Then I forgot about him. I was so absorbed by the problem of Granny Bell and her cottage and Leah Cringle and her trouble.

I had fears of Leah's taking some violent action. I did not see how she could face a family like hers; she did not seem to be equipped to rebel against them. I had visions of her drowning herself in the stream which ran through the castle grounds, looking like Ophelia with flowers in her hair. Or finding some other means of ending her life. I had tried to talk to her several times but could make no headway. She always insisted that nothing was wrong.

Then two mornings later when I went to the cottage it was to find that Granny Bell was dead.

No one talked of anything then but Granny Bell. The district nurse came to lay her out and Jacks the gravedigger dug her grave. I went to the funeral and Malcolm came with me. I realized that there again I had surprised them all. Susannah had never been to funerals on the estate, though Esmond had now and then. He had often promised to go and when he did not attend would go along afterwards to tell the bereaved family what had prevented him. It might not have been the truth but it mollified them to a certain extent because it showed that he knew what was due the dead.

So I created quite a stir by going and I was glad, for my presence and that of Malcolm seemed to add to the ceremony simply because those who attended thought it did.

I felt tears in my eyes as I listened to the clods of earth falling on the coffin and thought of poor Granny. At least she was at peace at last.

Malcolm took my arm as we walked away.

"You're really affected," he said.

"Who wouldn't be?" I replied. "Death is awe-inspiring."

"I know some who wouldn't, and who would find the death of anyone with whom they were not personally involved quite boring. That is just how you would have been once, Susannah."

He gripped my arm tightly and turned me round so that I was facing him. Moments like that were really frightening. I felt he must be on the point of telling me I was a cheat and a fraud.

"I often wonder..." he began.

"What?" I asked faintly.

"Susannah, what *has* happened to change you? You've become so...human."

"I always belonged to the species, you know."

"Flippancy solves nothing."

"Well, let me tell you I am just the same as I ever was."

"Then you put on a very good show of being something else."

"Oh, I was young and careless, I dare say."

(**271**)

"It was not a matter of youth and carelessness. You were...a monster."

I pretended to ignore that. I went on: "Poor Granny! She was a good woman. She did her duty here all those years and was so grateful for living in that dark little cottage and being able to make ends meet."

He was silent and appeared to be deep in thought, which was disquieting.

As we went back to the castle neither of us spoke very much.

The next morning there was a caller at the castle to see me. It was a young man called Jack Chivers. He was employed by several of the farms, working when he was needed.

I saw him in the small parlor which led from the hall. He stood before me, nervously twirling his cap round.

"I had to speak to you quick, Miss Susannah," he said. "I want to know whether I have a chance of Mrs. Bell's cottage."

"Oh, but..." I began. "Well, it is all but decided."

His face fell. "Then I'm sorry to have troubled you, miss," he said, and turned away.

There was something so despairing about the droop of his shoulders that I detained him. I noticed that he was about eighteen years old and good-looking.

I said: "Just a moment. Don't go yet. Why are you so anxious to have the cottage?"

"I want to get married, miss."

"Well," I told him, "you can wait awhile, can't you? There'll be other cottages in due course."

"We can't wait," he muttered. "Thank you, miss. I just thought there might be a chance."

"You can't wait," I said. And then: "Tell me who you are going to marry."

"Leah Cringle, miss."

"Oh," I said; and then: "Sit down a moment."

He sat down and I looked at him steadily. "Leah is going to have a baby, is that it?" I asked.

He flushed to the roots of his hair. Then he grinned, but it was not a grin of pleasure. Embarrassment and panic would describe it better.

"Yes, miss, that's about it. If we had a place to go to we could get married."

"Can't you get married without the cottage?"

(272)

"There'd be nowhere for her...Leah would have to stay at Cringles' farm. Life wouldn't be worth living for her. The only way is for us to get married on the sly...and then go into a cottage together."

"I see," I said. "Yes, I do understand. The roof has to be thatched, you know. You would want the place done up a bit."

He was staring at me incredulously.

I went on: "I can see how difficult it would be for Leah at Cringles' farm. I suppose I ought to say you should have thought of this before...."

"I know, miss. You always ought to...but somehow you don't. She's awful pretty and one day she was crying. Something had happened. Something's always happening at Cringles'.... It's all prayers and doing so much good and making everybody miserable. And then ... afore I knew what was happening ... and once it had begun it went on. I love Leah, miss, and she loves me and there's nothing we want more than our little baby...."

I felt a great lump in my throat. I don't care what Jeff says, I thought. I don't care what Malcolm says. I'm the Queen of the Castle.

"All right," I said. "You shall have the cottage. There's no sense in delay. Get married and move in. You can clean it up, can't you? Better say nothing until you and Leah are married. The Cringles are odd people."

"Oh, miss, do you mean it?"

"I mean it. The cottage is yours. Go and tell Leah and don't forget it's a secret...as yet."

"Oh, miss," he said, "I dunno what to say."

"In that case, say nothing. I know how you feel, so you have no need to tell me."

I rode straight over to Jeff's house. Malcolm was there. Malcolm was often there. One would have thought the castle was his by the way he concerned himself in its affairs.

I blurted out right away: "I've settled the business of the Bell cottage. Jack Chivers is having it."

"Jack Chivers!" cried Jeff. "He's only a boy. The Baddocks come before him."

"The Baddocks will have to wait. Jack Chivers is having it."

"Why?" demanded Malcolm.

I turned to him. "The castle estate is mine," I said. "I am

the one who makes the decisions. I have already told Jack Chivers that he can have the cottage."

"But it seems unreasonable," said Jeff soothingly.

"In fact there is a very good reason why he should have it. Leah Cringle is going to have his baby. They want to get married right away. They need the cottage."

Both of the men were staring at me.

"Imagine Leah Cringle's living with those dreadful parents of hers," I went on passionately. "To say nothing of the old grandfather. Of course, she can't. I have a strange feeling that if something isn't done she will do away with herself. It's up to me to look after these people. Leah and Jack Chivers are going to have the cottage and there is an end of the matter."

I could see that both men thought it was foolish to allow a woman to make decisions. She responded to the urge of the heart and they, being shrewd businessmen, knew that the head should always rule.

I laughed inwardly. It was for them to remember that I was the one who commanded.

The next day I went over to the cottage and as I stood in the bedroom I heard the door open cautiously. I went down the stairs. Jack Chivers was standing there with Leah. They were looking round with rapturous wonder. The transformation in Leah was miraculous. I had never seen anyone express greater happiness.

And I had done this.

I experienced one of those supremely happy moments which come rarely and are usually brief when they do.

"Come to inspect your new home?" I asked.

Leah ran to me. Then she did a strange thing. She knelt and, taking my skirt by the hem, she lifted it to her lips and kissed it.

"Leah," I said, fighting back my emotion, "get up at once. Tell me, are you going to change the wallpaper?"

During the next few weeks I was really happy, which meant that I could go for several hours at a stretch without remembering the sight of that devastated island and the terrible sense of loss for my loved ones; and at the same time I did not brood on the enormity of this masquerade which I had undertaken and ask myself how I could ever have been drawn into it.

The reason was that I was beginning to be more and more

involved in the affairs of the castle estate. I relished the involvement. I felt I had been born to do just that. If only I had been in truth Susannah, how contented I could have been!

I was delighted to see the change in Leah; she was a beautiful girl and happiness accentuated her beauty. She and Jack Chivers were in a state of bliss. They spent every spare moment in the cottage getting it ready; the roof had been thatched and the place was beginning to look very different from the way it had during Mrs. Bell's occupation. I found some curtains in the castle which could be cut down and fitted to the windows. Leah's gratitude shone out of her eyes.

Of course there was some opposition and particularly from the Baddocks. It seemed, was the comment, that some people were rewarded for their sins and the righteous sent empty away.

Jeff Carleton agreed with that. I don't think Malcolm did. However, it was my will and, whatever anyone thought about it, they could *do* nothing.

I managed to placate the Baddocks by promising them the next cottage which fell vacant and they were, to a certain extent, mollified.

I was discovering a new talent in myself. I had always been interested in people. I understood them because I could put myself in their place; and this stood me in good stead. I was beginning to win confidences and this was quite an achievement, for Susannah had been very unpredictable—showing friendship one day and seeming to be unaware of people's existence the next. But I was winning through. I knew this by the way they discussed their problems with me and that I was beginning to erase the impression Susannah had made on them and replace it with my own.

Not only did it please me to be able to help, but always at the back of my mind was the thought: Is it so bad if I can do good to them? If I can make them happier than they would have been under Susannah, can it be so wicked? It did not alter the fact that it was fraud, but I could do some good through it. Susannah was not here to enjoy this so I was not taking anything away from her. But this should be Malcolm's.

Malcolm! He was constantly in my thoughts. Ever since the day when I had said that Jack Chivers should have the cottage Malcolm and I had spent a good deal of time in each other's company.

Jack Chivers and Leah Cringle were married. I went to the wedding and to my surprise Malcolm came.

The church was almost empty. None of the Cringle family was there. They were still showing their disapproval because of the circumstances.

"Let them stay away," I whispered to Malcolm. "It's a happier occasion without them."

"As usual you are right," he answered.

I was so delighted to see Leah come down the aisle on Jack's arm, her fawnlike eyes radiant with happiness. She saw me there and tears welled into her eyes. I thought she was going to stop in her progress and come and kiss the hem of my skirt.

Outside the church we congratulated them.

"Oh, Miss Susannah," said Leah, "'twouldn't have happened but for you. I can't never do enough for you."

"Well, here you are, Leah. Mrs. Chivers now. You're going to live happy ever after."

"That's a command," put in Malcolm. "A command from Miss Susannah, and you know they always have to be obeyed."

Leah hardly looked at him. She was so shy. But her great doelike eyes were fixed on me.

When she and Jack went off arm in arm to the cottage, I stood for a few moments looking after them. Malcolm, I suddenly realized, was watching me.

"Susannah," he said softly.

I was afraid to look at him, for I guessed I should betray the emotion I was feeling.

"You've really made their cause your own, haven't you?" he went on. "I dare say they will ask you to be godmother when the baby arrives."

I did not answer.

He came a little closer. "They seem pleased with life," he mused. "There's a great deal to be said for marriage. Do you agree with me, Susannah?"

"Oh yes...of course."

"You contemplated it once yourself...you and Esmond."

I was silent. I was aware that I was on very dangerous ground.

"Susannah," he continued, "there are things I want to know."

"I think we should be getting back to the castle," I said quickly.

He had taken my arm. "What's the matter, Susannah?" he asked. "What are you afraid of?"

"Afraid!" I laughed, and hoped my laughter sounded convincing. "What *are* you talking about? Come along. I must get back now."

"There's something I have to discover," he added.

I was sure then that he suspected me. I started to walk very quickly, and he kept close beside me but he said no more.

When I was ready to leave for the rounds that afternoon he was waiting for me.

"Mind if I accompany you?" he asked.

"Of course not ... if you want to."

"I want to very much," he replied.

Strangely enough, he said nothing more to disturb me and I felt really happy that afternoon. I found great pleasure riding beside him in the sunshine. I tried to forget that I was here under false pretenses. I tried to believe that I really was Susannah, a Susannah who cared about helping people and found happiness doing so.

We went past the Thorns' cottage but did not call.

I said: "Miss Thorn has spent many years looking after her disagreeable old mother."

"A fate reserved for numbers of women."

"It's not fair," I said. "I'm going to do something for her if I can."

"What?"

"I've discovered Miss Thorn is full of anxieties. Think of the life she leads! Oh, I do wish I could make her happy."

We had ridden some way round the estate and entered the woods. To me they would always be enchanted woods because of that episode in my childhood.

"Let's rest here awhile," said Malcolm. "It was always my favorite spot."

"Mine too," I said.

"There's a wonderful view of the castle from here. It looks like something out of a painting."

We tied up our horses and stretched out on the grass.

This was the nearest I had come to contentment since my parents had died; and the realization suddenly came to me that I could find happiness again. There was something else

(277)

I had learned. My happiness was not entirely due to what I had been able to do on the estate. It was because of Malcolm.

He reminded me of my father. He was after all a distant connection. There was a strong streak of Mateland in him. I told myself that friendship with Malcolm supplied something that I needed to fill the terrible gap in my life.

He said suddenly: "How beautiful it is! Do you know, Susannah, this to me is the most beautiful spot in the world."

"You love the castle."

"Yes. You too."

"There is something enthralling about a castle," I added. "One thinks of all that has happened there. Just to look at it transports one back as far as the twelfth century and a hundred years later when the first Matelands came."

"You're well versed in the family history."

"Aren't you?"

"I am. But you . . . Susannah . . . you used to be so different."

That phrase always filled me with apprehension. "Was I?" I said faintly.

"I disliked you intensely as a child. You were a selfish little brat."

"Some children are."

"You were particularly so. You believed that the whole world existed to feed Susannah's whims."

"Was I really as bad as all that?"

"Worse," he said emphatically. "Even later. . . ."

"Yes?" I prompted, my heart beating faster.

"Since you came back from Australia I've been astounded. All that drama over the Chiverses' cottage and poor little Leah."

"There's nothing very unusual about it," I said. "It's a sad human story that repeats itself again and again."

"It's Susannah's part in it that's so unusual. You really cared, didn't you? And you've won little Leah's eternal gratitude."

"It was so little I did."

"You showed Jeff Carleton that you were in charge."

"Well, I am, am I not? He knows that."

"He knows it now."

"I suppose you think that a woman should not be in this position!"

He was silent for a while. Then he said: "It depends on the woman."

"And you think *this* woman is worthy?"

"Completely so," he answered gravely.

We were silent for a while; then I said: "Malcolm...you thought when Esmond died this would come to you...."

"Yes," he said, "I thought it likely."

"And you wanted it. You wanted it badly."

"Yes. I did."

"I'm sorry, Malcolm."

He laughed. "Sorry! Of course you mustn't be. It's what's called fate. I never really thought your grandfather would leave the management of the estate to a woman. He must have been very fond of you."

"You've done a great deal for the castle. I wish..."

"Yes, what do you wish?"

I didn't answer that. I could not tell him what was in my mind. So I said: "I suppose you will be going away. We shall miss you...Jeff and I."

He leaned towards me and put his hand over mine.

"Thank you, Susannah. I might be persuaded to stay."

My heart began to beat fast. What was he hinting? Could he possibly mean that he and I would marry...as Susannah and Esmond had intended to?

He was watching me intently. I thought, The moment has come. If he asks me to marry him I shall have to tell. And what would he think if he knew that I was a cheat and a fraud?

I heard myself say: "But you have your own life. What do you do when you are not here?"

He looked at me in puzzlement and I realized at once what a mistake I had made. Of course Susannah would have known what he did.

After a pause he said: "Well, you know Stockley has to be managed. Tom Rexon is a good manager fortunately. That's why I can always leave things to him. If there is a major decision to be made he can get in touch. Otherwise he's completely capable."

So his home was Stockley. I wondered where. I must be careful not to betray myself. It was so easy to take a false step and I saw that I had just made one. I had halted the flow of conversation. What had he been about to say? Whatever it was, he was not going to say it now.

He talked of Stockley and the difference between his estate

and that of the castle. "It hasn't the fascination of the castle, of course, but I love the old place. After all, it's mine."

And as I lay there listening to Malcolm I realized that I was making my position more complicated than ever because I was falling in love with him.

The idyl continued. Each morning we rode together. There was one occasion when my horse lost a shoe and we had to take her to a blacksmith. While we were waiting for the horse to be shod we went into the nearby hostelry and drank cider and ate hot bread with cheese. Food had rarely tasted so good and I was once more poignantly reminded of the time when I had picnicked in the woods with my parents and had had three wishes. If only I could have three wishes now. I should wish that . . . no, not that I was Susannah, but that I could be made the rightful heiress of the castle, and Malcolm could fall in love with me, and the third would be that I could forget the tragedy of Vulcan Island.

That was absurd. I would never forget but I might with good luck superimpose another image over the past. I might find the present and the future so enthralling that I should never be tempted to look back and long for the days before the disaster.

Why should I wish for these things to happen to me? I didn't deserve them. I had committed a mighty fraud and must not complain if I had to pay for my wickedness.

But how happy I could have been if things were different.

That day, I remember, we discussed the case of Emily Thorn.

I had at last broken through that reserve of hers and made her admit her fear.

I had cornered her in her kitchen only the day before. She had been so nervous. She said she would make me a cup of tea and I sat in the kitchen talking to her. Just as she had opened the tea caddy there was the sound of knocking from above. She had looked flustered, frustrated and anxious.

She dropped the caddy and the tea was spilled all over the table.

"Oh dear," she said, "what an idiot I am! Mother is right."

"It's nothing," I said. I took the caddy from her hands and spooned up some tea which had spilled onto the table.

"Go and see what your mother wants," I said. "I'll make the tea."

She went away and when she came back I had made the tea.

"Is anything wrong?" I asked.

"No. She only wanted her lemonade. She must have heard someone down here, Miss Susannah."

I could believe that. If she thought her daughter was with a visitor she would want to interrupt them.

Because Miss Thorn was distraught I came closer to her that morning over the cup of tea than I had ever been able to before.

She had been a lady's maid. She had enjoyed that.

"I had a lovely lady," she said. "She had lovely hair and I knew just how to make it look its best. She used to be ever so pleased with me. She'd give me dresses and ribbons and things like that. Then she got married and I could have gone with her, but Mother wanted someone to look after her so I had to come home."

Poor Miss Thorn, whose only glimpse of joy had been to dress another woman's hair and receive her castoff garments.

I then discovered the real source of her anxiety. That her mother made her life a burden was clear, as was the fact that she was condemned to look after her for the rest of her life. That she accepted, but when her mother died where would she go? She would have to find a post and somewhere to live. How could she do that? She would be getting old herself.

I said to her: "There's no need to worry. While your mother lives, things must remain as they are, but you must not be afraid that you will be turned out of the cottage before we have found something else for you. Who knows? I might decide I would like a lady's maid."

And as we sat in the inn I told Malcolm what I had said. He looked at me searchingly for a long time.

"This is not the way to run an estate successfully, you know, Susannah," he said.

"It's the way to run it happily," I replied. "The change in Miss Thorn is miraculous."

"You're behaving like a fairy godmother."

"What's wrong with fairy godmothers?"

"It's all right when they have magic at their fingertips."

"I have... to a certain extent. I mean I have the means to help these people solve their problems."

Then he leaned forward and kissed the tip of my nose.

I drew back. He raised his eyebrows and said: "I couldn't

help it. You looked so lovely, glowing with virtue." He put his elbows on the table and regarded me quizzically. "Tell me, Susannah, what happened in Australia?"

"Why do you ask?"

"It must have been something tremendous. Like St. Paul on the road to Damascus. You've changed. You've changed so utterly."

"I'm sorry but..."

"Sorry! It's not a matter for sorrow. It's one for rejoicing. You've become a new Susannah. You've become aware .... You've become vulnerable. I always thought you had a skin like an armadillo. All you wanted was your own way. But something must have happened in Australia...."

"I found my father, of course."

He was looking at me steadily and I was growing more and more uneasy.

"Now I come to think of it, you don't even *look* the same. I could almost believe...But then I don't believe in fairy stories. Do you?"

I thought of three wishes in an enchanted wood and hesitated.

"You do!" he cried. "Some old witch came to you, did she? She said: 'I'll make you what you would like to be and in exchange I'll take your soul.' Oh, Susannah, you haven't bartered your soul, have you?"

I could not meet his eyes. But I was thinking, Yes, perhaps I have.

"Don't let anything change you back, Susannah. Please stay as you are."

I just sat there looking at him and I knew then that I was in love with Malcolm Mateland. I felt exhilarated and then despair came to me as the hopelessness of my situation came home to me.

I was a cheat. I was afraid. This was nothing more than a masquerade. I must not let myself become too deeply enmeshed.

But what was the use? I already was.

A few more days passed. I saw Malcolm on every one. Janet noticed. I think I must have betrayed my feelings for him. She was very observant and sometimes made me very uneasy, for I fancied she watched me closely; but I had to admit that she had helped me out with her gossip on more than one occasion.

There was nothing subservient about Janet. She regarded herself as highly privileged and one entitled to speak her mind.

She said: "You and Mr. Malcolm are becoming very friendly. I reckon that's a good thing, if you ask me."

"I didn't ask you, Janet," I said. "But I suppose all friendship is a good thing."

"You remind me of someone I used to know very well. Always got an answer. Well, I reckon friendship *is* a good thing but when it's between such as you and Mr. Malcolm, it's a little bit more good than most."

"Oh?" I said.

"Well, what I mean is, you've got the castle and he wanted the castle, and he could be a great help in managing it . . . and I reckon if you're quite fond of each other . . ."

"Janet, you presume too much," I said.

"All right, all right," she placated. "Perhaps I do speak out of turn. But it could be a good thing and there's no gainsaying that. It could solve a lot of things and that's nice in itself."

So Janet had noticed. I wondered if others had too.

My nature was such that I would seize on an optimistic turn of affairs. I thought to myself, If Malcolm loved me, if I married Malcolm, if he shared the castle with me, what harm would have been done? I could let him take charge of things. I could always remember that he was the rightful owner. Could I, in such circumstances, forget my guilt? A wrong would have been righted. I would stand beside him, help him in what he wanted to do. It would be as it should have been on Susannah's death. It would just be that the heir of the castle had married me and thus I had become its mistress.

It seemed as though the gods of good fortune were offering me forgiveness on a plate.

It was a lovely euphoric experience. It made me feel that I was at liberty to fall in love with Malcolm, to marry him if he asked me and to live in peace for the rest of my life.

Perhaps in ten years' time when we had grown together and we had our children, I would confess to him. By then there would be no question of his not understanding and he would forgive me readily.

Oh, it was a happy solution. It seemed possible that it could come about.

We laughed together; we worked together; and I was happy. We discussed the castle constantly—what should be done and how we should do it. It was almost as though we were a partnership.

One day he said to me: "Have you ever thought of marrying now that Esmond is dead?"

I turned away. I dared not look at him. I knew that his feelings towards me were quite different from those he had had for Susannah, but that whenever we were on the point of getting to a closer understanding he would be repelled by some mystery he sensed between us. He could not believe in the change which had apparently come over Susannah and, while his emotions drew him to me, his common sense warned him against me. I think that sometimes he believed I would revert to the old ways and was asking himself whether I was playing a game of pretense. How right he was! And how often I considered making a confession. But I was afraid of losing him. I wanted to bind him so close to me that he could not escape, even if what I had done did fill him with horror. The force of my emotions was strong, as I believed his could be, but the guilt in me and the distrust in him lay between us like a two-edged sword.

I murmured: "Marriage is something not to be undertaken lightly. You, who have never married, agree with that, I am sure."

"I certainly have always felt it was a state into which one should not enter lightly. Esmond's death would have been a terrible blow to you. Was it?"

I turned my head away, feigning emotion.

"He was besotted about you," he went on. "I always felt sorry for him. You were so different then. Like another person. I should have been envious...now."

I raised my eyes to his face. I so much wanted him to put his arms about me and tell me he loved me.

He took me by the shoulders and shook me slightly.

"Something happened, Susannah!" he cried. "What? For God's sake tell me."

I wanted to confess then. I dared not though. I was as unsure of him as he was of me.

"My father died," I said quietly. "It was a great shock...."

He dropped his arms. He didn't believe me. That was not what he wanted to hear.

With a gesture of exasperation he released me.

He said no more, but I assured myself that one day . . . soon . . . he would. Perhaps he would ask me to marry him and then what should I do? Dare I confess?

Then I began to reason with myself. Why should there be need for confession? In marrying me he would automatically share the castle.

Why shouldn't that be the answer? Fate was offering me a way out.

Perhaps I should have known that was too good to be true. Life does not work out as smoothly as that.

I found the letters in a bureau in Susannah's room. It was a beautiful eighteenth-century piece which I had admired from the moment I saw it. It had several drawers which I used for the papers and diaries I had from Esmond's room.

I often went through these. They had been invaluable in teaching me about people on the estate and I found it very useful to study them.

I was in a state of euphoria, having spent almost the entire day in Malcolm's company. I had called in at the Chiverses' cottage and heard that all was well there; I saw that the curtains from the castle looked very grand and realized that they were a source of delight to Leah; but what I knew pleased her most was my interest in her. She looked upon me as a sort of protectress and that touched me deeply.

So I was ready for bed and I went to the drawer to get out the papers. I intended to sit up in bed and go through them, which had become a habit of mine. I opened the drawer and as I took them out I saw that some had become wedged in. I pulled at them, but they did not come away, so I knelt on my hands and knees to see if I could discover what was holding them.

I pulled gently and still they did not come away. I put in my hand to see if I could feel what was holding them. They were jammed. If I pulled the drawer right out I would release them. This I did. Then I realized that there was a secret drawer behind the one in which I had kept the papers. I put in my hand and drew it out. In it was a thin roll of paper tied up with red tape. I untied this and unrolled the paper. I saw that they were letters. My heart started to pound, for I realized they had been written to Susannah.

I knelt there for some seconds with them in my hands. I was not by nature a person who listened at doors or read other people's correspondence and I hesitated now as I had over Esmond's diaries.

Some instinct told me that these letters might contain vital information and that I must not be squeamish. I put back the secret drawer and pushed the other one into place in front of it and, chiding myself for being so foolish as to hesitate, I took the letters to my bed.

There I read them and after I had done so I lay awake considering their content. They had shattered me, those letters. I could only guess who had written them, but it seemed to me there was only one person who could have done so.

They were dated and in order, so I knew they had been written to Susannah just before she left England for Australia.

The first read:

Dearest and Most Wonderful (hereinafter and forever more known as D.M.W.) What bliss to be with you as we were last night. I never dreamed it could be so. And the best is yet to come. You have to do your part though and it won't be long. Wedding bells and the two of us here—the King and Queen of the Castle. You know how to deal with S.C. He'll do anything you ask. He's besotted. Clever of you to have reduced him to that state. Keep him like it. I don't ask how, but I understand and I'll try not to be jealous of your rural lover. We need his help to get the needful, for it has to come from a source where it can't be traced...just in case. If he supplied it, he'll be involved. Not that it will come to that. We're going to see that it works smoothly.

D.M.W., I'll have to write to you, for it won't do for me to be around at this time. You never know. We might betray something. So burn any letters I write as soon as you have read them. In that way I can write frankly. Let me know when S.C. gives you what we need. A pity he has to be brought in, but we'll deal with that after. The King and Queen will act.

To the day, my love.

Devoted Slave and Constant Lover
(hereafter D.S.C.L.)

I went on to the next:

D.M.W.,

So S.C. is holding off. Hasn't got it, he says. You'll have to get it from him. Tell him you want it for a face wash. They are bound to use it for something on the farm. Wheedle it out of him. I'm getting jealous. I think you're rather fond of him. I am sure you act your part well, but let's get this over and then no more of it, eh? I wish we could marry, but you won't, I suppose, until the coast is clear. You were always a devil, D.M.W. You want to keep one foot in each camp, don't you? You're not going to let go of Cousin E. until he's laid to rest. You want to be supreme, don't you? Remember I'm of the same blood. You know we're a reckless, scheming, ambitious brood. Mateland of Mateland. Burn this letter and all my letters. Get the stuff from S.C. and then make sure you use it. I'm getting impatient for you. I long for the day when we are you know where together.

My D.M.W.

Your D.S.C.L.

And the last one:

D.M.W.,

Have been frantically waiting to hear. What went wrong? Your mixture was not strong enough. Of course I know you had to avoid suspicion. Near to death...that's not good enough, is it? And S.C. quitting this life in that melodramatic way. A pity we had to use him. Still, you're right. We must not attempt it again for a long time. Yes, I agree . . . a year say. Then he can develop the same illness. That sounds very plausible. Who would have thought S.C. would have been such a fool? Let's hope he hasn't talked. That sort do sometimes. They make confessions. I wish we could have got the stuff without him. Too awkward though . . . buying it . . . or getting it through another source. We had covered our tracks well and then that fool calls attention to himself by that!

Now take heed, D.M.W. I like your plan. You're going away somewhere. You're going to look for your father, having discovered his whereabouts. That's fine. You shouldn't be there when it happens again. Fair enough. But I can't lose you all that time. I'll come out with you and then back...and in a year's time we'll have the whole thing settled. We have to be

(287)

patient. We have to think of what the reward will be…you
and I where we belong together.

It's really foolish to set all this down on paper, but I am
foolish where you're concerned…as you are with me. We've
fooled them all with our battles. We'll go on fooling them.
You'll hear when it's done and then you'll come home and you
and I will find that our antipathy was a mistake. We loved
each other all the time. Wedding bells and the castle ours.
Mateland forever.

Burn this as you have the rest. Do you realize that this letter
could condemn us? But so do I trust you. In any case we are
in this together.

I'll be at the castle very soon now and you will be making
your plans to leave. Be very loving to Esmond. But get away.
The Cs may be awkward.

With you soon,

Your D.S.C.L.

I was shattered. Those letters betrayed so much. Esmond
had been murdered. He was the victim of Susannah and her
lover. Susannah had attempted to kill him and her lover had
succeeded in doing so, thus making Susannah mistress of the
castle. Susannah had seduced Saul Cringle and he had provided her with the poison from which Esmond had died—
presumably arsenic since there had been mention of a cos-
metic. And she had been careless enough to leave these letters—incriminating as they were—in the secret drawer in
her bureau, in spite of her lover's urgent injunction to destroy
them. So I had found them. How careless she had been. But
perhaps she had had some ulterior motive in preserving the
letters.

I was trying to hold off the overwhelming fact that had
come out of all this. I did not want to examine it. I dared not.

I thought of being shut in the barn and seeing that horrible
thing dangling from the rafters. One thing was obvious. The
Cringles knew that Susannah had been involved with Saul
and, believing me to be Susannah, had confronted me with
that horror.

It was an explosive situation.

But staring me in the face was the fear which I could no
longer evade. One sentence kept dancing before my eyes.
"Remember I'm of the same blood…."

There was only one person who could have written that. Malcolm!

So he must know that I was an impostor. He must, for his letters revealed how close he had been to Susannah. He could not have mistaken me for her. Besides, considering their relationship, it was quite clear that he knew I was masquerading as her. Then why did he not expose me? If he did, the castle would be his. Why did he let me go on with the pretense? What did it mean? What had I walked into? I was a cheat, I knew. I was posing as another woman. But Malcolm, the man with whom I had fallen in love, was a murderer.

I could see no other possibility.

Malcolm was Susannah's devoted slave and constant lover. He was playing some game. What?

I felt sick with fear.

He must know that Susannah was dead, and he was a murderer. He was a clever actor. He must be to be able to delude me as he did. He cared for the castle. Of course it was for the castle he had done what he had.

And yet why did he not claim it now?

With Susannah dead, he could inherit. Why had he not exposed me?

Thoughts chased themselves round and round in my head. I did not sleep at all that night. I just lay there tossing and turning, waiting for the dawn.

I was filled with fear. I knew that some terrible climax was about to break.

I saw no one at breakfast. I went out to the woods. I could not face Malcolm. It seemed to me that he, no less than I, had been wearing a mask. When that strong and pleasant face was removed, what was beneath it? Something cold and cunning, shrewd, cruel, sensual and murderous.

I could not bear it. I had been so utterly deceived. I wanted to stop thinking of him, and yet I could not. I had already allowed my feelings to become too much involved. Moreover, I was not merely a girl who had put her trust in a man—a cynical man, capable of the vilest deeds—I was one who was herself tainted by dishonesty.

What a fool I had been! What a tangled web I had woven, and I was at the center of this mystery, intrigue and murder.

I must make things appear normal.

I returned to the castle for luncheon. Malcolm, I was

thankful to see, was not there. He had left word to say that he was lunching with Jeff Carleton.

Emerald and I lunched alone.

I listened to an account of her sleepless night and her inability to rest her back. Then I heard her saying: "I've written to Garth to tell him you're here. It's such a long time since he's been. He probably feels disinclined to come here now that his mother has gone."

After luncheon I went out again. I went into the woods and lay there, looking at the castle and thinking again of that magic day of my childhood. I suppose that was when it all started.

But how different I was now from that young and innocent child!

When I went back to the house Janet was in my room putting some things she had washed away in a drawer.

"My goodness," she said. "You look as if you've lost a sovereign and found a penny piece."

"I'm all right," I replied. "I'm a bit tired. I didn't sleep well last night."

She studied me in that way which I deeply resented.

"I'd say you didn't! Anything wrong, Miss Susannah?"

"No," I said blithely. "Nothing at all."

She nodded and went on putting the things away.

I heard the arrival of a rider in the distance. I went to my window and saw Malcolm. He pulled up his horse and paused for a moment looking at the castle. I could imagine the satisfaction on his face. He loved the castle as Susannah had, and as I was beginning to. It was haunted, this castle, haunted by the people who had lived in it—mainly the family of Mateland to which Malcolm, Susannah and I all belonged.

We loved the castle for a hundred reasons, not only because it had been the family home for generations but because of the spell it cast on us so that we would lie and cheat for possession of it—and some of us would do murder.

I did not go down to dinner. I pleaded a headache. I could not face Malcolm...yet.

Janet brought up my supper on a tray.

"I don't want anything," I told her.

"Come on," she retorted as though I were two years old. "Whatever the trouble, it's best not to face it on an empty stomach."

(290)

She was watching me anxiously. Sometimes I thought Janet really cared about me.

The night brought me no comfort.

When finally I reached what should have been blessed oblivion I was haunted by dreams of terror in which Esmond, Malcolm, Susannah and myself were involved.

In the morning I got up early and went down and tried to eat a little breakfast. While I toyed with the food, Chaston came in to tell me that Jack Chivers had come to see me. He was waiting outside and seemed very upset.

"I told him, Miss Susannah, that I would not disturb you at breakfast," said Chaston, "but he said it was so important and about his wife, so he prevailed on me to come to you."

"His wife!" I cried. "Oh, certainly you should disturb me. I'll see Jack Chivers at once."

"Very good, Miss Susannah. Should I bring him in?"

"Yes, please. Immediately."

Jack came into the hall. I took him at once into one of the small rooms. I thought he had come to tell me that Leah's pains had started, and I was worried because the baby was by no means due.

"What is it, Jack?" I asked.

"It's Leah, miss. She's quite upset."

"The baby..."

"No, not the baby, miss. She says she must see you. She says will you come as soon as you can."

"Certainly I will, Jack. What is it about?"

"She wants to tell you herself, Miss Susannah. If you could come..."

I was dressed for riding so I said we should go at once, and I rode over to the cottage with him.

Leah was sitting at the table looking very pale and frightened.

"Why, Leah," I asked, "what has happened?"

"It's my father," she told me. "He got it out of me."

"Got what, Leah? What do you mean?"

"He threatened to beat me, Miss Susannah. I would never have told ... particularly now ... I wouldn't have. But I was frightened ... not so much for me as for the baby. I told him everything and he said he'd get even. ..."

"What did you tell him?"

"I told him about you... and Saul."

"What about me ... and Saul?"

"Miss Susannah, he said he'd just about kill me if I didn't tell. I had to tell, miss. I had to because of the little 'un."

"Of course you had to ... but what?"

"I can't make it out, miss. It's like someone else come in her place. It's like you ain't Miss Susannah any more. You're good. I can see it, miss. It must have been a devil what possessed you. It's been drawn out now, ain't it, miss? I know they can do that. You're good now, miss. I ain't never going to forget what you done for me and Jack ... and the baby. Nor will Jack. But I had to tell him. . . . I had to tell him what you was while you had them devils in you."

"But what did you tell him, Leah?"

"All I knew. . . . My Uncle Saul was tormented, he was. He said his soul was lost. He'd go to hell. He used to talk to me. He always talked to me. He's saved me many a beating. He was good, Uncle Saul was ... but there's no standing against the Devil, miss ... and you had the Devil in you then."

"Please, Leah, will you tell me what you told your father."

"It was what Uncle Saul had told me. I'd seen you ... I'd seen you go in the barn together and stay there ... and then you'd come out and you'd be all laughing. It was the devils laughing, I know now, but then I thought you were just a wicked ... wicked witch. And Uncle Saul would be all shining in the face and looking as though he'd been with the angels ... till he remembered and then he was well nigh fit to do away with himself."

"Oh, God help me," I murmured.

"He used to talk to me. He talked to me the night afore he did it. He was in the field working and I took out his cold tea and bacon sandwich. We sat by the hedge and he said to me: 'I can't stand it, Leah. I'll have to get out ... I've sinned. Most terrible I've sinned. I can't see no way out. The wages of sin is death, Leah, and I've earned them wages.' That's what he said to me, miss. 'The Devil tempted me,' he said. And I said, 'Yes. Miss Susannah. She is the Devil.' Then he started to tremble and he said, 'I can't turn away from her, Leah. When she's not there I know it's wicked and when she's there it's only her.' I said to him, 'Ask forgiveness and don't sin again.' He said, 'But I've sinned, Leah. I've sinned as you don't know.' I said, 'Yes, you've sinned, but people do sin like that. Look at Annie Draper. She got a baby and after that she married Farmer Smedley and she goes to church regular

(292)

now and she's reckoned to be quite good. It's what they call repenting their sins. You can repent, Uncle Saul.' He kept shaking his head. Then he said it had gone too far. I had to find some comfort for him. I kept saying, 'It's the same thing, Uncle Saul. Whether it was with Miss Susannah like you...or a passing peddler like Annie Smedley.' But he wouldn't have it. Then he said this terrible thing. He said, 'It's worse than that. It's worse than fornication and that's enough to send me to hell. It's murder. Leah, that's what it is. She's asked me to help her do away with Mr. Esmond. She can't abide him. She's not going to marry him. You see, she wants the castle but not him.' I said, 'What do you mean? What's castle folks' affairs to do with you?' And he said, 'It's Miss Susannah. I've got to do what she asks. You don't understand. I've got to. I've done it. And there's only one way out.' I didn't know quite what he meant, miss...not until next day when they found him hanging in the barn."

I said faintly: "And this is what you have told your father?"

"I wouldn't have told, miss. Not after what you done for Jack and me. I wouldn't have told...but for the baby. I know it was devils in you, miss. I know it now. I know that without them you're good and kind. I wouldn't have told...but for harm coming to the baby. But I had to tell you what I'd done."

"Thank you, Leah," I said. "Thank you. I'm grateful."

"Miss Susannah," she said earnestly, "it was the devils in you, wasn't it? You're not going to be wicked again. You'll always be your own true self, won't you...kind and good so we can all feel safe with you?"

"I will, Leah," I cried. "I will."

"Miss Susannah, my father...he can do terrible things. He's too good a man not to fight what he thinks is evil...no matter where it is. He says he'll not let this rest. He's going to avenge Saul. He's going to do something...I don't know what. But he's a terrible cruel man...when he has to set wrong right."

"Leah," I said, "you mustn't get upset. Think of the baby."

"Oh, I do, miss. I think of all you've done for us. It was terrible when he come here. But I was frightened, miss, not for myself but for the baby."

"Don't fret. Everything will be all right," I said. I wanted to get away to think what this meant.

I left the cottage and went into the woods. I was trapped

now. I had thought to take on the custodianship of the castle and in doing so I had put on the mask of a murderess.

I was numb with fear, unable to plan. I did not know which way to turn.

Revengeful Jacob Cringle knew why his brother Saul had committed suicide. He knew that murder had been planned at the castle, and it had later been carried out.

He would not let the matter rest. He was going to pursue the murderers and bring them to justice. He was going to have vengeance for his brother's death.

I knew that murder had been planned. I had proof in the letters which I had found in the secret drawer. It was all beginning to fall into shape.

Unwittingly I had taken on the part of the murderess.

I was trapped in Mateland Castle.

As Cougaba had said: "Dat ole Debil" had been at my elbow. He had tempted me. He had spread out the glory of the castle before me and promised me it should be mine... in return for my allegiance to him.

And I had succumbed to temptation. Now I was here in a position growing hourly more dangerous. Caught in a trap of my own making.

I don't know how I got through the day. I could eat nothing, so I stayed out, pretending to be on estate business and that I had eaten at one of the inns.

I came in late in the afternoon. I would have to plead another headache. I could not face them that evening. I did not want to see Malcolm. He was as much involved in this as I was and when I thought of the letters I was nauseated. It was clear from them what his relationship with Susannah had been and what I could not understand was why he was leading me on to believe he accepted me. He must have known from the very beginning that I was an impostor. What game was *he* playing? I needed time . . . lots of it . . . to try to make sense of this.

Janet came in with a tray. "They're concerned," she said. "That's two nights you've not been down to dinner. What's wrong?"

"Just a headache."

"It's not natural for young girls to have headaches. You'd better see a doctor."

I shook my head and she left me.

(294)

When she came back for the tray she saw that I had eaten nothing.

She came and stood at the foot of my bed looking at me.

"You'd better tell me," she said. "In a bit of trouble, I'll be bound."

I did not answer.

"You'd better tell me. I might be able to help. I've helped you quite a bit, I believe, right from the start when you came here pretending to be Miss Susannah."

"Janet!" I cried.

"Think I didn't know? Think you could fool me? You might deceive poor Mrs. Emerald with her sight being like it is and her not taking much notice of anything but herself. But you don't fool me. I knew you were Miss Anabel's girl from the moment I saw you."

"You...knew!"

"Suewellyn!" she said. "I saw you once when you were a little thing. Anabel and Joel came. They were a reckless pair. Yes, I guessed who you were. You look that little bit like Susannah...but there's a world of difference in you two. I had to do my best for Anabel's girl. I was really fond of her. She was a lovely young thing. It was just what she would have done herself, I reckon. Oh yes, I knew who you were."

All I could say was: "Oh, Janet!"

She came round to me and put her arms about me. The show of emotion and affection was all the more effective because she was usually so undemonstrative.

She said: "There, little 'un. I'll do what I can. You shouldn't have tried to be Susannah. It's like a dove pretending to be a hawk. She had the Devil in her, Susannah did. There was them that saw it and knew it and yet couldn't resist her."

"It's gone so far..." I began.

"'Twas bound to. You can't do that sort of thing and not meet trouble sooner or later. Life's not a game of masks and pretends."

I said: "I don't know what to do. I'll have to go away."

"Yes," she agreed. "Go away and start something fresh. They'll look for you, though. Mr. Malcolm would want to know where you were, wouldn't he? You seem to have become fond of each other."

"Please..." I whispered.

"All right. All right. It's funny. He couldn't abide Susannah. It was the same with Garth. I reckon they were just

(295)

about the only two men who didn't fall into her arms. And they might have done with a bit of beckoning from her. Oh, she had all the wiles at her fingertips, that one. But she had the Devil in her...and I said it from the first."

I could not tell Janet about the letters. I could not tell her of Leah's confession.

It was enough that she knew who I was.

It gave me a little comfort.

I could feel disaster in the air. I was uncertain what to do, what to say. I had been totally deceived in Malcolm. All the time he knew. What was he planning for me? He had pretended to believe I was Susannah. Why? He had acted superbly. But perhaps I had too.

I was in a daze. I even thought of running away, hiding myself, going to Australia . . . working my passage over . . . going to Laura or the property and asking for sanctuary.

No, I would talk to Malcolm. I would say: "Yes, I am a cheat and a liar and you do well to despise me. But you are a murderer. You planned with Susannah to kill Esmond and then she went away and you did it. At least I did not kill. I only took what would have been Susannah's if she had lived. And I am her half sister. I know what I took is legally yours now...but you murdered for it."

I could not go yet. I had to see Malcolm first. I had to explain to him why I had done what I had and I wanted to know why he had pretended to believe I was Susannah.

The day passed uneasily. It was just before dinner when the blow fell.

We were going to dine in the small dining room as we did except when there were visitors. As I came down the stairs I saw a man in the hall.

When he saw me he stood very still. Then he came bounding towards me.

"Susannah!" he cried. Then he stopped short.

"Hello," I said, smiling. He was evidently someone I should know.

He merely stared at me.

I took a step down the stairs. He took my hands and his face was close to mine.

"It's nice to see you," I stammered.

Just at that moment Emerald came to the top of the stairs.

"I'm glad you're back, Garth," she said.

So now I knew.

"I haven't seen Susannah since she went to Australia," said Garth.

"No, you haven't, have you?" I said feebly.

"Let's go to dinner," put in Emerald. "Oh, here's Malcolm. Malcolm, Garth's here."

"So I see," said Malcolm.

I looked at him warily. He was the same as ever. None would have guessed that he could be capable of planning cold-blooded murder.

I tried to remember what I had heard of Garth. He was the son of Elizabeth Larkham, who had been companion to Emerald when Anabel lived at the castle. He paid periodic visits to the castle still.

We went in to dinner.

"How did you like Australia?" Garth asked me.

I told him I had enjoyed it till the tragedy.

"The tragedy?" Of course, I thought, he wouldn't have heard.

I said: "The island where my father lived was destroyed by a volcano which erupted."

"That was rather dramatic, wasn't it?"

"It was tragic," I said; and I was aware of the tremor in my voice.

"And you escaped luckily."

"I was in Australia when it happened."

"Trust you," said Garth.

"Now, Garth," said Emerald, "no sparring. I know how you two are when you have been together five minutes."

"We'll behave, won't we, Susannah?"

"We'll try," I added.

He asked several questions about the island and I answered with an emotion which I could not suppress. Then Malcolm changed the subject to that of the castle and we all joined in. I gathered that Malcolm did not like Garth very much, and I fancied the feeling was mutual. Once or twice I caught Garth's eyes on me and he looked as though he were puzzled.

I was getting more and more uneasy, for he was assessing me.

"She's changed," he said at length. "Do you think so, Malcolm?"

"Susannah?" answered Malcolm. "Oh yes, indeed she has. A visit to Australia had a marked effect on her."

"It was a considerable adventure," I reminded them, "and in view of what happened..."

"Yes, in view of what happened," said Garth slowly.

"Susannah is proving herself to be an excellent custodian...or should we say seneschal," said Malcolm. He turned to me, smiling. "I must say I was a little surprised."

"You didn't have much of an opinion of me then?" I murmured.

"I can't say that I had. I never thought you'd give the time and thought to the job. I didn't think you'd be interested enough in the tenants."

"So she is proving a model of virtue, is she?" said Garth. "I must say that shakes me."

"Garth, please..." said Emerald.

"All right, all right," said Garth. "Only I must say that the very thought of Susannah's sprouting wings amuses me. I'll have to get used to it, I suppose. What did you do, Susannah? Turn over a new leaf, repent the folly of your ways...or what?"

"I am interested in everything about the castle naturally."

"Yes, you always were . . . in a way. And now . . . coming into possession . . . I suppose makes a difference."

Somehow I got through that uneasy dinner hour. As we rose from the table Malcolm said: "I haven't seen much of you these last few days. Where have you been hiding?"

"I haven't been feeling very well," I told him.

A solicitous look came into his eyes. "You involve yourself too much with these people. A little is all very well..."

"I'm all right," I insisted. "Just a little tired."

I went up to my room.

I was thinking: I can't go on like this. Something will have to happen. I toyed with the idea of going down to Malcolm now and telling him what I knew. Perhaps I should confess to Emerald.

I took off my dress and put on a dressing gown. I sat at my mirror staring at my reflection as though for some inspiration as to what I should do next. The mask of Susannah was still on my face. But I fancied it had slipped a little

I heard footsteps in the corridor. They paused at my door and it was opened.

Garth stood there.

He was grinning at me. He came towards me and his eyes did not leave my face as he approached.

"I don't know who you are," he said, "but there is one thing I do know and that is that you are not Susannah."

I stood up. "Will you please leave my room," I said.

"No," he replied. "Who the hell are you? What are you doing here pretending to be Susannah? Looking a little like her, yes. But you can't fool me. You're a fraud. Who are you, I say?"

I did not answer. He took me by the shoulders and forced my head back. He brought his face close to mine.

"If anybody knows Susannah, I do. I know every inch of Susannah. Where is she? What have you done with her? Where have you come from?"

"Let me go," I cried.

"When you tell me."

"I...I am Susannah."

"You're a liar. What's happened to you then? You've become a saint, have you? So good to all the people. Winning the approval of second cousin Malcolm. What's the idea? You say you are Susannah. Then let's continue where we left off, shall we? Come, Susannah, you were never so retiring before. Do you realize how long it is since we were together?" He had pulled me to him and started kissing me...in a violent, savage sort of way. He tore at my dressing gown. He seemed to be working himself into a frenzy.

"Stop," I cried.

He paused and there was something demoniacal in his laughter.

"If you're Susannah," he said, "show me. You were never exactly shy. Insatiable, that was you, Susannah. You know you wanted me as much as I wanted you. That's why it was such fun."

I cried: "Let me go. I am not Susannah."

He released me. "Ah," he said, "now you are going to tell me the truth. Where is Susannah?"

"Susannah is dead. She died in the volcanic eruption on Vulcan Island."

"And who in God's name are you?"

"Her half sister."

"Lord save us. You're Anabel's brat. Anabel's and Joel's."

"They were my parents."

"And you were with them on that island...."

"Yes. Susannah came. I went to Australia to attend a friend's wedding and while I was there the volcano erupted. It killed everyone on the island."

"And so . . . you took her place." He looked at me with something like admiration. "Clever girl!" he added. "Clever little girl!"

"Now you will tell them, I suppose. I've confessed. And I'm glad. I can't go on with this."

"A good plan," he said, eying me speculatively. "You took possession of the castle, didn't you? One in the eye for Malcolm. What a joke!" He started to laugh. "Esmond died and that gave the castle to Susannah . . . and then little bastard sister comes along and decides she'll have it. I call that rich. I like it in a way. But it's not foolproof, is it, and when Susannah's constant lover and devoted slave comes along he finds a cuckoo in the nest."

I knew then that he was the writer of those letters. He frightened me.

"It was wicked of me," I said. "I realize that now. I'm going to tell them and I shall go away."

"You could be prosecuted for fraud, you little schemer. No, you mustn't confess. That's silly. I shan't give you away. I'll think of some way round this. So she's dead, is she? Susannah! She was a witch. She was an enchantress. You'll never be that, my dear little impostor. You haven't got what she had. Who else ever had? Oh, Susannah . . . I was thinking that tonight would be what it used to be. Why did she want to go to that wretched island? . . ." He was genuinely moved. He brightened suddenly. "Never let misfortune overwhelm you," he went on. "Never cry over what's done and dead and gone. I'm not going to, I promise you. *You've* got the castle now. All right then. I might let you keep it . . . if you'll share it with me."

"What do you mean?"

"Susannah and I were going to be married when Esmond died."

"You . . . you killed Esmond."

He gripped my wrist. "Never say that out loud. Esmond died. He had a recurrence of a former illness. This last time he did not recover."

It was all sickening. I was learning so much, but there was one piece of knowledge which gladdened my heart: I had made a mistake about the man who had written those letters; it was not Malcolm but Garth.

Mingling with the terror which Garth created was the delight that Malcolm had never been Susannah's lover and that he was not involved in the murder of Esmond.

Garth came close to me and put his hands on my shoulders. "You and I know too much about each other, little imitation Susannah. We shall have to work together and I see a way. Yes, I do." He lifted my chin in his hands and looked into my face. I shrank from him. I was afraid of the glitter in his eyes. "I came home thinking that this night Susannah and I would be together. I was starved for Susannah. And she is dead...that lovely, desirable, wicked insatiable witch is dead. That enchantress of men has gone. The Devil has taken back his own." He almost threw me from him and sat down heavily. He brought down his fist on the dressing table. Then he stared ahead. I wondered what he was going to do next.

Suddenly he began to laugh. "So you died, Susannah. You let me down by dying.... Never mind. I'll get along without you. You've sent me someone who looks a little like you. I could pretend she was you...at times." He turned to me. "Come here," he said.

"I shall do no such thing. Please go."

"I want to look at you. You've got to make me forget I've lost Susannah."

"I am going to leave the castle," I said. "You must go tomorrow."

"Indeed! The Queen of the Castle speaks. Never mind that she has usurped the crown and I know it. You think I'm going to be ordered about by you, do you? No, little Queen with no right to the crown, *you* are going to do as I say. Then you can go on being Queen for as long as I shall let you."

"Listen," I insisted. "I'm going to tell them. I'm going away from here. You can do your worst."

"Spirit!" he commented. "And not unexpected. If you'd been spineless you'd never be here, would you? I've a plan forming in my mind and it could be good for both of us. I fancy you, my little one. You are like Susannah...in a way, and that could be piquant." He took my hand and tried to draw me to him. "Let us put the matter to the test. Let us see if it would work. If I like you I'd marry you. And we'd rule together as Susannah and I promised ourselves we would."

"Please take your hands off me," I cried, "and go. If you don't I shall ring the bell and call for help."

"And what if I were to tell them what a wicked girl you are?"

"You may do so. I intend to tell them myself."

"I believe you would. That would be foolish. It would spoil everything. Malcolm would be proclaimed true heir and we don't want that, do we? No. Keep quiet. I'll make a plan. It'll be like planning with Susannah."

"I shall not make any plans with you."

"You have no help for it. It's either be kind to me or the end of your little game."

"My little game is over now."

"It need not be."

"If the only alternative is to go on planning with you it is definitely over."

"Nice words. Nobly spoken." He swayed on his heels, looking at me. "I like you more every minute. It was a bit of a shock finding you weren't Susannah. But it's no use harking back, is it? I'll go now...if you want me to. But plans are forming in my head. We are going to make a good thing of this . . . you and I together."

I could only say: "Please go . . . now. . . ."

He nodded.

Then he came over to me and kissed me hard on the mouth.

"Oh yes," he whispered, "I like you, little mock Susannah. You're going to come round to my way of thinking. We're going to work our way through this together."

Then he was gone.

I pulled my dressing gown over my shoulders; which were red where he had roughly handled me.

I felt sick and very frightened.

What could I do now?

As I sat there, there was a knock on my door. I sprang up, fearing that he had come back.

"Who's there?" I whispered.

"It's only Janet."

I opened the door.

"My patience me! What's wrong?"

I said: "Nothing . . . nothing. . . . It's all right, Janet."

"Don't nothing me. I know better than that. Garth's been in here. I saw him going out. What's he up to?"

(302)

"He knows, Janet."

"I guessed as much. I was afraid when he came. There was something between him and Susannah. There was something between her and a lot of them. She couldn't resist men ... and there's nothing that men like better than that."

"Oh, Janet," I cried wearily, "what am I going to do? I should never have done this."

"Well, you did, and what's done is done. It's brought you back to the castle and that's where you belong by rights. You should have come back and said who you were. I doubt you would have been turned away."

"Janet ... Garth ... who is he?"

"Elizabeth Larkham's boy. He used to be here a lot when he was young. Used to come here because his mother was here."

"Yes, I know that. But *who* was his father?"

"David of course. Elizabeth was supposed to be a widow, but, well, she'd been David's mistress before she came here ... and Garth was the result. She called herself a widow and came to be under the same roof as her lover. They're like that, these Matelands. Always have been through the ages, I reckon. Leopards can't change spots and Matelands can't change their ways either."

I was thinking: Mateland blood! Garth of course. Not Malcolm. I was deeply relieved because Malcolm was completely exonerated.

I found myself telling Janet all that had happened. It was a relief to pour it out. At least I knew that she was a friend. I told her everything about David's encounter with me on my way home from school and how Anabel had come to collect me and we had gone off together.

She listened attentively. She wanted to know how Anabel had lived on the island, about her happiness there.

"And did she ever mention me?" she asked.

"She did," I told her, "and always with affection."

"She should have taken me with her," said Janet. "But then I'd have been blown up and not able to look after you."

"What shall I do, Janet?" I asked. "I must tell them, of course. I'll tell Malcolm tomorrow."

"Yes," answered Janet, "but let's think about it first."

She sat with me until late and then I went to bed. I was so exhausted that, to my surprise, I slept through until morning.

The next day when I arose I learned that Malcolm had gone out and that he would be away all day.

That gave me a day's respite, for I had come to the conclusion that it should be to Malcolm that I made my confession.

I went down to breakfast. I was glad no one was there, for I could only manage a cup of coffee. While I was drinking it, Chaston appeared. Jack Chivers had come to see me again.

I took him into the small room off the main hall where I had seen him before.

"It's Leah again," he told me.

"The baby . . . ?"

"No, it's her father. She says to come to her as soon as you can."

I went upstairs, changed into my riding kit and rode over to the cottage.

Leah was waiting, her big eyes showing great concern.

"It's my father again. He's left this for you. He said I was to give it into your own hands."

I took the envelope she gave me, slit it, took out a sheet of paper and read what it contained.

I've got something to say to you, Miss Susannah, and I want to say it quick. You tried to murder Mr. Esmond and my brother was a help to you. He was a good man but you are a witch and there's not many can hold out against witches. Now you've got to pay for it. I want a lease to give me the farm for the rest of my days and then to be renewed for Amos and Reuben. I want new equipment and everything that can make the farm flourish again. You may say this is blackmail. Maybe it is. But you can't betray me without betraying yourself. Come to the barn . . . the one where poor Saul hanged himself. Come at nine tonight and have a paper with you promising me what I ask for, and I'll give you my word that I'll keep quiet about what I know. Fail me and the next day everyone will know what you got from Saul and the real reason why he killed himself.

I stared at the paper. Leah continued to watch me, her eyes full of anxiety.

I put the letter in its envelope and thrust them into my pocket.

"Oh, Miss Susannah," said Leah, "I hope it's not too bad."

I looked at her sadly. I thought: I shall never see the baby when it comes. I shall be far away. Where? I wondered. I should never see the castle again. I should never see Malcolm.

I don't know how I got through that day.

Janet came into my room during the morning. On impulse I showed her Jacob Cringle's letter.

"Looks like a bit of blackmail to me," she said.

"He hates Susannah," I replied. "I understand it. He thinks she was responsible for Saul's death."

"You mustn't go there tonight."

"I'm going to tell Malcolm when I see him."

"Yes," said Janet. "Make a clean breast of it. I don't think he'll be too hard. I think he's a bit soft on you. You were such a change...after Susannah. He couldn't abide her."

"I'll have to go away, Janet. I'll have to leave everything...."

"You'll be back. I just feel it in my bones. But wait and tell Malcolm. That's your best plan."

"So I thought."

I went out so that I did not need to come back for luncheon. I had another day here, for Malcolm could not be back until late. I would not speak to him today. It would be tomorrow.

I came back and went to my room. It was the middle of the afternoon. I took out Jacob Cringle's letter and read it again.

The strange thing was that I had been turning over in my mind the possibility of giving new equipment to the Cringles' farm, to give Jacob an incentive to work harder, for I knew he was a good farmer. I should in time have given him all he was demanding. But he hated me...because he thought I was Susannah. I wanted to tell him that I understood, he wanted vengeance. But how could I?

As I sat there, the letter in my hand, the door opened and to my horror I saw that it was Garth.

"Ah, the little impostor," he said. "Are you glad to see me?"

"No," I answered.

"And what have you got there?"

He snatched the letter from me and when he read it his expression changed.

"Silly man!" he said. "He knows too much."

"I am not going to see him," I replied.

"But you must."

"I am going to tell Malcolm as soon as I get the chance. There will be no need for me to see Jacob Cringle."

He was thoughtful, looking at me through narrowed eyes.

"If you don't see him he will come to the castle. He will shout the truth for all to hear. You should see him and explain who you are. Tell him that, and he'll have no case. Susannah is dead. That's the end of it. It's the only way."

"I think I should tell Malcolm first."

"Malcolm will not be back until late tonight. You have to see Jacob first."

I was thoughtful.

"I'll come with you. I'll protect you," he said.

"I don't need you with me."

"Very well. But it won't do for him to go about shouting all this." He tapped the letter.

"I'll see him tonight. I'll explain."

He nodded.

To my surprise he did not pester me further.

I had made up my mind. I was going to see Jacob Cringle. I was going to tell him that I was not Susannah, that I had never known his brother Saul and that Susannah was dead. Perhaps that would satisfy him and ease his craving for revenge.

Then I was coming back and I was going to tell Malcolm the truth.

I felt a sense of relief. My mad masquerade was coming to an end. Whatever the price asked, I must pay it and bear whatever was coming to me, for I deserved it.

The day seemed as though it would never end. I was glad when it was time for dinner, though I could not eat. Garth, Emerald and I kept up some sort of conversation. I can't remember what I said but, whatever it was, it was very vague, I am sure. I was thinking all the time of what I was going to say to Jacob Cringle and most of all how I would tell Malcolm afterwards.

I dreaded the evening and yet I could not wait for it to come.

When the meal was over I hurried to my room and changed into my riding habit. It was half past eight and my rendezvous with Jacob Cringle was for nine o'clock. It would take me ten minutes to ride to the barn.

Janet came in. She was very distressed.

"You ought not to go," she said. "I don't like it."

"I must go, Janet," I told her. "I have to talk to Jacob Cringle. He must have an explanation. His brother died and he blames Susannah. I took her place...and I feel I owe him an explanation."

"To write a letter like that...it's nothing short of blackmail and blackmailers are bad people."

"I don't think it is quite as simple as that. I think there is a difference in this case. Anyway, I've made up my mind."

As we stood there we heard the sound of a horse's hoofs below.

"That would be Malcolm," said Janet, looking at me steadily.

"I shall tell him tonight. As soon as I get back I shall tell him."

"Don't go," begged Janet urgently.

But I shook my head.

She stood still looking after me as I went out.

In the stables I mounted my horse. Malcolm's was there. So it *was* he who had just come in. One of the grooms would be coming soon to tend his horse, so I had to be quick.

I rode out of the stables. The barn looked eerie in moonlight. I had never got over my dread of the place since I had seen that horrible thing hanging there.

I tied up my horse and as I was doing so I heard the sound of a rider approaching. I thought it must be Jacob. I looked around me and someone was leaping down beside me. It was Garth.

"I'm coming with you," he said.

"But..." I began.

"No buts," he commanded. "You can't handle this alone. You need help."

"I want no help."

"But you're going to get it whether you want it or not."

He took my arm. I tried to shrug him off but he held on firmly.

"Come on," he said.

The barn door creaked as we opened it. We went in. Jacob was there with the lantern. I saw that the scarecrow was still hanging from the rafters.

"So you've come, miss," said Jacob, and broke off when he saw that I was not alone.

"Yes," I said, "I came. I've come to tell you that you are mistaken."

"Not me, miss. You can't talk me out of this. My brother Saul killed himself, they say, but it was you what led him to it."

"No, no. I'm not Susannah Mateland. I am her half sister. I took her place."

Garth was gripping my arm so strongly that it hurt.

"Shut up, you little fool," he muttered.

Then he said loudly, blusteringly: "What's all this about, Cringle? You're trying to blackmail Miss Mateland."

"Miss Mateland ruined us when she lured my brother to his death. We lost heart then. I want a chance to start again . . . that's all . . . to build up the farm . . . as she took him away from us, so she should give this to us."

"And what will you do, my good man, if I tell you that this night's work has lost you your farm?"

I caught my breath. "No . . . no, that's not so. . . ."

"I'll tell you what I'd say," cried Jacob. "I'd say I'd make this place too hot to hold you two. I'd have you brought to justice."

"Do you know what you have done, Cringle?" murmured Garth lightly. "You have just signed your death warrant."

"What do you mean . . . ?" began Jacob.

I screamed, for Garth had taken a pistol from his pocket and was pointing it at Jacob. But Jacob was too quick for him. He made a dash for Garth and caught the hand which held the weapon.

The two men struggled. I stood cowering against the wall.

Then the door opened and someone came in just as the pistol shot rang out. I stared in horror at the blood spattering the wall.

The pistol had fallen to the ground, and Jacob Cringle was staring at the body lying there.

It was Malcolm who had come in and the sight of him overwhelmed me with relief. He knelt beside Garth.

"He's dead," he said quietly.

There was a terrible silence in the barn. The light from the lantern shone on that macabre scene. From the rafters the horrible scarecrow dangled, his face turning towards us . . . with the red gash in its face where the mouth should have been.

And on the floor lay Garth.

(308)

Jacob Cringle covered his face with his hands and began to sob. "I've killed him. I've killed him. I've done murder. 'Twas Satan's work."

Malcolm said nothing for a moment. I thought the terrible silence was going on and on. It was like a nightmare. I could not believe it was real. I was desperately hoping that I should wake up soon.

Then Malcolm spoke. "Something has to be done...and quickly."

Jacob lowered his hands and stared at him. Malcolm was pale; he looked grim and determined.

"He's dead," he said. "There's no doubt of it."

"And I killed him," whispered Jacob. "Damned forever, I be."

"You killed him defending yourself," said Malcolm. "If you hadn't killed him he would have killed you. That's self-defense and no crime. We have to act quickly. Now listen to me, Jacob. You've let your lust for revenge get the better of your good sense. You're a good man at heart, Jacob, and you'd be a better one if you were not so self-righteous. We've got to act at once. I've thought of this rather quickly, so it may have flaws. On the face of it, it seems it might work. You're going to help me."

"W-what, sir?"

"After tonight you shall have a lease on the farm for yourself and your children, and you shall have the equipment to make the farm prosperous again. This lady is not Miss Susannah Mateland. She has been masquerading as the owner of the castle. You will understand in due course. But there could be trouble. A man has been killed tonight and no matter how it happened there will be questions asked and blame attached. You and I are going to set fire to this barn, Jacob. We are going to wipe out all trace of what happened tonight. We'll leave the lantern here among the hay. The fire has to seem accidental. Two people are going to appear to have died in the fire. Garth Larkham and this lady. This will be the end of Susannah Mateland as well as Garth Larkham."

He turned to me. "Listen carefully. You will go back to the castle, take as much money as you can lay your hands on. Take my horse, not your own. Leave yours here. Try not to be seen, but if you are, act naturally. Don't let it be seen that you are riding my horse, so don't take it to the stables. Tether it in the woods while you return to the castle. When you have taken the money come back to my horse and ride to Denborough station. It is a distance of twenty miles. Stay at the inn there and leave my horse. I will collect it tomorrow. Take the train to London. There is one at six in the morning. And when you are in London you will assume your real identity...and lose yourself."

I felt desperately unhappy. My masquerade was over and so was everything that was worthwhile to me. I could hear the coldness in his voice. He despised me.

He had, of course, every reason to. But at least he was giving me a chance to escape.

He said: "Give me that ring you are wearing."

I stammered: "My father gave it to me."

"Give it to me," he went on sternly. "And your belt and your brooch."

With trembling fingers I drew them off and gave them to him.

"They will provide some evidence of your presence here in the burned-out barn, even though they won't find your body. Well, Jacob, what do you say?"

"I'll do as you say, sir. 'Tis true I had no intent to kill him. It just went off."

"I think he intended to kill you, Jacob, to silence you forever. Give me the pistol. It comes from the castle. I'll take it back." He turned to me. "What are you waiting for? Count yourself fortunate. It's time you were off."

I moved away. He called after me: "You know what to do. It's imperative not to make a mistake. Get out...unseen if you possibly can...and don't forget, take the six o'clock train to London."

I stumbled out as though in a daze. I took his horse and rode back to the castle.

No one saw me as I went to my room. Janet was there, looking very agitated.

"I sent him off after you," she said. "I showed him Jacob's note and told him who you were."

"Oh, Janet," I said, "it's the end. I'm going away...tonight."

"Tonight!" she cried.

"Yes. You'll hear what happened. Garth is dead. But it's all going to seem different from what it actually was. And I'm to go right away...away from you all, Janet."

"I'm coming with you."

"No, you can't. It wouldn't work if you did. I've got to disappear and people have to think I was burned to death in the barn with Garth."

"I don't understand all this," said Janet.

"You will...and you'll know the truth. It's the end. It has to be the end. I must obey him. He said I was not to delay but to get away quickly. I must go. I must take what money I can. I'm going to London. I have to make a new life for myself."

Janet ran out of the room while I collected what money I could. It was not a great deal but with care it would last a few months. Janet came back with a bag full of sovereigns and a cameo brooch.

"Take them," she said. "And let me know what happens. Write to me. Promise. No...swear. Always let me know where you are. The brooch was given to me by Anabel. It'll fetch a nice little bit."

"I can't take this, Janet."

"You can and I'll be mortally offended if you don't. Take it . . . and let me know where you are . . . always."

"I will, Janet."

"That's a solemn vow."

She put her arms round me and we clung together for a few moments. It was the first time I had ever seen Janet show great emotion.

Then I left the castle. I went to that spot where I had tethered Malcolm's horse. I stopped only for a moment to look back at the castle shimmering ghostlike in the moonlight.

As I turned and rode away I saw a conflagration on the other side of the woods. I could smell the acrid burning and I knew that the barn was now on fire. It was destroying the evidence of what had happened that night. Garth was dead; Susannah was dead. The masquerade was over.

After the Masquerade

Three months have passed.

I suppose I am not unfortunate. Mrs. Christopher is good to me. I arise every morning at six-thirty, make her tea, take it in to her, draw the blinds and ask if she has had a good night. Then I have my breakfast, which is brought to me by one of the maids, a little grudgingly, for she does not see why she should be asked to wait on the companion. Then I help Mrs. Christopher with her toilet. She is crippled with rheumatism and finds walking painful. After that I take her out for her morning ride in her Bath chair. I walk along the promenade, for we are in Bournemouth, and she stops and chats with acquaintances while I stand by and sometimes get a bleak good morning addressed to me.

Then I take her back. And in the afternoon while she rests, I exercise the pekingese, who is a bad-tempered creature and about as fond of me as I am of him, which means there is a state of armed neutrality between us which could break into open warfare at any moment. I go to the lending library and choose books—romantic tales of love and passion—which please Mrs. Christopher. These in due course I read to her.

So the days drift by.

Mrs. Christopher is a kindly woman who tries to make life easy for those about her; and I appreciate this, having spent three weeks in the employ of a rich dowager in Belgrave

Square. I was what she called her "social secretary," which consisted of a variety of tasks, all of which were expected to be performed with the utmost speed and efficiency all at once. I think I might have endured the work but what I could not stand was the dowager's imperious temper. So I resigned and by great good luck found Mrs. Christopher.

I passed from humiliation to boredom; and I think that the latter was more bearable because I had experienced the former.

I kept my promise and write regularly to Janet. I gave her details of the dowager and Mrs. Christopher and I am sure she was shocked that such a fate should have befallen one of the Matelands, even if born on the wrong side of the blanket.

I heard from her what had happened.

It was presumed that Garth and Susannah had gone to the barn for some purpose and had taken a lantern with them. The lantern had overturned and set fire to the dry hay, which had gone up in flames in no time. They had been unable to get out of the barn and had been burned to death. Remains of Garth's body had been found and, although there was no trace of Susannah's, some of her jewelry and a belt she was known to have been wearing that day were identified.

Malcolm had taken over the castle. Cringles' farm was beginning to look as it had in the old days before Saul's death. Leah had her baby—a boy. She had been really upset by the death of Susannah.

That was all the news there was of the castle.

As for myself, I should be grateful that I got off so lightly. All I have to do now is to carry on with the life I'm leading and as time passes that reckless masquerade of mine will recede farther into the past.

As I walked the promenade with the pekingese snapping at my heels, as I brooded over the books in the library, I thought a good deal of Malcolm.

Of course he had been disgusted by my deceit. I was aware of that in the barn. Yet he had rescued me. He had saved Jacob Cringle from unpleasantness, for even though he was innocent of murder he would have had difficulty in proving it. And what could have happened to me? Suppose Garth had killed Jacob, I should have been in a very dangerous position. I could have been implicated in murder. I felt cold with fear when I thought of it. It might well have been that I should have been accused. There could certainly have been a strong reason for my wanting to be rid of Jacob. What would Garth have done and said then? He had been completely unscrupulous, I knew. Would he have slipped away and left me to stand accused? But I had been saved...saved by Malcolm. He had made it possible for the Susannah I had created to die, leaving me, Suewellyn, to go free and pursue my life.

I try not to think of him, but that is impossible. He is always in my thoughts. Sometimes when I am reading I will be saying the words without thinking of their meaning because my thoughts are at the castle in those days, now seeming so far away, when Malcolm and I rode out together and talked so earnestly of castle matters.

How I long to be there again! I want to ride under the gatehouse, to look at those gray impregnable walls, to feel the glow of pride in the home of my ancestors.

But it has all gone. It is all lost to me. I shall never see it again.

"You're dreaming," Mrs. Christopher used to say to me.

"I'm sorry," I would reply.

"Was it a false lover?" she asked hopefully.

"No...I never had a lover."

"Someone who never spoke?"

She patted my hand. She was romantic. She was living in the books we read; she cried for good people who were wronged and grew angry about the wicked ones.

She said: "You're too young to be shut away looking after an old woman. Never mind. Perhaps you'll meet someone nice on the promenade one day."

I grew fond of her as I think she did of me, and although I did not think she wished to lose me, I knew she would be glad if some handsome hero fell in love with me as I walked the promenade and carried me off to be his bride.

So I should not complain. When I thought of my dowager I was very grateful for the good fortune which had brought me into Mrs. Christopher's path.

It was a cold windy October day. It was always bitterly cold along the front on such days and I had been hard put to it to hold on my hat and keep control of the dog on his leash. He knew of my difficulties, I was sure, and kept sitting down, refusing to budge, so that I had had more or less to pull him along.

When I came in the maid said that Mrs. Christopher wished to see me.

She was excited, her cheeks pink, her hair slightly ruffled, for she had a habit of pulling at it when she was excited.

"There has been someone asking for you," she told me, her eyes round with curiosity.

"For me? Are you sure?"

"Quite. He said your name very distinctly."

"A man...?"

"Oh yes." Mrs. Christopher dimpled. "A very distinguished-looking man."

"Where is he?"

"I kept him here. He's in the drawing room. I wasn't going to let him go. I said you'd be coming back soon and I shut him in there with the *Lady's Companion*."

"Oh, thank you...."

"You'd better tidy up first, eh? Your hair's untidy...and perhaps you should put on a prettier blouse."

I tidied up a bit and went along to the drawing room.

Malcolm rose as I entered.

"Hello," he said. And: "Hello," I replied.

He stood looking at me. "So you live here. Companion to the old lady?"

I nodded.

"I should have come before," he said.

"Oh no...no.... It's good of you to come now. Is anything wrong?"

"No. Everything is going well."

"I hear from Janet."

"Yes, I found you through her. It worked out as I hoped. It was accepted that Garth and Susannah had gone to the barn together. There had been rumors about their relationship, so it fitted. There was a certain amount of searching for Susannah's body, but they were satisfied with the charred remains of the belt, and the jewelry was found. Janet identified it and others did too. I left your horse there to be discovered with Garth's and I went and got mine the next day. It all worked out just as I planned."

"It was a clever plan."

"So Susannah is now dead," he went on. "Leah Chivers was very sad but she's got her baby boy now and seems content."

"And the castle?"

"All going well. I have left it in Jeff Carleton's capable hands. He'll manage while I'm away."

"So you're going away?"

"I think to Australia."

"That will be interesting."

I wished he had not come. He brought home to me how much I cared for him, how much I wanted to be with him.

"I have a reason," he said. "I'm hoping to get married."

"Well...I wish you luck. Is it to be someone in Australia?"

"No. . . . But we shall go there after the ceremony . . . that's if she agrees."

"I dare say you will persuade her."

I wanted to shout at him: Go away. Why do you come here to taunt me? I said: "I suppose you were very shocked by what I did. You must have despised me for it."

"It was a shock in a way...but I think I must have known that you couldn't be Susannah."

"So...I didn't really deceive you."

"I disliked her heartily. I always did...from the time we were children. The change...it was too miraculous to be real." He paused. "I think I subconsciously felt that something was going on...something strange. Susannah could not have changed so much."

"Oh, then . . . I wish you well . . . in your marriage."

"Suewellyn, surely you see what I'm getting at. It all depends on you."

I stared at him.

"I wanted to come before. I regretted sending you off like that. It seemed the only way out of a difficult situation. Then I discovered dear old Janet knew where you were."

"Dear old Janet," I heard myself say.

"Now I have made a plan."

"You are good at making plans."

Then suddenly the whole world seemed to be singing, for he had taken my hands in his.

"This is the plan," he said eagerly. "I should go to Australia and there by a miraculous coincidence I discover my long-lost relative . . . second or third cousin . . . or something like that . . . Suewellyn anyway. She lived on Vulcan Island with her parents but happened to be visiting friends in Sydney when the eruption took place. She stayed in Sydney and when I was there I met a young woman and I was struck by her resemblance to my own family. We fell in love and married.

(316)

I persuaded her to leave Sydney and of course you know who she turned out to be. There's one hitch to the plan."

"What is that?"

"We'll marry before we go, but that will have to be secret. We'll go to Australia *after* our marriage. Perhaps we'll visit Vulcan Island. Or would that make you too sad? We want no more sadness. Then we'll come home...home to our castle. There's only one thing I have to find out."

"What's that?"

"Whether you agree."

I smiled up at him and I said: "I am not dreaming, am I?"

"No. You are very wide awake."

Then he held me fast and I just wanted that moment to go on forever. Mrs. Christopher's drawing room with its pictures of pugs and pekes who had ruled her in the past was to me the most beautiful place in the world.

So we went and told her and she beamed on us and said it was like one of the romances I read aloud to her and she was so happy for us. She didn't mind in the least having to put another advertisement in the *Lady's Companion* for someone to walk the dog and change the library books.

Within a month we were married. We left England on the *Ocean Queen* and most blissfully did I cross the seas to the other side of the world. We were so happy...more so because we had lost each other for a while.

We stayed in Sydney among the graziers and the successful miners; we went out to Vulcan Island. It was deeply moving to see the crescent-shaped canoes coming out to the ship. I stood there on the sandy beach and looked up at the Giant who had destroyed so much. He was quiet now. He had finished his grumbling. Already there were a few huts dotted about and the palm trees which had escaped the holocaust were fresh and green and laden with fruit. More would be planted. Perhaps Vulcan would be inhabited again.

In due course we came back to England, and there was the castle the same as it had been for hundreds of years.

The servants came out to greet the master and the new Mateland bride whom he had discovered in Australia and who had turned out to be his kinswoman, a Mateland herself.

Janet was there.

As soon as I was in my room she came to me. For the

second time she gave way to emotion. That was when I pinned onto her blouse the cameo brooch which I had kept for her.

Then she looked at me.

"So all's well," she said. "You've come through, eh? After all your sins...."

"Yes, Janet," I said. "After all my sins, I've come through."

NEW FROM FAWCETT CREST

☐ BORN WITH THE CENTURY   24295 $3.50
by William Kinsolving
A gripping chronicle of a man who creates an empire for his family,
and how they destroy it.

☐ NOT A PENNY MORE, NOT A PENNY LESS 24428 $2.95
by Jeffrey Archer
A story of high suspense. Four unlikely conspirators collaborate to
recoup one million dollars they had lost to an expert con man.

☐ SUCH NICE PEOPLE   24420 $2.75
by Sandra Scoppettone
The fabric which binds a family together is dramatically torn when
one member begins to act increasingly disturbed, and puts all their
lives in danger.

☐ SINS OF THE FATHERS   24417 $3.95
by Susan Howatch
The tale of a family divided from generation to generation by great
wealth and the consequences of a terrible secret.

☐ BLITZ   24419 $2.95
by David Fraser
A novel which dynamically depicts wartime London in a brilliant
composite of a populace under siege.

☐ SILVER NUTMEG   24431 $2.95
by Norah Lofts
Set on an exotic island, this is the story of a man who comes to love
his wife only after she has found happiness with another man.

Buy them at your local bookstore or use this handy coupon for ordering.

COLUMBIA BOOK SERVICE
32275 Mally Road, P.O. Box FB, Madison Heights, MI 48071

Please send me the books I have checked above. Orders for less than 5 books
must include 75¢ for the first book and 25¢ for each additional book to cover
postage and handling. Orders for 5 books or more postage is FREE. Send check
or money order only. Allow 3-4 weeks for delivery.

Cost $_____ Name_____

Sales tax*_____ Address_____

Postage _____ City_____

Total $_____ State_____ Zip_____

*The government requires us to collect sales tax in all states except AK, DE,
MT, NH and OR.

Prices and availability subject to change without notice.

8199

ROMANCE From Fawcett Books

☐ **A NECESSARY WOMAN** 04544 $2.75
by Helen Van Slyke
Mary Farr Morgan seemed to have everything—a handsome husband, successful career, good looks. She had everything except a man who could make her feel like a woman.

☐ **THE LAST ENCHANTMENT** 24207 $2.95
by Mary Stewart
Love, lust and betrayal in Camelot. The tale of King Arthur as seen through the eyes of the mysterious Merlin.

☐ **THE SPRING OF THE TIGER** 24297 $2.75
by Victoria Holt
A tale of intrigue and love. A young woman goes to Ceylon and finds herself in a marriage of thwarted passion and danger.

☐ **THE TURQUOISE MASK** 23470 $2.95
by Phyllis A. Whitney
Something hidden deep in her memory was the key to Amanda Austin's past. She didn't know it was also the key to her future.

☐ **THE RICH ARE DIFFERENT** 24098 $2.95
by Susan Howatch
This is the story of a young Englishwoman whose life, loves and ambition become intertwined with the fate of a great American banking family.

Buy them at your local bookstore or use this handy coupon for ordering.

COLUMBIA BOOK SERVICE
32275 Mally Road, P.O. Box FB, Madison Heights, MI 48071

Please send me the books I have checked above. Orders for less than 5 books must include 75¢ for the first book and 25¢ for each additional book to cover postage and handling. Orders for 5 books or more postage is FREE. Send check or money order only. Allow 3-4 weeks for delivery.

Cost $_____	Name_____
Sales tax*_____	Address_____
Postage _____	City_____
Total $_____	State_____ Zip_____

*The government requires us to collect sales tax in all states except AK, DE, MT, NH and OR.

Prices and availability subject to change without notice.

8204